The Last Act of Adam Campbell

About the Author

In one form or another, Andy has always been a write
school, he passed notes in class and scribbled rude wor
lamp posts. At university, he wrote a PhD in biochem
and forged tickets to various balls, and as an adver
copywriter, he has written adverts for everything from
food to booze. But it wasn't until he was well into his
ties that Andy started writing fiction. If he could w
letter to his younger self, it would urge him to stop me
about and get on with it. Andy lives in London with hi
and two little girls. Chances are, he's writing someth

Find Andy on Twitter and Instagram @andyjone
and on Facebook /andyjonesauthor.

Andy Jones

The Last Act
of Adam Campbell

HODDER

First published in Great Britain in 2020 by Hodder & Stoughton
An Hachette UK company

This paperback edition published in 2021

1

A CIP catalogue record for this title is available from the British Library

Paperback ISBN 978 1 473 68045 6
eBook ISBN 978 1 473 68046 3

Typeset in Sabon MT by Hewer Text UK Ltd, Edinburgh
Printed and bound in Great Britain by Clays Ltd, Elcograf S.p.A.

Hodder & Stoughton policy is to use papers that are natural, renewable
and recyclable products and made from wood grown in sustainable
forests. The logging and manufacturing processes are expected to
conform to the environmental regulations of the country of origin.

Hodder & Stoughton Ltd
Carmelite House
50 Victoria Embankment
London EC4Y 0DZ

www.hodder.co.uk

To Rooster and Mouse
'Just one more page.'
Daddy x

'Out, out, brief candle!
Life's but a walking shadow, a poor player
That struts and frets his hour upon the stage
And then is heard no more. It is a tale
Told by an idiot, full of sound and fury,
Signifying nothing.'

William Shakespeare, *Macbeth*,
Act V, Scene V

'Shit happens
And then you die.'

Traditional refrain

Act I

Chapter 1

Adam has been dying for eight weeks now, but he isn't getting any better at it. The fixation with time, the almost irresistible drag towards panic, the maudlin fascination with metaphor.

The fixation with time, for example, is not restricted to his too-few remaining months, but encompasses the smaller increments also; the start of a new day, the stealthy passing of an hour, the slow sweep of a minute, the inexorable tick of the kitchen clock — the hands moving forward, forward, forward, but the time counting backwards now, progressing steadily from some meagre number towards a final zero. Dr Sam suggested Adam stop wearing a watch. Adam did as the psychologist suggested, but you can't escape time. Sitting now in his parked car, listening to the engine cool and creak, he looks at the dashboard clock and sees that he still has eight minutes and a handful of diminishing seconds before the session starts. He should have left the house eight minutes later, used that time to drink a cup of coffee, read an article in the paper, put the dishes away, listen to a track, or maybe two, by Bob Dylan, Marvin Gaye or Johann Sebastian Bach — so many songs, so little . . . time.

The eight minutes are now seven, and Adam sits in his car, staring through the window at the carefully designed, sympathetically painted hospice, set out here on the border between the city and the surrounding suburbs. Set, if you like, on the border between one place and the next. The brochure makes much of the four acres of surrounding land; the trees, the lake, the view of distant hills — and they are, as advertised, spectacular. The leaves are fading from green now, moving through the spectrum of yellows, umbers and reds. Dying with — *and here's that compulsion to metaphor* – a style and grace that Adam can only envy.

'We're all dying,' a sympathetic friend might say, and more than a few have.

The cliché is well meant, but this pedantry is the privilege of the living, which, Adam supposes, is why he is here – in the land of the dying. In many ways, Adam is approaching his end the way a baby approaches life; clumsily, bewildered, frightened and with no small amount of tears. This crisis is, literally, existential.

And now, the familiar tightness across his chest and abdomen, the squeamish awareness of his wet heart beating faster behind his bones, a sensation of confinement and futility. Dr Sam taught Adam to focus on a single spot and slow his breath in order that his heart and mind follow.

He focuses on a single leaf, flattened against the windscreen, smooth edged and shaped like an eye or a teardrop. The colour scheme a mottled sunset of orange and brown, the veins sharp and stark like black lightning, a surviving patch of vivid green clinging tight to life. Adam concentrates his attention on the stubborn swathe of green, and breathes in to a count of one, two, three, four . . . and out to the same tempo. In . . . and out . . . and . . .

Half a year ago, Heather had insisted he leave the home they had shared for more than ten years. Three weeks ago – the enthusiastic tumour a newly named thing – he had pleaded with her to take him back in. A concession rather than reconciliation. Allowing Adam to spend his limited months under the same roof as his six-year-old daughter.

Nothing resolved; everything simply further fucked up.

He quit work and moved into the spare room, entertaining an idealised vision of Adam Campbell making the very best of this very bad situation. Stoic and pragmatic in the face of the inevitable, he would make Mabel's packed lunch in the morning, walk her to school, then fill his day with books, films, music and long lunches with dear friends. This done, he would collect Mabel from school, content and refreshed from a day well spent. He would help his daughter with her homework, play, create, impart wisdom and indulge. And long after Adam had gone, Mabel would remember those hours and days as a special time characterised by laughter and ice-cream and unaccountably good weather. His last months would be his best.

He would live even as he was dying. He would die well.

And yet. Two weeks ago, he had found himself struggling with George Eliot in the living room. Struggling with the turgid prose, struggling to get comfortable, struggling to block out the rhythmic whir of the motor insinuating poison through a silicon tube inserted into a major vein of his left arm – the pump, roughly the size of an old Walkman, bulky against his hip in the hospital-supplied bum-bag. And above that hum and drone, the insistent kitchen clock ticking in the next room. He put on music, something low and acoustic. For a moment it worked, smothering the murmuring motor, adding context to the slow Victorian novel. But the relentless, ruthless tick, tick, tick of the kitchen clock pushed through the spaces between the notes until it was all that Adam could hear.

He set down the book, walked through to the kitchen, lifted the clock from the wall, and swung it hard against the corner of the kitchen table. He swung again, smashing the glass cover and tin face, buckling the black hands and sending the batteries skittering across the tiles. He slumped to the floor, shaking and crying for the first time since the oncologist – *I'm sorry, Adam* – had delivered her own shattering blow.

Perhaps – as he bashed the clock face against the table and the clock hands tinkled to the floor – perhaps Adam felt this destruction would be cathartic. That he would laugh, cringe, mutter something whimsical about having needed only to remove the batteries. But there was no such sigh and no purging laughter. Just the sensation of roiling waves inside his head and belly, of the walls closing in on him like coffin boards.

And all of this at eleven-fifteen on a Monday morning.

Eight weeks ago, when the doctor had laid it all out – *Months, Adam. Perhaps a year* – there had been less than a week left in August. The last of the true summer months. And Adam's immediate thought – the bargaining stage, he supposes, albeit out of sequence, out of time – had been: *Give me one more Christmas.* And then, denial, anger: *Fuck that; give me two.* The anger had lent Adam strength. He felt, even as he sat there absorbing his diagnosis, that this defiance might sustain him.

It sustained him for seven weeks. Seven weeks during which he broke news, made arrangements, bargained with the mother of his child and returned to the home he had left six months previously under an altogether different shadow. But the defiance (as all medicines must) stopped working, and Adam reduced the kitchen clock to smithereens.

He cleaned up the mess, sanded the splinters from the corner of the table and in doing so found the legs somewhat loose. He fixed them next. Screwdriver in hand, Adam moved through the rooms, tightening hinges and handles and rails. He changed a dead light bulb in the bathroom, and bled the radiators ready for autumn – the morbid nomenclature of these tasks not escaping Adam's attention.

He made a sandwich and ate most of it, consigned George Eliot to the recycling and watched a *Monty Python* DVD. He collected Mabel at ten past three and they played and drew and watched cartoons.

By the end of his seventh week of dying, every door in the house swung silently and true, every crack had been vanished and every bulb burned bright. The following Monday, with nothing else reparable besides his mind, Adam sat in Dr Sam's office, focused on a single spot and slowed his heartbeat with his breath. They talked about mortality, fear, and the slow process of adjustment.

When Adam left work, his co-workers gave him a card and a bottle of thirty-year-old whiskey in a black and gold presentation box. These colleagues observe a code of flippancy – a compulsion to reduce significant events (weddings, births, divorce) to nothing more than banter. And Adam – some words expected of him – was tempted to joke that at least he had outlasted this single malt in its coffin-like box. But this, he sensed, this would be pushing the code beyond its limits.

Nevertheless, he felt a duty to show bravado – 'No time like the present, right?' – and had begun unwrapping the foil from the neck there and then. His boss, just a few years older than Adam, had gently taken the bottle from him. 'Save it,' he said, patting Adam's wrist. 'Save it.' And there were tears standing in the man's eyes. Later, several drinks down in a crowded bar, the same man had said to Adam: 'We're all dying, when you think about it.'

'He meant well,' Adam told Dr Sam.

'But . . .?'

'Well, besides being a cliché, it's bullshit, isn't it? He's not dying, not *actually* dying. Not like . . . not like me.'

'"We were born to die",' Sam had said, his delivery telling Adam the words weren't his own. And in response to Adam's silent enquiry: '*Romeo and Juliet.*'

Adam nodded. 'I'm not sure if that's better or worse.'

'Go on.'

'Well it's a damn sight more snappy, I'll give him that.'

A short laugh from Dr Sam; a tilt of the head inviting further comment.

'It's kind of bleak,' Adam said. 'Don't you think? The idea that we're doomed from the outset. From the day we're born.'

'When you put it like that: *doomed*. But what about *destined*? Does that change anything?'

'"We're all dying",' Adam said. 'It diminishes what I'm going through. Trivialises it.'

Dr Sam nodded at this.

'It suggests me and Derek are in the same boat, dealing with the same bad hand . . .'

The same rotten pancreas.

'But the other one . . .'

'"We were born to die",' repeated Sam.

'It's about inevitability. And it might be bleak, but at least it doesn't trivialise anything. It's . . . honest, I suppose. That's the best I can do. Sorry.'

Sam had seemed pleased by this.

'Did I pass?' Adam asked.

'Do you know why Shakespeare has endured for so long?' Sam said, then, answering his own question: 'He understood the human condition. Love, lust, fear, ambition. Death. He was particularly insightful on the subject of death, in my opinion.'

Adam, sensing there was more to Sam's discourse than an English lesson, sensing that the man was steering them somewhere and was soon to arrive, simply nodded and waited.

'Shakespeare understood our fear and fascination with mortality. He doesn't pretend death isn't tragic, but he shows us it can also be noble, beautiful, necessary. He shows us—'

'That we're born to die?' Adam interjected, and perhaps there was a note of cynicism in his quick reply.

Sam had smiled. 'That death is a part of life. The problem with this,' he said, using his palms to indicate both himself and Adam, 'is that – like your colleague – I'm not "in your boat". But I know men and women who are. A small group of us meet once a week and . . .' Sam laughed, a small apologetic sound. 'We talk.'

'About Shakespeare?'

'Amongst other things.'

'I'm not really . . . I studied geography.'

'It's not a literary thing,' Sam said. 'Nothing *academic*. I think you'd like them.'

'I don't know.'

'Will you at least think about it?'

Adam thought about it. He thought about it at home that night. He thought about it in the empty house the following day. And, really, what else was he going to do on a cold Thursday afternoon? After all, there are only so many clocks a man can smash.

'Life is a process of adjustment,' Dr Sam had said. 'And death is no different.'

Adam shifts his attention now from the leaf to the dashboard clock and sees he is one minute late for group therapy with Dr Sam and half a dozen others who are unlikely to receive calendars this Christmas.

He climbs out of the car and heads towards the entrance.

Chapter 2

The hospice is divided into quadrants, arranged in a cross forma-
tion around the central hub of reception and open-plan coffee
shop. The seating is soft, the framed prints colourful but subdued,
even the flowers in their vases project an attitude of empathy and
decorum.

The quadrants are named – pleasingly, to Adam's mind – after
the seasons, and a smiling receptionist directs him to a meeting
room at the far end of summer. Adam declines the offer of an
escort and, using the supplied floor plan, makes his way north-
west past private rooms, an art studio and a physiotherapy centre.
In other seasons, the map lists a hairdresser, crèche and non-
denominational chapel. There is an atmosphere of quiet bustle,
camaraderie and optimism and it makes Adam want to run
screaming to the car park, maybe kicking over a vase of empathetic
orchids in passing.

He rounds a final corner, arriving at a closed door painted in a
soothing green that merely intensifies his instinct to turn and run.
He hears laughter from inside the room, and checks the embossed
plaque – Summer: 4.b. – against the room number scribble on his
floor plan. This is it. He reaches for the door handle, closes his
hand around the cool metal . . .

A sound behind him, of someone shifting position or taking a
step.

The girl might be as young as sixteen, but is unlikely to be much
older than twenty.

'Are you here for the . . .' Adam hesitates to complete the question. Because to ask if she is here for the group, is to ask this girl
– who doesn't look old enough to buy a stiff drink – if she is dying.

'It's my first time,' says the girl.

Adam fights an urge to close his eyes and sigh. Feels an impulse – which he resists – to hug this girl and tell her how sorry he is.

'Me too,' he says. 'I'm Adam.'

The girl nods. 'Laura.'

And again, laughter from inside.

A look passes between Adam and Laura. Adam shrugs: *Shall we?*

Laura removes her right hand from her pocket and shows Adam a dull and tarnished fifty-pence coin. She tosses the coin high, catches and covers it on the back of her left hand. She looks at Adam.

'Tails.'

Laura looks at the coin, nods and returns it to her pocket. 'Lead on, Adam.'

Chapter 3

The chatter stops as the two newcomers walk into the room. Laura, half hidden behind Adam, counts the faces tilted towards them – five excluding the doctor, all somewhere past fifty with the exception of a single guy who she puts in the vicinity of thirty. This man wears a baseball cap, and a gold stud in his left ear. Crude, possibly hand-drawn tattoos show on both wrists, vanishing up the sleeves of an ill-fitting checked shirt.

'Tom,' says the man, and Laura fades back into Adam's shadow.

Dr Sam rises from his chair, arms extended and wide. Wild-haired and bicycle-clipped, he looks more like a busker than a clinical psychologist. 'You came,' he says. 'Wonderful, great. Come in, take a seat.'

There are three free chairs in the circle and Adam takes one adjacent to an older woman who shakes his hand and whispers a name Laura doesn't catch. There are two seats left: one next to Tom, the other beside a kindly-looking woman who could be the same age as Laura's mother. Both hold invitations in their eyes. Tom smiles, as if daring Laura to sit beside him; the woman looks at her with something more urgent and Laura walks across the circle of chairs to sit beside her.

'Erin,' says the woman. She touches Laura's wrist and her sympathetic smile makes Laura look away.

Sam claps his hands gently together. 'As we have two newcomers, perhaps we'll go around the circle and introduce ourselves. I'm Sam. Some of you – Adam, for example – know me from our individual sessions. Others – like Laura – have been referred from elsewhere. All of which I mention for nothing more than preamble. It doesn't matter how you came to be here, what matters is that you are here now.'

Erin glances across the room to the last remaining empty chair, and Laura notices other members of the group doing likewise.

'This is *your* group,' Sam says to the room as a whole. 'Take the sessions where you will, share what you want, and only what you want. I'm simply here to moderate, nudge and bring a box of books. Okay, enough from me.' He gestures to the lady on his left. 'This is Pat.'

Pat has smooth, plump skin with simple make-up and entirely pencilled-on eyebrows. She wears a pale grey headscarf printed with images of various breeds of dog.

'Hi,' she says, and she places her index finger against the poodle at her temple: 'Little b— bugger just here. Gliob— blastoma. Although not so . . . not so little any more. So if I say anything daft, don't hold it against me.' She turns to Adam. 'It feels strange to say welcome, under the c— circumstances. But, well, I hope you enjoy the g— g— group. I hope you enjoy it as much as I have.'

'Thank you, Pat. I'm Adam, and I'm . . .' *Glad to be here? Pleased to meet you?* But he isn't glad, he isn't pleased, and he feels it's important – here more than anywhere, perhaps – to be honest. 'I'm new to this. But . . . Dr Sam spoke highly of you all. So, here I am.'

A man wearing a football shirt laughs. 'Can't trust them doctors. No offence, Sam.'

Sam smiles, the corners of his eyes folding easily into well-worn grooves. 'None taken. And thank you Adam.'

Sam nods at the upright gentleman to Adam's left.

'I'm Raymond,' says the man in a pleasant Scottish brogue. Square of shoulder, clean-shaven and wearing an impeccably ironed shirt, he has the bearing of a retired army captain. 'Prostate,' he says with a curt nod. And he nods again to indicate that will be all.

The next lady along touches Raymond lightly on the shoulder. 'Thank you, Raymond. That was lovely.' And there is not one jot of irony.

'I'm Erin,' she says. 'It was in my ovary.'

Erin touches the teal ribbon on her cardigan, a membership badge to a club no woman would want to belong to.

'They took it out, but it . . .' Erin puts her hand to her belly and rubs it in a widening circle that takes in her sides and chest and neck. 'So . . .' Erin shrugs, 'there you go.' She wipes a tear from her cheek and reaches into her bag, withdrawing a large Tupperware tub. 'Nearly forgot.'

The inside of the container is dotted with condensation, and the tub hisses as Erin lifts the lid. The smell, when it reaches Adam's nostrils, is both sweet and acrid – it brings to mind over-ripe fruit, vegetable peelings, compost.

'Spinach, goji berries, ginger and turmeric,' Erin says. 'I call them chemuffins. Like chemo, but in a muffin.'

Adam laughs politely. 'Sounds . . . good.'

He catches the eye of the man in the football shirt. The man shakes his head, subtly but emphatically, and the message is clear: *No, Adam. They're not.*

Erin holds the tub towards Adam. 'Please.'

He suffers waves of nausea, but the sickness is at low tide now and Adam's specialist has impressed upon him the importance of taking in sufficient calories. He selects the smallest muffin available. Erin offers the box to Laura, but Laura has read the room – the pinched lips and flared nostrils – and declines politely.

'Just eaten. But thank you anyway.'

'Anyone else?'

The assembled bodies mutter excuses and make apologetic gestures of firm refusal.

'I'll leave them here,' Erin says, placing the tub on the floor, 'in case anyone changes their mind.'

Adam bites into his muffin and knows instantly that no one will. 'Lovely,' he says around clenched teeth, and Pat touches him gently on the knee. She taps it once, twice, as if to say: *Good boy.*

This business done, Erin turns to Laura, and as she does, Adam slips the revolting lump of calories into his jacket pocket.

Laura puts a thumbnail between her teeth, removes it, adjusts the scarf bundled around her neck, clamps her hands between her knees. 'I'm Laura,' she says. 'Stage four skin cancer. Well, melanoma, but same difference, I suppose. I've got three mets in the brain.' Erin makes a small noise of anguish. 'But . . . they've got me on immunotherapy; sort of the new thing, so . . .' She wavers her palm up and down. 'So I guess we'll see.'

She turns to the man in the football shirt. His hair is shaved close to his skull, but on closer inspection – the islands and continents of dark stubble in a sea of pink skin – she sees this is done out of necessity rather than choice or affiliation.

'Thank you, darling,' says the man.

'Laura,' says Laura.

'Course, course you are. Thank you, *Laura*. I'm Vernon,' he says, addressing this to Laura and then to Adam. 'Cancer of the bowel, spread all over the shop. I've had the lot – surgery, radio, chemo, trials, you name it, but . . . well, here we all are. The end of the line club.'

There is a beat of silence as the room waits for a response; for some objection, perhaps, to this brutal candour. None comes.

'No use in dressing it up,' says Vernon. 'Get enough of that at home.' And there are several low murmurs of agreement. 'So, yeah, that's me.'

'It certainly is,' says the young man with the baseball cap and tattoos. And I'm Tom.' His voice, now that he's used it to form more than a single syllable, is cracked and thin.

He has a long curving scar from the hinge of his jaw to the hollow between his collarbones; neat and almost certainly surgical. Laura's hand goes to the concealing silk scarf piled around her own neck.

She has lost count of how many scarves she owns, but it seems her mother can't leave the house without bringing a new scarf back with her. 'To keep you warm,' her mother says, regardless of the month. Or 'It matches your eyes.' Or your coat, or your shoes, or that pair of socks your aunty bought you. But what her mother is saying, of course, is 'This will hide the scar where the surgeon removed your lymph nodes.'

Wrapping me in cotton wool. Or silk, or cashmere or merino wool, just so long as we keep that scar hidden.

The young man with the tattoos points to his own scar. 'Tonsil cancer,' he says. 'Which is a right liberty considering I had 'em out when I was nine.'

Laura leans forward. 'You're joking.'

Tom shakes his head. 'T*iiiny* bit left,' he says, 'and a tiny bit is all it takes, apparently.' He has the voice of an old smoker, but there is a lisping aspect too that slides over the words *waste* and *ice-cream*. 'Spread, too, so they took a bit of my tongue for good measure. Still, my mum always said I talked too much.' Tom takes a sip from a bottle of water and winces.

He rests his hand on the empty chair to his left. 'No Nadeem today?'

Sam smiles a smile that perhaps they had all been anticipating. 'Nadeem had a bad few days. Some complications.'

'Is he . . .?'

'He's in hospital. I had an email from his wife last night. Sending Nad's apologies for missing group.'

Some affectionate laughter.

'He's okay, though?' asks Pat.

'He's not good.'

'When will he be back?' Erin asks. 'I expect he'll be back next week?'

Adam watches this slow teasing out of the obvious fact concerning this man he has never met, and – to judge from Sam's expression – never will.

'His wife has asked me to pass on Nadeem's email address, for those that don't have it already.'

Vernon clasps his hands behind his head. 'Shit. Sorry, I . . .' He shakes his head. 'Shit.'

Sam leans forwards, faces Vernon with his elbows resting on his knees, his hands clasped lightly together. His posture invites the man to continue.

'It's just . . ,' Vernon shakes his head. 'Empty chairs,' he says, his voice slowing, quietening and trailing off. 'Empty chairs waiting to happen.'

Adam watches the slowly settling reactions. Watches the doctor shift his attention to Laura. Sam mouths *Okay?* And Laura nods, although Adam — well versed in bravado — sees the slowness, the heaviness, in this simple movement.

It occurs to him that perhaps this — the steady ebb of members — is part of the point. The way a therapist might present an arachnophobe with a large spider in a glass jar. Exposing and then inuring the patient to the thing he fears.

Silence falls about the room, and the members of the group reach into bags, pockets and folders, each producing a thin sheaf of paper, some crisp, others creased and dog-eared as if from repeated handling.

Sam rises from his chair and hands a set of stapled-together pages to Laura and another to Adam.

Adam scans the evenly spaced text, his eyes drifting over pages of quotes, each attributed to William Shakespeare and referencing the play or sonnet from which it originates. His eye is drawn to the word 'minutes', and he reads:

> 'Like as the waves make towards the pebbled shore,
> So do our minutes hasten to their end;
> Each changing place with that which goes before,
> In sequent toil all forwards do contend.'

Another:

> 'Golden lads and girls all must,
> As chimney-sweepers, come to dust.'

He turns to the last page and reads the final quote:

> 'We cannot hold mortality's strong hand.'

Death, he realises; these words – of course – are all concerned with death. Adam looks across to Laura, her head dipped towards the sheet, lips moving as she reads.

She is familiar with some of these words: *What dreams may come when we have shuffled off this mortal coil*, she knows is from *Hamlet*, and likewise, she recognises Juliet in the line: *Death, that hath suck'd the honey of thy breath, Hath had no power yet upon thy beauty*.

' "He that cuts off twenty years of life . . ." ' Pat pauses to make sure she has the attention of the group. ' ". . . cuts off so many years of fearing death." '

Tom dings an imaginary bell. 'Johnson, University of Life. Is it *Julius Caesar*, Jeremy?'

'Ten points, Johnson.'

Vernon whacks Tom with his rolled-up notes. 'It's printed on your sheet, you numpty.'

Sam indulges the horseplay for a moment before asking Pat: 'And what was it about this one in particular . . .?' He taps his index finger against his own sheaf of papers.

'Nadeem,' says Pat. 'He's had a long . . . b— battle.'

Vernon sighs. A heavy breath of exasperation rather than empathy or concurrence. '*Battle*.'

Pat looks taken aback. 'Oh, I'm s— sorry. Did I . . .?'

'I've had cancer for seven years,' Vernon says. 'And whatever else anyone says – the missus, the kids, the lads down the pub – there's no battle. A battle's a fight; they come at you and you come right back at them. You've got a chance in a battle. But this . . .' He holds up his hands as if presenting himself as evidence. 'You hold out for as long as you can.' He gathers himself, masters the tremor that has crept into his voice. 'You hold out. But it ain't no battle. Sorry, Pat.'

Pat shakes her head. 'Don't apologise. I u— understand. And I agree with you. Completely. What I meant is it's . . . it's frightening. You suffer in all kinds of ways, but the fear hangs over you, *every day*. Until . . .' She smiles. 'I can't put it any better than Mr Shakespeare, I'm afraid.'

Vernon nods, his defiant posture softening. 'You put it perfectly,' he says. 'I just . . .' He shrugs. 'You know . . .'

Laura *mm-hmm*s in agreement – yes, she does know – and the confident, unequivocal tone of it quite surprises her. Vernon turns to face her, clearly expecting some elaboration. The others, too, are looking at her, waiting, as if she had cleared her throat to attract their attention.

'I . . . at home, I mean, or in school, it's . . . everyone treats you like . . . like you're . . .'

'Like you're going to break,' says Erin, sniffing into her tissue.

'Exactly,' says Laura. 'But here, you're all . . . well, you're a bit more . . .'

'Irreverent,' tries Tom.

Vernon gives him another tap on the head with his roll of quotes.

'Honest,' says Laura.

Adam leans forward in his seat. 'Is it okay if I read one?'

'Please do.'

'I vaguely remember it from school. Macbeth has just heard that Lady Macbeth's died, although I can't remember how. Anyway:

' "Out, out, brief candle! Life's but a walking shadow, a poor player that . . . struts" ' – his voice falters – ' " . . . a poor player that struts and frets his hour upon the stage. And then is heard no more. It is a tale told by an idiot . . ." ' He is crying freely, but is entirely unselfconscious.

' "An idiot, full of sound and fury, signifying nothing." ' Adam clears his throat into the tense hush of the room. '*Macbeth*. Act five, scene five, lines twenty-three to twenty-eight.'

'Thank you,' says Sam, and Pat leans gently into him with her shoulder.

Adam nods. 'It's good,' he says, almost to himself. 'It's good to be here.'

Chapter 4

They called her Mabel because every time one of them suggested a name, the other would say, 'Maybe.' *Annabelle? Maybe. Dorothy? Maybe. Zoe? Maybe.* It became a call and response that amused them more than it had any right to do, and they dismissed pages of names for the pleasure of rolling out their shared chorus. *Evie? Maybe. Ruby? Maybe. Sarah? Maybe.* And then Adam, or maybe it was Heather, had said, 'Maybe we should call her Maybe?' From which it was only a small step to Mabel. Which, once mooted, was met with the answer: 'Definitely.' Six years and five months later, their chorus has become a nickname and an in-joke. *Can I stay up ten more minutes? Yes, Maybe. Can I have a try of your wine? No, Maybe. Will you live here forever now, Daddy? Maybe, Maybe. Maybe.*

As he waits for her across the road from the school gates, Adam is aware of the other parents watching him. After all, Adam is great gossip; the errant husband recently returned, and, oh, under what awful circumstances. Heather has shared the news with a small group of friends, but it's no secret that in a primary school playground, tittle-tattle spreads faster than headlice.

Or maybe he is being paranoid; perhaps they are staring because of the giant pumpkin he is attempting to hold nonchalantly under one arm. Halloween is still two weeks away, but as it is likely to be Adam's last, he was determined to bag the biggest pumpkin available. And they don't come much bigger than this.

The gates open and the parents, the grandparents and nannies move through to the playground where they will collect their charges. There is a tree in the far corner and Adam makes his way towards this, standing apart and avoiding eye contact with those who seek to make it. He feels knocked about, and it's hard to know how much is down to the malady and how much the cure.

They give him drugs once a fortnight; a day in hospital during which he is attached to a drip for more than four hours while three different and equally nasty chemotherapies are introduced into his system. Then they send him home with a slow pump that administers a fourth poison over the next forty-six hours. For the next few days, Adam feels as if he has flu. And not simply a headache and a runny nose; this is the real deal – his muscles ache, his *skin* aches, he has the shivers, the sweats, profound fatigue and nausea. On day five or maybe six, he begins to feel normal again, although normal, it must be noted, ain't what it used to be. And then, on day fifteen, they do it all over again. Maybe twelve times in total, if his body holds up.

Today is day five, and without this tree at his back, Adam might just slump to the ground. The pumpkin, held in two hands now, feels like it is gaining weight and he aches from fingertip to shoulder.

Unattended pre-schoolers toddle and run about the playground with a reckless vigour Adam would pay for if he could. Their mothers huddle and cluster, heads tilted inwards as they talk in low voices. Some angle their shoulders towards him, they invite him to meet their eyes: *Come in*, their bodies say, *come and tell us all about your terrible, terrible news*.

A bell rings, classroom doors open and children emerge at great speed, propelled by the pent-up pressure of a hard day drawing rainbows and spelling 'cat'. They barrel out of the doors on perfect legs, shouting, laughing, clapping – and here is Mabel, skipping towards him, holding the hand of her latest best friend. Her tiny body smashes into him with the force of a rampaging animal. Her friend Holly stands one step back, hands held at her sides, waiting. Her face is set in a wide-eyed smile of unflinching courtesy that is more sinister than endearing.

'Daddy, Daddy, can Holly come for a play date to our house? Pl*eeeaaase*? Can she, Daddy?'

'Oh, *hello*, Mabel. And how was your day?'

'Good.'

'Hi, Holly, how are you?'

'Good.'

'Can Holly come to our house, Daddy? Holly can plait hair.'

'Daddy's a bit tired today. Another time, maybe?'

'We don't mind if you're tired. It's okay.'

'Thank you, sweetheart, it's just . . . Today's tricky. Perhaps another time?'

The answer isn't the one Mabel wants, and her disappointment drags the smile from her face. 'Why not?'

'I've tried to explain, sweetheart – Daddy's knackered.'

'What's knackered?' asks Holly.

'Very, *very* tired,' says an adult voice at Adam's shoulder.

Dianne, Heather's closest friend from the school-mum crowd. Privy to everything, and adept in the emotional sleight of hand necessary to project sincere sympathy and absolute disapproval.

'How *are* you, Adam?'

'Good,' he says, aware that he sounds like every child currently undergoing similar interrogation by an adult. 'Okay,' he adds.

Dianne kisses him, but only on one cheek. She is a large, robust woman, at least an inch taller than Adam, and when she squeezes his shoulder, Adam feels she might leave finger marks. 'Sturdy' is the word Adam's father would have used to describe Dianne; this said in the admiring tones of a man who shared a bed with a woman capable of smothering him, effortlessly and in a number of ways.

Holly looks up to her mother. 'Why is Mabel's daddy knackered, Mummy?'

'He's always knackered,' says Mabel. 'Mummy says he needs extra rest.'

Dianne regards Adam with a tight-lipped smile. 'We could arrange a play date at our house, if you like?'

'Can we, Daddy? Can we?'

Heather doesn't work Fridays, so Adam has Mabel to himself for three rapid hours four days a week. If he's lucky he has two hundred of these precious windows left, and it pains him to give up even one. But, he understands that it will be good for Mabel. He understands, too, that the time is not so far away when he and Heather will become reliant on such acts of kindness. So he smiles. He says, 'Yes, Maybe.' He says, 'Thank you, Dianne. Perhaps sometime next week? Or the week after that?'

'Anytime. Any time at all.' The children are chattering between themselves, distracted by a particularly interesting leaf on the ground, and Dianne drops her voice, moves a half-step closer. 'You'll fight this,' she says. 'I know you will.'

The doctors deal in probabilities rather than absolutes.

Everybody is different, Adam, but this therapy could *give you an additional five months.*

So . . . Adam hesitating with the simple mathematics of six plus five. *So eleven? Eleven months?*

On average, yes.

So it could be more?

Yes, Adam. But, also . . . it's just an average. That's important to remember.

Two months ago now.

'They can do so much, these days,' Dianne whispers.

'Yes.'

'I know a lady, lovely lady' – her voice goes silent as she mouths the word *cancer* – 'of the . . . somewhere in the tummy, I think. Anyway . . .' – and for reasons unfathomable, she chooses to mouth the words: *full remission*. 'So, we must stay positive.'

'Right,' says Adam. 'Yes. Mabel, come on now.'

'You too, missy,' and Dianne scoops up her daughter as if she weighed no more than a doll, hoisting her high overhead and depositing Holly on her broad shoulders. The little girl laughs and claps as her mother squats down to retrieve her school bag.

'Daddy!' Mabel reaches up towards Adam. 'Shoulder ride!'

Dianne grimaces. Mouths *Sorry*.

Her habit of hitting the mute button is contagious, and Adam mouths back: *It's fine*.

'Can I?' says Mabel.

'Definitely, Maybe,' Adam tells her.

He squats down, feeling his bones creak and his muscles pull tight. 'Put your backpack on,' he says as he sets the pumpkin on the ground. 'Daddy's got a pumpkin to carry. Two pumpkins including you.'

Mabel claps her hands together. 'I'm not a pupkin.'

Adam laughs at the slip. 'Oh yes you are. Okay, *Pupkin*. Let's get you on board.' And as he lifts her onto his shoulders, Adam is aware of Dianne bracing herself to catch a dropped child. How she intends to do this with Holly on her shoulders is beyond Adam, but he suspects this woman could handle it.

Mabel in place, his left hand on her left ankle, Adam scoops up the orange boulder masquerading as a pumpkin and braces it against his right hip. All he has to do now is stand. He flexes his thighs and they send a message to his brain asking what the hell it thinks it is playing at. The brain tells the legs to shut up and push, and they begin – grudgingly – to comply. It would be easier if he could wear the effort on his face, grunt and swear, but pride forbids this. Instead, Adam fixes a stupid smile on his red face and drives slowly upward, bracing his back and guts and neck for stability and rising with the slow determination of a rocket attempting to escape gravity. He wobbles, and Dianne flinches like a wicket keeper, but Adam continues his painful, determined ascent until he is standing at full height, with a child on his shoulders and a colossal pumpkin under one arm.

Dianne relaxes and celebrates by bouncing Holly on her shoulders. 'Giddy up then,' she says.

I'll do my best, thinks Adam, and he puts one foot in front of the other, and then the next.

'Do you think you can carry me all the way home, Daddy?'

'Maybe, Maybe, Maybe.'

Chapter 5

Halloween is two weeks away, but her parents have already decorated the house with woollen cobwebs, rubber bats, silhouettes of witches and ghosts cut from black cartridge paper. As if she were eight rather than eighteen. As if, a voice whispers in her ear, this might be her last October. Her father bought a pumpkin at the weekend, a ludicrous thing the size of a troll's head, and then carved it alone when Laura declined to join in the 'fun'. It sits on the gatepost – early for its own party – and bares its teeth at her when she returns from school, the shops, or a walk around the quiet block; a fresh candle every evening flickering disapproval at her churlishness.

Out, brief candle, she thinks, remembering the man – Adam – crying when he read *Macbeth*. A bit embarrassing really, but he seems like an okay sort of bloke.

She is sitting cross-legged on the living-room floor, leaning back against the sofa, a stack of university literature scattered at her feet, the prospectus for Nottingham in her hand. Her father has the road atlas from the car, has it spread open in his lap. 'Nottingham,' he says. 'Nottingham . . . Nottingham.'

Laura's mother sits in the corner of the sofa and she stretches out her leg, gently touching her foot to Laura's shoulder. Her mother's sock smells of fabric conditioner and the cotton is ticklish against Laura's cheek.

'So,' she says, 'tell us more about this group.'

Laura shrugs. 'Nothing much to tell. Bunch of terminally ill people reading Shakespeare quotes and having a cry.'

'Crying?' Her mother sounds concerned.

Laura shrugs again. 'What do you expect? They're dying.'

26

Her father clears his throat. He flips a page in the atlas: 'There we are . . . B5.'

'Did you make any nice friends?' her mother asks.

After Adam read the *Macbeth* bit, they had moved on to suicide.

The boy with the tattoos and the wrecked voice – Tom – had asked: 'So how did Lady Mac cop it, then? Doesn't say, does it?'

'Suicide,' Dr Sam said. '"His fiend-like queen, who took her life with violent hands." Or words to that effect.'

'Is . . . is suicide still a sin?' Erin asked, addressing the question to Pat. 'Not that I . . . I never would, I just . . .'

Raymond had cleared his throat in obvious disapproval. 'Last refuge of the weak.'

'Or the terribly desperate,' Pat suggested. She turned to Erin. 'It depends who you talk to. But no, not necessarily. We're a *little* more e— enlightened these days.'

Vernon chuckled. 'Whatever you say, Sister.'

Laura raised an eyebrow at this, to which Pat responded by producing a crucifix from beneath her purple jumper. 'You're a nun?'

'Almost,' Pat told her. 'Nuns, by and large, live in convents, monasteries, that kind of thing. I'm more of a free-range nun,' she said, crinkling her eyes in a way that suggested this was a joke she had used before.

'Nundercover,' Tom added.

'Very good,' Pat said. 'I might steal that one.'

Sam did his gentle handclap. 'Why don't we break into twos?' he said, and already Laura could feel Erin claiming her.

'There was a lady called Erin,' Laura says to her mother.

'Oh, really?'

Erin had cried when Laura told her she was hoping to go to university next year, but she seemed to have the knack of doing this pragmatically and without drama, just getting on with it in the way of someone with, say, a runny nose.

'Her daughter's at Liverpool. Doing Geography.'

'That's nice. Does she like it there?'

'Sounds okay,' Laura said. 'She likes the clubs, apparently. And there's a Beatles museum and good shops.'

'I used to love Paul,' her mother says. 'Although I didn't care much for Wings.'

'Liverpool,' says her father, turning to the index at the back of the atlas. 'Liverpool, Liverpool . . . Liverpool.'

'Here we are,' her father says. 'L . . . 7.' He jabs his finger onto the page, as if catching the university and holding it in place.

'Honestly?' says Laura. 'Just look on the iPad. If you really must.'

'Can't trust them.' He picks up a length of string now, holding it against the motorways and A-roads that connect the university to their house. 'And anyway, your mum's hogging the iPad.'

Her mother wrinkles her nose at this and snorts.

'God,' Laura says under her breath.

Applications don't close until January, but the longer she leaves it, the longer she has to listen to her parents' opinions, anxieties and general nonsense on the subject. Since her diagnosis, she has noticed a tendency in them both towards a sort of measured urgency – the premature pumpkin on the gatepost; the cinema visits on opening weekend, her father mapping the fastest routes to every university in the country.

Wherever she goes, she can't get there soon enough.

When she started in the sixth form (for the first time) she had picked A levels that would qualify her for medical school. She could have been there right now, cutting open cadavers with her course mates. But her own body had had different ideas; sprouting cancer cells – at the very same moment, perhaps, that Laura was studying cell division in her textbooks. And despite it all – the shock, the drugs, the hospital visits – she still sat and passed her end-of-year exams. One A and two A stars, thank you very much. More than good enough to apply for medicine.

But the world was different now.

With an uncertain span of time ahead of her, Laura knew with sudden and profound clarity that she did not want to burn five years lugging heavy medical textbooks to and from the library. Did not, in all likelihood, *have* five years. And as for hospitals and doctors' surgeries, she's seen enough of those to last a lifetime – however long that might prove to be.

Laura had worried that her parents might freak out when she told them she wanted to start the sixth form again, changing A levels, changing paths. But they had received the news with surprising composure. A few tears, obviously, but basically, 'Whatever makes you happy, Laura. Whatever makes you happy.'

Reclining in his armchair, her father is holding his piece of string to a plastic ruler, muttering again as he converts centimetres to miles, miles to hours.

'The Royal has a good reputation in oncology,' her mother says.

'I'm picking a university, not a hospital.'

'One hour, forty-five minutes,' her father says. 'Give or take.'

'Well I'm not going there. The reading list's all Victorian.'

'Are you sure?' her mother says. 'It will be good to have you . . . you know, close.'

Laura picks up the Edinburgh prospectus.

'Okay.' Her father turns to the index at the back of the atlas. 'Edinburgh,' he says.

Laura shouts, 'Dad, will you please not!'

'I'm just . . .'

Laura is tired and hungry. She can't eat until after she has taken her final dose of today's tablets, and this, as much as anything, is making her irritable.

'If I . . . if something happens,' Laura says, 'it won't make any difference whether I'm ten minutes or ten hours away.'

'Laura,' her mother's voice, soft, patient, 'your father and I are just—'

'Well, just . . . just don't, please.'

A beeper sounds on her father's wristwatch, and half a second later an alarm pings on her mother's phone. Laura's mobile is upstairs in her bedroom, but it, too, will be pinging a reminder for Laura to take her medication.

It will beep again tomorrow morning, tomorrow evening, and twice a day every day until she beats the cancer or the cancer beats her.

'You're lucky,' Dr Suleiman had said eighteen months ago, when Laura's blood tests confirmed her as eligible for immunotherapy.

'Lucky is winning the lottery,' Laura had wanted to say.

Her doctor flicked his index finger against the sheet of paper listing the genetic markers in Laura's blood. 'We have a chance to *significantly* extend survival.'

Her mother had asked the question that was inside all of their heads. And when the doctor hedged, her father pushed.

'There's a good chance of getting another three years.'

'A chance?'

'Fifty per cent.'

Her mother's voice shaky with disappointment. 'Three years?'

'Five years ago, there would have been . . .' The doctor shook his head, smiled apologetically. 'This is cutting edge.' As if that made three years any less fleeting.

'Fifty per cent.' Her father's grip had tightened around Laura's hand to the point where it was uncomfortable.

'What's exciting,' the doctor said, his tone a little too gleeful, 'is that *if* we see three, there's a good chance we'll see five. Maybe more. In some cases we're even seeing a lasting response.'

He didn't use the word 'cure', but it's there on the internet if you look for it.

Her father's grip had relaxed on Laura's hand.

'A lasting response?'

'There's a long way to go,' Dr Suleiman said. 'But like I said' – and again, he flicked the page containing Laura's result – 'you're lucky.'

Her parents began to cry then, as if the miracle were nothing more than a formality. But Laura was replaying the exchange, trying to remember how many times the good doctor had used the words *luck* and *chance* and *maybe* and *per cent*, each one stacked on top of the last like a teetering pile of pennies.

Her father stops the alarm on his watch, and Laura and her parents sit in the ringing silence. Laura doesn't move, she waits, daring her parents to tell her what this insistent beep – the beep she has been obeying twice a day for the last eighteen months – means: *Time to take your miracle drugs, Laura*.

In the hospital car park that afternoon Laura's eye had been drawn to something in the gravel beside their car. Her parents – arms around each other and just giddy with hope – didn't notice as Laura bent and scooped up a scuffed and dinged fifty-pence coin. She turned it over, and printed beneath the sweep of Her Majesty's jowls was the year of Laura's birth. *Lucky Laura*. She stuffs her left hand into the depths of her hoodie pocket and finds the familiar coin. Runs her thumb along its seven edges and seven corners. She can distinguish the two faces by feel now, but she guesses first – *tails* – before checking the orientation of the coin in her palm. Her thumb moves over the surface, feeling the flat spaces that surround Britannia and confirm her guess. Fifty-fifty, but you take your luck where you can find it. 'I'll go and . . .' inclining her head '. . . you know.'

Her father nods and closes the atlas. Laura gathers up the prospectuses, shuffling together the yeses and the nos into a single pile, which she tucks under one arm as she stands.

'I'll put supper on,' her mother says. 'How does fish fingers and chips sound?'

Kid's food, Laura thinks, and then she nods. 'Yes,' she says. 'That sounds nice.'

Chapter 6

Laura is early this week but the room is noisy with bodies and voices when she arrives. Vernon and Raymond are setting out chairs, and Adam is showing a picture of something – his kid, probably – to Pat.

'You came back,' Erin says, going to Laura and hugging her.

'More fool you,' says Vernon, winking. 'More fool you.'

'Awful weather,' says Erin. 'Look at you, you're soaked.'

Erin unzips Laura's hoodie, pulling it from her shoulders and off her arms. Laura doesn't mind the fuss as much as she might have guessed, and Erin carefully drapes the hoodie over one of several large radiators lining the room.

'Want me to take your scarf?'

Laura's hand goes to her neck. 'No, it's . . . fine.'

'But it's wet, sweetheart.'

'It's fine. Honestly.' And Erin receives the message in Laura's eyes.

'Sorry, sweetheart. It's the mother in me. Always fussing.'

'Not late, am I?' says Tom. 'Cats and whatnot out there.'

His voice sounds painful. As if his words are crudely carved and splintered, scraping his throat as he forces them out.

'There's space on the radiators,' Laura says. 'For your coat.'

'Lovely,' says Tom. 'Thank you.'

And when he drapes his coat over the radiator he looks like a thing drowned.

'Like a cat crawled out of a sack,' Tom says, as if reading her thoughts, and Laura looks quickly away.

One by one the group find their seats, the regulars landing in a similar pattern to last week. Vernon checks his watch. 'He's late.'

'Perhaps he's been delayed,' says Erin.

Raymond grumbles.

'You could die waiting,' says Tom, and this is met with some laughter.

'Would anyone like a muffin?' Erin asks, but it turns out no one is hungry.

Vernon checks his watch again. 'I was this late when I was working, they'd have given me the tin tack, believe you me.'

'What did you do?' Adam asks.

Vernon crosses his arms. 'Every boy's dream job.'

'Footballer?'

'Nope.'

'Astronaut?' tries Raymond.

Vernon laughs. 'Yeah, right. I was a train driver. Thirty-five years and a hell of a lot of miles.'

Raymond perks up at this. 'I was an engineer,' he says.

'Trains?'

'Telecoms.'

'Snap,' says Tom.

Raymond regards Tom doubtfully.

Tom holds an invisible telephone to his ear. 'Hello,' he says in his sandpaper voice. 'I believe you were involved in an accident that wasn't your fault.'

Six faces look at him the way a lover might regard a partner who has just confessed to infidelity.

Erin breaks the silence. 'That was you?'

'Well, not every time. But . . . yeah. Sorry.'

'Always when the footy's on,' says Vernon.

'Or when I'm in the bath,' says Pat.

'Some people appreciate the company,' Tom says, but this buys him no leniency.

There is a knock at the door and seven heads turn towards it. The door opens slowly, as if the person on the opposite side is pushing against great resistance.

'Is this . . .' A lady's face peers around the half-open door. 'Dr . . . Dr Sam's group?'

'Don't tell me,' says Vernon, 'he's running late?'

Laura recognises the woman now from the reception desk where she was employing her carefully modulated happy-but-not-*too*-happy smile. The smile is gone. To look at this woman now – this disembodied head, peering around the half-open door – you might imagine she had never smiled in her entire life.

They all sense this. The trepidation and solemnity of this woman who, it is clear now, has no intention of crossing the threshold into the room.

'He's . . .' tears sheen her eyes. 'It's so awful,' she says. 'It's just so awful.'

Chapter 7

The rain has stopped, and they sit around a table in the beer garden of the Mermaid pub. Rain drips hypnotically from the spokes of the large parasol and Tom watches the droplets swell, tremble . . . fall. Each newborn drop oblivious to the tragedy of its predecessor, or its own imminent and inescapable fate.

The seven sit in quiet contemplation. They meet eyes and read each other's thoughts. They sigh and they shake their heads.

'Do you think he was coming to see us?' Erin says. Her tears forming, Tom notes, at the same unhurried pace as the raindrops on their parasol. 'Do you suppose he was on his bicycle because he was coming to see us?'

They consider the question in silence. Looking for the answer in the shifting clouds, on the backs of their hands, on the surface of their drinks.

'Maybe he had other people to see,' Adam says. 'Beside us.'

'It's possible,' says Pat.

'Either way,' says Vernon.

'*Dead*,' says Tom, and they have all tried this word several times since hearing the news. As if to believe this thing, they first need to say it.

'Dead,' says Laura, perhaps in answer to Tom. Or simply letting escape the heavy syllable that occludes all other thought.

Tom takes a slow sip of Guinness. 'It's so . . . ,'

'Tragic,' says Adam.

'Well, yes. But I was going to say ironic.'

They all look at Tom.

'I'm not trying to be glib. But . . . you know what I mean?'

35

Pat puts her arm around him and squeezes. 'We know what you mean.'

'At least it was quick,' Vernon says. 'At least he didn't . . . well, see it coming, if you'll pardon the whatnot.'

' "He that cuts off twenty years of life," ' says Laura.

'Shit,' says Tom.

'Aye,' says Raymond.

'Was he married?' Erin asks. The Tupperware tub of muffins sits on the table like an unexploded bomb. 'Does anyone know if he was married?'

No one knows.

'It must be terrible,' she says. 'To lose someone you love.'

They mutter and nod and fidget with their drinks. These people who are all the 'someone' that some other one will soon lose.

Erin drums her fingers on the lid of the tub. 'I don't suppose anyone wants one?'

Heads shake, palms are raised, polite refusals are muttered.

'I know they're awful,' Erin says.

'Don't be daft,' says Vernon. 'It's just . . . I'm just . . .' He puts a hand to his belly.

'Brian makes them, you see. My husband.'

'Oh.'

'He means well. And I haven't the heart to tell him they're . . . well, awful.'

'They're not *that* bad,' Adam says.

Tom nods. 'To be fair, they really are.'

Erin laughs. 'I throw them away,' she says, her tears continuing their silent work. 'I lie and tell him everybody ate one. I hate to lie, but . . . he's so pleased with himself. That he's doing something. You know . . . to help.'

'Here,' Vernon says, dragging the tub towards himself and popping the lid. He removes one of the muffins and places it on the table in front of him. 'Tell the old man that Vernon had one.'

'You're going to eat it?'

'I'm sick enough, darling. But I've took one, and that's the truth.'

Tom reaches into the tub and removes a muffin. 'And you can tell him Tom took one too.'

Erin dabs at her eyes, she mouths the words *Thank you.*

'And me,' says Pat, helping herself to a muffin and passing the tub along to Laura.

'And you can tell him I took two,' says Adam.

Vernon gathers all the muffins together and deposits the lot in a nearby bin. 'Delicious,' he says, dusting his palms together. 'Very . . . hempy.'

Erin blows her nose into a napkin. 'You're all so good. I love you all. Honestly, I do.'

Vernon lays his hand on top of Erin's. 'And we love you, too, darling.'

Erin sniffs. 'I'll miss you,' she says. 'I'll miss all of you.'

'Well I'm not doing anything next Thursday,' Tom says.

'Me either,' says Vernon.

'No,' says Pat, 'neither am I.'

'You mean . . . meet?'

'Why not?' says Vernon.

Laura feels Tom's eyes on her. 'Sure,' she says. 'I'm in.'

Raymond fiddles with a beer mat. 'Is it . . . wise?'

Vernon sneers at him. '*Wise?* I'll tell you what's not *wise*, and that's sitting at home feeling sorry for yourself. *Wise.*'

Raymond shrugs. 'Only asked.'

'Well,' says Vernon, 'now you've only been told.'

'Life goes on,' says Erin.

'Well,' says Tom. 'Until it stops, it does.'

'Anyway,' says Pat, 'I rather think Dr Sam . . . I think he'd want us to carry on. Don't you?'

They all do.

'We'll need somewhere,' Raymond says. 'Somewhere to meet.'

'Leave it with me,' Pat says. 'I have f— friends in high places.'

'Dead,' says Erin.

And everybody nods.

Chapter 8

The pumpkin stinks. Sweet and with an echo of something he can't quite identify. It's on the tip of Adam's brain, but Adam's brain is preoccupied with the rising tide of nausea in Adam's belly.

'Daddy? Are you okay, Daddy?'

'Fine, Pupkin.'

It's been a week since he bought it, but the pumpkin remains as tough and unyielding as potter's clay. The muscles in his forearms ache, the palms of his hands are sore.

Mabel laughs. 'Are you having fun, Daddy? I'm having fun.'

He is still reeling from the news of Dr Sam's death. The sudden, indiscriminate nonsense of it. The vicious fucking irony.

'Yes, Maybe. I'm having *lots* of fun.' And he's become rather adept at this nailed-on smile.

Much about Adam's current situation might pass for ironic – like the time he dedicates to his daughter now that his time is running out.

All the mornings he left for work while Mabel was still asleep, and the nights he returned to find her curled beneath her blanket, as if – for all he knew – she had never left her bed. Adam spending his good health in the office, in airports and windowless meeting rooms. Instead of school concerts, parents' evenings, cake sales and sports days.

Is it ironic, or simply tragic?

And the six months alone in a rented flat, wondering what it might take and what he would do to earn his way back into this house and Heather's heart. On some of those nights, drunk and ashamed and self-pitying, he had wondered – and here's your irony – if he wouldn't be better off dead.

And another; the one with which he is currently contending. Adam is hungry. But Adam can't eat. The sight of food, the smell and idea of it, sends bile up his oesophagus, twists his guts and brings sweat to his brow. Today he has managed – through sheer effort of will – to consume half a banana and one bottle of fortified meal replacement. Adam can't eat, and yet Adam is – see his ribs, his wasting legs, the bones in his back – starving.

'Your face is wet, Daddy.'

Mabel pushes her fingers into the glistening pile of scooped-out pumpkin. Adam has pumpkin under his nails and in his hair. The smell is like hands around his neck, like fingers shoved down the back of his throat.

He swallows. 'It's sweat, darling.'

'Why are you sweating, Daddy?'

'Because this pumpkin, Pupkin, is very hard to carve.'

It's taken almost an hour to hollow out the gourd and carve its simple oval features. The effect – an accident of incompetence and pragmatism – is reminiscent of Edvard Munch's *The Scream*. Or so Adam tells himself.

The pumpkin leers at him through its narrow mouth, but for the first time since they began this project, Adam believes they might finish.

'Nearly there.'

'Can I do the last bit?' Mabel asks.

They are sitting on opposite sides of the table, and Adam rotates the pumpkin through 180 degrees so that it is facing his daughter. 'Be careful,' he says, handing her the serrated steak knife.

Adam shakes out his tingling fingers. 'Peripheral neuropathy,' the nurse told him; a side effect of his medication and 'neither uncommon nor anything to worry about'. As if that made it any less frustrating or his fingers any less clumsy.

Mabel's current favourite activity is making necklaces; stringing alphabet beads onto coloured twine and spelling out the names of her friends and favourite animals. She wants Adam to join in

– pleads and bargains and *insists* – but Adam's fingers are too numb and clumsy for this simple game. So he finds alternatives: Play-Doh, paper aeroplanes, pumpkin carving.

'Will you come trick or treating?' Mabel asks.

'You bet I will.'

'Will you dress up?'

'Absolutely.'

'Will Mummy come too?'

'Probably. Maybe.'

'I like it when you and Mummy and me do things.'

'Me too. Be careful there – if you cut your fingers off, Mummy will be *very* cross with Daddy.'

'And it would hurt lots.'

'Yes it would,' Adam says. 'It really would.'

'Would Mummy shout at you? If I chopped all my fingers off?'

The visual is reflexive: his daughter's severed fingers, tiny, prawn-like, beaded with blood and curled in shock. Adam's stomach heaves.

Vomit, Adam thinks. That's what this pumpkin smells of; it has the sweet, sharp aroma of freshly regurgitated food. And the realisation only adds to the effect. 'Yes, baby,' he says. 'Mummy would shout. So be careful.'

'Would she scream at you and cry like she used to when you weren't friends any more?'

'I'm sorry about all of that, Mabel. It was . . . I'm sorry you saw all of that.'

'It's okay. It made me sad though.'

'It made me sad too.'

'Why weren't you and Mummy friends?'

'I was silly, Pupkin.'

'Silly how?'

'I . . . wasn't very nice to Mummy.'

'Why not?'

'I made some mistakes. Don't pick your nose, sweetheart.'

Mabel inspects her finger then moves it towards her mouth.

'No!'

She wipes her finger on the front of her T-shirt, leaving a tapering smear of shining fluid. 'What mistakes did you make, Daddy?'

'I did . . . I had an . . . it was only once, one day. Well, a night, really, one night, not that that . . . you know, makes it any better.'

'You're confusing me, Daddy.'

'Right, sorry. Okay, let's take your friend. Holly.'

'Where?'

'What I mean is, she's your best friend, right?'

'She's my bestest friend.'

'But remember last week when she wasn't?'

'Last week she was best friends with Zadie. I don't like Zadie.'

'Well, Mummy was— Mummy *is* my best friend. But for a moment, I had another best friend.'

Mabel thinks about this. 'Like Mummy's new friend Jamie?'

Adam draws a deep breath, and whether it's the thought of Jamie or the smell of pumpkin, his stomach folds in on itself.

'Is Jamie Mummy's best friend now?'

'It's complicated, Maybe.'

'That's what Mummy said.'

Mabel intrudes her index finger deep into her nostril, and it is no longer a question of if Adam will be sick, but when.

'Don't do that, Pupkin.'

He pushes his chair back from the table, and the chair legs squeal on the tiled floor, a sound Adam feels in his skull as much as it rings in his ears. Mabel removes her finger, and with it a shining gobbet of yellow snot. The mucus is attached to both finger and nostril, pulled into a quivering rope of decreasing thickness as she moves her finger away from her nose.

Standing is a matter of will as much as muscle. Adam flexes his legs; he braces his hands against the table and pushes downward with everything he has. Which turns out to be not very much. His bottom rises slowly from the seat, and as it does, his face tilts towards the table. The smell of pumpkin – the sweet stench of puke – enfolds Adam's mouth and nose like a filthy rag.

Mabel watches with fascination as the snot rope snaps and reforms into a perfect yellow pearl on her fingertip.

The pile of chopped-up pumpkin meat is the same colour as Mabel's snot.

She moves her finger towards her lips.

Adam is halfway to standing now, but he pauses under a wave of vertiginous nausea.

Mabel's tongue extends towards the blob of snot and guides it into her waiting mouth.

Adam vomits.

He vomits into the hollowed-out pumpkin, and he has a moment to marvel at just how much was inside his empty stomach. He vomits hard and copiously. Mabel shrieks, hands raised either side of her face in a parody of *The Scream*, in a parody of the pumpkin in front of her. And in response, the rapidly filling pumpkin begins, itself, to vomit. It dribbles and spills her father's sick from its oval mouth, the spew rolling and spreading onto the table, and from there – in a slow waterfall of banana and fortified milk – onto Mabel's bare knees.

As his daughter screams, Adam can't help but wonder if this constitutes yet another irony. He lowers himself back to his chair. The nausea has passed with astonishing rapidity, and as he surveys the mess of pumpkin and vomit, Adam begins to laugh.

'What's funny?' Mabel asks.

'Life,' Adam says. 'Life is funny.'

And to his immense relief, Mabel laughs too.

Chapter 9

Pat pushes her key into the lock of the front door, and before she has time to twist it one quarter-turn anticlockwise, she hears Hitchens gruffing from the kitchen at the back of the house.

'Only me,' she calls, stepping into the hallway.

The big crossbreed is getting old now – although how old, she can only guess – and the dog huffs and grumbles as he exits his basket and comes to greet Pat. When she found him at the shelter they had estimated the boisterous mutt was around two. Five winters later, and taking dog years into the equation, Hitchens must be around fifty – but he wears it well; better, at any rate, than his owner. Hitchens yawns theatrically, emits a low and lazy two-part woof then pushes his broad head into Pat's thigh.

'Hello to you too. Hello Hitchens. Hello boy.' She pats his withers and massages his chops until Hitchens, satisfied, turns back to the kitchen and huffs out another low syllable.

'Okay. Okay. Let me get my coat off.'

Hitchens watches with his unique brand of reluctant patience as Pat struggles through the slow and clumsy process of removing and hanging her heavy coat.

'I know it's late. I know. I had to see Father Michael.'

Hitchens waits.

'About the hall, yes. Lovely man. Even if he is an A— Anglican.'

Hitchens makes a noise like an extended sigh and nods his head towards the kitchen.

'Yes,' Pat says. 'I'm ready now.'

Hitchens goes ahead and sits in front of the cupboard where Pat keeps the cans of good stuff. An adhesive label on the head-high cupboard door reads: *Dog food & dog treats*. Another says: *Breakfast cereal*, but Hitchens couldn't care less about cornflakes. Pat fetches a can of the good stuff and Hitchens relocates to a position in front of the draining board upon which lies his terracotta bowl.

Pat finds the can opener in a drawer labelled: *Knives, forks, spoons & so on*.

The labelling is a work in progress, driven – for the time being, at least – by caution rather than necessity. Her mind is beginning to fail; trivial glitches for the most part, but they are worrying. And it's not simply a matter of finding and identifying, but also of understanding.

Two weeks ago, she couldn't remember how to change the channels on her television. Having turned the box on, Pat went to the kitchen to make tea. But when she came back and sat in her armchair, she simply could not fathom how to remove the insincere talk show host from her screen and replace him with the news. She knew it could be done, and done easily, but the trick of it had gone. 'Change,' she said to the television. And when it didn't, she repeated the command in a louder voice, despite knowing that this would never work. It wasn't until she thumped the arm of the chair and sent the remote control clattering to the floor that the answer fell back into her head. Now the remote control bears a label explaining: *Turns on TV. Change channel and volume*. This punctuated with a round smiley face, because otherwise, a Sister might just throw her remote control right through the sodding TV screen.

Hitchens's bowl has a label too, this one covered with a strip of clear sticky-backed plastic to stop the ink from running in soapy water: *Hitchens's food goes here*.

She sets the bowl in front of her patient companion. She rubs his tummy as he bends to the food. 'And food goes here,' Pat says. 'I wonder if we'll need to label you. Shall we label you, Hitchens?' Hitchens doesn't look up from his dinner. 'Okay. Perhaps not just yet.'

Pat understands that the day is steadily approaching when she will no longer be able to look after Hitchens, when she will no longer be able to keep him. And without Hitchens, Pat will have little reason left to carry on. So if labelling the drawers and the dog bowl delays that day, by however long, then it's a job worth doing.

She shakes herself. *No need to dwell on that just yet.*

'I'll see you up there,' she says to Hitchens.

Hitchens gruffs.

Pat brushes her teeth, removes her headscarf and the little make-up she wears, then washes her face. Her hair has grown back in a thin but even baby fuzz, but it doesn't grow longer than an inch or so now. Not long enough or thick enough to hide the surgery scar above her right ear.

She undresses and pulls on her pyjamas – a pinstripe jacket and trouser set that reminds her of her father. All Pat wants to do is sleep, but she needs to check in with the boss first.

In her professional capacity, Pat will tell the devoted they can pray anywhere – standing up, sitting down, stuck in traffic or in the middle of the crowd at a heavy metal concert. God is everywhere, after all. But Pat prefers to say her prayers kneeling down. *Force of habit* – as the bad joke goes.

She takes an embroidered cushion from the rocking chair and places it on the floor in front of her bed. *How silly*, she thinks, *kneeling beside a perfectly good and comfortable chair.* But yes, old habits do die hard, and kneeling in this way, more than opening a connection to God, connects Pat to herself as a seven-year-old girl.

Seven-year-old Patricia, kneeling at her bed on young and pliable knees. Twice a day; first 'think' in the morning and last 'think' at night – an innocent malapropism that carried more truth than the child understood.

No one instructed young Patricia to do this; her parents believed, of course, and they attended mass every week, but they never preached or insisted. They never needed to. Pat prayed with the diligence of one who felt the certainty of God, Jesus and the

Holy Spirit in her heart and in her head. She prayed with the gullible, idiot faith of a child. Aged ten, she announced that she had heard the calling and her mother cried tears of joy – a joy that doubled inside Pat's chest and doubled again and again until it filled her up. And maybe that, rather than the presence of God, was the thing she felt in her heart?

Her life in Christ has put Pat in the same room as the best and the worst humanity has to offer. She has taught primary-school children to read and write and wipe their own bottoms. She has given The Spiritual Exercises to convicted murderers, thieves and paedophiles. And no one, Pat has learned, clings to faith with a tighter grip than a child or a mortal sinner. The children because they know no better, the convicts because they have no better option.

Pat has ministered to the dying, too; slowing bodies just a handful of heartbeats from – if your faith holds – heaven. But as their bodies failed, Pat felt their grip on faith begin to slip. She has held the hands of many men, women and old ordained souls who have, with terminal clarity, seen through the thin film of their willed belief to a yawning expanse of nothingness and disappointment.

And Pat knows exactly how they feel.

The doubt slow growing and insidious like the tumour behind her scarf of tiny stars.

'We all have crises of faith,' Father Michael had said, and Pat was both dismayed and reassured that the Anglicans were trotting out the same line as her crew. 'It's God's way of testing us.'

Why would he do that? Pat had wanted to say. But she knew the answer; she has given it more times than she can remember: *To show us how strong we are.*

Kneeling now beside a perfectly good chair, Pat says, 'I don't feel strong.'

She has tried to unravel her doubt but it's a big and messy knot. And the stakes, now, are high. It's all well and good to clap your hands and sing about life everlasting when the future is laid out in a long line before you. But when life is fast expiring, those hand-claps can sound hollow.

Pat's head begins to throb and she reaches for the tablets in her bedside drawer, pops one from its foil packet and swallows it with a sip of water. Last night her head hurt with such feroc-ity she practically levitated off the bed. It hurt like hell. It hurt like the devil. Pat muttering prayers, writhing and groaning like a woman possessed. Hitchens had pushed his muzzle against her hand, gruffing and whimpering and staying by her side until the tablets kicked in and the pain dulled to somewhere in the region of bearable. Thank God for painkillers. Thank God for Hitchens.

She puts two fingers to her temple, moving them in a circular motion as if this might calm the malevolent lump pushing her brain all out of shape, making her lose words, forget objects and, maybe too, question her faith.

Hitchens patters into the room, his claws tapping out his approach on the floorboards. Pat reaches down and lays her hand gently on his snout.

'I'm afraid I haven't got very far.'

Hitchens gives out a low snuffle and sits upright, resting his front paws on the bed, beside Pat's. He sits quietly, big head bowed, waiting.

Pat looks towards the crucifix hanging above her bed; just another aid to memory, perhaps, like the labels on her kitchen drawers.

Pat lets her eyelids fall closed.

As a child, her prayers expanded outwards like concentric ripples from a thrown pebble. She would pray for herself, her parents, her aunts, uncles, cousins and grandparents. For her friends, her teachers. She would pray for everyone in the village, the country, the world. And anyone else, Lord, who I might have left out.

She learned, later, that prayer needs focus, and she wonders now where to direct her mind. She visualises the group, and in particular the three she has come to think of as the youngsters. Tom, Adam, and that poor brave child, Laura.

'Three is not too many. I think God can handle three.'

And Hitchens snuffles in agreement.

'Right,' says Pat. 'Let's pray for the y— youngsters.'

Chapter 10

'It's big,' says Erin. 'Don't you think?'

Compared to the sympathetic cosiness of their usual room in the hospice, the Anglican church hall is stark, bright and big enough to comfortably accommodate a barn dance. And it probably has.

'Play a good game of hide and seek in here,' says Laura.

'Bloody huge,' says Vernon.

'Warm, though,' says Tom, leaning against a radiator. 'Can't go wrong with warm.' And the vast room adds an echo even to Tom's cracked and fragile voice.

Laura turns on the spot, taking in the space around her. The Anglican church hall is high roofed and bright with light, the main space several metres longer and wider than the badminton court marked on the parquet floor in white tape. Additional to this is a fully functional stage at one end, and a galley kitchen at the other, beside the main entrance.

'Imagine the heating bill,' Vernon adds. 'Bloody hell.'

Raymond is inspecting the windows – four on each wall – in the manner of a surveyor or a reluctant buyer. 'That's the third one,' he says, indicating a cracked pane. 'Putty's rotten, too.' He holds his palm to one of the radiators, then raps his knuckles against the metal casing. 'And that needs bleeding.'

'Bloody hell,' says Vernon. 'It's *DIY SOS* over here. I thought we was doing Shakespeare.'

'Forsooth,' says Tom. 'Thy radiators do clang.'

Adam is perched on the edge of the curtained stage, feet dangling a foot or so above the floor.

'The Bard would approve.'

'Thank you,' says Tom.

'I meant the hall.'

The mention of Shakespeare triggers memories of Dr Sam, and as they land in the heads of the seven, a quiet falls about the room. They each feel it and understand that the others do too.

Vernon looks to the rafters and crosses himself. 'Doc.'

'Feels like a long time ago,' says Erin. 'Already it feels like a long time.'

Vernon puts his arm around her shoulders. 'Life goes on, darling.'

'Until it stops,' says Erin. 'Didn't someone say that?'

'Must have been someone very wise,' says Tom.

'See if you're wise enough to find some chairs,' says Vernon.

'This really is some hall,' says Laura.

Pat rolls up the kitchen shutter. 'F— friends in high p— places,' she says. 'And if I'm not mistaken . . . one of them's left a cake.'

They are sitting in a loose circle, close to the kitchen. Initially Tom and Raymond had arranged the chairs in the centre of the room, but the effect was one of being adrift or marooned. So they dragged their chairs into the corner, nearer to both the kettle and the conveniences.

They each have a mug of tea or coffee in their hands or at their feet. An eighth chair serves as a table, upon which sits a stack of side plates, a knife and a round floral tin crammed to its perimeter with the vicar's wife's fruitcake.

'That reminds me,' says Erin, producing a perspiring tub from her bag. 'Don't let me forget to throw these out.'

'No danger of that,' says Tom, taking Erin's chemuffins and setting them on the kitchen counter.

'I think it has brandy in it,' says Raymond, biting into a wedge of fruitcake that could hold a barn door open.

'Brandy?' says Vernon, leaning in. 'Go on then, cut me a sliver.'

'Anyone else?'

No one else.

Erin and Adam are feeling nauseous. Tom's throat is sore, Pat has a headache and Laura's immunotherapy tends to give her diarrhoea – although she keeps this to herself, saying instead that rich food doesn't mix with her drugs.

Raymond replaces the lid on the cake tin.

'What's that say?' Tom asks.

Raymond tilts the tin so that Tom can read the white, handwritten label.

'Cancer group.'

There is a collective sigh.

'Just in case,' says Tom. 'Just in case for one single minute, we might forget.'

Pat breaks the following beat of silence. 'F— forget w— what?'

Tom smiles. 'Can't remember, Sister. Can't remember.'

'In which case,' says Pat, reaching into her bag, 'shall we begin?'

And one by one, they reach into their bags and pockets for Dr Sam's printed sheets. But without Dr Sam, with, instead, the spectre of his recent and sudden passing, no one is sure how to proceed.

Laura's sheet is highlighted in a rainbow of colours, the margins crammed with notes and annotations.

'Been busy?' says Vernon.

'Oh, I, er . . . we had homework.'

'What . . . off Dr Sam?'

Laura shakes her head. 'Drama and Theatre Studies.'

'That's an A level?' asks Tom.

'You'd be surprised. We had to write a proposal for a one-act play incorporating one or more classic works of fiction.'

Vernon chuckles. 'As you do, darling. As you do.'

'So I thought, well . . .' And again she holds up the Bard's collected musings on death. 'As it's almost Halloween, how about a sort of mash-up of all Shakespeare's best deaths.'

'Sounds lovely,' says Erin.

Laura shrugs. 'I tried it as a ghost story – you know: Banquo,

Hamlet's dad, Caesar. The "sheeted dead", Shakespeare calls them.'

'Every day's a school day,' says Vernon.

'But it was . . . I dunno, a bit *Christmas Carol*. Then I thought about . . . well, about us.'

Pat points first to herself then draws a circle in the air, taking in the remainder of the group. 'Us? What about us, love?'

'Therapy, you know. Shakespeare as therapy. And then . . .' She shrugs, colours slightly, makes a gesture with her hands as if swapping something back and forth.

'Let me guess . . .' Tom leans forward. 'Shakespeare *in* therapy?'

'Yes!' Laura claps her hands together, her former embarrassment displaced with a wave of candid enthusiasm. 'Exactly. Shakespeare on a psychiatrist's couch, talking about his death fixation. Stabbings, drownings, sword fights, poison, heartbreak and so on. And then use that – the session – as a sort of frame story to show all the, you know, death.'

'Like *Shakespeare in Love*,' says Vernon.

'But with more stabbing,' adds Tom.

'I love it,' says Pat. 'I just adore it.'

'Clever,' says Adam. 'Very clever.'

Laura shakes her head in a display of bashful modesty. 'I only got a B for it,' she says. 'And I think Mrs Jones went easy on me 'cos I've got cancer.'

'Oi!' says Vernon. 'Don't do yourself down. I could never come up with something like that.'

'Well I think it would make an excellent play,' Pat says. She pauses meaningfully, glances across the room to the vacant stage. 'Don't you think?'

Tom gets it. He smiles and nods. 'I think, Sister. I definitely think.'

Laura looks flustered. 'Oh, I don't really . . . it was just . . . just homework. Just a bit of fun.'

'Fun's good,' says Tom.

'A play?' says Erin. 'Are we talking a play?'

'Why not?' says Vernon. 'What else we going to do?'

Raymond has been quiet up until now. 'Are you sure this i—'

'Listen, *Eeyore*,' says Vernon. 'If you ask if this is wise, there'll be one more murder on the list, you get me?'

'I've always wanted to be in a play,' Erin says.

'We could sell tickets,' Pat suggests. 'Raise some money for charity. I mean, if that's okay with you, Laura?'

'Me? Why me?'

'It's your play, sweetheart.'

'I wouldn't say—'

'What about the hospice?' says Adam. 'Give the proceeds to the hospice.'

The suggestion is met with a volley of approval.

'Shall we?' asks Erin, turning to Laura. 'Do a play for the hospice?'

Laura stares at Erin, this request, this mad idea that she may or may not be responsible, for hanging in the air like an echo. The others too are watching her, like children waiting for permission to play.

'Well, I suppose I could . . . cobble something together. If you like?'

'I'd like that a lot,' says Erin.

'Pass me that,' Pat says, extending a hand towards the vicar's wife's cake tin. And from her bag, she produces a blank adhesive label and a pen. She sticks the label on top of the one that reads *Cancer group*. 'Now all we need is a name,' she says.

'The Dead Good Actors,' tries Tom.

'The Shakes,' suggests Vernon.

'Poor Players,' says Adam. 'You know, from *Macbeth*?'

Raymond clears his throat. '*A Midsummer Night's Dream*,' he says. 'There's that group of actors, Bottom, Quince and the others.'

'Right,' says Erin. 'The play within the play.'

'The Rude Mechanicals,' Raymond says. 'That's their name.'

'The Rude Mechanicals,' says Pat, testing the sound of it. 'Now I do like that.' She turns to Laura. 'What do you think?'

'Me? I . . .'

'Yeah,' says Vernon. 'This' – gesturing around the circle – 'I mean, this was all your daft idea, after all.'

Laura blushes. 'Well I wouldn't go as . . . you know, as far as . . .'

'Well I just did, darling. So what do you say?'

'I like it,' Laura says. 'I . . . yeah, I like it a lot.'

Pat uncaps her marker pen and writes the three words on the clean white label.

'So it's official,' says Erin. 'We're actors.'

'Cross that off your bucket list,' says Vernon, and the comment is met with knowing laughter that grows and multiplies and echoes all the way to the roof.

Act II

Chapter 11

They joked about their bucket lists – creating overblown fantasies involving wild locations, exotic food, famous people. But really, what kind of person's dying wish is to drink champagne in a hot-air balloon? To base-jump off the Golden Gate Bridge? What day-numbered woman, in her right mind, would want to eat lobster with Tom Cruise?

The answer is simple: these are the parlour-game contrivances of men and women who have worked, travelled, partied, loved. These are the blasé fancies of men and women who have lived.

Laura did her best to join in, but she struggled to fake any enthusiasm for a balloon ride, a safari, a Michelin-starred restaurant. Because diverting as the fantasies may be, there are other items Laura wants to tick off first.

Take, for example, sex.

Because for sure, dying young is a tragedy, but dying a virgin – well that's just embarrassing. A concept brought into sharp focus in double English just three days ago.

The year she restarted her A levels – new subjects, new outlook, new silk scarf in school colours – Laura had found herself in a hinterland between the upper and lower sixth forms. Her friends of the previous year, of the previous six years, had advanced to the upper sixth. With one foot out of the school gate, they were preoccupied with talk of exams, grades, applications and which universities promised the best social life. They hadn't yet left school, but they had absolutely moved on.

Whereas Laura's new classmates had their own friends. Bonds and loyalties and secret knowledge formed over the five-year ascent from playground to sixth-form common room.

Laura belonged to neither group, and in the periods between classes she haunted the common room – translucent and unsettling – like a bad omen. In some ways, the afternoons at the hospital were a relief.

It's a little better now that she has finally advanced to the upper sixth. But whilst Laura may be accepted, she has learned that her history – her glaring mortality – sets her apart. On Halloween, for example, a bunch of them went drinking in town, but Laura only found out about it after the fact. She doesn't blame them; after all, who wants to be reminded of death at a Halloween party? They have better things to do, like get drunk, flirt and – as in Tiff Jennings's case – screw one of the bar staff in the car park.

It's all anyone's been talking about, and by extension, who else is a member of the cherry club. On her first trip through the sixth form, Laura had a pretty good idea who had lost it, who hadn't and who was pretending. At least with this group, her own status is something of a mystery, although – and you can see it in their eyes – they can probably guess.

So much about Laura's situation – the scar on her neck, the diarrhoea, the flip-a-coin prognosis – is beyond her control. She has been well and truly fucked by cancer. But so far, by nobody else. This last, though, is within Laura's powers to address.

Sitting at the small desk in her bedroom, surrounded by exercise books and the first five pages of *Shakespeare in Therapy*, Laura takes a single sheet of paper and tears it in half, first down its length and then again widthways.

She picks up a green biro and writes in capital letters across the top: LAURA'S BUCKET LIST.

And underneath this, she writes the words: *Don't Die a Virgin*.

Chapter 12

Adam is a ghost.

But this is not so unusual. The pavements tonight are crawling with zombies, vampires, witches and a great many black cats. Children clutch buckets and carrier bags full of sweets, and a surprising number of houses are adorned with cobwebs, fairy lights, hanging bats and pumpkin lanterns. One is cordoned off with yellow incident tape, the bloody legs of a mannequin jutting upwards from a wheelie bin.

So much effort, Adam thinks. And is, again, somewhat embarrassed by his hastily cut sheet. But what his costume lacks in finesse and preparation, it makes up for in originality. Adam, as far as he knows, is the only member of the *besheeted dead* haunting the neighbourhood tonight, and his get-up has drawn much admiration and comment.

This is the first time he has trick or treated with Mabel and Heather. There is, of course, a corollary to this – that it is also likely to be the last – and Adam has expended no small amount of effort in not thinking about it. A tall order when you're dressed as the dead.

Last Halloween Adam was working late and he can only assume this was true of the year before. Not so different from a ghost, after all. The year before that, Mabel would have been three, so perhaps they didn't venture out into the cold dark streets for sweets. He wishes they had.

Heather is going out later, so they had planned a quick turnaround. All Adam had been required to do was feed Mabel, get them both into costume (one witch, one mummy) and be ready to leave at six o'clock. She wrote the time on his hand just to be sure.

Mabel was ready by five-thirty and Adam went upstairs to shower and bind himself in several rolls of toilet tissue.

He woke half an hour later to the sound of Heather coming home from work, the door banging firmly closed. Adam foetal on the loft-room bed, wearing nothing more frightening than a towel and his loosening skin.

Several seconds later – enough time for Heather to find Mabel alone in front of the TV – Heather shouted up the stairs: was Adam okay, and was he ready?

Yes, he shouted in response. And yes.

Heather gave him the five-minute warning.

No time for the mummy get-up, it took him one minute to splash water on his face and brush his teeth, two minutes to pull on socks, underwear, jeans, shirt, jumper. And another two to find a pair of scissors and mutilate what turned out to be a very expensive sheet.

Heather was waiting with Mabel as Adam floated down the stairs.

Mabel clapped; Heather narrowed her eyes and shook her head.

Other men joke about how long women take to get ready for a night out, for work, for bed. And Adam had enjoyed the fact that Heather didn't conform to the stereotype, which, in any case, he had always suspected a little contrived.

In the time it had taken Adam to destroy the bed linen, Heather had changed out of her hygienist's scrubs and into matching boots, jeans and polo neck. All black, all – as far as Adam could tell – bought new for this evening. Three hundred seconds ago, her hair would have been a tangle of tied-back chaos; erratic, half escaped and harbouring fugitive pens. Now it hung loose, even, and (a lunchtime appointment at the hairdressers, he assumes) approximately two inches shorter than it had this morning. Black eyeliner exaggerated the already feline shape of her eyes. A hairband fitted with kitten ears her single concession to costume.

Then again, Heather had a date with Jamie tonight, and it wouldn't do to turn up with a black nose and drawn-on whiskers.

'Nice hairband,' Adam said.

'Mummy's a cat.'

Adam meowed, then immediately wished he hadn't.

'Come on,' Heather said. 'We're late.'

Standing beside Heather now – as they watch Mabel trot confidently down another front path – Adam detects the smell of perfume on the chill breeze.

'She looks adorable,' Heather says, and Adam makes a noise of agreement. 'The Rice Krispie warts were a nice touch.'

'Thank you.'

Heather looks at Adam, takes in his besheeted form and shakes her head.

'I fell asleep,' he says.

'I can see that.'

'I'll buy a new sheet,' Adam says.

'Too right you will. This' – she tugs a fold in Adam's costume – 'is Selfridges Egyptian bloody cotton.'

It's dark, but Adam notices a small and reluctant smile on Heather's lips.

'I assumed it was one of the crappy ones.'

'Why would you assume that?'

'Because it's on my bed.'

'You . . . idiot.'

Mabel comes running towards them. 'Who's an idiot?'

'Say silly,' Heather tells her. 'Idiot's not nice.'

'But you said idiot.'

'That's right,' says Adam. 'Naughty mummy.'

Mabel laughs.

Heather shakes her head. 'I'm allowed.'

'Why are you allowed?'

'Because Daddy's an idiot, sweetheart.'

'Oh,' says Mabel, apparently satisfied by this line of rhetoric. 'I see. Here.' She holds out two lollipops. 'The lady gave me these for you.'

'But I have no hands,' Adam says, raising his arms and floating the sheet out in front of him. 'And no mouuuuuth.'

'You could eat it through your eye-hole, Daddy.'

'I'm not Daddy, I'm a very . . . very . . . sc*aaary*' – Adam lurches at his daughter – '*ghost!*'

Mabel squeals and runs ahead, pumpkin bucket swinging at her side.

'Well she seems to be okay with pumpkins,' Heather says.

'Despite my best efforts.'

They amble after Mabel. 'How are you feeling today?'

'I'm okay.'

'That's what you always say.' A hint of exasperation in her voice.

They have argued since Adam's return; there have been raised voices and tears and firmly closed doors, but nothing to disturb the neighbours. Nothing to compromise their uncomfortable civility. Besides, they both understand that this awful situation is temporary; that the air will, sometime soon, clear itself.

'I'm scared,' he says, and he had no warning that these words were waiting to emerge. As if, on this of all nights, they have taken on a life of their own.

Heather puts a hand to Adam's sheet, somewhere in the region of his arm. 'Scared? Of . . .'

Of dying?

Of course. But more than that. Scared of my next cycle of treatment, the side effects I have now and the ones to come. Because there are always more to come.

'Of getting worse,' Adam says. 'Of Mabel watching me get worse. Mabel and you.'

'Maybe I should take some time off?'

'I'm fine,' he says. 'Just . . . being . . .' He shrugs. 'I'm fine.'

They walk a short way in silence. 'You have to tell her,' Heather says.

'I know. Just . . . not just yet.'

'You can't keep putting it off.'

Adam might beg to differ, despite knowing Heather is, as usual, entirely correct. She unwraps her lollipop and puts it into her mouth.

'You'll spoil your appetite.'

Heather glances at him. 'Don't try and change the subject.'

'Or are you and Jamie just going for drinks?'

She shifts the lollipop from one side of her mouth to the other.

'Or a movie, maybe?'

'Adam.'

'I just . . . there's no use pretending noth—'

'What are you pretending?' Mabel comes scampering towards them.

'You've got the ears of a bat,' Adam says.

Mabel puts her hands to the sides of her head. 'I'm a witch!' Whatever she collected at this latest doorstep, she's already eating it.

'Don't eat all your sweets at once,' Heather tells her. 'You'll make yourself sick.'

'Like Daddy,' Mabel says. 'Yeauuurk!'

Grateful for the cover of his sheet, Adam closes his eyes and sighs silently.

'What were you pretending?' Mabel asks again.

Lots of things, Adam thinks.

'Nothing,' says Heather. She checks her watch. 'Five more minutes, Maybe. Then Mummy has to go.'

'To see Jamie?'

'Yes, honey.'

'Can I stay out with Daddy?'

'Maybe, Maybe. Now go and see if you can get me something with chocolate on it.'

'Okay.' Mabel twirls on the spot then runs ahead to the next lantern-lit doorway.

Adam and Heather follow, and Adam bumps Heather amiably with his shoulder. 'You look nice.'

'Don't.'

'I'm not being . . . I mean it. You look . . . nice.'

Heather bumps him back. 'Thank you.'

At the next house, Adam sits on the low garden wall and emits an involuntary groan of relief.

'Okay in there?'

'Feet ache a bit. But it's not too bad.'

Although this is not entirely true.

A new side effect – the soles of his feet are red and inflamed, peeling in places as if they have been nastily sunburnt. A hairline fissure has split the fold of one toe and it feels raw despite a layer of cotton dressing. *Palmar plantar*, his chemo nurse told him. *Not uncommon*, and Adam, anticipating the couplet, had finished it with her: *And nothing to worry about*.

Heather checks her watch again. 'You should head straight back.'

'I'm good for a little longer.'

'She's got more than enou—'

'I'll be fine. Honestly. I'll be fine.'

Heather draws a long bracing breath through her nose. *Okay*. 'So . . . when are we going to tell Mabel?'

'How many dates have you had with Jamie?'

She looks at him, expressionless. 'Four.'

'Number five tonight?'

'That would be four plus one, Adam, yes.'

Adam pauses, because he does not want what he says next to sound bitter, petty or resentful. Even if he is feeling all of these things in dozens. 'Is he nice?'

'He has a job and all his own teeth. He's funny.'

'Jackpot.'

Heather allows herself a smile.

'I'm sorry,' Adam says. 'For spoiling . . . you know, everything.'

'Yeah.' And then Heather tilts her head, waiting for an answer to her question. 'So?'

'After Christmas.'

'But . . .'

But . . . nothing.

They both understand that the shadow of Adam's looming death has the potential to ruin what, in all likelihood, will be Adam's final Christmas.

'Christmas,' Heather says.

Mabel skips towards them, a chocolate frog held in her outstretched hand. 'When is Christmas?'

'Eight weeks,' Heather says.

'That's *aaa*ges!'

'It'll go quick,' Heather says. And Adam thinks, *Tell me about it*.

Heather kisses Mabel. 'Don't stay out too late.'

And before Adam can stop himself, he answers, 'You too.'

They watch Heather go, watch her remove the kitten ears from her hair and vanish into the darkness.

Adam reaches out from beneath his sheet and takes hold of Mabel's hand.

'Can we stay out longer, Daddy?'

'Yes, Maybe. We can stay out as long as you like.'

Chapter 13

Last week, to avoid appearing ungrateful, The Rude Mechanicals divided up the vicar's wife's fruitcake and took slices home, wrapped in sheets of kitchen roll. When they arrived today, they found a fresh cake in the tin. Raymond has a slice and Vernon a 'sliver' but as slivers go, this is a good one.

Vernon wipes crumbs from his mouth. 'So, how you getting on with the script, boss?'

'I made a list.' Laura reaches into her bag. 'All the best deaths: Cleopatra, Brutus, Hamlet and Laertes, Mercutio, the Duke of Clarence and so on.'

Tom raises his hands, fingers curled like the claws of an animal. 'Exit pursued by a bear?'

'Definitely. Yes. And I thought, if I read them out, maybe we could put our hands up. Choose how we want to, you know . . . die. Mind you,' she says, 'most of you, all of us, I think, are going to have to die more than once.'

Vernon slaps his thigh. 'I'll die as many times as you like, sweetheart.'

Erin looks hesitant. 'Sorry to interrupt, but . . . I was wondering, I've been wondering about when? When we're going to do this. Because . . . well . . .'

'None of us are getting any younger,' says Vernon.

'Exactly,' says Erin. 'Exactly.'

'Right,' says Laura. 'I see what you . . . well, there's a lot of lines to learn. A lot of . . . deaths.'

'How long do you think we'll need?' Pat asks.

'More a case of how long we've got,' says Vernon. 'Know what I mean?'

Silence.

'November now,' says Adam, almost to himself, and Laura watches him count off the months on his fingers. He stops on his ninth finger, somewhere in the region of July.

'Christmas soon,' says Tom.

'Too soon for a play,' says Pat.

'And no one does anything in January,' Adam says. 'Kind of a . . . dead month.'

'We're going to Cape Verde in February,' Erin says. 'Two weeks. I hope that's not a problem.' She looks to Laura as if for permission.

'God no. Of course not.'

'The Ides of March,' Raymond says, portentously.

'Come again?'

'*Julius Caesar*,' says Tom. 'If I'm not mistaken.'

Raymond nods. 'March fifteenth. Four and a bit months.'

'P— poetic.' But Pat's tone seems to say something else. *Optimistic*, perhaps.

Vernon puffs out his chest. 'Reckon I'm good for March.'

Adam nods. 'March is good. If it's good for everyone else, that is?'

March is good for everyone else.

'The Ides of March . . .' Tom says. 'How's the rest of that go? Beware, or something?'

'Beware the back of my hand,' says Vernon, showing said piece of anatomy to Tom.

'Fair enough.'

'Okay, boss. You was saying something about best deaths.'

Vernon calls her boss with a warm smile, and Laura has rather taken to the epithet. She smooths out the list resting on her knees. 'Yes, best deaths.'

She pushes her free hand into her pocket and finds the coin she hasn't yet rubbed thin. She takes a breath. 'Right. First up, *Romeo and Juliet*. I thought it made sense for me and' – an infinitesimal hesitation – 'Tom to do that. Do those.' She forces herself to look up, as if this is really no big deal.

Tom meets her eyes. When he smiles he favours the left side of his mouth, and his left eye closes in what might or might not be a wink. 'Sounds good to me.'

Laura writes their names against those of the star-crossed lovers, and as she does she thinks of the short bucket list buried in her bedroom drawer. In her peripheral vision, Laura thinks that Vernon may be grinning, a suspicion confirmed when Pat bumps him with her shoulder. Her cheeks feel warm, but she presses on. 'Mercutio and Tybalt,' she says, 'the first of our duels.'

'I'll have a bit of that,' says Vernon. 'Adam, care to join me?'

'Sure. Why not?'

Laura scribbles their names on her list. 'Next up, Desdemona. Smothered in bed.'

Pat raises a hand. 'I think I can m— manage that.'

'Any smotherers?'

Vernon goes to speak, but Raymond has already raised his hand.

Chapter 14

Tom had considered wrapping up and watching the fireworks in the park; after all, this is surely the last chance he'll get. But it's bitter tonight – a single degree according to his know-it-all phone – and Tom is losing his insulation. Cachexia, if you want to get medical. Wasting away, if you prefer your English plain. Call it what you will, the cold hits Tom hard in the bones and teeth, and tonight the cold is cruel.

This is the kind of weather that snatches homeless people in their sleep, taking them from a drug-induced stupor to a more permanent rest. And Tom should know; he's spent more nights than he cares to remember with nothing more substantial than a sleeping bag and a cardboard box between him and the stars. He knows what it's like to wonder, as you hunker down and shiver, whether you will sleep tonight. And if you do, will you wake again the following morning. He knows men who didn't.

But it's warm inside and Tom will sleep well in his bed tonight. Swaddled in three blankets to compensate for the flesh he can't hold on to.

From his third-floor window – *his* window – Tom's view extends for miles, and the sky is illustrated in full colour from displays small, large and back garden all across the county. Also, Laura is sending live updates from somewhere down there on the ground. Blurry pictures and sardonic commentary of what he's already seen from a broader perspective. But he likes this contact.

The microwave pings – *his* microwave – and he can smell the hot chicken soup even before he opens the door to the small and slightly bashed-up oven. The first mouthful hurts his throat, and Tom swallows two mouthfuls of cold water and then a third with half of a powerful painkiller. He could take a whole, but these blissful tablets make him nervous. Tom leaves the soup to cool and fetches his phone from beside the bed.

He turns the phone over in his hands, still not quite used to the fact that he owns something so desirable, intact and frankly beautiful. Not the latest model, of course, but a marvel, nevertheless. He can play music on it, watch films, shoot zombies, read books – although he prefers to do this the old-fashioned way. There's a sticker on the back; a happy green frog, croaking out a voice bubble: 'Well done!' A unicorn too, although this one has nothing to say and the sticker is partially torn.

'They'll probably come off,' Pat had said. But Tom likes them, amused by the idea of some boy or girl attaching stickers to their parent's phone. She hooked him up with the microwave too, via some Christian society that specialises in the poor. After last week's rehearsal, she pulled him aside and asked if he was busy.

'Not hitting on me, are you, Sister?'

'You wish. Now, get your coat. We're going to see a nice lady about a microwave.'

He'd told her about the werewolf some time back. Just a story to make her laugh, about the man – he assumed it was a man – that left thick black hairs in the communal shower and – somehow – in the sink of the shared kitchen. Pat had laughed but she had also quizzed Tom, rather thoroughly with hindsight, on the extent and quality of the amenities in his flat.

The nice lady was called Iris, and she must have been waiting for them. Before Pat and Tom had even reached the counter, Iris produced a microwave oven in a cardboard box along with four pairs of socks and as many tins of chicken soup. Heinz, too, not that supermarket knock-off stuff. Tom asked how much, and Pat told him it was taken care of. He considered protesting, but knew that it would be a charade, and one Pat would be wise to.

So he said thank you, instead, and kissed Pat on the cheek.

'I wondered,' Iris said, 'could you use this?' And she pushed the phone towards Tom as if it were nothing more exciting than a can opener.

He had a phone, of course, but it didn't do what this one does, and the '5' button tended to stick. 'You kidding?'

The woman laughed, but, no, she said, she wasn't kidding.

So he said thank you again, and this time he kissed Iris too.

Lying on his bed, Tom opens the latest message from Laura. A picture of her gloved hand holding a sparkler: *Mum and Dad bought sparklers! Like, I'm 9 or something!* – and an emoji of a cringing yellow face. Meant, Tom assumes, to communicate naffness.

When Tom was nine, his mother would give him cigarettes. By the time he was as old as Laura is now, he was smoking heroin in derelict buildings. He doesn't think his mother ever bought him a sparkler.

Tom wonders if Laura would still flirt with him if she knew where he'd been, where he'd slept, what he'd injected into his arm and what he had done to get it. He hopes she wouldn't. Tom makes no secret of his past life, but neither does he use it as a conversation-starter. Pat knows some of it, and the more established members of the group – Vernon, Ray, Erin – have probably guessed. Adam too, perhaps, but he doubts Laura has put the pieces together. Not yet.

She's funny, clever, brave. Pretty, too, and, if Tom understands correctly, the only Rude Mechanicals with a realistic chance of seeing another Bonfire Night. He is saddened that a girl like that would flirt – if that's what it is – with a guy like him.

Some Romeo.

Tom breathes on the phone's black glass and polishes it to a high shine with his sleeve. He clicks on the Facebook app, although he has no friends yet. He has found people he knows, old school friends, old school enemies, old colleagues. But Tom isn't looking to connect with these former acquaintances. His interest extends as far as one woman.

He has scrolled through every one of her sporadic posts, zoomed in on every picture and read all the likes and inane comments that go with them. Pictures for the most part taken in a generic pub that Tom recognises as the White Lion. This woman is in her late forties. She pouts at the camera, her lips thick with make-up, her eyes lined and glazed. Sometimes there is a man, different men in different pictures. Sometime she angles the camera downward so that her cleavage is on show. Occasionally, this woman posts pictures of herself in bed, her dyed hair carefully fanned on the pillow. In these pictures, Tom thinks the woman looks lonely. She shares videos from reality TV shows, 'lols' at funny clips of people falling over, signs petitions to have paedophiles hung, bankers jailed, immigrants deported. Her 'friends' have a lot of tattoos. The pictures don't show it, but her eyes – Tom knows – are the exact same colour as his own.

He could add her as a friend now, but Tom hesitates. The woman who shares his surname seems happy after a fashion, and he worries that contacting her might compromise that. Tom and his mother haven't talked – have had no contact of any kind – for more than five years, and this woman doesn't know whether her son is alive or dead.

The fact is, he stands somewhere between the two, and why say hello when any day now it will be followed by a great big goodbye.

Hey, Mum, I've got a place of my own.

Did you get a job?

No, Mum, I got cancer.

Thanks to the lump in his neck, the surgery, the medicine and the frankly lousy prognosis, the Pathway team have classified Tom as 'a priority need'.

What's that mean? he'd asked.

It meant a roof over his head. Granted, said roof is a little low and has a brown stain in one corner, but it's *his* roof and it keeps the rain out. His single bed, his wardrobe, his table and his chair. He has clean clothes and two pairs of trainers. He has bought himself a plastic kettle and two mugs in case he has company. And right there on the small table, perhaps the most amazing thing of all – a set of keys to a solid door.

To keep out the werewolf and other assorted nutters. Because, let's be honest, the neighbours leave a little to be desired. These other 'priority needs', with their screaming kids, violent boyfriends, dangerous habits and foaming addictions. Someone plays loud drum 'n' bass in the middle of the night. Someone shits on the concrete stairs between the third and fourth floors. Someone – the werewolf, surely – howls at night, full moon or not.

Sure, the place is a little west of perfect, but perfect would do Tom's head in. Besides, Tom has had a heck of a lot worse.

Truth is, Tom has never had it so good.

The Pathway team apologised for moving him here; the miles in the hundreds from his old stomping ground. They said they were sorry for the inconvenience – of putting distance between him and the people he knew: the users and dealers and the muttering men with mental illness like gravity. Neuroses and fears and delusions that threaten – through proximity and irresistible drag – to take hold of you, too, to pin you down and crush you with their weight.

Sorry, they said. *But this is where the accommodation is*, pointing at three dots on a map. *There*, Tom said, picking the place furthest away from the shop doorways and railway bridges of London. Picking the place where he knew no one and no one knew him. They asked Tom if he needed help moving his stuff, and Tom had laughed until his throat hurt.

His phone vibrates in his hand.

Another message from Laura: *Want to grab a coffee sometime?*

And how to answer that without being a dick?

He looks again at Facebook. At his meagre profile with no pictures, no likes and no timeline. He types in his mother's name – Rachel – and brings up her profile. His finger hovers above the button urging him to 'Add Friend'.

But best, perhaps, to let sleeping dogs lie.

Or maybe he's afraid that his mother will reject him. She has form, after all, in that department.

Tom opens up the text message from Laura and replies: *Coffee sounds good*.

He turns the phone over in his hand and smiles at the approving frog on the back. 'Well done!' says the frog.

'We'll see,' says Tom.

His throat has settled now, and he takes his soup to the window, where he can better watch the fireworks.

Chapter 15

He would rather not see his body, but it's hard to avoid in the bath-tub. His legs – once a point of minor pride – have lost much of their hair and are shedding muscle too. His knees appear swollen, and it's possible that they are. Ideally, the water would be warmer, but this temperature is easier on his sore feet.

He is almost comfortable, but this luxury comes at the expense of soaking a pair of good towels. The taps are on the wrong end of the tub, and without a double layer of towels for padding, they would dig into his back, leaving bruises like fat thumbprints over the bony planes of his scapulae.

He is acutely – painfully – aware of his anatomy, and in more detail than he ever wished to know.

The pump – whirring impassively on the toilet lid – is connected to a PICC line. A thin plastic tube that enters Adam's body via the brachial vein in the hollow of his left elbow. From there, the thin tube travels upwards through the vein of his upper arm, hangs a left at the subclavian then terminates at the superior vena cava where it can drip chemotherapy directly into Adam's heart.

Either arm would have done, but since he is right-handed, the left sounded like the better option. But that was before Adam real-ised the bath taps are on the wrong end.

Adam needs to keep his cannula-stuck arm dry. He needs to dangle this arm, the left arm, over the edge of the bath. And to do this he has to recline against the taps, his back to the window full of fireworks, facing nothing more wonderful than the bathroom door. He could shower, of course, but this involves binding his arm in clingfilm, and besides, he's been on his feet for long enough today.

The local bonfire was a mile and a half away; a short enough walk, but the display went on for over an hour, and the walk home is largely uphill. There was blood in his socks when he undressed.

Because of the pump, he had to be careful to keep Mabel on his right side, away from his tubes and the bum-bag full of toxic medicine.

'What's that, Daddy?'

'It's a bum-bag.'

A giggle. 'Bum?'

'It's where I keep my spare bottom.'

'No it *isn't*. What is it? It's making a noise.'

Heather raised an eyebrow, shrugged: *You're on your own.*

'It's medicine, baby.'

'Like Calpol?'

'Something like that, yes.'

'Why is it Calpol?'

'You know Daddy's not been feeling very well?' Heather said.

'He was sick on my pupkin.'

'Right.'

'And he's *always tired*.'

'Well, the medicine will help with that.'

'Will you be better now?'

'Let's watch the fireworks, shall we? Look at that one.'

'But why does it make a noise?'

'It's hard to explain.'

'I want to see it.' Mabel reached across Adam's waist and tugged hard on the canvas bag at his hip.

'Fuck! Mabel!'

When the nurse jammed twelve inches of silicon tubing up Adam's veins, she had used local anaesthetic. And it still hurt. As Mabel tugged the tube in the opposite direction, Adam felt it dragging like wire from shoulder to elbow.

'Jesus. I'm . . . it's okay, Mabel. Don't cry, baby. I'm sorry. It just . . .' People were looking at him; this man who uses the F-word to his six-year-old daughter. Another father shaking his head. A woman tutting and pulling her own child closer. Adam squatted on his haunches. 'I'm sorry I shouted, Mabel – you gave me a shock, that's all. Are you okay?'

Mabel sniffed and said that she was. But she removed her hand from his and took hold of Heather's instead. They lit sparklers and Mabel came back to herself with the resilience unique to small children. And God knows, she's going to need it.

The tube is still taped in place; there's some redness around the insertion point but no blood. Tomorrow a nurse will come to the house, disconnect the pump and flush out his line. And two weeks later they will do it all over again.

He hears movement on the landing and his eyes go to the bathroom door.

'Okay in there?'

'Good, thanks.'

'Want me to strip your bed?'

'Thank you, no. I'll do it tomorrow.'

'Sure?'

'Sure.'

Not for the first time, Adam reflects that he doesn't deserve Heather. He hates the idea of this character Jamie, but he wants her to be happy, to have someone in her life – although he would prefer she waited until after his has ended. Adam hopes Jamie will treat Heather better than he did. Which, he understands, is setting the bar low.

Adam blinks, and as his eyes come into focus, so too do a series of short horizontal lines marked on the doorframe in variously coloured biros and felt-tip pens. The lower lines are faded now, whilst the uppermost, the more recent, are crisp against the white paint. The highest of these lines is a little lower than the top of their growing daughter's head.

Silly place to do it, really, but this is where they started and it's where Heather will continue to record Mabel's upward progress long after Adam has gone. He remembers marking the first, less than a dozen inches from the ground. Mabel could barely sit, let alone stand, and Adam had held her wobbling in place, naked and pink from her bath, while Heather drew a line above the soft fluff of their daughter's head. The pen, he assumes, produced from somewhere in the depths of Heather's own hair.

A good memory.

It would have been Heather's idea; exactly the sort of silly spontaneous thing that first attracted him to her, that he came to love, and then took for granted until – life, routine, fatigue – the spontaneity stopped.

Memory.

The duality of the word strikes him now – what the living retain and the dead become. Erin told the group how she is preparing a memory box for her daughter, Jenny. Pictures, gifts, special books and souvenirs from twenty shared years as mother and daughter.

Adam likes the idea of leaving a memory box for Mabel, but he has scant memorabilia compared to Erin and Jenny. For the most part, his and Mabel's shared memories exist only inside their heads, and while Adam's will soon wink out like spent fireworks, Mabel's will slowly lose colour and fade to grey. Will she remember him snapping at her tonight? Will she remember his death? He thinks not. He hopes not.

Adam was thirty-one when his mother and father died on the same day and in a foreign country. And even that brutal shock has faded somewhat over the last thirteen years. It no longer brings tears to his eyes or causes him to double over with nausea. Instead, he feels their loss like a dull ache, no more troublesome than the morning stiffness in his back that would – before he became sick – fade under the hot water of the shower. That backache can last all day now, and likewise, with his own demise in sight, the memory of his parents' death hurts more than it has for many years.

There's a line about your parents fucking you up, a poet or an author whose name Adam can't recall. Although he's confident it wasn't Shakespeare. 'They fuck you up, your mum and dad.'

And while some may fuck you up with neglect or indifference or an unreasonable weight of expectation, Adam's parents fucked him up by dying. And by leaving him with enough money to drink himself to death before his next three birthdays. He was making good progress too, until he met a dental hygienist who gave him an ultimatum – get your shit together or find another girl to watch you piss away your life.

And whilst fate clearly had plans of its own for Adam, it would be no exaggeration – or only a small one – to say he owes the last ten years to Heather. Not least because as well as herself, Heather gave him Mabel.

And just look how you repaid her.

The water is turning tepid. If the taps had been on the correct end of the bath, he could use his big toe now to let in half a gallon of hot water. But this way, he gets to remember Mabel, chuckling toothless against the wall, squirming in Adam's hands while her mother marked the first line of her growth on the doorframe.

'You can't have everything,' Adam whispers.

'Want a cup of tea in there?'

The shock of Heather's voice makes him jump.

'I made you a tea.'

'Oh,' says Adam. 'Right. Thank you.'

'Shall I come in?'

Adam looks around the room, at his nakedness, at his prominent ribs, his thin legs and the tube trailing from his arm.

'Adam?'

'I . . .'

His towel is beyond reach, on the back of the door, which now opens a crack.

'I'm coming in.'

Adam lays one hand across his groin, hiding himself from the mother of his child. The woman who would be his wife if she hadn't become pregnant while they were planning not a baby, but a wedding. The latter put on hold, where it has remained for almost seven years. On the upside, at least Heather wasn't able to divorce him.

'Hey.' Heather keeps her eyes fixed on his as she comes into the room carrying a mug of tea.

'Hi.'

'I'll put it . . .' She looks at the toilet, where Adam's pump sits gently whirring medicine up his arm. 'Can I move this?'

Adam twists and reaches for the pump. As he does, the towels at his back slip. 'Shit.'

'Here,' says Heather, 'let me.'

She puts the mug of tea on the floor, then replaces the towels across the taps. This done, she places Adam's pump carefully on the floor and sits down on the lowered toilet lid. She picks up the tea and takes a sip. 'Do you mind?'

'No. Of course not.' Although he would be grateful for a good covering of bubbles. The layout of the room is such that Heather is sitting behind Adam's line of sight, and he comforts himself with the notion that if Heather is looking at his fading body, at least he doesn't have to watch her doing it.

'How you doing in there?'

'I feel awful.'

'Sick?'

'No, about Mabel.'

'She's forgotten all about it. She's talking to *Lady McFluff*.' The last words spoken with light-hearted admonishment.

'Yeah, sorry about that too. Seemed like a . . . you know.'

Heather takes another sip of Adam's tea. 'It was a sweet idea. I suppose.'

The idea was to give Mabel something that would die before Adam. Something to introduce her to the concept of death before Adam explained that death was coming for him. So Adam bought a fish.

'They never lasted more than a week when I was a kid. Must have flushed a dozen of them.'

'Well, that was then.'

'Right,' says Adam. 'They can do amazing things with goldfish now.'

He hasn't heard Heather laugh for a long time, and the sound of it now surprises him. It makes him smile.

The man in the pet shop asked Adam if he had a tank, and Adam said no, could he get a bowl. The 'bowl' the man showed Adam cost eighty-five pounds and came with an LED light, bubble tube, air pump and filter cartridge.

'Don't you just have a normal, you know, *goldfish* bowl?'

'This is a goldfish bowl.'

'But without all the whatnot.'

'Whatnot?'

'Pump, filter and . . . all that.'

'Without *all that*, the fish'll die.'

'Right,' said Adam, regarding the small fish in the plastic bag. *That's kind of the point*.

Including gravel, fish food and a few ornaments it had cost over a hundred pounds.

'Odd name for a goldfish,' Heather says.

'I wanted to call it Little Macduff.'

'Because?'

'He led by example,' Adam says.

Heather passes the mug of tea to Adam. 'Sorry, I drank most of it.'

'Anyway, Mabel heard Lady McFluff, so it's Lady McFluff.'

'Perhaps it's a lady fish?'

'Perhaps. She doesn't have a penis as far as I can see.' Mabel has a tub of bath toys and, in the absence of any concealing bubbles, Adam would be grateful for any one of them right now. 'Thanks for the tea.'

'You're welcome.'

'Thanks for . . . you know, everything.'

'It's fine.'

'I know it must b—'

'It's fine,' Heather says. 'What else am I going to do?' And her voice has picked up an edge.

Adam passes the tea back to her.

'You look thin,' she says.

'Well . . .'

'I'm sorry. I . . .' When Adam turns to look at Heather, he realises she is crying.

'Hey, it's okay. I feel okay, you know. Really.'

Heather wipes her eye with the knuckles of one hand. 'I broke up with Jamie.'

'I'm sorry.'

'No you're not.'

He decides not to counter this contradiction. 'You liked him?'

'I did. But . . . anyway, it's probably best for . . .' Heather inhales.

'What? For now?'

'For Mabel,' Heather says. 'Best for Mabel. And you don't get to be indignant, Adam. You lost that right, okay?'

'I know. I'm sorry.'

Heather stands and passes the tea back to Adam. 'You should get out. I'm bringing Mabel up in ten minutes.'

Heather is almost through the doorway when Adam says, 'Why?'

'What?'

'Why did you and Jamie break up?'

'He's . . . he's not my type.'

'When did you figure that out?'

'When he told me he'd cheated on his wife.' And she closes the door behind her.

Chapter 16

Jenny surprised her today by coming home early for the weekend. A bag full of dirty laundry, her hair chopped short – too short, Erin thinks, but it's good to experiment. They had supper as a family and stood in the back garden with mugs of tea, watching the fireworks near and far. Jenny brought a packet of sparklers home with her, and the three of them traced circles and 'X's and love-hearts in the blue-black air.

Such a lovely surprise.

But even as they laughed and painted shapes with light, Erin could sense her daughter's restlessness and it came as no surprise when Jenny said she might 'pop out' to meet friends at the pub. 'You don't mind, do you, Mum?'

Erin was disappointed, but she didn't say so. Even with Jenny in the pub, the house is warm with the echo of her recent arrival. Her laundry drying on the rack gives off the damp scent of a child returned. They will have breakfast together – whenever Jenny emerges from her room – and this knowledge is warm inside Erin's breast. She visualises Jenny's tired and pillow-creased face at the kitchen table, her messy hair that will grow back soon enough. Perhaps Erin will make pancakes.

While Brian watches the news, Jenny takes three unused sparklers from the packet and carries them upstairs to place in Jenny's memory box. *Our last Bonfire Night*, she thinks. *And such a lovely surprise.*

Chapter 17

Laura should have taken the umbrella. Instead, she snapped at her mother and told her to stop treating her like a child. She anticipated and cut off her mother's response.

'I know I'm your *child*. But I'm not ten.'

'The app says there's a forty per cent chance of rain.'

Laura's hand closed around the coin in her coat pocket. 'Which means a sixty per cent chance of not rain.'

'It won't do any harm to take it.'

Not true. Laura was meeting Tom later, and there was no way she was doing it with a pink polka-dot umbrella hanging off her wrist. 'I'll pass.'

'Well take a coat with a hood.'

'It makes my face itch. I'll see you later.'

'When will you be home?'

'I said – later.'

'Well . . .' A wounded look on her mother's face. 'Supper at—'

'I know. I have to go.'

It's bad enough that she's spent the day feeling guilty, without the added ignominy of her mother having been proved right. She really should have brought the umbrella.

She wonders if he can hear the water squelching in her shoes as she approaches the table. 'Been here long?'

Tom – composed, warm, dry – checks the time on his phone. A beaten-up item with a frog sticker on the back. '*Juuuust* over an hour and a half.'

'Oh my God, I'm sorry. Did I get the time . . .' She checks her watch. 'I thought . . .'

'I came early,' Tom says. 'I like to see how long I can make a coffee last before the staff start getting twitchy.'

Laura sits down. 'And how did that go?'

Tom takes his hands from around the coffee cup, rotating them slightly outwards as if presenting himself as an exhibit – the tattoos, the damaged face, the frayed baseball cap. 'About five minutes.' When Tom smiles, he reveals a set of wide white teeth that clash with the rest of him. 'Maybe four.'

Laura laughs; she nods at his almost empty coffee cup. 'Need another?'

'I'm good. Thank you. You're leaking.'

'I'm what?' She picks up her cup and inspects it and then her top for spilled coffee.

'I mean you,' he says. 'Your hair.'

Her hair, perfect when she left school, is now hanging in mad wet coils and a small puddle of run-off has formed on the table. As well as this, her scarf is soaked and cold rivulets of water are meandering down her back.

'Should have brought a brolly,' Tom says, indicating a yellow collapsible hanging off the back of his chair.

'You sound like my mother.'

'She sounds like a sensible woman.'

'Well you don't have to live with her.' Along with his coffee, Tom has a glass of water. 'Done with that?' Laura asks.

Tom slides it towards her. 'Thirsty?'

Laura drinks the last of the water then sets the empty glass on the table in front of her. She gathers her hair over one shoulder and then wrings it into the glass, half filling it with cloudy rainwater. 'Sorry. Not very . . .' – *attractive* – 'classy.'

'You going to drink that too?'

Laura laughs. 'I'll stick with coffee. Sorry' – indicating her hair – 'It's a nightmare.'

'It's amazing. I mean . . . you're lucky you didn't lose it.'

Laura nods. 'Lucky me.'

'Sorry,' Tom says. 'My filter's . . . rubbish.'

'The girls at . . . in my class,' Laura says, 'they were gutted.'

'That you had . . .?'

She laughs. 'When my hair didn't fall out.'

'Wait, what?'

'They were going to shave their heads. Out of solidarity. Raise money for charity. Have something . . . compassionate to put on their uni applications.'

Tom pulls a face. 'That's . . . I don't know what that is. Weird? Cynical?'

Laura shudders as another stream of cold rainwater trickles down her back.

Misunderstanding the nature of this shudder, Tom reaches across the table and – oh my God – puts both hands on top of hers. 'You okay?'

Laura goes with it. Nods bravely. *Yeah, I'm okay. But best keep holding my hand for a while longer. Just in case.* She makes a determined effort to not smile.

Another droplet of rainwater runs down her back. And then one more. She senses restlessness in Tom's hands and decides she will be the one to break contact.

Tom takes a tiny sip of coffee as Laura unwinds her scarf and drapes it across the back of her chair. His eyes locate the scar on her neck.

Laura raises her eyebrows: 'Snap.'

'Bar fight?' Tom asks with a playful smile.

'You should have seen the other girl.'

'It's neat,' Tom says. 'Your scar's very . . . neat.'

'My mother doesn't think so.'

'It must be hard for her.'

Laura huffs. 'Sure. I just wish she wouldn't be so . . . I don't know, *suffocating.*'

Tom's gaze drops, and his eyes drift over the artwork (amateurish, now that Laura has a chance to observe it at close quarters) on his hands and arms. A faded blue swallow nests in the space between his thumb and index finger; a misshapen Pac-Man on the opposite hand, chasing dots around his wrist. Trying not to stare, Laura picks out dice, a cross, a cartoon bomb, an angel, a heart, more than one rose, a scroll holding the word 'MUM'.

'How did your mum take it?' Laura says. 'When she found out about your . . .' She puts her fingers to the scar on her neck.

'She doesn't know,' Tom says. 'We're . . . estranged, I suppose.'

Laura's face flushes hot, and she knows this will make the scar on her neck turn livid. 'I'm sorry, I . . .'

'You weren't to know.'

The mood has changed, and Laura feels all of a sudden like a child – beyond her depth and unsure how to proceed. 'Did you have an argument?'

'You could say that. I sold her telly.'

Laura hesitates, but Tom's demeanour is light and open. 'I assume she hadn't asked you to?'

Tom laughs. 'You assume correctly.'

'What happened?'

'Chucked me out. And rightly so.'

'How old were you?'

'Sixteen going on stupid.'

'*Sixteen?* Where did you go?'

'Friends, friends of friends, strangers and weirdos. Squats, doss-houses.' Tom shrugs. 'Doorways.'

He holds Laura's gaze and she wonders at his frankness, wonders if it is a form of self-protection; a test, perhaps, to weed out those that might look down on him.

'I'm sorry,' she says. 'That sounds . . . awful. Just . . . fucking awful.'

Tom nods. *Yes it is.* 'So don't steal your mum's telly. And . . .' she watches Tom's features as he decides whether or not to finish his sentence, 'maybe listen next time she offers you an umbrella.'

'I'll take it in to consideration.' A copy of *Romeo and Juliet* is splayed open and face down on the table beside him. She points her chin in the book's direction. 'Been rehearsing?'

'Never read it before. Thought I should get the, you know, big picture.'

Laura picks up the book; an RSC publication, the cover showing two pairs of entwined legs partially covered by a white sheet.

'I guess that's their wedding night,' she says.

'There or thereabouts.'

'Do you think they . . . you know.' She blushes.

Tom laughs. 'What? *Consummated* the marriage?'

He articulates the verb as if scandalised, and this relaxes Laura. 'I mean, it doesn't say, does it? In the play.'

Tom paints a pair of square brackets in the air. '*Shags her*. Must have missed that bit.'

'So you reckon?'

Tom meets Laura's eyes, holds them for a second and then looks away. 'Well, they weren't exactly big on hanging around, were they?'

'That's why it's so romantic.'

'It's why it's so tragic,' Tom says. 'They didn't have to die.'

'Er, I think that's the point.'

Tom laughs again and concedes the rally. 'That's why you're the one in charge.'

Laura accepts the compliment. 'So,' she says. 'Tell me about stealing your mum's TV. Unless . . . unless that's too personal.'

Tom shakes his head. 'My life's an open book. Even if it is a bit dog-eared.'

Laura's hand goes to *Romeo and Juliet*. 'All the best books are.'

Chapter 18

They're taking their break in front of the stage, the chairs arranged in a semi-circle a few feet back from the empty boards. They are quiet; eyes fixed on the floor at the foot of the stage, on a scattering of raisins and fruitcake crumbs.

'Maybe it doesn't like cake?' Tom whispers.

'Course it likes cake.'

Pat nudges Vernon with her elbow. Mimes the act of turning down a volume switch.

Several times this afternoon she's seen him sipping from a hip flask. Not furtive, exactly, but neither without discretion. The drink — she assumes it's the drink — has accentuated his edges, emphasising Vernon's natural tendency to dig, tease and needle. Well intentioned, perhaps, but less well received.

Critiquing his fellow actors' performances, Laura's script, the very words of William Shakespeare. He even went as far as to suggest Raymond black up for his turn as Othello. Not seriously, Pat assumes, but poor old Raymond didn't know which way to turn.

'Oops,' he says now, holding a finger to his lips and dropping his voice to a stage whisper. 'Course it likes cake,' he says. 'It's us it don't like.'

Raymond asks, 'You're sure you saw it?'

Erin nods, although nobody sees this as their attention is focused on a crack in the boards on the front of the stage. 'Bolted right through that gap.'

'Maybe try it with one of your muffins?' Laura suggests.

'I thought we were trying to lure it out, not frighten it off?' says Tom. 'No offence.'

'None taken.'

'Exactly,' says Pat, eyeing the crumbs. 'None taken. Maybe he's w— watching us.'

Laura: 'Or she?'

'Hah,' says Vernon, as if at a sudden jogging of memory. 'A lady mouse, I'll bet it is.' He waits for someone to beg elaboration. And when no one does, Vernon carries on as if they had. 'There's this tribe I read about. Africans. Or maybe I saw it on Discovery. Anyway, these . . . Ubutu, Mambodo, summink like that, if a fella dies, in the tribe—'

'The Manchego?' Tom asks.

Laura, sitting next to Tom, laughs under her breath, and Pat detects a growing closeness between the two youngsters.

Vernon continues: 'So if this fella dies without having kids, they bury him with a dead mouse.'

'Why would they do that?'

'Well, it's a lady mouse, see. So's the fella can have kids in the everafter.'

'That's awful,' Erin says.

'For the mouse?' Tom asks. 'Or the Manchego?'

Laura sniggers.

'I think it's dreadful for both,' says Erin. 'It's not . . . humane, is it?'

Vernon turns down his bottom lip. 'I think they've got a point, personally.'

Adam sighs out loud. He's been quiet today, slow moving and clearly suffering. Twice, he's hurriedly excused himself, pale and sweating, and they have all – even Vernon – carried on as if they couldn't hear him retch and spit and groan in the gents' toilets. But this sigh is clearly one of exasperation rather than affliction.

'What's that?' Vernon asks, turning to Adam.

Adam shakes his head: *Nothing*.

'Let me ask you a question,' Vernon says, and he sweeps his eyes around the semi-circle, making it clear that this question is for everybody. 'If that's okay?' This last directed at Adam.

Adam gestures for Vernon to continue. As if there were any possibility he might not.

'What's the meaning of life?' he asks. 'Huh? Anyone?'

'To enjoy yourself?' Laura says, not quite burying the note of enquiry in her voice. As if eager that her answer be marked correct. 'To enjoy your life.'

Vernon shakes his head. *Nope.*

'To be a good person,' Erin says. 'That's what I think.'

'Aye,' says Raymond.

Again, Vernon shakes his head. *Sorry. Wrong.*

'There is no meaning,' Tom says. 'It's a happy – or tragic – accident.'

You're not even trying.

Vernon turns to Pat. 'Sister?'

God made me to know him, love him and serve him. This is what the priests and nuns drummed into Pat both as a schoolgirl and as a postulate. But her mother's kitchen wisdom always rang with more truth. More humanity. 'I'd say the most important thing is to leave the world a better p— place. In whatever f— form that takes. And there are many.'

Vernon waggles his head with indulgent deliberation. 'I'm not saying that's not a nice thing to do, Sister. A nice *sentiment*. But it ain't, in my humble opinion, the meaning of life.'

'Please,' says Adam. 'Put us out of our misery.'

'You,' Vernon says, pointing at Adam, 'you know already. You too,' directing the finger at Erin.

'Children?' Erin asks.

'Ding. We have a winner. The meaning of life, see, *is* life. The only reason we exist is to reproduce, procreate and squeeze out babies.'

'All of those things?' Tom asks.

'And I've had' – Vernon holds up both fists and uncurls, one after the other, a thumb, four fingers, and another thumb – 'six. Anything else, in the grand scheme, is simply meaningless.'

'So is my life meaningless?' asks Pat.

'And mine?' Laura adds.

Tom raises a hand. 'Meaningless over here,' he says. 'Well, to the best of my whatnot.'

'That's not what I'm saying.'

'It s— s— sounds like you are.'

'Any prick with a dick can get someone pregnant,' Tom says. 'Excuse my language, Sister.'

Pat winks and floats a sign of the cross towards him. 'Ten Hail Marys before bed.'

But Vernon will not be derailed: 'All's I'm saying is, there is no *higher* meaning than having children. Right, Adam? Erin? Raymondo?'

Raymond stands. 'My wife had a child,' he says. 'I didn't.' He places the lid on the cake tin and takes it to the kitchen.

'Nice one,' says Tom, but Vernon appears not to hear.

'Having Jenny,' Erin says, 'might be the only . . . the only really meaningful thing I've done. But . . . but I don't agree . . .' She wipes a tear from her cheek. 'I agree with Pat,' she says. 'Not you.'

'What about men and w— women that a— adopt,' Pat asks. 'Does that mean anything? Does that m— measure up in your book?' And she wonders if the note of barely suppressed anger is as evident to the others as it is to her.

Laura leans in. 'What if your children die? Does that cancel out your meaning? Will it cancel out *my* parents' meaning?'

Pat's eyes go to the stage, to the pillow resting on the chaise. By her estimation, Pat has a good fifteen pounds weight advantage on Vernon, and she thinks he'd have a hard job fighting her off if she were to take that soft white pillow and press it to his face.

'Course not,' Vernon says, 'but I—'

'Here's a question,' Tom says, and while all the other voices have risen, his remains quiet and deliberate. 'What if you have kids and abandon them? What if you have kids and neglect them? Or abuse them? Does your life still have meaning then?'

Vernon hesitates, and Pat whispers a prayer for God to please stop this man's tongue. And just in case God isn't home, she claps her hands and says, 'Anyone fancy doing a spot of ac— acting?'

Adam heaves himself from his chair. 'I have to go. I feel awful.'

'Actually, I . . . I think I might be done for today, too.' Erin turns to Laura. 'If that's okay?'

'Summink I said?'

Erin turns to Vernon. 'Take some cake for your wife,' she says. 'I expect she deserves it.'

'Good for you,' Vernon says quietly as he watches her leave. 'Good for you, darling.'

Raymond returns now with a dustpan and brush. He gets down on his knees and sweeps the cake crumbs onto the pan.

'Not leaving any supper for our little friend, Raymondo?'

'The worst thing you can do with vermin,' he says, and he pauses just long enough for the last word to find its rhyme, 'is encourage them.'

Vernon lets out a long and weary sigh. 'Too true, Raymondo. Too true.'

'Got the energy to smother me one more time?' Pat asks.

Raymond stands and bows. 'For you, Desdemona, anything.'

'I'll wrap the cake,' Vernon says. 'Everyone taking some?'

Everyone is taking some.

Pat places a hand on his knee. 'And don't forget an extra big slice for Mrs V.'

'I never do,' Vernon says. 'How could I? She lumbered me with all them bloody kids.'

Chapter 19

They told him the nausea would get better. No, it *might* get better, or *could* get better, or *tended* to improve. As with everything else, the doctors never promise – shading any optimism with an arsenal of caveats and qualifiers. This medicine, for example, *might* give him eleven months, whereas the milder regimen would *likely* give him only nine. The difference amounting to a small number of weeks, a scattering of days. But all days are not created equal. And this nausea has *not* improved.

This afternoon he vomited like a dog, into the hedge beside the bus stop. His bus arrived as he was heaving weak tea and high-calorie meal replacement into the shrub. He assumes the laughter was schoolchildren – going home or skiving off – with a grand-stand view from the top deck. His hand is scratched from attempt-ing to steady himself against the bush. From grasping at twigs.

Despite leaving rehearsals an hour early, he was late collecting Mabel from her play date. But if Dianne was inconvenienced, she didn't let on. Adam declined the offer of a lift home, not wanting to vomit over the seats in Dianne's Volvo.

Sitting on the toilet now – a necessary expedient – with a glass bowl between his knees, Adam retches again.

Mabel's voice from the other side of the closed bathroom door: 'Are you okay, Daddy?'

This nausea is a full-body thing. He feels it in his lungs, in his shoulders, on the nape of his neck. He is shivering and sweating nausea.

'Fine,' he says. 'I'll be . . . I'm fine.'

'Can we do it again?'

'Yes baby. Do it again.'

He hears her footsteps retreat along the corridor, her bedroom door closing. This is Mabel waiting in the wings, preparing for her big entrance.

The Christmas play is four weeks away, and the parts have been assigned. Mabel's has four lines, which Adam would bet good money did not feature in the original text of *A Christmas Carol*. Likewise, Mabel will be dressed as a robot – a costume she wanted to start making immediately.

'We have four weeks,' he told her.

'But I want to do it now.'

'We don't have the stuff. Boxes, foil.'

'We have boxes.'

'Not the right boxes.'

'We can get them. Now.'

'We have to go *home* now.'

'I don't *want* to go home.'

Adam tried to explain, to be patient, to empathise and understand. Mabel insisted, sulked, cried not fair. So Adam snapped and told his excited six-year-old daughter to stop being a brat.

'What's a brat?'

'A brat is horrible.'

And then, of course, Mabel cried. 'You always make people cry,' she told him, stamping her foot for emphasis. 'You're a brat!'

They walked the rest of the way home in silent, but gradually dissipating loathing.

Time, he supposes, is elastic for children. Four weeks can loom with the immediacy of tomorrow, and a five-minute walk can have the calming effect of a good night's sleep. He sees this clearly now, because his world has been subject to the same distortions.

There are minutes that feel like hours. And days that pass like moments.

'Ready?' shouts Mabel.

'Ready.'

He hears her bedroom door open, footsteps approaching down the corridor. Then silence.

'I'm waving my hands,' Mabel says. 'Like a spooky.'

She is already a centimetre taller than her most recent mark on the doorframe and Adam wants to reach through the bathroom door and touch her face.

'I've stopped now. Ready?'

'Ready.'

'I am the Robot Ghost,' she says, 'of Christmas Future. Ooooooooo.'

Adam sets the bowl down on the floor, then claps. 'Brilliant,' he says. 'It was very spooky.'

'And then I say: "Follow me." But spooky as well.'

'Great.'

'Shall I say it?'

'Yes.'

'Okay then. Follow meeeeee. Beep.'

'Blimey, Mabes, that's scary.'

'Were you frightened?'

'Terrified.'

'Okay then, I'll do my next bit now. It's mostly pointing and waving, though. Shall I say what I'm doing?'

'Please. Yes.'

And while Mabel beeps and makes invisible gestures behind the door, Adam begins the clean-up operation in the bathroom. Unlike Mabel, he does not narrate this process blow by blow.

He cleans himself first; wipes his backside, washes his hands and his face. The chemotherapy coursing through his system is toxic, designed – in yet another irony – to kill. To kill the cancer cells, for sure, but there is collateral damage – his hair, his hands, his feet, his aching joints and roiling nausea. This poison churns within his bodily fluids – his blood, his piss and vomit are all contaminated, they are toxic too and must be cleaned fastidiously. Adam dons rubber gloves from the bathroom cabinet and cleans the toilet bowl inside and out. He cleans the flush, the sink and the taps. Overkill seems an appropriate phrase. But this is a necessary precaution. The doctors suggested he sits down to urinate, lest he leave a poison splash on the seat. He has been instructed to flush the toilet twice, with the lid down. So yes, this clean-up is essential. It takes time, however, and to buy more of this commodity, Adam slows Mabel down by asking questions and requesting repeat performances of the actions he can't see through the closed door.

'And now I do my 'nother line,' Mabel says.

'Give it to me,' Adam says, unpeeling the gloves and returning them to the plastic bag he keeps at the top of the cabinet.

'Mend your way, Ebbyneezer.'

Adam washes his hands once more for good luck, then squeezes a line of toothpaste onto a Spider-Man toothbrush. His gums have been bleeding. They *may* get better, the nurse told him. But in the meantime, a soft-bristled kids' toothbrush is easier on his mouth. An upside – and you take 'em where you find 'em, Adam – is that Mabel thinks this is fantastic.

Adam opens the bathroom door now.

'Spider-Man teeth!' Mabel shouts.

Adam nods, brush in mouth.

'And my last line is, I stop moving like this, like I'm *stuck*?'

'Yes.'

'And I say: "I must leave now, but can you plug me in first please? My battery is flat." And then I go floppy like this. Like I died. But I'm just a robot so it's okay.'

Adam pulls her towards him. His reflection blurs in the bathroom mirror and his eyes gloss over with toxic tears.

Chapter 20

The big drama at school yesterday was Tiff Jennings's period being two days late. Which is really just a cover story for Tiff Jennings reminding everybody that she lost her virginity two weeks ago. 'But I'm so regular,' she says, attended to by a tight circle of concerned friends who surely see this for the pantomime it is. None of them are particularly great actors. If you ask Laura, they would all be secretly delighted if it turned out Tiff really was up the duff with a barman's baby.

In addition to the treatment side effects Laura has now are those she might have in the future. Such as spontaneous diabetes. Such as infertility. Motherhood isn't something she's given much thought to; she's been kind of preoccupied with having cancer.

Fair play to Tiff, though, she's throwing herself into the part. They sit four to a table in English, and to the mock horror of her entourage she used the corner of a metal ruler to scratch two short lines – one for each day she is late – onto the inside of her forearm. The lines raised into stark welts against Tiff's perfect white skin. But she didn't break the surface. This is, after all, only a part she is playing.

Laura has a pair of good scissors in her pencil case, and she imagined herself coolly walking over to Tiff's table and placing the scissors in her hand: 'For tomorrow,' she would say.

Sitting at the desk in her bedroom, an open textbook before her, Laura takes the scissors and runs her thumb along the sharp edge. The cold metal tickles her skin.

There are side effects, too, that don't appear on the comprehensive lists that come with her various medications. Laura, for example, would never have considered herself a cynical girl two years ago. She never would have considered herself hard. Quite the opposite.

'You need to toughen up,' her father would say. Laura crying with a tummy ache, grazed knee, a rash of nettle stings on her calf.

This desk is where it started. Or where it first came to their attention. Laura hunched over her revision, annotating a cross-section of the human brain and scratching absentmindedly at her right shoulder. A dark black mole that itches like an insect bite.

Hypothalamus, pituitary, medulla oblongata. She is so engrossed in her revision that she doesn't notice when the mole begins to bleed. A red bud blossoming on the shoulder of her clean white shirt. It's only when her fingers go again to her shoulder and come away sticky, that Laura freaks out.

She has a scar on her shoulder now from where they removed the mole. Others from the removal of various lymph nodes. Her father doesn't tell her to toughen up any more. She only has to bump her hip against the table and his face is a mask of concern. His voice – *Are you okay, poppet?* – rising by half an octave.

There is no such thing any more as a minor graze. Everything is a major fucking incident. A stubbed toe, a headache, a paper cut. Ice packs, aspirin, anti-bacterial sticking plasters. It's enough to drive a girl to self-harm – but, Lord, can you imagine the drama?

She doesn't mind the fuss. It's the lack of continuity. Because all it does – this shift towards the sympathetic – is to remind her that a cut finger is the very least of her problems.

And so Laura wears her own mask. Tough, glib, indifferent.

She rolls up her sleeve and peels back a plain salmon-coloured plaster. The burn underneath is still raw from where her wrist touched the edge of the grill pan two nights ago. The pain was fast and intense, but she didn't cry out. She went quietly upstairs, dressed it with a sticking plaster and changed into a long-sleeved T-shirt.

Today, Tiff Jennings performed the drama of relief. Her period – was there ever any doubt – had come in the evening, and now she cried the tears of a crisis averted. She's not having a baby, after all. Lucky Tiff.

The meaning of life, according to Vernon, is to create life. To 'squeeze out babies', as he so delicately put it. Does that mean Laura's life will be a lesser thing if it comes at the cost of her fertility? Laura doesn't know the answer to this question. Perhaps there is no answer. Perhaps the question itself is null. She likes Vernon, but anyone with half a medulla oblongata can see the man is more fool than philosopher.

She purses her lips and blows a narrow stream of air over the wound on the inside of her wrist. The cool air is instantly soothing and when her breath runs out, Laura fills her lungs to capacity and blows again, making it last as long as she can.

If Laura ever has children, and one should fall and take the skin off her elbow, Laura will not tell the child to toughen up. She'll kiss it better, make a fuss and fill the bathroom cabinet with brightly coloured sticking plasters.

Chapter 21

The system isn't perfect, but neither is life. Neither is death. Philosophical pragmatism notwithstanding, however, Hitchens is growing impatient. He nudges Pat's calves with a force that speaks of exasperation, the weight of him upsetting her balance and doing nothing for her concentration. She has the dog food and the bowl, but she is temporarily baffled as to how she might go about getting the food out of one and into the other. The sticky notes tell her where things are and what things do, but they're next to useless if her brain won't tell her what particular thing she needs at any given time. Like now.

Hitchens yips and turns tight circles at her feet.

'If you would just give me a m— moment. I m— might be able to work this thing out.'

He barks, irritated. *Food*.

'I've had rather enough of cantankerous old m— men today, thank you very much. Without you making m— matters w— worse.'

The memory of Vernon ushers in the memory of the cake, and specifically the two slices in her shoulder bag.

She empties the contents of the bag onto the kitchen table, roots out the fruitcake and places a slice in the dog's bowl. In his eagerness to get at the food, Hitchens almost nuzzles the bowl from Pat's hand as she sets it on the floor. She worries; is it okay to give cake to dogs? Surely it is; people feed their pets all sorts, and the stuff Hitchens sniffs and licks when they're out walking . . . infinitely less desirable than a small slice of fruitcake. And it doesn't require a can opener, which is a bless—

'A *can opener*,' Pat says out loud. 'See, dog, I told you I'd get there.'

Hitchens grumps. *Whatever. Got cake.*

Pat begins returning items to her bag. Tissues, tablets, books, a diary, two pairs of spectacles, an unopened bag of buttermints she doesn't recall buying but which she peels open now, popping one of the sweets into her mouth. She is hungry today and will cook something nice for supper – a chicken casserole, perhaps; that way she can save down small portions for later in the week.

Also on the table is Pat's swimming costume and cap, her goggles and a towel that folds up into a bundle barely larger than a facecloth. And here is another example of the fallibility of the system – the sticky notes don't tell Pat what she can no longer do, what she no longer needs. She hasn't swum since August, when she threw a fit in the local swimming pool, thrashing the water with her eyes rolled back in her head, frightening the children – frightening the lifeguard, in fact, although the boy can't have been more than eighteen himself.

'Exertion,' her oncologist had speculated. Pat had been only halfway through twenty slow lengths, alternating breaststroke with backstroke. When she was younger she swam on the school team and brought home enough medals to fill two shoe boxes. 'You're lucky you didn't drown,' her oncologist said. These doctors have a funny idea of luck. He suggested Pat stop swimming until they ran a scan and some further tests, and once the results came back he upgraded that suggestion to a firm recommendation. Which was now redundant; the swimming pool would only admit Pat with the written consent of her doctor. Pat didn't ask, not wanting to put her doctor in the awkward position of having to refuse, and, anyway, not wanting to terrify any more children or lifeguards.

After her fit in the deep end, Pat had managed (with the help of the ashen-faced lifeguard and some undignified shoving from a man in green Speedos) to exit the pool upright and conscious. Next time, all concerned may be less lucky. Yet her brain had forgotten or ignored this excruciating recent history when Pat had packed her bag this morning, looking forward to twenty gentle lengths on the way home.

Hitchens looks up and woofs gently. He has eaten much of his cake, but has enough left to keep him anchored to the bowl.

'I'm fine,' Pat says. 'Just being silly.' She dabs at her eyes then blows her nose into one of the many scattered tissues, and Hitchens returns to his cake. 'Let me clear this up, then I'll get your m— main course, yes?'

Fine.

Pat returns the rest of the items to her bag, and drops a selection of papers, wrappers and receipts into the bin. She has leaflets from two organisations that take in abandoned pets, and she puts these to one side. She should dump her swimming gear in the bin along with the old receipts, but not today, and she gathers the items into a neat pile and puts them in the airing cupboard in the hallway. It crosses her mind to add a label to this small dry bundle: *You can't swim.* But Pat resists. There is a lido a bus ride away – it's too cold now for any but the hardiest or most determined souls, and if Pat were to go early enough there would be fewer people still. It's a possibility. The cold combined with the exertion might, of course, finish Pat off, but – she smiles – perhaps that wouldn't be such a bad way to go.

Better than the alternative. A hospice staffed by nuns, the beds occupied by more of the same and a good flock of rambling, shouting, farting priests. Pat could refuse; choose a more secular locale in which to fade out. But wouldn't that be ungracious, after all the church has done for her? They gave her a life, and she owes them a death in return.

Pat has worked in one such hospice, owned and funded by the church. In St Bernadette's, she changed beds, administered tablets, washed old and confused nuns beneath a concealing sheet. They were – despite all expectations – among the happiest days of Pat's life. But she does not want to end her days surrounded by prayer and piety and a religion that might be nothing more than make-believe. She wants to die at home, with music on the radio and Hitchens at her side. But Hitchens can't help Pat to the bathroom, he can't fetch water or bring Pat her tablets when she is too weak to climb out of bed.

In the kitchen, Pat checks the fridge and finds chicken thighs, carrots, an onion and some rosemary that hasn't quite gone. Potatoes, too, just beginning to sprout, a leek and half of a yellow pepper. The prospect of cooking cheers Pat, and she washes her hands then starts in on the peeling. This simple action triggers a collage of memory from childhood; of helping her mother prepare the vegetables for Sunday dinner, of stewing apples and rolling out pastry until it was the exact thickness of a blue saucer. Afterwards, the three of them would go for a walk, or if it was cold, stay indoors and play whist. And Pat sees their hands in her memory; the red-backed cards fanned between her parents' small fingers – as if her mother and father had been made to match each other, both constructed of fine and tiny parts. Pat's hands – swimmer's hands, her mother said – were bigger than her mother's at age twelve, bigger than her father's the year after that.

Recalling Vernon's proclamation that the meaning of life is to create life, Pat is offended not on her own behalf, but on that of her now deceased parents who never produced children of their own. And how dare that man? They raised Pat and loved her and gave her, if not everything she wanted, then everything she needed. *Almost everything.* Her parents lived to be eighty-three and eighty-six, and they took their good, small-handed, long-living genetic material with them. Pat wonders what became of her birth mother and father – did they have strong swimmer's hands? Did one succumb to the same cancer that will take Pat?

Chopping the leek into thin half-moons, Pat feels no regret. She has lived a full and happy life. She has, in her small way, improved the lives of others and – by her mother's reckoning – lived a life of meaning.

In her capacity as an undercover nun, Pat has a ready answer for the inevitable: *Do you have children?*

'I've had hundreds,' she says.

And after a good pause, she tells the enquirer about more than thirty years working in primary school. Of teaching the alphabet to more than one thousand tiny humans, introducing them to the

Egyptians, the Romans, Charles Dickens and Ludwig van Beethoven. Sticking plasters on their knees and drying their tears with her thumb. She has a cardboard trunk in the living room, stuffed with Christmas, birthday, and thank-you cards written in so many hundred tiny hands.

Does she regret that none of those hands were the same shape as hers? Perhaps. She has heard childlessness described as an ache or an absence, but Pat doesn't feel this. What she aches for is companionship, for love and intimacy.

She has wine in the fridge. Less than a glass gone, and that drank more than a week ago. The wine will be sour now, but she adds a healthy glug to the chicken casserole. Her mother used red, even with chicken, but Pat is sure her mother will forgive this minor transgression.

Hitchens trots over to Pat now, licking his chops and making low noises.

'Can you give me five minutes, mister?'

Hitchens, his belly full of cake, woofs and waddles back to his basket.

'Thank you. I won't be long.'

I can wait.

She places a lid on the casserole, sets an egg-timer for thirty minutes and drops the timer into her cardigan pocket. She opens the can of dog food and opens the kitchen drawer to retrieve a fork.

Sitting on a chair at the small table, Pat digs the fork into the open can and twists out a lump of jellied meat. She looks through the dark kitchen window and imagines a shed at the foot of her small garden, a single window lit from within – the man she shares her life with fixing a lamp or mending the leg on a rickety chair. The radio is on low, and – like her father – the man hums while he works.

'Supper in thirty minutes,' she says to the ghost in her shed. And she imagines him turning off the light, and coming inside to wash his hands and eat with her at this small table.

Hitchens gruffs from his basket; he yawns and stands.

'I know. I know.'

She lifts the fork of dog food to her mouth, takes the meat off the tines with her teeth and chews. *This is odd.* A quiet voice at the back of her mind. And again, she digs the fork into the can.

Hitchens barks.

'Yes,' she says, the fork halfway to her lips.

The dog barks again, louder and with urgency.

'What now? Silly pu—'

The food. The food.

And Pat knows, she understands, smelling the dog food just inches from her nose.

Somehow she manages to feed Hitchens first, scooping the shining meat into his bowl as he dances around her feet. And then she goes upstairs, vomits and brushes her teeth twice.

She wakes from a bad dream, flustered and afraid.

It's some time after three in the morning – the time when old priests and nuns slip quietly away. In the dream, Pat lay dead on these sheets, Hitchens standing astride her chest, taking bites from her face and neck. A calm and bloodless consuming of her flesh. *The body of Pat.*

Would Hitchens do this if she dies in her sleep? She supposes he might.

Pat is not concerned for herself – the body is simply a vessel – but she wouldn't wish that discovery on the people who would eventually find her. What was left of her. More of a concern would be the implications for Hitchens. No family would take him after he had tasted human flesh. He would see out his days in a kennels – a hospice, if you like – for old hounds. Unless, of course, they put her boy to sleep for the sins of his nature.

Pat levers herself into a sitting position, swings her legs from the bed and goes through to the bathroom to pee. This done, she plods downstairs to check she did in fact turn off the chicken casserole. She did, but the thought of eating it now – the phantom taste of dog food in her mouth – makes her feel queasy. Maybe Hitchens will eat it.

He's curled in his basket, and dreaming of what? Something nice, Pat hopes.

She strokes his shoulder gently, so as not to wake him, and on her way back upstairs, she closes the kitchen door behind her. She closes her bedroom door too. Just in case.

Chapter 22

Vernon can't sleep.

The cancer's in his colon, but bits of it have spread to his liver and lungs and he's been having difficulty catching breath. He wakes several times a night, chest heaving for air – dreams of drowning, and tonight, a nightmare in which he was being smothered with a gigantic pillow.

His wife has learned the knack of sleeping through this, and Vernon is glad. She does so much and God knows she needs her kip. He shuffles down the stairs, a descent of thirteen steps that takes him close to two minutes. The last thing Maggie needs is to find him cold and broken-necked at the bottom of the stairs. *What's the word? Ironical. Now wouldn't that be ironical?*

In the kitchen, he boils a kettle, washes the remaining dishes, two mugs, one plate and one fork.

Six days ago, Pat sent him packing with a whole quarter of the vicar's fruitcake, and Maggie only got to finishing it last night. Good cake, the missus said, but reckoned it was a bit heavy on the raisins and a touch dry by that account. Vernon told her about the mouse, about them all sitting round watching a bunch of crumbs and the mouse not falling for none of it. 'Too many raisins, see,' Maggie said; she always could make him laugh.

He left out the bit about him being a proper tit with all that 'meaning of life' business. She's heard the riff before, and even though it's her that went through labour half a dozen times, she buys it no more than Pat did nor any of the rest of them.

Maggie. Everything that's good in his life he owes to her. His home, his family, the life they've built around them.

Besides making him laugh and sleeping through his snoring, she guides him past the worst parts of himself. She tells him, in other words, when he's being a proper tit. She wouldn't have stood for that nonsense today. *Vernon, she'd say, you don't half talk some nonsense.* And Vernon would not have disputed the obvious fact. The nonsense would have blown over, he would have apologised, made a joke, moved on. He wouldn't have upset a room full of good people who he has come to love like family.

He's a better man when Maggie's in the room. A marginally better man for having her in his life.

And what does she get out of it? Earplugs for his snoring and the occasional slice of leftover cake. But he loves her, see. He loves her true, and she – God bless her – loves him back. *What a lot of sins love forgives,* he thinks. *And what a lot it prevents, too.*

He makes tea, strong with a good nip of whiskey, and carries it into the living room. Photographs everywhere of his beloved girls and boys. All grown up and left the nest. And good kids, all of 'em. You can't play favourites with your kids; you love 'em all, completely, but Geoffrey is perhaps the most like Vernon, and there's no one to blame for that tragedy besides Vernon himself.

Not a favourite, exactly, but of all of his girls and boys, he worries about Geoffrey the most. The boy – *boy!* Six foot two and wide as a window – has a good job now, driving wagons all over Europe, and Vernon when he says his prayers, prays that Geoffrey will keep this one. The boy's a hot-head, ruled by his passions and set off easily. Maybe if the lad had someone, a steadying influence like his mother, maybe then life would fall easier into place for him. Maybe if he had a kid of his own, someone other than himself to think of – isn't that what Vernon's kids did for him? Gave him purpose, helped him become a better man. Although this last task remains a work very much in progress.

Three of his kids have children of their own now, and Donna is due her second in February, making him a grandfather for the fifth time. He'd like to live to see that day.

Give me Christmas and get me to February, he says to Maggie. *And I'll settle for that.*

But he will get what he's given and the thought of only one more Christmas terrifies him, though he'd never admit it. If he makes it to next May he'll be sixty-five. But that's not nearly enough.

Vernon shuffles around the perimeter of the room, stopping at every framed picture and fixing the images of his children in his head. He mutters his love to each one. Tomorrow he will pick up the phone six times and tell them all over again.

He stops finally at a picture of Geoffrey. He's tossing his nephew – Donna's first – above his head, and the camera caught it just right; his son and his grandson both open-mouthed and smiling the same smile at each other. And doesn't Geoffrey's life have meaning, despite him not being a dad in his own right? Of course it does – look at that picture; look at the tear forming now in his father's eye.

Pat said that the meaning of life is to leave the world a better place, in whatever form that takes. And she's right, isn't she? You only need look at that picture to see the truth of it.

He was a berk at the last rehearsal, and he'd take it back if he could. Like so much else that is done and later regretted. He'll be a better man tomorrow, he tells himself. He might even tell Pat she was right – so long as she promises to keep this information to herself.

Vernon lowers himself onto the sofa and sips his tea, watched from every wall and flat surface by the faces of his children.

Chapter 23

'Does your mum take you shopping ever?'

'Not as much as she'd like,' Laura says. 'But . . . we have different tastes. She'd have me all in pink and frills.'

Erin takes a top from one of the racks and holds it against Laura's chest. 'Something like this?'

Laura laughs, blushes. 'No, this is nice.'

Erin squints at Laura, letting her eyes lose focus. Imagining her daughter standing in Laura's place. According to Erin, Laura and Jenny are around the same height and build. Laura maybe a little taller. But close enough for Laura to act as a stand-in – an understudy – to help Erin pick something out for her daughter's birthday.

'Do you think she'd like it?' Erin asks. 'It's so hard to tell.'

Laura shrugs; she doesn't know Jenny from Eve. For all she knows Jenny could be into metal or skate or – who knows? – pink and frills. 'It's nice,' she says. 'I like it.'

Erin bites her bottom lip. 'Would you . . . try it on?'

'What?'

'I'm sorry, I . . .'

Laura takes the top from her – pink, but salmon pink, not fairy pink. A little blousy in the shoulders and scalloped at the cuffs, but no frills. 'I don't mind.'

After rehearsals Laura had hung back, hoping to catch Tom alone, to see if he wanted to go for coffee again. In her imagination, Laura saw this coffee extending into a trip to the cinema, hands touching on the arm rests, her head tilting sideways against Tom's, her knee pushing against his, his hand on her leg, kisses and hands outside, maybe back to Tom's flat, maybe all the way.

But Tom said he had a hospital appointment, so, 'Some other time, maybe?'

And then Erin tapped Laura on the shoulder, that look of appalling desperation in her eyes. 'I wondered if I could— if you're not busy, that is, if you might do me a favour.'

And how do you say no to a dying woman?

In the changing room, Laura removes her top, revealing the new bra she is wearing for the first time today. No childish cotton whitey, either. Agent Provocateur, and pennies change from two weeks' allowance. She has a credit card, but it's connected to her father's bank account and – despite his sincere 'Whatever you need, Laura' – he doesn't need to see over a hundred quid's worth of 'mini brief and nude bra' on his statement.

Laura laughs at the absurdity of it all.

'Okay in there?'

'Fine,' Laura says. 'Just . . . something in my throat.'

Corpsing.

That's what Raymond had called it. Involuntary laughter on stage. And there's been a lot of that today.

They were rehearsing the death of Cleopatra and her hand-maids, which involved two snake-bite fatalities and much – unscripted – reference to asps. Fat asps and thin, shaking one's asp, does my asp look big in this, and 'please refrain from staring at my asp'.

'It's worse than *Carry on Cleo*,' Pat said, referencing some old film Laura has never seen but from which everyone else could quote by heart.

'One of my favourite films,' Vernon had said, but it was clear he was only teasing.

Teasing in a playful way rather than with the antagonism and edge of last week's rehearsal. It was Raymond who brought them all down to earth today, his weapon of choice being a complete absence of tact and introducing them to that awful term: *Corpsing*.

A reference to dying on stage, perhaps. But this was a theory Laura kept to herself.

In truth, Raymond had done them a favour. The laughter dried up and they were able – which was the whole point, after all – to continue with their rehearsal.

Laura pulls on the pink top and steps out of the changing room.

'It's lovely,' Erin says. 'You look' – she reaches up and – 'Do you mind?' – uses both hands to hold Laura's hair back from her face. She squints. 'You look lovely. Just . . . lovely.'

'Will you buy it?'

'What do you think?'

Laura nods. 'Does she have a boyfriend?'

'Same boy she was seeing in school. Nice boy, but . . . I shouldn't be saying this, but I think she should move on.'

'Dump him?'

'It sounds harsh when you put it like that. But . . . she should be . . . broadening her horizons. Trying new things. Meeting new people. Taking risks, don't you think?'

'I think you sound like a cool mum,' Laura says.

'Oh bless you, darling. I'm far from cool, but . . . when you go through what we've been through, it changes you. Changes your outlook.'

'Yes,' Laura says. 'It really does.'

'When you go,' Erin says. 'When you go to university, you make sure to do it all. Try everything, go out, say yes to things. Won't you?'

'Yes.'

'Do you promise?'

'I promise.'

She ducks back into the changing room to change into her own clothes. Through the curtain, she says, 'What would you think if she brought a boy like Tom home?'

Erin doesn't answer, and Laura has time to wonder whether she has gone back to the shop floor, before Erin replies: 'He's a nice boy. A very nice boy.'

Laura steps out of the changing room and Erin takes hold of both her hands. 'I think if Jenny met a boy like Tom, she should . . .

you know, go for it.' She squeezes Laura's hands for emphasis. 'Yes?'

Laura nods.

'Good girl.' Erin takes the top from Laura and drapes it over her arm.

'You should get a clean one,' Laura says.

'I will. But this one's for you.'

'Really, there's no need. I . . .'

'Don't you like it?'

'It's lovely, but—'

'What did I say about saying yes to things? Hmm?'

'Thank you.'

'Close enough,' says Erin. 'Close enough.'

Chapter 24

If there is one place Tom loves more than his new home, it would have to be the library. The warmth and space and quiet, the sense of being a part of something, of sharing something, of being enfolded by all these stories. He reads at home, of course, but he is more focused here. No one screaming in the stairwell, no one revving a moped outside his window, no one screwing noisily in the room above. Stories in their own right, he supposes, but some stories are better than others.

In the show he will die as Romeo, King Duncan and Banquo – heartbroken, assassinated and betrayed. He will also drown in wine; get stabbed through a curtain; and 'Exit pursued by a bear', presumably then to be mauled and devoured. Grand deaths and farcical ends in equal measure. But Tom knows all his lines, and he is not here to rehearse.

In this warm library, he reads purely for pleasure.

He has written a list: *Shakespeare plays to read before I die*. At seventeen titles, he feels this is not too ambitious, but he needs to focus. He needs the library.

If he could have his time again – *and oh, if only* – Tom thinks he might enjoy being a librarian. He slept in a library once, leaving the toilet window open five minutes before closing time, and then clambering through from the outside several hours later. An old and sometimes successful trick he had pulled off in a train station, a swimming baths and a dole office. More often than not, he would return to a building to find the window closed or the alarm set, but people are lazy and they make mistakes. Worst comes to worst, you get a few hours in a cell which, on a wet night, is infinitely preferable to a cardboard box.

Successfully through the library window, Tom had spent the next five minutes standing still, listening for an alarm, the approach of a car, an opening door, booted feet. They didn't come. What he should have done was sleep in the bathroom, be grateful for this safe, dry space. But on the other side of that door and down a short flight of steps there were comfortable chairs, a staff room with a kettle, and rows upon rows of stories.

He opened the bathroom door, and when no bells began ringing, he made a cautious descent of the stairs. Over the next hour – moving slowly, staying close to the walls and the ground – Tom gathered a dozen books, stacking them in a pile of maybes before selecting one with which to read himself to sleep on a pile of cushions in the Classics section.

He fell asleep with Holmes and Watson on his chest.

He woke in full sunlight to the sound of two librarians discussing – somewhat disappointingly – last night's TV.

The stairwell was in plain view of the reception desk, the librarians' voices somewhere in the vicinity of the staff room. No time to return anything to its proper place, Tom fastened his jeans, pulled on his coat and left the pile of books behind, the Sherlock Holmes forever unfinished and unsolved. He made it as far as the second step before a nervous voice asked, 'Can I help you?'

Tom pulled up his hood and continued ascending the stairs.

'Stop, wait.'

Another voice. 'Call the police, Muriel.'

Tom took the remainder of the steps at a casual trot, vanished into the bathroom and – *Exit pursued by a librarian* – out of the window.

Everyone knows Shakespeare's most bizarre piece of stage direction. But until Tom read *The Winter's Tale*, he had been ignorant of the context.

Antigonus is abandoning an infant to the elements and savage animals. And as punishment for this barbaric act, he is – and rightly fucking so – killed in one of the most horrific ways imaginable. Gored and clawed and pulled apart; his chest torn open, his skull crushed in slavering jaws. Difficult, one assumes, to convincingly pull off on an Elizabethan stage, hence the cop-out stage direction: *Exit pursued by a bear*.

Laura has had the idea that, maybe three or four times throughout the show, Tom will run across the stage with the bear still hot on his heels. But Tom has come to believe this is missing the point. He thinks they should play it straight and restore the opening phrase from Antigonus's edited soliloquy: 'the spirits of the dead may walk again'. Because surely this is a message their audience will want to hear.

He will mention it to Laura at their next rehearsal.

She wanted to go for coffee again today. But Tom told her – a white lie – that he had a hospital appointment. She volunteered to go with him; to 'hold your hand', she said in that guileless way of hers that is both endearing and nerve-wracking. But Tom demurred, again – a hasty, ramshackle construction of excuses about waiting times and superstition.

They have had coffee twice now; the last time, Laura was early, a seat towards the back, and a little more make-up than usual. He enjoys her company, she's bold and smart and sincere and brave. She wore a pink T-shirt to rehearsals today, and watching her Charmian swoon to the floor, Tom felt a stab of desire that he has not experienced for a long time.

But for all of Laura's qualities, her judgement leaves something to be realised. See her idea to reduce the poetic justice of *The Winter's Tale* to a piece of Benny Hill knockabout. See her inviting a loser like Tom for coffee.

And so Tom, stabs of desire or no, will exercise the discernment Laura lacks. He will couch and duck and demur and tell little white lies.

Tom watches a young father reading to his child – a boy or a girl, Tom can't tell. He doesn't remember his mother ever reading to him – but she brought him up single-handed, and Tom could be a difficult child. He learned from an early age not to ask questions about his father, particularly when his mother had been drinking.

She never knew him, was all she would say. And what that means, Tom can only guess – *Another unsolved mystery, my dear Watson*. His father may be dead for all Tom knows, killed by drink or violence or perhaps by cancer of the throat. Tom feels nothing when he considers this. He feels more affection for the foster families whose faces and names are also lost to time. Even the woman who punched out one of Tom's teeth for stealing from her purse. He remembers her arms – white, stringy and dotted with sores – but not her face. And he recalls that she gave him sweets right after knocking out his front tooth. More poetic justice, perhaps. Or simply one more farce.

But when he thinks about his mother, he has the sense – like that abandoned Sherlock Holmes – of a story unfinished. A book within his grasp whose final chapter he has not read. Tom pulls his phone from his pocket and opens Facebook, his mother's page already loaded. And before he has a chance to hesitate or lose his nerve, he hits the button that will send a request of friendship to the woman who – as she was wont to remind him – endured forty-seven hours and forty-eight minutes of labour to bring Tom into the world.

What would his mother make of Laura? Tom thinks.

And what would Laura make of his mother?

In the final scene of *The Winter's Tale*, the Queen is magically restored to life. Tom thinks this might be a pleasing coda to The Rude Mechanicals' – at last count – twenty-eight deaths. And he thinks Laura would play the part perfectly. He'll mention it when he tells her his concerns about the bear.

Chapter 25

It's a big scene today, Tom and Laura rehearsing the entirely unnecessary double suicide of Romeo and Juliet. As Pat watches from her seat in front of the stage, the sheer pointlessness of their deaths frustrates her to the brink of anger. And it's all the fault of the interfering Friar Lawrence – who in his 'wisdom' thought it was a good idea to fake Juliet's death, rather than simply spiriting her away to Mantua where her true love was waiting. *Typical clergy.*

'They're very good,' says Erin. 'Don't you think?'

Erin is wrapped in a blanket and shivering. She has no energy for acting today, and barely enough strength to cross the room. Even so, she had no intention of missing a rehearsal. ('After all, it's better than anything on the telly.')

'Proper couple of star-crossed whatnots?' says Vernon.

Pat goes to nudge him with her elbow – a reflexive reaction to the man's frequent lapses of tact. But this comment about Tom and Laura is spoken quietly and with sincerity, or perhaps even affection, and Pat keeps her elbow to herself.

Besides, he's only saying what Pat was thinking. That despite their different backgrounds and a significant age gap, there appears to be something between Tom and Laura beyond their obvious chemistry on the stage.

Pat can count the boys she has kissed on the fingers of one hand. Gerald Hawley; Michael Stockton; the captain of a competing swimming team and although she allowed this boy to caress her breasts (above her cardigan), she cannot remember his name. And on the fourth finger, a man with eyes the colour of envy – Father Declan Corrigan. Six years older than Pat, but seemingly a lifetime wiser as they talked and sometimes prayed (his voice, even when whispering, held a resonance Pat felt behind her ribs) in the quiet corridors and rooms of St Bernadette's hospice.

He took mass in the hospice chapel, and more than once Father Declan asked her to help dispense the Eucharist. She did this with him at bedsides, too. If the patient slept, she would part their dry lips, and bow her head as Father Declan placed a crumb of wafer – 'the body of Christ' – on the revealed tongue.

They died at night more often than not, in the still hours before dawn – and Pat would sit with Declan as he whispered the last rites over their beds. The shared intimacy made Pat's heartbeat quicken, and as a new shift approached, she found herself hoping – she dared not pray – that God might expedite the death of one more priest, so Pat could sit close to Father Declan and feel his reverberant voice inside her chest.

And then old Father Hughes had passed, at a time of night when the air feels still and sound travels lazily. Big spaces between the ticks of wall-mounted clocks. A ward sister found Declan drinking coffee with Pat, and told him that the old priest was in Cheyne–Stokes now – his breath faltering and slowing.

In the event, Father Hughes held on for another forty minutes. A wavering and protesting inhalation . . . stasis . . . and the warm breath stealing out again from his tired lungs. Then stillness, maybe two seconds, maybe three. Before again, one more defiant breath. They sat and prayed, and Pat dabbed the priest's lips with wet cotton wool. Once or twice, Pat and Declan exchanged glances: *He's really dragging this out?* And finally, the last breath left the old man's dead body and his thin chest was still.

Declan stood and went around the bed, opening a low cabinet containing the priest's effects. Pat gave him a look. 'Whiskey,' Declan whispered, vanishing the bottle into the folds of his cassock. 'No use to him now.'

They drank it from plastic cups – a quarter bottle between them – in the shadows at the bottom of the garden. The heat of the single malt offsetting the chill of the pre-dawn air. 'Deadmun's whiskey,' he called it. 'Very rare. Aged in . . .'

'Aged in life,' Pat said.

And then a different pause . . . a different stillness. He took Pat's hand in his and they each understood that to speak would be to ruin this. So they kissed quietly, Pat dropping her plastic cup to the ground and placing her hand against his cheek. There was heat in this, and urgency and the promise of perhaps a different life. They clung to each other and tasted Father Hughes's whiskey on each other's mouths. Stretching this time out – knowing they must return to the ward, and thinking that perhaps they did not. Perhaps they could just walk away and not look back.

But they did return, something – duty, fear, naivety – taking them back to the wards and the slow-ticking clocks that held their secret now in the spaces between the seconds. They kissed two nights later, and then again one excruciating week after that. But they never spoke about what they were doing. They would exchange a glance, walk quietly outside, hearts thudding, and then kiss and breathe and cling to each other as if for life.

And then Father Declan was gone.

No words and no goodbye. Pat stayed at the hospice until the end of the year, watching the old priests and nuns die, and then crying to herself at the bottom of the garden.

He will be an old man himself now, Pat thinks. His brown hair white, his resonant voice thin and high. Perhaps he has gone the way of Father Hughes – some younger priest or nun or nurse filching the whiskey from his bedside cabinet.

She is jolted from this reverie by the sound of a generic ringtone. Pat, like Erin and Vernon on either side of her, reflexively checks her phone.

The ringing continues; the sound, she now realises, coming from somewhere at the back of the hall.

'Sorry,' says Adam. 'I think it's mine.'

Adam rises from his seat, walking to the row of coat hooks near the door. He takes the phone from his jacket pocket and glances at the screen. Number not recognised.

'Hello?'
'Mr Campbell?'
And he knows from the tone that this is not good news.
'Yes. That's me.'
'It's about Mabel.'

Chapter 26

Adam can't remember the last time he was in a graveyard, but it would have been to lay flowers on his parents' adjacent plots. Around the anniversary of their deaths, he imagines – so March. Maybe three years ago, maybe four. For the first half-dozen years after they died, he visited every 3 March, no matter what day of the week it landed on, arranging holidays or rescheduling meetings so he could be there. Then one year, the reasons lost to him now, he spent that day elsewhere.

We move on.

It took Adam years.

It's taken Mabel a little over one hour. He can hear her laughter as she scampers about the headstones with her friend Holly. To hear them, it's hard to imagine Mabel sinking her teeth into Holly's arm earlier this afternoon.

'I'm so sorry,' Dianne says. Again.

'It's fine. Honestly. And I'm sorry about Holly's arm.'

Dianne laughs. 'Well, good for Mabel. She's a tough . . . you know. Sure you don't want some.'

'Go on then.'

Dianne snaps an arm off her gingerbread man and passes it to Adam.

The chain of events: Dianne told Holly that Adam had cancer; Holly told Mabel; Mabel bit Holly.

Adam takes a bite of gingerbread man.

'I shouldn't have told Holly,' Dianne says.

'And I should have told Mabel sooner.'

'Holly was asking if she could have a play date at yours, you see. And play dates are bloody hard work. Even for me, and I'm . . . I'm not . . . you know. Sorry.'

Andy Jones

'It's . . .' Adam waves it away. 'It's fine.'

Dianne sighs. 'Well, you know what they're like when they zero in on something?'

'I do.'

'So I told her you were sick. Very, very sick. And she said how sick, and . . .'

'And you told her.'

'I did. I told her.'

According to Mrs Gibbons, the girls' teacher, things got ugly during rehearsals for *A Christmas Carol Lost in Space*.

Holly's Robot Ghost of Christmas Past costume is already complete, and as such she was wearing it at today's rehearsals. Mabel's Robot Ghost of Christmas Future, however, is still a work in progress, and as such Mabel had to rehearse in school uniform. There was some teasing. Mabel became upset. She protested that her daddy hadn't made her costume because he was tired, but when he did, it would definitely be better than Holly's, which – according to Mabel – was 'rubbish and stupid'.

'He's tired because he's dying of cancer,' Holly told her. 'And anyway, you're stupid.'

So Mabel bit Holly. And then burst into hysterical, hyperventilating tears.

The girls run towards them now, their voices bright and joyous, and Adam imagines this cheering the dead the way it cheers him.

'We found a good one,' Mabel says.

'Agatha,' says Holly. 'She was . . .' Holly consults the paper in her hand. 'She was seventy-five!'

'Wow,' says Dianne. 'Best one yet.'

Adam holds out his hand for the paper. 'Let me see.'

He has taught them to subtract one year from the next, including the tricky business of crossing millennia. They are terrible at this, and a quick glance at Agatha's dates tells Adam she died at the tender age of twenty-four. But now is not the time for mathematical pedantry.

'Brilliant,' he says. 'And I love the name.'

'Mabel found it!'

'Well done, Mabel.'

'Can we do another?'

Dianne looks at Adam. 'Sure,' Adam says. 'Why not?'

And the girls scamper away.

'Do you think it counts as homework?' Dianne asks.

There have been many questions from Holly and Mabel: *Do the dead get bored? Cold? Hungry? Lonely? Does it hurt?*

'Maths and metaphysics,' Adam says. 'Key stage one.' And Dianne laughs.

'Heather always said you were funny.'

Adam sighs.

'You okay?'

A week after his last cycle of chemo, Adam still feels flattened. He is constantly tired, but has difficulty sleeping. When he does, he frequently wakes soaked in sweat. Despite a potent anti-emetic, he struggles against a constant undercurrent of nausea. His hands and feet hurt. His skin is tinged with yellow and he has bruises on his back. His throat is sore. There is a ringing in his ears. He can feels the bones of his backside.

'Those seats were small,' says Adam, referencing his earlier conversation with Mrs Gibbons.

Dianne chuckles. 'Made for smaller bums than mine, that's for sure.'

After Adam had finished talking with Mrs Gibbons, he went to find Mabel in the lunch hall, where she was chatting happily to a teaching assistant and eating a bowl of pink ice-cream.

Adam sat beside his daughter and placed a kiss on her forehead. 'Is that strawberry?'

Mabel stared at him the way only a child can. Hope and fear and fragile innocence in her eyes. 'Is what Holly said true?'

Adam nodded.

The tears came slowly, Mabel's face contorting as if they were thick and viscous and painful to cry. A small, high sound – *No, no, no* – as she clenched her hands into fists and pressed them against her ears, as if by this means she could unhear the news that her daddy is dying.

Adam watched her ice-cream melt as he held her to his chest. In the kitchen, the muted – as if for them – rattle and clatter of cleaning. Life going on. Perhaps he heard someone stifle their own tears.

And then the questions: *Why? How? When?*

And inadequate answers: *Everybody does. I'm sick. I don't know.*

Adam dipped his finger into the pink puddle of Mabel's ice-cream.

'Hey! That's mine!'

'I thought you were finished?'

Eyes red and swollen, cheeks flushed, Mabel scooped up a spoonful of pink goo. The tears still rolling, but there was composure now.

'I don't want you to die, Daddy.'

'And I don't want to leave you, Maybe.'

'Can I have more ice-cream?'

Adam laughed at this. 'Maybe later. Let's go home now.'

Dianne was waiting in the foyer, asked if Adam wanted to talk, wanted coffee.

He wanted both, and it was a clear December day so they ordered them to go, Adam's feet bringing them here. 'Where the dead people sleep. Where you can talk to them anytime you like.'

'Are all the dead people here?' Mabel had asked.

'Not all of them.'

'Are Granny and Granddad here?'

'They're somewhere else, sweetheart.'

'What do you do when you miss them?'

A finger to his temple. 'I talk to them in here. I close my eyes and I can see them in here.'

And this had seemed to do.

The children's voices carry in the quiet graveyard as they run and hide among the old slabs and stone angels. Adam hopes Mabel will play here, after he is below ground. He doesn't believe in an afterlife, but he likes to think her laughter will find a way to reach him.

'You lost your parents young?' Dianne asks.

Adam hitches a short ironic laugh. At the absurdity of life and death and dying. 'They were on holiday,' he says. 'A boat accident.'

'Shit.'

'Weren't even sixty.'

'Too young,' Dianne says, her voice trailing off on the last word.

Adam told the girls that no, the dead don't get bored, or cold, or hungry, or lonely. Death was like sleeping, he said. A sleep from which you didn't wake. And this answer landed softly, floating down along the shallow parabolas of a feather or a leaf.

'We found another!' Mabel skipping towards him, skipping along the gravel path, and over the threadbare surface of these winter plots.

'Who is it?'

'Charles,' says Holly. 'Like in our play who wrote *A Christmas Carol Lost in Space*.'

'We'll have to correct that one,' Dianne says from the corner of her mouth.

'He was forty-eight,' says Mabel. 'Look.'

They're almost right, this time. Charles was forty-seven when he met his maker.

'How old are you, Daddy?'

'I'm forty-four.'

Forty-five in June, maybe.

'Can we do another?'

'One more,' Adam says. 'And make it a big one. A really big one.'

The girls hold hands as they run off among the dead.

'This is a nice graveyard,' says Dianne.

'Yes. Yes it is.'

Chapter 27

Left to his own devices, Brian would eat take-away every night. Forced to cook, his prime objective is expediency. A matter of combining the minimum of ingredients in the least amount of time. Nuance comes in a ketchup bottle.

But that's no way to eat. No way to live.

Erin looks over Brian's shoulder and sees the onions have softened and browned. '*Now* you can add the mince.'

'You sure?' Brian says. 'There's a bit there looks a little peaky.' But he's joking.

'And while the mince is cooking you can grate the zest of a lemon.'

'Do what?'

'A lemon, you . . . lemon. And just the skin.'

It's brought them closer. This process of domesticating her husband after more than twenty years of marriage. Of teaching him how to 'drive' the washing machine, iron his shirts and cook a meal that doesn't taste like it came from a can.

'Remember Jenny and that lemon wedge?' Erin says.

Brian screws up his face in a bitter wince. 'Owinge!'

Their daughter would have been two, maybe a good bit younger. Toddling around and fumbling with words: *Mamma, Dadda, yes, no. Teddy, dolly. Miwk, nana, owinge.*

The memory is faded at the borders, a snapshot without context. Whether they were at home or in a restaurant, for example, neither can recall. The memory consists simply of Jenny picking up a lemon wedge, mistaking it for an orange and taking a good bite with her tiny white teeth. And then the baffled frown, the look of betrayal and slowly dawning indignation: 'Owinge!'

They have told the anecdote a hundred times, but only now does it occur to Erin that this was perhaps Jenny's first realisation that the world is not always fair. That life can be cruel. She considers adding a lemon to the memory box she is preparing for her daughter. Or something lemon-flavoured. She almost mentions this to Brian, but to do so would be to raise the veil on the reason they are here teaching Brian to cook a non-awful Bolognese. It would – as Jenny says – be something of a buzzkill.

'So what do I do with this?' Brian asks of the lemon zest. 'Chuck it in?'

'Quick on the uptake tonight, aren't you?'

'And it makes a difference?'

It makes a difference to me, Erin thinks. 'All the difference in the world,' she says.

Brian scrapes the lemon zest into the pan. 'Owinge!'

And they laugh all over again.

Chapter 28

The Christmas season is – in Tom's experience – the best time of year for shoplifting. Increased security, for sure. But the chaos more than makes up for that. Big crowds, arguing couples, crying kids. The shelves are brimming, and a young man doesn't look out of place contemplating the stacked perfume bottles and silver trinkets. And everything is so much easier to shift afterwards. Who doesn't want authentic Chanel No 5 for a tenner? A Hugo Boss wallet for a fiver? Small, desirable, high-ticket items, easily concealed in the underpants.

It feels better to be browsing the aisles as a paying customer. No anxiety about being collared, no guilt after getting away scot-free. Although he never felt that regret as keenly as he feels it now. And not necessarily for the miniscule dent he made in the profits of these department stores. (*They build their losses into the prices*, a friend had said. *We're just keepin' 'em honest.*) But for the effect it had on him. Because he can't take it back. Because it was cheap and tawdry. Because it was Christmas, for fuck's sake.

'How about this?'

Tom turns to see Laura holding a bottle of Chanel No 5, and laughs. This hurts not only his throat but his side, and he winces.

'Okay?'

Tom nods. *I'm fine.*

But fine is not great, and he is becoming less fine by the week. He has a new ache – somewhere between his ribs and his right hip. Sometimes the ache becomes a stabbing pain that takes his breath away. He has put his hand to his side – afraid of what he might feel, but all he felt were ribs. His jeans are a twenty-eight-inch waist, but three of those inches are concertinaed around his hips and he will need to find a new pair in the charity shop. He had an appointment with his oncologist yesterday, but didn't attend because what, after all, can anyone do? He has his various medications, his painkillers and his meal-replacement supplements. So unless someone's come up with a cure in the last couple of months, another trip to the hospital's just a waste of time and bus fare. So he's fine. Not great, perhaps, but fine, and fine will do for now.

'Is it too corny?' Laura asks of the perfume and Tom's reaction towards it.

'Too classy, probably.'

'Well you can't give her gin.'

Tom regards the elaborate bottle in his hands, replaces it on the shelf. 'At least I know she likes gin. Well, that or vodka.'

His mother accepted his Facebook friend request almost immediately. Although it was another three days before either of them spoke, Tom testing the waters by liking several of his mother's posts before plucking up the courage to comment: 'Nice dress.' This received a small blue thumbs-up but no reply.

No declarations of joy, surprise, relief, anger. No questions, no words.

Just a simple blue thumb.

Tom sent her a short message, asking how she was, telling her he was clean, suggesting lunch sometime might be nice.

And then two days later, yesterday:

'How about Christmas?' A Santa Claus emoji and a single 'x'.

'Thanks,' Laura says. 'You know, for' – she gestures around the store, at the decorations, the tinsel, the Christmas jingle piping through the sound system – 'for involving me.'

'You're kidding, aren't you? I should be thanking you. In fact – *thank you* – I am thanking you. Thank you.'

Laura goes to speak, hesitates, then goes for it all the same. 'I thought you might be . . .' A shrug. 'I don't know. Avoiding me.'

Tom makes a face that suggests this is a ridiculous idea. 'Why would I do that?'

Laura blushes, shrugs again.

They rehearsed the deaths of Romeo and Juliet today. Tom had been dreading it, picking up on a palpable awkwardness, or maybe even an over-eagerness from Laura. Possibly both. But it had been okay. Better than okay; it had been good. They managed three run-throughs with no jeering from Vernon, no clashes of teeth, no corpsing from the principles.

It helps, Tom supposes, that they never actually look at each other. Juliet being asleep for the first kiss, and Romeo dead for the second. Although he felt Laura's breath as she hovered above him, felt the warmth coming off her skin, and the tickle of her hair against his face.

As they were packing away the chairs, Laura asked if Tom had time for coffee. Perhaps she saw him hesitate, because she intercepted any objection before he could form it. 'And "no" isn't an acceptable answer.'

'How about instead you help me buy a Christmas present for my mother?'

After Tom had messaged his mother, they texted, her punctuating the notes with smiley faces, hearts, more kisses. And then she called. She called *him*. They talked until Tom's voice was raw.

'So just the two of you?' Laura says.

'She had a boyfriend, apparently, but . . .' He walks his fingers across the air.

'Shame.'

'He sounds like a dick.' He takes a sip from a bottle of water.

'Did you tell her?'

Tom wavers his palm, half up, half down. 'Told her I had cancer. Having treatment.'

'What did she say?'

'I don't think she believed me at first.'

'What?'

'I dunno. Thought I was trying an angle, or something.'

'But she knows now?'

Tom nods. 'Most of it, not . . . One thing at a time.'

Tom leads off, turning at random into an aisle stacked with toys and novelty items. Flashing antlers, ridiculous sweaters, an elf that drops his trousers at the sound of a handclap.

'I sent my applications,' Laura says.

'That's great.'

'Edinburgh, Durham, Cardiff, Portsmouth, Liverpool.'

'Liverpool? I thought you didn't like Liverpool.'

'It's okay.'

'You said it had a stuffy reading list.'

'It's the closest one. Easy to visit.' She blushes. 'If . . . if you wanted to.'

Tom picks up a glass jar filled with multi-coloured glitter. It's labelled 'Reindeer Food'. And the cynicism of it – a twelve-quid jar of glitter – makes his fingers itch. He returns the expensive glitter to the shelf. 'When does term start?'

'September.'

'September's a long time away. You know?'

'Not *that* long.'

'Well that depends on your . . . what I mean is, you shouldn't . . . I mean you should pick the place that's best for *you*. It's going to be your life for three years. More maybe. You've got to pick a course you love, not one that's . . . you know.'

Laura inspects her nails, tucks her hair behind her ears. 'I was just . . . just conversation, that's all.'

And now who's the dick.

He picks up a Magic 8 Ball from one of the shelves and gives it a good shake. 'Should Laura go to Liverpool?' He watches the ball settle. '*Ask again later*. Well that's just hedging.'

'Got to pass my exams first.' She stuffs one hand into the depths of her pocket. 'I mean . . . who knows what's going to happen.'

And it's clear to Tom that this last 'who knows?' pertains not to Laura's exams – which she will obviously smash – but to her health. He wants to tell her that everything will be fine. That the results of her next scan will be as positive as the results of her mocks. But he knows how trite this sounds, how blasé and dismissive. So he says nothing, even though he believes it to be true. He believes it because he sees it standing before him, wrapped in a woolly hat and red silk scarf. He sees it in her skin, her eyes, her shy smile.

'What?' Laura says.

Tom shakes the Magic 8 Ball again. 'Will Laura pass?' he says. 'With flying colours?' He waits as the ball makes up its mind, and crosses his fingers even though there is no need for such superstition.

'What does it say?'

Tom shows her.

'*Outlook good,*' Laura reads. 'Hmm. I like this ball.'

'Maybe I should get it for my mum,' Tom says.

Laura shakes her head. 'Outlook bad.'

They continue up the aisle, but Tom doesn't yet relinquish the ball. Laura plucks a silk scarf from a rack. 'Simple, stylish.'

Tom inspects the price tag. 'Jesus! It's a . . . a big hankie.'

'It's Liberty.'

'*A* liberty, yes.'

'Now you sound like my dad.'

'Well he's a sensible man. Cos that' – he hands the scarf back to Laura – 'is criminal.'

And that, Thomas, is a little rich, considering you'd have stuffed that scarf right down your boxer shorts five years ago.

'Here.' Laura unwraps the red silk scarf from around her neck. Holds it out to Tom. 'Practically brand new.'

'I . . . I couldn't.'

'Why not?'

'It's yours.'

'I've got twenty. I don't even like it.'

'It's lovely.'

'Get it dry cleaned and give it to your mum then.'

'Thank you. Honestly. But I can't.'

Laura takes the Magic 8 Ball, shakes it: 'Should Tom take the scarf for his mother?' She holds out the answer for Tom to read.

'*It is decidedly so,*' he says.

'Can't argue with the Magic 8 Ball.'

Tom takes the scarf and wraps it around his own neck. 'Thank you.'

Laura shakes the ball one more time, watches as the fluid swirls and settles. She takes a step towards Tom and kisses him lightly on the lips.

'What was that for?' Laura, he has come to realise, has an entire lexicon of shrugs. This one, he thinks, says *Why not?* Or *Just because.*

'I like you,' Laura says, her skin colouring, but only slightly.

Tom smiles, 'I like you too.'

They set off walking down another aisle. Standing maybe a little closer than they were before. 'I'll visit you wherever you go,' Tom says. 'Portsmouth, Edinburgh, Liverpool. If I . . . I'll visit you anywhere.'

Chapter 29

The logic of a six-year-old goes like this:

If dying is just like sleeping, then sleeping is just like dying.

Adam has heard his daughter cry a dozen different ways in the last twelve hours, but when she woke at one-thirty in the morning, she was screaming.

Adam's room is directly above hers. He jolted into consciousness from a deep sleep, confused and in something close to panic. The room was wrong – not the bedroom he shares with Heather. Where was she? Who was screaming?

And then reality congealed around him; he was in the attic room – there because he was an adulterer and he was dying. And his daughter was screaming for her mother. When he got to Mabel's bedroom, Heather was already there, holding Mabel to her chest and whispering soothing noises into the child's ear. She waved Adam away, so Adam went downstairs to fill the kettle.

By the time Heather plods downstairs the water has cooled, and Adam has to boil the kettle again to make tea. While they wait – the kettle cracking and protesting at having to do this all over again, and at *this hour* – Heather tells Adam of Mabel's bad dream. Non-descript and nonsensical, but frightening and threatening death. And then of how, when Heather had tucked Mabel back into her bed, the tears had started again because sleeping, Mabel explained, was like dying. And Mabel didn't want to die.

'Shit, I'm . . . it seemed like a good idea. At the time.'

'Yeah,' Heather says. 'I get that.'

He recalls Mabel skipping through the graveyard, determining the ages at which the buried corpses breathed their last breaths. 'What was I thinking?'

Heather puts her hand on his, the heat from her mug passing through his skin to his bones. 'It was very brave. Very thoughtful.'

'Really?'

'Yes. Really.' Heather withdraws her hand from his, sips her tea. 'She seems to have settled.'

'You look tired.'

'Thank you, Adam.'

'I mean . . .'

'It's fine. I do. I am.'

'What did you say to her?' His eyes flicking towards the ceiling. 'To settle her.'

'Told her to think about Christmas.'

The word sits between them. Heather's parents will be coming for Christmas lunch, all five of them around the table like any other family. Except they aren't, are they? Adam hasn't seen his 'almost-in-laws' since before Heather asked him to move out, and he struggles to imagine himself pulling a cracker with either of them.

'Did you see her Christmas list?' Heather says.

Adam knows Mabel's Christmas list by heart, and he intends to get her almost everything on it: *a dolly, a dress, a teddy* . . .

'A cheesecake?' he says. 'What kid wants a cheesecake?'

'Ours, apparently.'

'At least we can do something about that one.'

Heather looks up from her tea, her mouth turns down and when she cries she looks exactly like Mabel.

Item nine on Mabel's list: *A sister.*

'I'm sorry,' Adam says.

'Don't.'

'About everythi—'

'Yes. Yes, you're sorry. I know. I . . . I don't know how to do this, Adam.' And the tears are flowing freely. 'I'm sad, and tired, and angry, and afraid and . . .' She shakes her head, looks at Adam and then punches him on the shoulder. Her jaw clenches as if she'd like to do it again, only harder.

'I fucked everything up, didn't I?'

Heather nods. *Yes. Yes you did.* 'And the worst thing. Well, not the *worst* thing, obviously, but . . . God, Adam. I've even enjoyed having you in the house again.'

'Thank you for . . . you're a better person than I des—'

'I did it for Mabel,' she says. 'It wasn't for Mabel, I . . . I don't know.'

Heather stands, goes to fetch a sheet of kitchen roll, wipes her eyes and blows her nose.

'You'll be okay,' Adam says. 'You know that? I'm insured, and the mortg—'

'Not now. I . . . not now.'

'I'll make a will and then we—'

'I slept with Jamie.'

'What?' Adam swivels around in his chair so that he is facing Heather. 'You . . .'

'Twice,' Heather says. 'I just thought you should know.'

Adam holds her eyes as this new information sinks in. He stands and goes to her, puts his arms around her shoulders and hugs her while she cries.

'It was nice,' Heather says. 'To have somebody want me like that. And . . . and I thought, *is that why you did it*? Because I wasn't . . . because . . .'

Adam shakes his head. 'No.'

'Then why?'

'I don't know.'

'Not good enough.'

'We weren't in a good place,' Adam says. 'But that wasn't your fault.'

'So you fucked someone else?'

'Heather.'

She untangles herself from his arms. 'I'm tired. Thank you for the tea.'

Heather goes upstairs, and Adam gathers up the cups and the teapot and takes them to the sink. And what was it Mabel said?

You always make people cry.

'Yes,' Adam whispers. 'I always do.'

Act III

Chapter 30

The sun rises over the sea here, turning the grey water into hammered bronze, and the light is sharp against Pat's eyes. Her headache has abated; even so, a pair of sunglasses would be wonderful. But who leaves the house at 5 a.m. in mid-December with sunglasses? *You'd have to be losing your mind*, she thinks, and laughs to herself. Not that there's anyone else here.

She doesn't know what time she woke with her head splitting open because her eyes were blind. She might have panicked, but the pain was all-consuming. Had she the presence of mind to make the bargain, Pat would have gladly traded her eyes for a reprieve from this pain. Instead, she simply screamed into her pillow. Groped in the dark for her tablets and knocked a glass of water to the floor where – a miracle – it bounced but did not break.

After the pain ebbed – after eternity – and her eyes remembered how to focus, there was blood on the pillow. Pat touches her tongue to the inside of her cheek, feeling the puckered flesh where she must have bitten herself.

By then it was minutes past three, so who knew how long she'd been whimpering into her bed linen. Hitchens was barking downstairs, so Pat went to him, tickled his muzzle and told him she was okay.

Because of the devil in her brain, Pat isn't allowed to drive. A fact she only remembered after defying the prohibition for close to an hour. Driving east through quiet roads, the world belonged to her and Hitchens alone. Hopefully, she can find a repair company prepared to tow a perfectly good car an hour west. Otherwise she will have to simply leave it here to rust.

The sea is molten gold now. It's bitterly cold but the beauty of the beach could make a lady forget, and Pat removes the scarf from her head. The frigid breeze ruffles her short fine hair and it feels like heaven.

Hitchens runs towards her, bounding along the shoreline then veering suddenly into the foam – testing this element from which his ancestors crawled. Does he remember it somewhere deep in his old genetics? Do we?

Hitchens slows to a lazy trot as he approaches Pat, the ball held in his strong curved teeth.

'Good boy,' she tells him. 'Good dog.'

Hitchens flattens himself on the wet sand, tail flipping excitedly from one side to the other.

'What? You want me to throw this again?'

Hitchens keeps his chin on the sand but lifts his backside in an attitude of readiness. *The ball, the ball!*

Pat scoops up the ball with the plastic launcher, and Hitchens is ten yards and running before she has completed her swing, throwing the ball a satisfying distance across the beach. The dog races after the ball not in a straight line, but along a shallow anticlockwise arc. A primal hunting instinct, perhaps. Or merely further proof that Hitchens is a very daft dog.

The sea is beautiful. Pat sits on the sand and unzips her boots. Once she has removed these, she removes her socks and places one inside each boot. She rolls her trousers past her calves – still solid, still strong.

The water isn't so cold. An initial shock, but this passes quickly. A quote comes to her and she speaks it out loud:

' "Like as waves towards the pebbled shore,

So our minutes hasten to their end;

Each changing place with that before,"

– something something – "they do contend." '

Words to that effect, Pat thinks. Close enough. And nary a hesitation nor a stutter.

She looks to the clouds and their fat bellies are daubed with amber, under-lit by the sun and beginning to shift.

Hitchens runs headlong into the waves, challenging them and

barking at them and scampering like a pup. And Pat feels his energy like warmth on her face.

Looking down towards her foot, Pat realises she is knee deep in the sleepy waves. Feels now the cold penetrating her flesh and creeping inward to her bones. 'Catch my d— death,' she says. But she continues. She walks further out, the water rising to her thighs, and shrieks with cold and defiance. Hitchens barks and Pat whoops a reply. *Yes, boy, this* is *fun.*

The tide is slow, lazy and oh, to dive beneath it and come up swimming. The water is lapping at the hem of her coat now, and already she can feel the weight of the North Sea dragging at her clothes.

Ophelia, she thinks. *We should do Ophelia.*

Drowned in her madness and her grief. 'Mermaid-like', wasn't that the line? And how beautiful. What a beautiful way to die. The water welcomes her like an old friend, and her pockets are full of waves.

She could go now, Pat thinks. And wonders again why she came here in a car she cannot drive home. Was it really whim?

Hitchens paddles towards her, the ball between his teeth.

Would he follow if Pat continued to wade and then swim away from the shore? She doubts he would, no more than he would follow her off a cliff. But Hitchens is daft, and he just might. 'Would you f— follow, Hitch?'

Hitchens woofs. *Water!*

Pat takes the ball, fits it to the launcher and throws it as hard as she can to the shore. Hitchens paddles after it, his feet find sand and he runs in pursuit. With Hitchens distracted, Pat could go now, dip beneath the hammered gold waves and – mermaid-like – swim to peace.

But what about the play? It would be a shame to miss their big night, and selfish to let those brave people down.

She hears voices. Someone unseen calling to another dog. Pat turns to face the shore – Hitchens turning circles and yipping at Pat to come and play. He will bring great joy to someone, like he has brought great joy to Pat. Tonight she will read some of those leaflets from the kennels and start to make the plans she has been putting off.

And then the show in three months' time.

Pat can do three months.

Putting a hand to an inside pocket, she locates her purse. That's good; she's going to need to buy some dry clothes and hire a tow truck.

She begins walking back to shore.

Chapter 31

Mabel's robot costume is attracting the attention of the pizza restaurant's other customers. More than one has winked or nodded their approval.

Adam accepts that he's biased, but it doesn't change the fact that Mabel blew the other robot ghosts clean off the stage. He must have spent over forty hours designing, sourcing parts, cutting, assembling, painting, and fitting an array of fairy lights to give the effect of a flashing LED panel.

For its intended purpose – housing the Robot Ghost of Christmas Future – it was, and there is no use in being modest, close to perfect.

Not so much when it comes to housing a hungry six-year-old girl.

The body is wide and deep, so Mabel is unable to reach around the boxy torso to access the mouth port. Which, anyway, is too narrow to admit a standard slice of Margherita. Nevertheless, Mabel refuses to remove even the head of her costume. And who can blame her? It's magnificent.

Mabel's head swivels towards Heather. 'Robot Mabel thirsty.'

'Robot manners?'

'Pleeeeaze.'

Drinking is less of a problem. Adam has connected four conventional straws into one long tube, through which they can pipe lemonade into their daughter's mouth with only minimal leakage.'

'Robot Mabel hungry. Pleeeeaze.'

Adam loads a small piece of pizza onto a fork and inserts this into the mouth port. The pizza is taken. 'Thank you. Beep.'

Heather glances at him and the look says: *How long can this go on?*

Adam smiles an apology. 'It's good though?'

'It's brilliant. You were brilliant, Mabel.'

'*Robot* Mabel knows. Thank you. Beep.'

Last year, Adam had arrived late for Mabel's Christmas play. How late, he can't recall, but late enough that the show was underway and Heather had been forced to give up the seat she had been attempting to save for him. And so Adam watched from the doorway, jostling for position with the other tardy parents and consoling himself with the fact that there would always be next year, and the year after that, and so on for ten years or more.

But – as any ghost of Christmas Future could attest – Adam would have been wrong.

This year, they had front row seats, reserved for them by Mabel's teacher. 'Here,' she said, eyes glistening, 'I think you'll have a better view from here.'

Adam thanked Mrs Gibbons and took his seat. The weight of two hundred pairs of eyes pushing against the back of his skull so that Adam wanted to turn and run. Heather reached across and took his hand. She squeezed it, and her touch said: *It's okay.*

He had taken additional painkillers and an anti-emetic prior to the performance; the combination leaving him feeling both torpid and a little weirded out by the sci-fi–Dickens mash-up. Despite the drugs, Adam began to feel giddy at the approximate mid-point of the performance, his chest tightening, sweat on his back, the familiar bile rising in his throat. Mabel had not yet made her entrance, so Adam resisted the urge to step outside for fresh air, instead focusing on a single spot – a tinfoil star above the stage – and attempting to slow his breath and regain his composure. And then the coughing started. A compulsion to clear his throat at first, developing quickly into a weak but persistent cough. Heather passed him a bottle of water. This helped for all of thirty seconds. The cough was louder and more forceful now, distracting the young actors. Heather's grip tightened on his hand and Adam willed the cough to subside, but the cough was impervious to such things. Adam stood – 'I'm fine, just a cough' – and walked the length of the centre aisle, past well meaning smiles, concerned eyes, baffled children and the late-arriving fathers at the back. Outside Adam let go with a full hacking cough that hurt his lungs and throat, but once it had passed, so too did the feeling of giddiness and nausea – as if the violent breaths had cleared his head and revitalised his blood.

When he returned to the hall, Mrs Gibbons was standing before the stage and leading the room in a spirited rendition of 'Jingle Bells'. Adam had assumed this was simply part of the performance, but as he made his way to his seat (relieved faces, awkward smiles) he realised with dawning horror that the performance had been halted for his benefit. Mrs Gibbons smiled at him, hit the chorus one last time, and then steered the players back to their marks. There was some confusion as the young actors struggled to remember their places and lines, but this was met with genuine laughter, and the play continued to its conclusion with no further interruption.

He stood and clapped – and cried – with the other parents, the tears a mixture of sentimentality and relief. Adam had made it to the final bow without having a seizure in the aisle and ruining not just this wonderful show, but the Christmas futures of one hundred small and impressionable children.

Adam feeds Robot Mabel another morsel of pizza. Heather delivers a further infusion of lemonade. She is eating a salad. Adam is sipping champagne and stealing occasional croutons.

Adam is aware of the lasts, piling up behind him. Some – the last time he climbed a tree or skipped a pebble over water – will have slipped by unnoticed and unappreciated. Others – his final Bonfire Night, the last time he will see Mabel totter about on stage – he has known for what they are, understanding their finality as they approached, unfolded and ended. Maybe that's why he felt compelled to order champagne tonight.

'Sure,' Heather said. 'Why not?' Perhaps intuiting Adam's thought process.

But there's more to this bottle of overpriced fizz than sentiment. He has a piece of paper in his pocket that he has not yet – the timing is delicate – shared with Heather.

His life insurance policy has come through, paying off the not insubstantial mortgage on their house. The news provoked mixed feelings.

The house is Adam's, but he will transfer ownership to Heather as quickly as his solicitor can arrange it. Plus – when Adam does eventually shuffle off – there will be an additional pay-out from his former employers. All in all, Heather and Mabel will be well taken care of. And this is something to celebrate.

On the other hand, Adam knows that insurance companies are not in the habit of writing cheques if there is any possible way of avoiding doing so. And yet, they have written this one. They have reviewed Adam's situation, sent his scans and medical reports to an impartial expert, and that expert has confirmed what Adam already knew. He will never carve another pumpkin, never again hold his child's hand before a bonfire, and never ski another black run. So, yes, let's have the bubbles. But for now, the envelope that makes the sweet thing bitter stays inside his coat pocket.

Heather catches his eye. 'Okay?'

'Sorry, miles away.'

He raises his glass and waits for Heather to do the same. 'Cheers,' he says. They touch glasses, and then clink them against Mabel's lemonade.

'Cheeerz. Beep.'

Adam sets down his glass. Sees something in Heather's expression. He mouths the word: *What?*

She touches her nose, frowns. Adam copies the gesture and his fingers come away sticky with blood. Not much, but more than he'd want Mabel seeing. He grabs a napkin and gets up from the table.

The toilets are down a flight of stairs and Adam has to steady himself on the banisters as he descends. The giddiness has returned. Now that he is moving, his stomach hurts too, despite the additional painkillers. In the bathroom, Adam dabs at his nose with damp tissue – he risks a gentle blow and clears a lump of congealed blood. And here comes the nausea, the prickling sweat on his brow, a liquid quality to his legs. Adam coughs then retches. He doubles up over the sink and spits blood. And when he vomits, the bile and bubbles are flecked with red.

Adam counts to ten. Breathing deep and focusing on a single spot – a chip on the bathroom mirror – the way Dr Sam taught him. He rinses his mouth with tap water until the water runs clear. And then he counts to ten again.

Climbing the steps back to the restaurant is no easy feat, and Heather is watching the stairs as he reaches the top. He waves at her – *nothing* – mimes holding a phone to his ear, and steps outside to call the number his cancer nurse gave him.

Someone takes his name, listens to his symptoms and puts him on hold. Within a minute, he is talking to a consultant, and Adam's first emotion is embarrassment. *Sorry to bother you. Probably nothing. A small amount of blood.*

The doctor assured Adam he had done the right thing, and asked a list of questions: *Where is your cancer, how advanced, what are you taking, what other symptoms are you experiencing?* She asked if his urine was dark, was he lethargic, did he have a fever. And Adam answered yes, yes, and possibly. She asked if he had tenderness in his arms or legs, and Adam realised that he did.

The lady told him not to panic, but to call a taxi – or an ambulance if he preferred – and make his way to the hospital.

Chapter 32

Wrapping a book shouldn't be a difficult job, but Tom has already ruined two sheets of paper and his teeth taste of Sellotape. On his last attempt he gave himself a wicked paper cut and came close to throwing the bugger out of the window, but the bugger – a leather-bound volume of Shakespeare's complete works – cost the best part of a hundred quid. Perhaps this – the book's value, its history and meaning – is why he is having such trouble.

There were cheaper editions, and in better condition too. But this slightly worn volume is eighty-eight years old and a thing of fragile beauty. One thousand three hundred and fifty-two pages so thin they are semi-transparent. Blue leather binding with gilt details on the spine and cover. A ribbon that is crimson where it has been hidden between the pages of *The Tempest* but faded to coral pink at the top where almost a century of sunlight has fallen across it. This last moves Tom the most.

He will give it to Laura at their next rehearsal. Ideally, wrapped in nice paper without ripples, tears or Sellotape marks. He is aware that Laura might misinterpret a gesture of friendship as something deeper. But she is perhaps the best friend he has ever had, and this is surely Tom's final December.

Laura's scarf, dry cleaned and pressed into a perfect square is already wrapped and ready to hand to his mother on Christmas Day. It doesn't look like much, regardless of what Laura's mother must have paid for it. And Tom is worried his mother will say something dismissive; that she will mock or scoff at this elegant and under-stated item. He should have bought the gin, but it's too late now.

Tom has sketchy memories of childhood Christmases. Strangers in the house, people singing, shouting, a tree that kept falling over until someone – his father? Another man? – opened the living-room window and threw the tree, tinsel, lights and all, into the front garden. He remembers that tree being there for a long time, the tinsel remaining long after the needles had dropped.

When Tom was perhaps nine, his mother had been pregnant over Christmas, and he has an unreliable image of this in his mind. His mother big-bumped and paper-hatted. Dancing in the front room with a man whose face Tom can't bring to mind. There was always drink, and many mornings Tom would creep through the house while his mother slept, drinking stale backwashed beer and the dregs of cheap wine. Smoking ground-out cigarette and joint butts. The Christmas when she was pregnant was different to the others – she didn't fall asleep in her chair, trip on the stairs, piss herself or hit Tom. He remembers that.

But she still lost the baby, and for a while Tom went to live with another family. That was difficult, but he doesn't blame his mother. Life was hard for her too. Tom doesn't remember any Christmas at home after that one.

Perhaps this – his last – will be the best Christmas Tom has ever had. It won't take much.

Finally, he manages to find the right balance of tension in the wrapping paper – simple holly leaves and red berries – drawing it tight across the leather cover, without tearing a hole at the corners. He bites off one more length of tape and secures the paper in place. Then again at the opposite end. Easy.

He imagines Laura taking this book from a shelf in fifty years' time – because Laura, like this book, is a survivor. She will take the book down from a shelf and read it in her favourite chair. And when she does, perhaps she will think of Tom.

He weighs the heavy, wrapped volume in his hands, running his fingers over the flat surface. He turns it over and notices, after all, that one of the troublesome edges has worn through. He covers this with a small square of tape. And if you squint, you'd never know it wasn't perfect.

Chapter 33

It's a little after six in the morning when the taxi drops Adam at home. But Heather – wild-haired and swollen-eyed – is sitting in the kitchen in her pyjamas, nursing a cup of coffee.

She gets up when Adam walks through the door and hugs him gently. And then she begins to cry.

Adam holds her. 'Are you okay?'

From somewhere, Heather manages a short laugh. 'I should be asking you that.'

'I'm fine.'

Heather sniffs, unwraps herself from Adam and wipes her eyes on the sleeve of her pyjamas. 'Fine,' she repeats. 'I think we have different ideas of fine, Adam.'

He nods towards the ceiling. 'How's Mabel?'

'Still asleep. You want coffee?'

'Please.'

Heather flicks the kettle on. 'I told her you'd had a call from Santa. That you needed to choose the dolly and the cheesecake.'

'And she went for it?'

'They believe what they want to believe, don't they? Next year she'll probably . . .'

Next year.

Perhaps it's a mercy that Adam will never see Mabel reject Santa, or cry when someone reveals that she has been lied to by her parents. He will miss the feared hormonal years, the unsuitable boyfriends with cars and acne, the sight of his daughter drunk or heartbroken. But it doesn't feel like a mercy.

'She was awesome last night, wasn't she?'

'She was. Took me thirty minutes to convince her she couldn't sleep in her robot costume, but . . . yeah, she was awesome.'

After hanging up on the helpline last night, Adam called a taxi and then stepped back into the pizzeria and whispered to Heather that he had to go. He told her he was fine, just a precaution. And he absolutely refused when Heather said she and Mabel would go with him. 'Please,' he said. 'Please keep this normal.'

And so Heather stayed and fed pieces of pizza to Robot Mabel, while Adam went to hospital. They took blood, ran tests, performed a scan. He called from the hospital and told Heather everything was okay, even though no one had said any such thing.

'You're up early,' Adam says.

Heather laughs. 'Haven't slept. Not really.'

'I'm sorry.'

'Not your fault.'

'Have you had breakfast?' Heather shakes her head. 'Let me make you some.'

'There's no need.'

'I'll make eggs. I need to . . . do something.'

He gets up from the table, adds a lump of butter to a pan and puts it over a low heat.

'So?' says Heather.

'So . . .'

Adam is something of a mess. His bile duct is blocked, the result of an infection for which he is now taking antibiotics. His tumour has metastasised to his liver, and whilst this was inevitable, it was no less of a shock.

'But what about the chemo?'

Adam had asked the consultant the same question.

'Well, chemo kills cells, Adam. It's a blunt tool. It's why your hair is falling out, why your feet are sore. The *hope* is that the chemo will inflict more damage on the cancer cells than on the rest of you. But that's not always the case.

'Like in my case?'

'Yes, Adam. Like in your case.'

They fitted a stent to his bile duct, and this should lead to an easing of some symptoms. At the very least, he should lose some of the yellow in his complexion. He has a small thrombosis on one lung, but the adjective does little in the way of mitigation. Adam will likely need to take oral anticoagulants for the next month, with the possibility of progressing to daily injections for the following six months. Or, in other words, for the rest of his life.

'The chemo wasn't agreeing with me,' Adam says.

'So?'

He cracks two eggs into the pan and mixes them with a wooden spoon. 'Toast?'

Heather shakes her head. 'I can do that.'

'Let me.'

She lets him.

'I'm off the chemo,' Adam says. 'For now.'

'But . . . don't you need it?'

'It's only for a few weeks. A "chemo holiday", they called it. Get me through Christmas. I'll feel less sick, have more energy. Maybe even eat Christmas dinner.'

'And then?'

Adam seasons the eggs with salt, pepper and basil. 'We'll see. A trial drug maybe. Or something less . . . punchy.'

Less potent, too, and this is the bargain – fewer days but better days, and Adam has made his peace with this. He has no say in the matter, but even so, the transaction sounds like a good one. The right one.

'A trial?' Heather repeats.

The gambler's choice: if it works, the therapy will buy him more time. But if it fails, the cancer in his liver will progress unchecked, wrecking that 'clean-up' organ and leaving Adam unable to tolerate further therapy of any kind.

'In which case, we would be looking at purely palliative care, Adam. Pain management. Keeping you comfortable.' *While you die.*

'If I'm eligible,' Adam says to Heather. 'But . . . I'm good. They took that port out of my arm, for one thing. So I can have a bath without wrecking your towels now.'

'That is good.'

He plates up the eggs and sets them in front of Heather.

She lifts her coffee cup, then puts it back on the table. 'I kept the champagne.'

'What?'

'From last night. I brought it home, and half a Margherita pizza.'

'You want champagne?'

Heather shrugs. 'It's probably flat.'

'Aren't you working?'

'I'll phone in,' she says. 'Tell them something came up.'

'Why?'

'Because something did. And because you'd do the same for me. Wouldn't you? Besides, I'm knackered.'

Adam laughs. 'Thank you. I . . . thank you.'

He fetches two champagne flutes from a cupboard and places them on the table.

'Just a small one,' Heather says. 'Then after we've taken Mabel to school, maybe we'll watch a movie? Drink champagne and fall asleep on the sofa?'

Like the old days, Adam wants to say. But this moment is close to perfect, so he says nothing and pours two small glasses of flat champagne.

Chapter 34

Today the vicar's wife's fruitcake is topped with a layer of marzipan and a frosting of white icing. A pair of green-icing holly leaves at each corner. It looks beautiful. Although it remains, as ever, largely untouched.

'Pass me a mouse,' Pat says. Her bandana today is printed with a festive snowscape. On top of this she wears a paper crown in fir tree green.

Tom hands a box of chocolate mice to Pat. 'You know they're full of booze?'

'Drunk mice,' Adam says. 'Trust Vernon.'

They all smile at this.

Raymond adjusts his crown. 'Quiet without him.'

'He'll be fine.'

'Yes, he'll be fine.'

According to Vernon's wife, he is 'struggling'.

She turned up at the door but refused Pat's invitation to come inside and meet the group. 'I won't,' she said. 'This is your thing. He just wanted you to have these.'

'Chocolate mice?'

'He said you'd understand.'

Pat laughed. 'I think I do. Are you sure you won't come in? There's sherry.'

Maggie declined, saying she wanted to get back for Vernon. That he was having a bad few days. That he was, she said it again, her eyes shining with tears, 'struggling'.

Before leaving, Maggie hugged Pat. 'He's had such a good time with you all. It's really . . . it's made a difference. Thank you.'

The rafters in the hall are hung with decorations – tinsel,

balloons, cardboard angels blowing trumpets. It's only a few days until Christmas, and as such, today's gathering is less of a rehearsal than a Christmas party. Pat brought sherry; Adam brought Christmas crackers. Erin's chemuffins were laced with cinnamon and orange zest, but this made them no less offensive, and they are, as usual, safely stored in the bin. Tom, to Raymond's chagrin, has put out a few crumbs of Christmas cake for the mouse, should he care to join them.

The song on the radio changes to 'Candle in the Wind'.

'I love this,' Erin says, and she giggles. 'Sorry, I . . .' and she laughs again.

Pat hands her the chocolate mice. 'You need one of these,' she says.

Erin takes the chocolates and passes the joint to Pat.

'Easy now, Sister,' Tom says.

Pat regards the joint with faux innocence. 'It's medicinal, right?'

Laughter is the best medicine, Tom thinks. And this weed has been responsible for a good deal of that commodity this afternoon.

'Definitely,' he says. 'It's definitely medicinal.'

The marijuana – two pre-rolled cigarettes – came from Erin's daughter, Jenny. She is home for the Christmas holidays, and two days ago had tentatively suggested Erin join her for a smoke.

'It did help,' Erin said. 'With the pain. And I slept so well. Funny dreams though.'

Laura laughs and shakes her head. 'I feel funny. Good funny, though. Not, you know, *funny* funny. Can I have another mouse?'

Pat hands her the box of mice. Then she offers the joint to Raymond.

He has removed the batteries from the smoke detectors so the others can indulge without setting off an alarm, but this doesn't mean he condones this wild behaviour, and Raymond leans away from the joint, as if it might contaminate him by proximity. 'No thank you.'

'You're sure?'

'I'm positive.'

And this, like most comments this afternoon, is met with laughter.

Adam accepts the joint and takes a long drag.

'I think this might be my funeral song,' Erin says. '"Candle in the Wind".'

This has been the main topic of conversation throughout the afternoon.

The Rude Mechanicals' funeral songs:

Pat – 'Over the Rainbow'. (*Not one of those dreary old hymns like 'The Lord is my Shepherd'.*)

Laura – 'Knockin' on Heaven's Door'.

Adam – 'We'll Meet Again'.

Raymond – 'The Lord Is My Shepherd'. (*As you're not using it, Sister.*)

Erin is humming the opening bars to 'Candle in the Wind'.

'Lovely song,' says Pat.

'What's that candle line in *Macbeth*?' Laura asks.

'"Out, brief candle!",' Adam says. '"Life's but a walking shadow".'

'Do you think that's where he got it? "Candle in the Wind"?'

'Has to be,' says Pat. 'Has to be.'

'Might be a bit . . . weird,' says Tom. 'For a funeral song.'

'Weird? It's Elton John.'

Tom studies Erin's face for signs of irony and finds none. 'There's a line,' he says, 'about Marilyn being naked when they found her dead body.'

'Really?'

'Really.'

'Oh,' says Erin. 'Well, back to Robbie Williams then.'

Pat offers the joint to Tom.

He holds up a hand. 'I'll pass.'

'Your throat?'

My habit. 'Something like that. Anyway, there's enough passive in here to put a hippy to sleep.'

'Sherry?'

Tom mimes a small amount, and Pat pours a drop into his mug.

'Thomas,' Erin says. 'You still haven't told us your song.'

Tom holds out two hands in a gesture that says: *Isn't it obvious?* 'Bowie. "Ashes to Ashes".'

'You being cremated?' Raymond asks.

'I don't think so. Haven't really thought about it.'

'So?'

'Major Tom,' says Tom.

And something Tom had never before appreciated: David Bowie is one of those rarefied stars of whom everyone believes they can perform a passable impersonation. Marilyn Monroe, John Wayne, Sylvester Stallone, David Bowie.

Pat attempts the chorus of Tom's funeral song, she gets as far as 'Funk to funky' then trails off, stopping before Mr Bowie completes the couplet with a revelation about Major Tom's not so heroic habits. Tom watches as Pat trots through the lyric in her head; he hums along with her and then says aloud the words that she is too tactful to speak.

'A junkie,' says Tom.

He smiles apologetically, and this simple gesture, it seems, is enough to complete the parallel.

Erin puts a hand to her mouth. Raymond winces. Adam regards the joint in his hand, drops it into a mug of cold tea. Pat lays a hand on Tom's knee.

Laura stands, calmly picks up her bag, then walks across the room and out of the door.

Raymond clips Tom around the back of the head.

'What?'

He nods towards the door. 'Go.'

Tom goes.

Laura is sitting on a wall outside. Waiting.

Tom sits beside her. 'You okay?'

Laura nods but doesn't look at him.

'Sorry. I thought you knew.'

'I knew.'

'I didn't mean to be . . .' He huffs a laugh. 'To be me.'

'You're fine,' Laura says. 'You're more than . . .' She's still a little buzzed from the joint, the sherry, the drunken chocolate mouse. She laughs. 'These cancer folk know how to party, right?'

'Like it's 1999,' Tom says.

She looks at him, notices the clumsily wrapped book in his hands.

Tom passes it to her. 'Open it on Christmas morning.'

'Thank you. I . . . I didn't expect . . .'

'We're friends, right?' He looks at her meaningfully.

Laura picks at a corner of tape, but Tom puts his hand on hers. 'Christmas,' he says.

Laura unzips her bag, removes a perfectly wrapped cube, big enough to hold a mug or a small bottle of aftershave. She doesn't hand it to Tom, instead holding it in her lap.

'It was the other stuff,' she says.

'Other stuff?'

'Ashes to ashes,' Laura says, and she is crying. Slowly and inconspicuously at first, but as Tom holds her hand, the tears come apace, Laura's shoulders shaking, her breath catching in short, fast gasps.

Tom puts an arm around her shoulders and pulls her gently against him. They sit and watch the passing traffic until the tears slow and subside.

Laura hands him the gift-wrapped box. 'Christmas.'

Tom goes to say thank you, but Laura leans in and kisses him. She reaches across and puts her hand to his cheek, extending the kiss and letting her lips separate around his. Tom returns the kiss then, gently, breaks it off.

She goes to kiss him again, but Tom pulls his head away. 'I like you,' he says. 'A lot, actually. But you've got—'

'Don't.'

'It's just that—'

'I'm tired of people telling me what's *best* for me,' she says. 'So I hope you're not about to do that. It would be *such* a disappointment, *Major Tom*.'

Tom shakes his head. 'I wouldn't want to disappoint you.'

'Then don't.' And she kisses him again.

When they return to the hall ten minutes later, Bing Crosby is crooning the daylights out of an up-tempo 'Jingle Bells', Adam is dancing with Pat, and Raymond is jiving – it has to be jiving – with Erin.

'Check out Raymond.'

'Got moves,' Laura says. 'I mean, *really* got moves.'

Tom extends his hand to Laura. 'Shall we?'

Laura takes his hand.

And whatever else happens, this is absolutely, without exception or close second, Tom's best Christmas ever.

Chapter 35

Christmas Eve falls on a Sunday this year – an annoyance to the diligent faithful, who will have to attend mass again tomorrow for the main event. Outside Father Declan's church, Pat watches the parishioners shake his hand as they exit via the small door at the rear of the chapel. They thank him for the service, wish him a merry Christmas and assure him they will see him in the morning. Some, Pat observes, make a point of avoiding him – these, the pragmatically faithful, will stay home, open presents, fry bacon, maybe add a splash of champagne to their orange juice. And good for them. Others will have opted for the lesser lapse of missing today, knowing they can make quick amends on the Big Man's birthday.

The congregation dwindles now, only a few stragglers – old ladies for the most part – still bending the priest's ear. He must be cold. A few have given gifts, and these sit in two carrier bags at the old priest's feet. He has noticed her, but has shown no sign of recognition. Pat sat at the back of the chapel with Hitchens, and at those points in the service when the congregation knelt in prayer, the dog joined in, resting his paws beside Pat and dipping his daft head in contemplation. The performance drew one or two chuckles and perhaps the same number of indignant tuts. Declan, from the front of the chapel, had smiled.

As the stragglers say goodbye and Declan turns to the door, Pat approaches.

'It was a lovely service.'

'Thank you,' his face moves through a sequence – familiar to Pat – of partial recognition and frustration.

'Are you local?'

'Passing through,' she says.

A lie, just ten minutes after mass. But only a small one. Father Declan was easy to find in the Catholic directory, and Pat was relieved to learn that his parish wasn't in Scotland, Ireland, or the Isle of Wight. Even so, a four-hour round trip on the train for a forty-five-minute mass is hardly 'passing through'.

'Do we . . .?'

'Pat,' she says. 'Sister Patricia. We worked together once. At—'

'St Bernadette's!' And he puts his arms around her shoulders and pulls her into a strong embrace. 'Patricia. Patricia. I remember it like it was yesterday.'

They sit on a pew at the front of the quiet church, cups of tea in hand, a pot beside them resting on a hymn book. Declan, again, lobs the tennis ball to the back of the chapel and Hitchens lollops after, his toenails echoing off the parquet floor.

'What's his name?'

'Hitchens.'

'Suits him.'

Declan takes a bite of the cake Pat brought in a small plastic tub. 'Good,' he says.

'It's Anglican,' she tells him, and Declan slaps his thigh as he laughs. 'The v— vicar's wife, she puts b— brandy in it.'

'Well they have that much right'.

'This is a nice church.'

'My fifth. My last, I imagine.'

The six years he has on Pat seem heavy now with life and tiredness. He is an old man, his hair gone, his skin lined, a network of fine red veins on the tip of his nose. But his voice is still rich and deep and handsome.

They have covered the preliminaries and courtesies, glossing and skipping over more than three decades of life. 'You're a long way from home,' Declan said after Pat told him where she lives. Pat had nodded, *yes*, and Declan, she believes, understood. But Pat decides now to make it explicit.

'I came to say—' The word has slipped away. It's the opposite of hello, but what, for the love of God, is the opposite of—'Goodbye,' Pat says. 'I came to say goodbye. Because . . .'

'Because we never did,' he says. 'I'm sorry.'

Pat has one hand on her knee, and Declan rests his own on top of hers. She sets down her tea and places her free hand on Declan's – as if worried he might withdraw it. 'You had your calling.'

'I did.'

Pat looks towards the altar. She remembers the old ladies shaking Father Declan's hand outside. The look of love – devout love – in their eyes and she thinks perhaps Declan did the right thing. This is a good life, serving the community, making the world a better place – in whatever form that takes.

'We were young,' he says.

'I . . . Did you ever have d— doubts?'

'About my calling?' He takes a sip of his tea. 'Sometimes.'

'Lately,' Pat says, 'I've been . . . unsure.'

'About your choices?'

'About my f— faith. But I suppose, one follows after the other. What if . . .' She indicates the altar, the stained glass, the vaulted ceiling, the Stations of the Cross. 'What if it's all . . .'

'A load of hooey?'

Pat laughs. 'Right. H— hooey.'

Hitchens returns with the ball, and Declan slides his hand out from between Pat's.

'And what do you think?' He scratches between the dog's ears. 'What do you think, Hitchens?'

Hitchens grumps.

'I agree,' Declan says, and he rolls the ball up the aisle. 'It doesn't matter,' he says to Pat.

'How can you say that? Here.'

'I'm a doddery old priest. We get to say all sorts of things the youngsters can't. It doesn't matter, Pat, because we'll know soon enough.' He smiles. 'We'll be proved right, or we'll rest in quiet blissful ignorance. So, it doesn't matter.'

'Well what does?'

'Living a good life. And . . . I think we've done that. Don't you think we've done that?'

Pat would like to think so. She reaches into her bag. 'I nearly forgot,' she says, removing a wrapped bottle.

Father Declan takes it from her. 'You shouldn't have.'

'It's Deadmun's,' Pat says. She waits for Declan to acknowledge the joke, but it fails to land.

He furrows his brow. 'Deadmun's?'

'It's . . . whiskey,' Pat says. 'It's whiskey.'

'Curse of the clergy, hey? Thank you, Pat. I wish I had something for you. But . . .'

Pat waves this away. 'I ambushed you.'

'No,' Declan says. 'This is nice. This is . . . it's lovely.'

Hitchens has abandoned the ball for now, and is instead running up and down between the pews, chasing mice or chasing shadows.

'Five parishes,' Pat says. 'Is that a lot?'

'It's . . .' Declan looks to the altar as if searching there for the answer. 'It's not so unusual.'

'Moving?'

Declan shrugs. 'The Anglicans . . . I think they might be on to something, don't you think?'

'Marriage?'

'We're human, after all,' Declan says.

And Pat wonders, of the four times Declan has been moved from one parish to another, how many times were because he had been 'human'? And just how human had he been? She feels silly now. They kissed on three different nights, more than thirty years ago. The whiskey – the Deadmun's that has slipped from Declan's memory – Pat has always thought was an excuse rather than a reason. But perhaps she was wrong.

She has clean clothes folded at the bottom of her bag, and she blushes at her stupidity and naivety.

'Deadmun's . . .' Declan says, inspecting the wrapped bottle in his hand, as if seeing through the paper to the whiskey beneath. 'The priest?' he says. 'In St Bernadette's.'

Pat smiles. 'Yes. We . . .'

Declan puts his hand again on Pat's. 'Yes,' he says. 'Special times.'

Hitchens makes his way towards them, snuffling and grumping and impatient. *Home. Home.*

Pat stands. 'I have a train.'

Declan rises too, and with considerable effort. 'To be young again,' he says.

Pat nods. *To be young again.*

They hug once more and they take their time, clinging tight, as if to life.

'I missed you.'

Pat kisses his white-stubbled cheek. 'I missed you too.'

'You'll come again?'

Pat nods, she says yes, and tells her second lie of the night.

Chapter 36

The nursing home is decorated with cheap paper chains, and Christmas carols are playing at low volume through the wall-mounted speakers. The nurses and carers flit with a quiet festive bustle – some wear tinsel in their hair, or sing along to the music, but they are careful not to agitate the residents.

It's early, not yet ten on Christmas morning, and Raymond's heart goes out to these jolly angels who should be at home with their own. He brought chocolates for the staff – not simply because they deserve it, which they do, but because Raymond reckons that if he treats them well, then they will be more inclined to treat Judith well. For Judith he brought nail polish.

She used to call him her toy-boy, although Raymond was past forty when they met, and Judith only a few years older. He liked the pet name, though; found it endearing and a little risqué. It spoke of sexuality, that thing so unwieldy to Raymond and so natural – amusing, even – to the woman who would become his wife. He called her his old girl, and though she acted offended, it always made her smile.

Her hand rests on the arm of the chair as Raymond carefully applies varnish to her nails. He's become rather good at this over the last thirteen months.

'You look well,' he says, and Judith's eyes drift in his direction. They slide over his face, pausing ever so briefly at his eyes, and then she is looking over his shoulder.

Raymond's compliment is no platitude.

At seventy-six, Judith is one of the younger residents here. He sits sometimes with the old boys and dears, listening and nodding while they spout their looped nonsense. They like to have their hands held. Raymond worries that he might bruise or break their delicate old bones, and holds them with great care as the owners twitter and drool at something buried deep inside.

Judith's hands are fat and warm, and when he squeezes them she squeezes back with great vigour. Her legs and shoulders are round with flesh, her skin plump, her eyes clear despite their lack of focus. She could last another ten years, another twenty. Lord knows she might even get the certificate they had always laughed about: *Congratulations on not dying yet; signed her Majesty the Queen*. Although Raymond would bet all he has that Judith will long outlive their current monarch.

And all that he has is no small amount. Which, too, is an issue.

He blows on her fingers to dry the varnish on her right hand, and Judith smiles.

When they married, Judith's son Philip was just old enough to get plastered at the reception. And this he did. When he called his mother all those vile names, his legs were loose and his words slurred – but everybody heard them.

When Raymond stepped between them, he received a punch on the ear for his gallantry and would no doubt have taken several more had Philip not been hauled away by the best man, kicking and spitting and turning the air filthy.

They have spoken since, but infrequently. Initially when Philip needed money. Often, they helped; other times – either because they couldn't or wouldn't – they refused. The gratitude at the former paling against the loathing that met the latter. But time heals. To an extent. And Philip is married now with a child of his own – an eight-year-old boy called Hugo, who he and Judith have seen perhaps a dozen times. Perhaps less. And not at all in the last two years.

Philip didn't have a father to raise and guide him and show him how to be (or not to be) a man, but that's no excuse for not visiting your mother. Raymond hopes that Philip will come today and bring the boy.

But this hope is a small one.

If there is a mercy to any of this, it is that Judith is now insulated by dementia. Insulated from her son's indifference. Insulated from everything.

He moves to Judith's left side, and sets that hand on the arm of the chair. 'Robin red,' he tells her. 'Nice for Christmas, I thought.'

Judith's eyes drop to her nails, but this is simply a trick of timing.

One of the nurses stops beside them. She has a mug of tea for Raymond, and two individually wrapped chocolates.

'Thank you, Ness.'

Ness puts a hand to Judith's cheek. 'He's well trained, isn't he, Judith? Happy Christmas, darling.'

Judith blinks.

Raymond unwraps a chocolate and holds it before her lips. She blinks at this, opens her mouth like a baby, and Raymond feeds her the sweet.

'So I'm fine,' he tells his wife. 'My knees creak in the mornings. But I still walk on the common every day. There was a crust of ice at the edge of the lake early today, but it will have melted by now.'

Some toy-boy, Raymond thinks. *Creaky knees and frozen puddles.*

They used to talk so easily, and not just about their ailments or the weather. Music, books, food, nature, politics, film, religion. They could talk about the colour of the grass and lose themselves for an hour debating shades of green. But it doesn't work when there's only one doing the talking.

'The group is keeping me busy,' he says. 'Macduff, Brutus, Laertes . . . Othello.'

I would not have thee linger in thy pain, Othello says as he smothers Desdemona. And although their circumstances are different, the sentiment is the same.

If Judith survives Raymond, his will leaves everything in trust to pay for her ongoing care in this quiet home. Without it, she would be transferred to some state-run pit where she'll be lucky to have her backside wiped, let alone her make-up done. And when she's gone, what's left will go into another trust for her grandson.

If Judith goes first, and Raymond feels wretched with guilt for hoping she does, then he will sell the big house that only serves to magnify his loneliness.

He will rent a small place near the coast, and use it as a base from whence he will travel to all the places he has never seen: Vietnam, New Zealand, Costa Rica.

Verona, Venice, Denmark.

He'll travel until either he or the money runs out. And anything left can go to charity. Prostate cancer, probably, but he is yet to decide the specifics.

He finishes Judith's nails and blows on the fingers of her left hand. 'You look beautiful,' he tells her.

Judith's mouth opens, forms a neat 'o' and then closes.

Raymond rises to his feet. 'I'll see you tomorrow, old girl.'

It disturbs her now to be kissed; she tenses and recoils, this woman who was always so confident and warm. So in place of a kiss, Raymond squeezes his wife's fat hand one last time before he leaves.

Chapter 37

And she has to do this all over again tomorrow. A different set of grandparents, aunts and uncles asking about school, giving her too many presents, squeezing her flesh, watching her eat, watching her sit and read, watching her every single move.

Laura cuts a slice of turkey and feels her grandmother's eyes on her as she lifts it to her mouth. She lowers the fork back to her plate, the turkey untouched, and hears a small but gratifying sigh from the opposite end of the table. She takes a sip of wine instead. The scandal of it.

But, hey, you're afforded a certain licence when everyone worries this Christmas might be your last. Presents Laura has received today: a silver necklace and matching earrings with sapphire studs. A second set of earrings, rose-gold and shaped like tiny daisies with rubies at their centre – 'in case one set clashes with whatever scarf you're wearing'. Scarves, of course. A leather jacket and suede boots. Vouchers, tokens, cash. New headphones. A satsuma, a box of chocolates and a pencil case for Christ's sake. And more tomorrow from Gran and Gramps mark two. They are spoiling her in case they never get another chance to do so. And Laura wonders how they will feel if they have to go through the same rigmarole next year. And the years after that. How many leather jackets can one girl wear? How many Christmases until they revert to buying her naff jumpers?

And the most beautiful thing she has ever owned – a leather-bound collection of Shakespeare's complete works. A note inside on a square of paper: *A lifetime – Happy Christmas. Tom.* No 'x', but Laura had her 'x' sitting on the wall outside the church hall and the memory of it brings colour to her cheeks.

'Are you hot?' her aunt asks. 'Turn the heating down, Ruth.' This last directed at Laura's mother.

'I'm fine,' Laura says.

She slides her phone from her pocket, glances at it beneath the tablecloth. Still no messages – but this is a special time for Tom, and Laura understands. She wishes she had bought him something less frivolous for Christmas. Something to match her beautiful blue-leather book.

'No phones at the table, poppet.'

Laura ignores her father and types out a short message: *Hope you're having a good time with your mum. Happy Christmas. Again ☺ xx*

She puts the phone away.

'Aren't you hungry?' Her grandmother.

Her father: 'She's fine, Doris.'

Her mother: 'You should eat something, though, sweetheart.'

'Good turkey,' her uncle says. 'Really moist.' And this might be the third time.

Laura lifts her fork, chews and swallows the morsel of turkey. Smiles: *Happy now?*

Her grandfather says, 'Can you play charades, Laura?'

As if, presumably, her cancer might preclude mime.

Laura holds up a single finger: *One word*. She nods her head: *Yes*.

Her grandfather looks confused. Which is, to be fair, normal.

'You should eat your sprouts, Laura.' Her grandmother points at Laura with her fork. 'She should eat her sprouts.'

'Greens,' her uncle says.

Her father puts a hand on her elbow. 'Not your favourite, are they, poppet?'

'Might put some colour in her cheeks,' her grandfather says.

Might cure my cancer, Laura is about to say, but her father gets in first.

'Who wants green cheeks, right?'

Laura sighs. Sips her wine.

'Full of iron,' her grandma says.

'Fine. Fine.' Laura picks up a sprout in her fingers and shoves it into her mouth. The table watch as she chews with exaggerated movements of her jaw.

Her grandma nods, satisfied. 'Good girl.'

Laura puts a hand to her pocket and finds the familiar fifty-pence coin. Found in the hospital car park over a year ago, minted in the year of her birth and – *just like me* – scuffed and dented with accumulated damage. She feels its edges through the denim of her jeans and makes a promise to herself: *If I'm here next year, I'm spending it somewhere else. Up a mountain, in a jungle, down a river. Anywhere but here.*

Her uncle clears his throat. 'This turkey really is delicious.'

And it's all Laura can do not to laugh.

Chapter 38

When Jenny was six, she used to call it 'Monolopy', and that's what they've called it ever since. This is their tradition – the three of them playing Monolopy around the coffee table after Christmas dinner, a box of chocolates, a bowl of nuts, something nice to drink. You can't play a good game of Monolopy with two, but Erin's wish is that Jenny, when she has children of her own, will keep this tradition alive.

Her fingers go to the necklace they bought her this year. A fine gold chain strung with three stars – one for each of them. She looks at her daughter, arranging her money into neat piles. A year from now, this necklace will hang around Jenny's neck. It will suit her, which is why Erin had steered Brian to this particular piece of jewellery – 'If you were thinking of buying anything along those lines.'

He's done well today. Him and Jenny cooked the whole meal themselves, and even though the bird was a little dry and the gravy thin, they've done a good job. Washed up too.

She worries about Brian looking after himself, and they have to share the blame on that one. Him for never helping around the house, her for putting up with it. But he's learning under Erin's watchful eye. Learning to fry the onions before the mince, to separate the whites from the darks, and to clean the glassware before the pans. They say you can't teach an old dog new tricks, but Brian, God bless him, is doing his best to prove them wrong. He baked those awful wonderful muffins, after all. And if that's not love, then tell me what is.

Still, she should have put her foot down sooner, while she was still healthy. It would have saved many tears and set a better example for Jenny – what she should expect and put up with in a man. Perhaps she will talk to Jenny about this later tonight – when Brian is sleeping in front of the film. This can be the lesson she passes on.

Never be anyone's dogsbody. Never settle for less than you deserve. Don't give up your dreams to wash someone else's undies.

But she mustn't do Brian down. They are both products of their generation, after all. Erin did all the laundry and the housework; Brian puts bread on the table, puts up shelves and takes out the bin bags on a Sunday night.

He's young enough to marry again; still strong, still handsome. And he's a good man when all is said and accounted for. But if he does marry again, Erin hopes that she, whoever *she* is, won't take Erin's place around this Monolopy board. This is their tradition.

Brian lands now on Park Lane – a prime property – and Erin already knows he won't buy it.

Jenny has Mayfair, and she sees a potential deal in the offing. 'Buy it, Dad. It's *Park Lane*.'

Brian looks at his pile of money, and he could easily afford it. But – a product of his generation – he shakes his head. 'Got to keep some back' – Erin knows the rest and says it with him: 'For rainy days and emergencies.' And he rhymes the two contingencies, just like he always does.

He thinks he's teaching Jenny an important lesson, and Erin loves him for it. Even though he's wrong. Life is too short and too precious to miss a sunny day for fear of a rainy one later. Living that way is to take your life for granted. *Better to take some risks*, Erin thinks.

It's Erin's turn to roll the dice, and of course it's her imagination, but even this feels like effort today. Her bones are heavy and her blood slow, is how it feels. Her lungs small and pinched. But no pain today, and on balance, this is a good exchange.

The dice takes Erin to Chance, and the card directs her halfway around the board to Go, where she collects £200. Enough for four houses on the pale blues.

'You're spreading yourself thin,' Brian warns.

'I'm feeling lucky,' Erin tells him. 'And you can go and get me a sherry.'

'Me too,' Jenny says.

Erin winks at her daughter.

This is a better lesson, she thinks, and she will share it with Jenny tonight. Better to take risks, than to take life for granted. And never fetch your own sherry when there's a perfectly good man on hand.

Chapter 39

Get me well for Christmas. The prayer on Vernon's lips every night for the last eight days. And perhaps this – shivering and sweating under his blanket, no appetite, no energy – perhaps this isn't any right-thinking person's idea of 'well', but he's still here, and that will do. It will have to.

As Lady Macbeth says: 'Things without all remedy should be without regard.'

Too true, darling. Too true.

They bought him the DVD for Christmas, and this is what they're watching now. Vernon with all his kids – all his 'pretty chickens', as Macduff would say – gathered beside him. Squashed onto the sofa, two to a chair and the lad on a beanbag at his feet. Yeah, this'll do.

He has a whiskey in his hand, but can't drink it. The smell, though, is something wonderful, and this, too, will do. Do very nicely, thank you very much.

Watching this young actor doing Macbeth – a movie star, apparently, but Vernon has never heard of him – watching this movie star read Macbeth's lines, Vernon sees the story all over again. Sees it brought to life, and the joy of it, the magic of it brings tears to his eyes.

His children, though, are restless. Maggie's set the nippers up in the big bedroom with a DVD of something from that *Toy Story* lot. Vernon's guessing most of the big 'uns would rather be up there with them. And Macbeth's not long done the king in.

'The wine of life is drawn,' Macbeth says, and Vernon savours the words.

'Listen to that,' he says, and his voice is parched. 'Poetry.'

The lad makes a noise. Neither a yes nor a no. Just a noise to let Vernon know he's been heard. A lot of death in *Macbeth*. And perhaps this is all a bit near the knuckle. Not exactly festive.

Vernon inhales the sweet vapour coming off his whiskey, as if this might wet his dry lips. 'Don't know about you lot,' he says, 'but – no offence, mind, and I'm very grateful – but isn't that film with the big elf fella on BBC?'

'*Elf*, Dad. It's called *Elf*.'

And his chickens all fall about laughing.

'What you reckon?' he says. 'Let's whack it on, hey?'

The lad changes channel and settles back at his father's feet. Maggie rests her head against his shoulder. She smells of the perfume he bought her – Chanel No 5.

Yeah, Vernon thinks. *This'll do just lovely.*

Chapter 40

Tom sits on the bed listening to the sounds of Christmas. *Antony & Cleopatra* lies open on his belly, Bruce Willis in his dirty vest is on the TV, and even with the volume off, it makes him laugh. He listens to people in the flats above, below and beside him. Good sounds today, for the most part. Laughter, singing, excited shouting. Music and television. Someone, he thinks, dancing. Rows, too – of course – but nothing violent. Nothing frightening.

Tom picks up the Magic 8 Ball from the bedside table. His present from Laura, and he smiles every time he holds it. Despite having discovered that the ball is a little disingenuous.

Tom shakes it now. 'Is my mother having a happy Christmas?'

The ball swirls as it makes up its mind: *Without a doubt.*

'Well that's good.'

Her ex-boyfriend turned up two days before Christmas with flowers and who knows what else. Excuses, flattery, promises. 'We're going to make a go of it, Tommy. You understand?'

Yeah, he understands. Fuerteventura, sixty-eight quid return on easyJet. 'Some sun'll do me good, Tommy.'

'Of course.'

'I mean, mad not to at that price, right?'

'Sure.'

'After all, Tommy, we waited this long, another week or two won't kill us – oops, no offence – will it, love?'

'Course not, Mum.'

'I knew you'd understand. Happy Christmas, Tommy.'

'Happy Christmas, Mum.'

Perhaps it's for the best, Tom thinks. But why think when he owns an all-knowing Magic 8 Ball.

181

'Is it for the best, 8 Ball?'

Signs point to yes.

Tom loves his Magic 8 Ball – loves that Laura bought it for him – but he's learned its trick and seen through its insincerity. Still, he supposes the ball means well.

The ball, Tom has discovered, has twenty answers and he has catalogued them all. Ten of those are positive, from an absolute *Yes*, to an optimistic *Outlook good*. Five answers aren't answers at all, rather equivocations and requests to *Try again*. Only five answers are negative. The trick is to ask the right question.

Tom's stomach rumbles beneath the splayed-open paperback. The local minimart had a deal on turkey-flavoured cup noodles so Tom bought four. He ate one for breakfast, but that was several hours ago.

He shakes the obliging ball. 'Should I spoil myself and have another?'

As I see it, yes.

Good, because those cup noodles are something special.

While the kettle boils, Tom checks his phone.

No messages from Mommie Dearest. And no surprise there.

Another from Laura. One of many delivering a blow by blow account of what sounds to Tom like a perfect Christmas. But to hear it from Laura, it's an interminable ordeal bordering on child abuse. Not that these missives aren't funny, just that they're a little . . . contrary.

She sends him kisses, she misses him, she loves the book, she wishes she'd bought him something more exciting, she hopes he's having a great day, hopes his mother likes the scarf, she'd love it if they could chat.

He doesn't like lying. But neither does he want to lay it all out right now. Too complicated, too embarrassing. Laura would make a fuss and want to meet. She might even invite him to her house. And Tom would be obliged to say no.

He knows all of this because the 8 Ball told him so.

So Tom hides behind the excuse of poor reception. Answering perhaps every fifth message: The ball is perfect, he misses her too, his mother loved the scarf, he can't call right now.

Tom opens the latest message from Laura.

Exhausted. Going to bed now. Hope you had an amazing day. Give your mum a kiss from me. And here's one for you X. Happy Christmas. Xx (Okay, three for you!)

Nice.

Tom types out a reply: *Keeping them all for myself! Sweet dreams x*

Thumb over the send button, he hesitates.

He rattles the Magic 8 Ball: 'Am I making a big mistake?'

Ask again later.

'Sure,' Tom says and he sends the message to Laura.

He will tell her the truth in a few days' time. But today is not the day. Today is for family.

The kettle has boiled, and Tom pours the water into the waiting cup noodle. It smells amazing.

Chapter 41

He's doing Christmas end to end. Twenty-four hours ago, he was out here sprinkling icing sugar on the back step and imprinting reindeer hooves with a halved potato. The day has minutes left in it now, and he and Heather sit on the back step, on a cushion brought outside from the sofa.

She taps ash from the cigarette and blows smoke towards the sky. Clear tonight and dotted with stars. Heather is wrapped in the scarf and hat Mabel bought her. Adam is wearing a thick coat, but the tingle of cold air on his scalp is soothing, and it's helping keep him awake after a long day.

Heather doesn't smoke. But her father left his cigarettes behind, and – as she will sometimes do when she visits her parents – she has taken one from the packet. She used to steal them as a teenager, and has long suspected her father knew this but turned a blind eye.

Heather's free hand goes to the necklace at her neck. Fat wooden alphabet beads spelling out: *Mummy*. Adam's necklace reads: *Daddy*.

Ostensibly, the beads were a present for Mabel, but Adam understands – a look from Heather – that they are for him. Adam's fingers still tingle with peripheral neuropathy, but these beads are big enough that he can handle them without dropping them all over the floor. They bought him socks too. Twenty pairs of seamless, cotton and silk socks in mad designs and vibrant colours. The in-laws bought him bath oil, towels and new pyjamas. All of it perfect.

Adam had been dreading this afternoon – Christmas dinner with the parents of the woman he let down so very badly. But Arthur and Gillian were friendly, compassionate, loving even. His sins forgiven, it seems, or at least overlooked under the shadow they didn't discuss. There were knowing looks, of course, searching glances and meaningful embraces. Some tears, too, but no melodrama. They played games, ate, laughed.

'That cracker,' Adam says to Heather.

And she hides her face in her hands and groans.

The joke in Mabel's cracker: 'What did Santa suffer from when he was stuck in the chimney?'

Arthur went for 'flue', which had seemed like a pretty good guess to Adam.

Mabel went for 'cancer'.

And after a beat of only two or three seconds, Adam laughed, and everybody else joined in.

The printed answer: Claustrophobia.

Heather looks at the cigarette and her eyes well up with tears.

'Hey.' Adam puts an arm around her shoulder. Heather doesn't shrug him off. 'What's up?'

Heather stubs the cigarette out on the back step. 'Nothing. Just . . . tired, I suppose.'

'Sure?'

Heather shakes her head. 'What if I die, Adam?'

'What?'

'Who will look after Mabel if I die?'

'You can't think like—'

'I can't *help* thinking like that. Because . . .' She turns to Adam then looks quickly away.

'Listen,' says Adam. 'You're going to live a long and healthy life.'

'You can't say that.'

'Like your parents. Like your dad, who smokes twenty a day and is healthy as a farm horse.'

'But—'

Adam shakes his head. 'Not going to happen. Because it can't. Because we've had all our bad luck now and because . . . because you can't believe anything else. Okay?'

Heather inhales the cold air. She nods.

'But you might want to give the fags a miss.'

'Right.'

'And don't take up parachuting.'

Heather laughs. 'But I love parachuting.'

A single firework arcs across the sky, the sound following a second later.

Adam has one more present to give Heather. He's hesitated throughout the day, unsure whether this gift is one too many, but Christmas – his final Christmas – is fast running out. He reaches into his coat pocket and pulls out an envelope.

'Don't be angry.'

'What is it?'

'Open it.'

Heather tears open the envelope and removes a Christmas card – Santa on the beach, a cocktail in his hand. 'Happy Holidays' printed across the top. Heather opens it and finds what looks like a credit card printed with an image of palm trees on a tropical beach.

'Travel vouchers,' Adam says. 'For you and Mabel.'

Heather frowns.

'For after,' Adam says. 'After I . . . I thought a holiday . . .'

Heather wipes a tear from her eye, punches Adam lightly on the shoulder. 'Stupid. Thank you.' And she kisses his cheek. 'Stupid.' The tears come freely now, falling gently down the contours of her face.

'Where will you go?'

Heather looks at the card, turns it over, but this reveals nothing more than a barcode on an expanse of white.

'There's enough,' Adam says. 'Wherever you want to go, there's enough.'

'But . . .'

Adam shrugs. 'What else am I going to spend it on?'

Heather replaces the voucher in the card, the card in the envelope.

'Seriously,' Adam says. 'Don't lose it.'

'Okay. I won't.' Heather leans into him. 'How long has Christmas got left?'

Adam checks his watch and sees that Christmas was yesterday by more than a minute. He replaces his arm around Heather's shoulders. 'Five more minutes,' he says.

'Happy Christmas, Adam.'

'Yeah. Happy Christmas.'

Chapter 42

They're struggling to get going. The Rude Mechanicals have had only a ten-day break, but in that time a whole new year has ticked over, and the fact has not escaped these men and women that it may be – will likely be – their last.

They are weighed down by apathy. As if the momentum they had found is now working against them. Adam is pensive, Erin distant, Raymond more taciturn than usual and Pat unusually quick-tempered. Vernon is back in the room but it's clear he is not back to himself; *he looks smaller*, Tom thinks, visibly diminished inside two jumpers and a jolly bobble hat. Even the creaking radiators seem reluctant to get back to work.

Laura and Tom have lost their momentum too, the awkwardness between them as palpable as the cold.

Three days after Christmas Laura and her parents visited relations in Scotland, only returning last night. She and Tom have messaged and they talked on the phone on New Year's Eve. But now, in the company of these lethargic Mechanicals, it is as if they have become strangers all over again.

By the time Tom arrived for rehearsal, the room was half full and the hug with which he greeted Laura was clumsy; the kiss indecisive, not sure whether it was supposed to land on cheek or mouth and ending up somewhere in-between. They laughed it off, neither quite sure where to look or what to say. It's Tom's fault of course; he is still carrying a lie of omission – 'Christmas was fine. My mother was fine' – and he won't relax until he lets it go.

They have run through a few scenes: Cleopatra and her attendants dying by asp, Adam stabbing Tom through a curtain, Vernon running (limping) onto his sword. Only Raymond smothering Pat had any feeling to it, but Pat – 'Commend me to my kind L— L— L— L— Jesus Christ! Commend me to my Lord' – stumbled over her lines and chastised herself like a naughty child.

Laura called a break and the collective relief was unanimous and absolute.

Raymond has taken a piece of cake backstage where he is currently – the sound of his hammer ringing through the hall – boarding up a broken window, but the rest of the Mechanicals have as much enthusiasm for cake as they appear to have for the rehearsal.

'First day back's always rough,' Adam says.

Pat shrugs.

'I wouldn't know,' says Erin.

'Bad for jumpers,' says Vernon.

Tom pulls at his sweater. 'Christmas jumpers?'

'Suicide jumpers. On the lines.'

Erin shakes her head. 'Poor souls.'

'Bloody inconsiderate,' Vernon says.

'They're obviously not . . . you know . . . right.'

'Well be *not right* in the privacy of your home, innit? Stick your head in the oven, not in front of my . . .'

. . . he registers the change in acoustics first, the quiet that comes when you have captured the undivided attention of a group. No talking, no movement, as if the room itself leans in. And then their expressions. Erin, Pat, Adam – they are appalled, not so much by the subject of his discourse as the manner in which it is told. With no regard, no . . . *what's the word?* . . . no compassion. He sees the way Laura watches him, and Tom and Raymond – their mouths tight at what he's about to say next. If Maggie was here, she'd jab her elbow into his ribs: *Vernon*, she'd say, stretching his name over the full length of its syllables, *that's people you're talking about. People with families.* And Vernon would accept the point; he'd back right off while the going was only moderately shoddy.

He meets Erin's eyes and smiles an apology, a retraction, an acknowledgement of his clumsy and crass insensitivity . . .

'You're right, Erin love. Of course you're right. Poor whatnots.'

Erin smiles and it seems to Vernon that her eyes say *thank you*.

He imagines Maggie at his side. Imagines her shaking her head – *Incorrigible, you are. Incorrigible* – but she's smiling too, because her corrective elbow is no longer needed. Not this time, at any rate.

'We should, maybe we should do O— O— Ophelia,' Pat says.

'From Hamlet?' Laura asks. 'Does she . . .?'

'S— suicide,' Pat says. 'More or less. She d— drowns.'

Laura furrows her brow. 'I don't . . . are you sure?'

'Off stage,' Pat says. 'Gertrude describes it to Laertes. It's b— b—' She closes her eyes, takes a slow breath. 'Beautiful. We could lay me – Ophelia – on the stage, flowers, a b— blue sheet for water.'

'I'll do Gertrude,' Erin says.

Pat says to Laura: 'What do you th— think?'

She doesn't have a chance to answer.

There is a shout of what might be pain, or possibly triumph from backstage. And then: 'Got ya, ye wee bugger!'

Tom raises an eyebrow. 'Do you reckon there's anything left to fix?'

Pat laughs. 'Can't be.'

'Only us,' says Vernon.

Raymond emerges from backstage, something held in his right hand. 'Hope nobody's squeamish.'

Tom's mouth falls open when he sees the thing in Raymond's hand. A part of him hopes that it's a prop, but the rest of him knows that it's not.

'Is that a mouse?'

'It was,' Raymond says, brandishing the trap and the back-broke mouse pinched under the sprung hammer. 'It's a dead mouse now.'

'A mouse trap?' Erin says. 'Did you . . .?'

'Half a dozen of 'em, baited with cake.'

He is beaming with uncommon pride, but his smile fades in the face of six blank expressions.

Erin turns away. 'You . . . killed it?'

'It's vermin.'

'It's a living *thing*.'

'How could you? Of all people – how could one of us?' Her eyes are brimming with angry tears. 'How could you end a life, Raymond?'

'I thought—'

'Get that thing away from me,' Erin says, her voice rising until it is high and shrill. 'Take that thing away!'

Raymond takes a step back, turns one way and the next as if he has suddenly lost his bearings in the wide-open space of the hall. 'I . . . I'm sorry,' he says quietly. 'I'll get . . . I'll take it . . .'

Raymond walks briskly to the back of the hall and pushes through the door leading out onto the street, there, presumably, to dispose of his kill. The group sit in silence for a moment, not knowing what to say or do next. Vernon struggles up from his chair. 'I'll go and see if he's . . .'

'He's fine,' Erin snaps. '*He's* just fine.'

Vernon puts a hand on her shoulder. 'He means well.'

Erin sniffs. '*Means*.'

'Right,' says Vernon. He nods at Tom and Adam. 'Why don't you two help me round up the rest of them traps.'

Chapter 43

The postcard – a montage of Greek ruins – is held together with Sellotape, having been torn into quarters approximately ten years previously.

The message on the back reads:

Dear Adam,
The Greek islands are beautiful, a bit too hot for your father, but it gives him an excuse to have a beer with his olives! Yesterday we saw some fab ruins (folk might say the same of us, 'a pair of old ruins', ha ha!). Today we're going to a local market – and your dad's already moaning. Only joking! Oh, and we signed up for a boat trip later in the week. They catch your fish and cook it right there and then.
Ya-sas! As they say. Love you, son – Mum and Dad x

By the time the postcard arrived in England, his parents were dead. The boat was called the *Lady of Athens*, and it was designed to carry eight. When it capsized, six miles out from the coast of Limnos, there were fifteen on board, not including the captain, who was later found to be intoxicated. Three people, excluding Adam's parents but including the drunken captain, survived.

The house is empty – Heather and Mabel are in Devon for the weekend – so Adam is at liberty to shout, scream or swear. But the anger, like his mother's handwriting, has long since faded.

It would have been his mother's idea. The holiday, the trip to the ruins, the local market, the fatal boat trip. It was always her idea – shouting for him and his father to put their coats on, get in the car, grab a brolly. Day trips into town, to the coast, to a funfair, whatever was happening or available. That's what made her Mum. And objecting – albeit half-heartedly – was what made Dad Dad. 'Your dad's already moaning' his mother had said in the postcard, and Adam doesn't doubt it, despite the 'ha ha!'. But Adam wishes – as he has wished ten thousand times before – that on this one occasion, his mother had said: *You know what Doug, you're right. Let's give the boat a miss.*

She led him to his death. No use pretending she didn't. But Adam knows, too, that his father's life was richer, happier and altogether more enjoyable for the hand of his mother tugging at his old man's sleeve.

They died too young, but they never saw death coming, and Adam clings to this. There was no slow decline, no pain or loss of dignity. No fear, excepting the brief intense minutes during which their boat tilted into the Aegean Sea. And they didn't live to see their only son die.

Adam holds the postcard to his lips, pressing them to the blue x at the bottom – the last kiss his mother gave him – and then he drops the postcard into a black bin liner.

He's already filled two bags, and will fill many more before the weekend is done.

The living room is piled with boxes, folders, battered and dusty bags, envelopes and photographs, souvenirs, papers, legal documents, ticket stubs and books.

This is the evidence of his life, of his time.

After Adam's parents died, he spent weeks clearing their house, from the contents of the garage to the food in the cupboards. Bagging up old bed linen and clothes, throwing out his mother's make-up, his father's electric razor. He kept wallets of photographs, their wedding album, a few ugly ornaments, and threw everything else out. It was a shitty job, devoid of nostalgia, uplifting reprieves, or happy discoveries. It was joyless, depressing and – bundling your mother's favourite dress into a bin liner – guilt-ridden.

And so, while Adam has the house to himself, he is doing the job he doesn't want to leave to Heather after he has gone. He was invited to join them – for Heather's sister's fiftieth birthday – but Adam declined. Heather's sister never did like him, and besides, this job needs doing – and if not now, then when?

There is an inclination towards brutality – throw everything – but some things he should (photographs) and must (legal documents) keep. And some things – the clothes on his back, his toothbrush, whatever book is splayed open on his bedside table – he will inevitably leave behind.

Included in this latter category is the collection of 'treasures' bestowed upon Adam by Mabel since his return from marital exile. These precious gifts include pages of drawings and scribbles, found petals and interesting stones. Craft projects brought home from school. Flowers made from lollipop sticks, abstract conglomerations of cardboard and glue, paper chains. And – his favourite – two tiny and surprisingly well-proportioned figures made from pipe cleaners and tinfoil: 'Me and you,' Mabel told him, laying the figures side by side on his pillow.

These things, he will keep for as long as he lives.

Treasure notwithstanding, he has made several trips up and down the stairs, crawled into the loft space and explored the garage's hidden depths. He feels – in this task of clearing out his life – cleansed. As if the weight of every bag filled is a weight lifted.

Among the items Adam doesn't want to keep but can't bear to throw is the bottle of thirty-year-old Scotch given to him as a leaving present by his colleagues. He was tempted – alone in the house – to drink it while he works. To get good and drunk and all that this entails – nostalgia, bluster, tears. But Adam never was a drinker, and now, more than ever, it is important he clings to the health he has.

Three weeks after Christmas, Adam has been accepted for the clinical trial. He has a bottle of pills in the kitchen; an engineered molecule designed to 'reprogramme' his immune system. To help his body distinguish, in the words of his clinician, 'between self and non-self'. Whatever's in the bottle, Adam's blood is pumping, his feet are healing and he hasn't vomited in weeks. 'Not a cure,' his clinician told him. 'Time. That's what we're aiming for here, Adam. Time.'

Throwing out clothes, ticket stubs and old phones is easy. Cathartic, even. But he struggles with the photographs. Old school friends and teachers whose names he can't recall. University friends, colleagues, and faces that hold no associations. He has not looked at these pictures for many years, but consigning them to the black bag feels like an insult. People who meant something at one time but no longer do.

Adam has a list – people to whom he wishes to say goodbye. The friends he would invite, say, to a fiftieth birthday party. Those who sent (or whose partners sent) Christmas cards. The people he would miss if it were them taking a bottle of time-buying tablets instead of Adam. They meet for lunches and breakfasts, and on occasion for drinks or supper. The breakfast dates are better, as his friends tend not to drink at these early rendezvous, or to drink less at any rate. And groups are preferable to one-on-ones where emotions are more liable to spin out of control. There's more laughter in groups.

Many of the names on this list are crossed off now, not merely though industry, but through an ongoing process of pruning. These mornings and afternoons with old acquaintances are mornings and afternoons Adam could spend with Heather, Mabel, or his new friends, The Rude Mechanicals. These are precious slices of time, and he has no issue being selfish with them. But still, there are a few names left, a few old friends with whom to share a coffee and an insincere promise to 'do this again'.

One of these, he supposes, will be Penny.

In this picture they are in a bar somewhere. A bar anywhere. They are suntanned and smiling, although Adam's eyes are a little unfocused. Arms around each other's shoulders, heads touching, Adam holds his fingers in a peace sign while Penny blows a kiss towards the camera. There are more pictures in the envelope. Adam shuffles them from front to back; beach scenes, bars, strangers, cocktails. Ibiza – and the last holiday they took together. In the pictures, they look like they are in love.

Close, he supposes, but close doesn't count; close is nowhere near where love is concerned. He knows this, because he knows now how the real thing feels. As opposed to its counterfeits – lust and recklessness.

When his parents died, Penny was there. They were just good friends then. Perhaps they had shared a drunken snog or two, but they weren't an item. They didn't sleep together until they went to Greece to collect his parents' bodies. And all these years later, he still feels the guilt – at allowing himself this moment of happiness, this excitement, while his parents lay in boxes just a few miles down the road – like bad food in the pit of his stomach.

There was no chance for them, really. Everything was tied to his parents' death and Adam resented Penny for that. He picked arguments, declared his love and then withdrew it, begged forgiveness and hurled blame. The relationship lasted from the March of his parents' death, when they had flown out as friends and returned as lovers, to the end of that summer, when they flew to Ibiza as a couple but came home sitting at opposite ends of the same plane. After a period of cooling off, they reverted to being friends, but they met less frequently and with less affection. But always on or around the anniversary of his parents' death. Sometimes they'd get drunk; once or twice they ended up in bed. After the first few years, the hook-ups became phone calls, and eventually these became messages or email, but Penny never forgot to contact him in the first week of March.

She did it ten months ago. An email asking after Adam and his family, and then the news, maybe not all that surprising, that Penny had separated from her husband of five years. 'Marriage is hard,' Adam told her in one of those emails, a conversation they continued over two bottles of wine almost twelve years to the day that his parents had died. They drank small bottles of vodka in Penny's hotel room, and continued their conversation in bed.

If he could change one thing about his past, it would be this infidelity. Not his parents' deaths, because without the chain of events that set in motion, Adam wouldn't have met Heather, and without Heather, there would be no Mabel. His parents, he knows, would understand.

They would understand, because they understood love.

He has worried about sudden death. It's rare – but it can happen to a cancer patient just as it can happen to anyone else. For the most part, cancer patients don't drop dead, they fade out. But that fading, that wearing thin and wearing out, it increases the chances of, say, a fatal stroke or embolism or whatever else might finish you off. He worries about this because he doesn't want Heather, and even less so Mabel, to return home one day and find him dead on the sofa, the toilet, the living-room rug surrounded by photographs of the ex-girlfriend with whom he trashed ten years of love, friendship and trust.

Adam places the photographs of him and Penny into the bin bag. Then he ties the bag off and carries it outside.

It's dark, but he has one more room to clear.

In one box, he has photographs that he thinks Mabel might one day enjoy. And maybe Heather, too. Pictures of Mummy and Daddy when they were happy. Pictures of Granny and Granddad on the day they were married. Pictures of Adam when he was a fat-legged boy with a mop of straw-blond hair.

In another box, the deeds to the house and details of Adam's bank accounts, pension funds and savings. Two years after his parents died, a Greek insurance company wrote Adam a cheque for €1.9 million – £360,000 per parent after tax and legal fees. A good chunk of that he squandered on drink, a car that he subsequently wrote off and temporary friends. He travelled, too, but this wasn't the cultural experience it might have been, rather a fog of small rooms, crowded bars, one-night stands and loneliness.

And then he met Heather. It was Heather who talked him into using what money he had left as a deposit on a house – this house. And tomorrow, Adam has an appointment with a solicitor who will advise him on the most efficient way to transfer the house to Heather and put a sum of money in trust for Mabel. He will sleep better when this is done.

With this thought in mind, Adam approaches the final room, hesitating on the threshold before entering. In what used to be 'their' bedroom, but where Heather now sleeps alone, he checks what used to be his bedside drawers, and is surprised to find Heather has not already emptied their contents into the bin. The two drawers contain a broken watch, receipts, pens, a pair of headphones. Cufflinks, instruction manuals, a walking map of the Cotswolds, earplugs, a train ticket, a tester bottle of aftershave. The cufflinks will go to Mabel. And perhaps when the weather changes, he will take a train for one last walk in the Cotswolds. Everything else, Adam drops into a bin liner.

He closes the drawers and walks around to the other side of the bed.

He sits on the bed for a moment, pretending that is all he is doing. He reaches out a hand to Heather's bedside drawer and – as if this has just occurred to him – pulls it open. He inspects it from where he sits – imagining this removed, casual perusal is less of an intrusion than if he were to root among the contents on his hands and knees.

Make-up, three hairbrushes, face cream. An inexplicable sock. A small box which once contained chocolate truffles but now holds seven of Mabel's baby teeth wrapped in tissue. He shakes these into his hand and lines them up across his palm. He feels they might mean something, but if the tiny white teeth know what this is they aren't telling.

In the next drawer is a torch, and this makes Adam's heart drop. As far as Adam knows, Heather never kept a torch in the bedroom while he slept beside her.

There are cards from Mabel. None from Adam. Tissues, hair slides, a lid without a jar.

And here, at the back, a pale grey ring box.

After this house and the written-off car, this is the most money

Adam has spent on a single item. Enough to put Mabel through university for a term or two. To buy her first car, or pay for a wedding. If it's still there.

It is. A single diamond set in a platinum band. Not thrown away or flushed down the toilet.

Adam puts the ring back in the drawer. And when he stands from the bed, he smooths out the tell-tale creases from the covers.

He wakes in a panic sometime before four. Pulls on his clothes, a coat and a pair of shoes. Outside, he unknots three bin bags before he finds the one containing the postcard from his mother. He folds it into his back pocket, reknots the bag, then goes back inside to make tea.

Chapter 44

Ideally Tom would be sitting beneath a tree, a book in his lap, spring in full and violent bloom. The campus lawns singing with new green; the blackthorn beneath which he sits exploding with blossoms. Students would be gathered in groups: this one tossing a frisbee, that couple necking, a huddle over there with a guitar.

But this is January in the north of England and a man could die of exposure out there. So instead, Tom is browsing the university gift shop. Any other shop like this, he'd have attracted the attention of the store detective by now, but Tom, in his second-hand coat and baggy jeans, fits right in here.

Tom thought they should practise on the train, but Laura – out of shyness, perhaps – was reluctant to engage.

Tell me, Ms Hargreaves, what made you choose the study of English literature?

I just love books, you know. Chick lit, erotica, stuff with vampires.

And what of the classics?

Fifty Shades, The Girl on the Train. *Classic.*

This place, these beautiful buildings, this opportunity, this life.

Just a joke.

'Aren't you nervous?'

'Faced worse.'

And you can't argue with that.

Tom had imagined buying a scarf from the gift shop, but they are £45. An umbrella with the university crest is £35; a replica of the redbrick library inside a snow globe is £45. A teddy bear £28; a fountain pen £105; a paperweight £12.50; a sodding key ring £11.

He handles the items, feeling their quality, the cold surfaces and surprising weight. But he's watching the families. The proud parents with nervous offspring. Laura's parents wanted to drive her here, but Laura was having none of it. Tom feels a little guilty about denying them this day, but they will have many chances over the years to visit their daughter wherever she goes.

Tom picks up a snow globe and imagines himself sitting inside the snow-struck library. His head dipped over a large and perhaps leather-bound book. Was this ever a possibility? It's easy to blame circumstance, the bad hand of parents, the rotten influences, the shit luck. But people with worse have done better, so who's really to blame?

If Tom filled his head with books instead of pumping his blood full of shit, maybe he could have done this. Maybe he wouldn't be dying of what is surely a self-inflicted malady. *It's as if*, Tom thinks, *he's lost two lives*.

And these kids, who don't know how lucky they are. Filling baskets with expensive souvenirs of a future they haven't yet lived.

Tom slips the snow globe into his pocket.

Professor Jencks leans forward. 'So, Laura, tell me about school?'

This wood-panelled room is exactly as Laura had imagined. Shelves of books, a grand view, even the cluttered desk and uncomfortable chairs. Even the professor – white-haired, bespectacled, a pointy white beard – *just* as she imagined.

It's as if it was meant to be.

She tells Professor Jencks about school.

Tom was nagging her on the train about not taking this seriously, but he dropped out of school at fifteen, so who's he to be lecturing her? Honestly, she almost wishes she'd brought her parents. But not really.

It's been like a date, taking the train up here on their own. There's a buffet car on board, so maybe they'll have a glass of wine on the trip home. Maybe see if she can wangle an invitation back to Tom's place. But she's not holding out too much hope. He's been different since the holidays. Since that *bitch* who calls herself his mother stood him up on Christmas Day. Tom and Laura are still close, they go for coffee, talk on the phone, they've even been to see a movie. But five minutes of kissing and Tom always breaks off, makes some glib comment, moves them on, says he has to go home. She's asked to see where he lives, but Tom makes excuses, says it's a mess, says it's an embarrassment, says, 'Some other time.'

'What other time?'

'Let's take it slow,' he says.

And Laura thinks, *Slow is a luxury we don't have*.

She says nothing but pulls a face. And Tom says it again: 'Let's just take it slow.'

Professor Jencks – a Dickensian name if ever there was one – makes a few notes in a hardback jotter. 'So, why English?'

'Well, you know I was sick?'

Jencks nods. 'Yes. Terrible, really terrible. And . . . how are you?'

Laura nods. Brave face. She tells him how she is, what she's been through, her hopes for a lasting response.

'In some ways, it's been a blessing.'

His reaction is as expected. 'How so?'

'I've met some amazing people,' Laura says.

And she tells him about The Rude Mechanicals. Jencks is very impressed by this.

' "Wise men ne'er sit and wail their loss but cheerily seek how to redress their harms." '

Laura smiles uncertainly as Jencks waits for a response.

'*Henry VI*,' he says.

Her hand goes to the seven-sided coin in her pocket. 'Shakespeare?'

He nods. *Yes, Shakespeare*. 'And this group, it inspired you to pursue a degree in English?'

Laura shakes her head. 'Originally – before I got sick – I was going to study medicine. But, well, something like this' – indicating herself – 'it makes you reassess your priorities.' She is *nailing* this. 'I realised I didn't want to spend my career working eighteen-hour days in a hospital. I mean . . . life's too short. You only live . . . you know, once.'

Jencks strokes his beard. 'You think English is an easy option?'

'I . . . what I meant . . . ha, I mean . . . no. Not at all.'

Jencks nods. 'It's a demanding degree. Do you think you have the stamina, the *drive* for that?'

She can feel herself blushing. 'Yes,' she tells him, sitting straighter. 'I'm studying for three A levels and running a theatre group. I've got the drive.' *I've got drive in spades, you stuffy old prig.*

'Good,' Jencks says. 'That's good.'

'Do you have the drive?' Laura says, in mock pomposity.

'He was just seeing how you stand up to pressure.'

Laura finishes her wine. She feels tipsy and is quite enjoying the sensation. She's never had alcohol on a train before.

'You've hardly touched yours.'

'You have it,' Tom says, sliding his glass across the table.

She wants this to be a shared experience and pushes the glass back to Tom. 'It's yours.' Maybe it will loosen him up a little. 'Anyway,' Laura says. 'Four more to go.'

'You might still get in to this one.'

'You already said that.'

'Sorry. What do you want me to say?'

'Don't be like that.'

Tom takes a sip of his wine and winces. 'I'm sure you blew his tweed socks off.'

'His socks were still on,' Laura says. 'I checked.'

It's warm on the train, but Tom, still in his coat, clutches his arms across his chest. The swallow tattooed on his left hand nested into his right armpit. On the table between them is a newspaper folded open at the 'quick' crossword, which – some English student – remains largely incomplete almost two hours into their return journey.

Laura picks up the biro, places her left hand flat on the table and begins to copy Tom's swallow tattoo onto her own pale skin.

Tom watches with a look of idle amusement. 'Suits you.'

'You think.'

'Sure, and you could get an anchor on the other hand.'

Laura checks her watch. 'Want to do something when we get back?'

'It's late,' he says.

'Not really.'

'Your parents'll be worrying about you.'

'I'm not ten. God, Tom.'

'I'm not saying that. I'm saying . . . they care about you, that's all. They give a shit.'

Tom turns to the window, stares at the passing shadows of nearby trees. It feels much later than it is.

Laura helps herself to a sip of his wine. 'Have you called her yet?' *His mother.*

Tom shakes his head.

'Are you going to?'

Tom laughs and turns to face Laura. 'Probably. I'm a sucker for punishment.'

'I'm glad. I mean, not about the punishment bit, but . . . I'm so mad at her.'

' "They fuck you up, your mum and dad." ' Then, affecting a foppish voice, 'Do you know who said that, Ms Hargreaves? Hmm?'

'Oh, was it Shakespeare?'

'Larkin,' Tom says. 'But close enough.'

He pulls the snow globe from his coat pocket and sets it on the table between them.

Laura rotates the globe through a full turn, as if looking for clues. 'What's this?'

Tom points to the library. 'That is where you are going to read Larkin, Shakespeare, Austen, Dickens, and some scary Russians. Look,' he says, beckoning Laura to come closer. She leans in. 'There you are, see. The beautiful one in the third-floor window.'

Laura leans over the table and kisses him.

'Here . . .' He places the globe in Laura's hands.

'You bought this for me?'

'Kind of.'

'Oh my God, Tom. Thank you.'

'But . . . do me a favour?'

Laura wrinkles her brow: *What?*

'Give it to your folks? When you get home, give it to your folks and tell them it's from you.'

The words inside Laura's head are: *I love you.*

She takes the globe and shakes up the snow. 'Absolutely,' she says. 'Absolutely.'

Chapter 45

She sleeps deep tonight.

A sleeping tablet pulling her down, beneath the pain that has been waking her with tears in her eyes for a week without relent. But she sleeps soundly tonight. Lying on her back, head sunk into the soft pillow, one arm across her chest, the other thrown back so that her forearm rests against her head in a pantomime attitude of exasperation. Although her smile contradicts this – peaceful, and gently animated as she dreams.

Watching the dream, rather than participating, she sees herself on an empty stage, standing before an anticipant crowd. Brian and Jenny are there, waiting for her to begin. She turns on the spot and sees the rest of the cast standing behind her; they smile and nod and Erin relaxes. She understands that she must speak Hamlet's lines.

In rehearsal, these lines are Adam's, but he has given them to her now, and this feels correct. Erin takes a step forward.

' "Thou know'st 'tis common; all that lives must die,
Passing through nature to eternity." '

Jenny smiles up at Erin, and Erin speaks the next lines directly to her daughter:

'So be bold,' she says. 'Take chances. And never fetch your own sherry.'

Brian blows a kiss to his wife.

In their bed, Erin's husband lies on his side, facing her, the fingers of his right hand resting gently on her belly. Her stomach tenses now as her heart rate spikes. Assailed by infection, medication and an asymptomatic accumulation of fluid, her heart struggles and falters and seizes. Her stomach is as rigid as a board, and her husband pulls his hand away and tucks it beneath his own chest.

In her dream the hall is empty, and when Erin looks behind her, she sees that she is alone on the stage. She turns back to the rows of empty chairs. No, not empty, a woman sits alone – her mother. Her mother waves, and nods. *It's okay. Erin, sweetheart, everything is okay.*

And now Erin is seated beside her mother, watching herself on stage. And whilst this is impossible, it is fine, because her mother is holding her hand and her mother's hand is warm.

In her bed, Erin's body spasms; her legs and arms contracting with all their feeble strength. Her hands clench, her smile tightens into a grimace of exertion. Outside the bedroom window it begins to rain, and Erin's sleeping brain imports the weather into the dream.

She and her mother are outside now, in the fields where Erin played as a child. Her mother opens an umbrella and they huddle beneath, its brightly coloured segments casting red and yellow shadows on Erin's bare knees. Her mother nods: *Go on . . .*

' "To die," ' Erin says, ' "to sleep;

To sleep: perchance to dream: ay, there's the rub;

For in that sleep of death what dreams may come." '

The landscape is deep in shadow and Erin shivers against the cold. Her mother wraps her arms around Erin and hugs her daughter to her bosom.

In her bed, Erin shudders, and then relaxes as the tension leaves her body.

Her heart stops fighting, beats once, twice, then falls still. Her blood flows for another set of seconds before settling into stillness within the quiet vessels of her body.

Erin slips from sleep into unconsciousness. The grimace on her lips relaxes back into a smile.

When her husband wakes in the morning, Erin will be gone. Still smiling and at peace.

Act IV

Chapter 46

Adam sits in a firm chair in his attic room, the afternoon sunlight bright through his closed eyelids. The voice on the meditation app tells Adam to focus on his breathing: 'If your mind wanders,' it says, a North American twang to the accent, 'simply let the thoughts go, and return to your breath.'

Easy for you to say, Adam thinks.

He thinks of Erin and feels his cheeks and lips and eyelids compress.

And who's next? Can you tell me that?

He attempts to let this thought go. But some thoughts are more stubborn than others.

'In, and out,' the voice says.

Because it's one of us.

'In . . .'

One of us is next.

'. . . and out.'

And it was all going so well.

The show is perhaps eight rehearsals away; they have a running order now, a beginning, a middle and an end. They are accumulating props and wardrobe – rubber snakes and wooden swords, cloaks and crowns. Raymond – chastened and contrite, but still with the group – has acquired half a dozen standing lamps and table lamps for what Laura called 'practical lighting'. Placed strategically around the stage, they will illuminate individual scenes, while the rest of the stage lies in shadow. The week before last they introduced the drowning of Ophelia as recounted by Gertrude, and Erin was . . .

Erin was . . .

'When a thought intrudes,' the voice says, 'simply acknowledge it, and then release it.'

I don't want to release it.

And then last week happened. They made small talk, growing restless and checking their watches without comment. Because Erin was never late. Even when she was sick, Erin was one of the first to arrive.

They waited fifteen minutes before Laura suggested they start without her.

'Probably stuck in traffic,' Vernon said.

And they all agreed this was almost certainly the case.

'Focus on the feeling of air entering though your nose,' says the voice. 'Feel it flow into your lungs.'

Your accent is really annoying, thinks Adam.

And he lets this go.

They phoned Erin after an hour, but the call went through to voicemail. Her cheery voice apologising for not being able to come to the phone.

'Maybe she's got an appointment,' Pat tried.

And they all agreed this was a possibility.

It wasn't until they were folding away the chairs at the end of the session that Raymond said what they were all thinking. That he hoped Erin was okay.

Her husband called Laura with the news later that evening. And Laura – a job no teenager should have to do – called everyone else.

He sits in his black suit that is too big for him now, baggy at the shoulders and cinched at the waist with his ever-constricting belt.

'Feel the air nourish your heart,' says the voice.

'Oh fuck off!' says Adam.

There is a knock on his bedroom door simultaneous with this outburst.

'Daddy?'

'Maybe?'

The door opens a crack, Mabel's face peering – hesitant, afraid – through the gap. Her chin dimples as she prepares to cry.

Adam goes to her, squats down on his stiff knees and puts his hands on her shoulders. 'I'm sorry, little one. I wasn't shouting at you, it was . . . I was talking to the lady on my phone.'

Mabel glances at Adam's phone, face up on the floor.

'Lady?'

'Feel your blood carrying your breath—'

Adam shuts off the phone. 'That lady.'

'Is she your friend?'

'She helps me meditate,' Adam says. 'Kind of.'

'Why did you shout at her?'

'Oh, I was . . . it was . . . I was being a bit grumpy.'

'Why?'

Because my friend died, and because before long I will die too.

'I'm just tired, little one.'

'Mummy thought you might have fallen asleep.'

Adam has a vision of Mabel pushing open the door some weeks or months from now and finding him cold in bed or slumped to the floor. He pulls her to him and kisses her hair. He will have to talk to Heather about this, about putting safeguards in place.

As he hugs Mabel, Adam feels something hard and angular pressing into his ribs.

'What's . . . what you got there, Mabes?'

She holds up a glass jam jar. It's filled with water and a fine layer of yellow silt that catches the light. Mabel shakes the jar, and the particles – gold glitter, he sees now – rise and swirl inside.

'I made it in ferrapy.'

Mabel attends weekly sessions with a school counsellor, working through any anxieties, talking about life, demystifying death. They play snakes and ladders and talk about life's ups and downs; they read stories in which little bunnies die; they draw pictures of angels. And, apparently, fill jam jars with glitter.

'What is it?'

'My jar of calm.'

She sits cross-legged on the floor and tugs Adam's hand for him to sit opposite her. Mabel gives the jar a good shake and sets it on the carpet between them.

'And what do we do now, Mabes?'

'We watch it.'

So Adam sits and watches the tiny specks of gold turn and tumble inside the jar, drifting and rising and slowly sinking to the bottom. Mabel still has hold of his hand, and he feels her thumb rub the skin below his knuckles.

He takes a breath and feels his shoulders relax, feels his mind soften.

They sit like this for many breaths, until Adam hears a car approach, slow and stop. The driver hits the horn once.

'I have to go now,' Adam says, working his way to his feet. His eyes are wet with tears, but his heart feels as though it has been unbound. As if some restrictive membrane has been pierced and cut away.

'Do you think we could do this again tomorrow?' he asks.

Mabel jumps up in a single movement. She turns on the spot, her skirt floating up around her knees. 'Of course,' she says. 'We can do it every day, Daddy.'

Chapter 47

'The hall feels bigger,' Vernon says.

There was a reception after the funeral, but after a single drink, The Rude Mechanicals left together. Leaving Erin's family and old friends to reminisce about times they were not a part of. No one said as much, but these six, with cancer hidden beneath their suits and smart clothes, can only have brought to mind less happy times. So they drank their drinks and made their excuses. It felt right that they should come here – it's rehearsal day, after all, and the hall is theirs.

Tom takes off the suit jacket and hangs it on the back of a chair. 'I'll get it cleaned,' he says to Raymond.

'It's yours,' Raymond says. 'I don't need two.'

The thick wool suit would have been too big for Tom even when he was healthy, and healthy was some time ago. But it's well cut and if he stands up straight it hangs well enough. A bit 80s maybe, but Tom was an 80s baby after all. 'You sure?'

'I'm sure.'

You'll likely need it again, Tom imagines him saying. And by the silence in the room, he's not the only one.

They have pulled seven chairs into a circle, but no one has taken a seat. Perhaps because when they do, there will be one seat still empty. So they stand, awkward, not knowing what to do next.

They all have mud on their shoes.

'I'll miss her,' Tom says. 'I already miss her.'

'She loved this group,' says Vernon.

Murmurs of agreement.

'She'd want us to . . . you know, carry on. Put on the best sh— sh—'

The hesitations have become longer and more frequent. Given time, Pat was always able to land on the word or a suitable substitute, but this is no longer the case.

'Show?' suggests Laura.

Pat points a finger at Laura: *Correct.* 'Put on the best show we can.'

'Agreed,' says Vernon. 'I mean, if it was me that . . .' he nods towards the ceiling, to the sky beyond. 'Well, I'd be bloody cheesed off if you didn't finish the job.'

'We'll need to . . . reorganise,' Laura says.

Adam has his arm around her shoulders. He squeezes her gently.

'Going to need another handmaid for Cleopatra,' Tom says. 'One of us.' Nodding at the other three men.

'Or roll b— both of them into one,' says Pat.

Laura removes her jacket. 'That could work.'

Other coats come off too, hung on chairs or over radiators.

'I don't have a script,' Laura says. 'But I think I know it. I mean' – she looks at the other five – 'if you think we should.'

'It's why we're here,' says Vernon.

Pat clears her throat. 'Do you think . . . would anyone m— mind if I said a p— p—'

'Prayer?'

Pat shoots her finger at Tom. 'Prayer.'

'So long as you're not trying to convert me.'

'Never. You're p— p— perfect. Perfect as you are.'

Tom nods: *This is true.*

They gather together in a circle. Pat takes a piece of paper from her pocket, unfolds it and begins to read:

'Our Father, force of nature or otherwise . . . who may or may not be in h— heaven.'

There are a few chuckles at this.

'Whatever is thy name. Give us this d— day . . .' Pat pauses and wipes a tear from the corner of her eye. 'And perhaps just a few more weeks b— besides.' She smiles and makes sweeping eye contact with each of the Mechanicals before continuing:

'And forgive us our bad acting. As we forgive those who acted bad against us. Lead us not into stage fright, and deliver us from corpsing. For this is our last act, and these are our glorious new friends. For ever and ever . . .'

They say the last amen together.

Vernon crosses himself, and finishes the action by blowing a kiss across the circle to Pat. 'Amazing.'

'It's nonsense.'

'It's amazing nonsense,' Tom insists.

Pat shakes her head. 'Right,' she says. 'Shall we . . . do some acting?'

Raymond clears his throat. He is the only one who has yet to remove his coat. 'I'm sorry,' he says. And he tilts his head towards the door. 'I have to go.'

'Now?'

'Yes. I . . . I'm leaving.'

Vernon takes a half-step towards Raymond. 'Leaving?' But they have all heard the finality in the old Scot's tone.

'I'm . . .' His face is a study of conflict and regret. 'You'll be better without me.'

Pat puts a hand on his elbow. 'Raymond. Whatever it is, we c— c—'

'No. I can't. I'm sorry.'

'But why?' Adam asks.

'It's not . . . for me. It's . . . it's just not for me. I'm sorry.'

'And what about us?' Vernon asks, his voice rising.

Raymond shakes his head. 'I'm sorry.'

And they watch him walk slowly to the door and leave.

'He'll come round,' Vernon says.

'I wouldn't bet on it,' says Tom.

Pat rubs Vernon's shoulder. 'We don't know what other people are going through.'

'Now what?' says Laura.

'We crack on,' says Tom.

'There's only five of us.'

'The show must go on,' says Adam. 'Right?'

And the other four nod in agreement. 'Right.'

'Just . . .' Tom holds up his index finger for emphasis. 'Just nobody else die, okay?'

And they all agree this is an excellent idea.

Chapter 48

Snow.

Ten days into February and the park is coated in thick pleats of glistening white powder. Tomorrow it will be sunny, the temperatures touching double digits, and this is no doubt the last time Adam will leave footprints in the snow. But rather than feeling melancholy or bitter about this, he is grateful and happy to have been given one more snowball fight, one more snowman.

He woke early from a fretful sleep, the light peeping through his curtains tinged an uncanny blue. They dressed and breakfasted quickly, made a thermos of hot chocolate and took the fattest carrot they could find from the fridge.

It's early, and the park is quiet, but soon it will be overrun and the snow will be carved up, revealing the threadbare green beneath. But just now, the cold air retains a touch of magic.

Sitting on a bench, he watches Heather and Mabel roll snow into a growing ball that will form their snowman's head. Adam's hands are numb with cold and his back aches from the effort of constructing Mr Flakey's base and torso. He is heavy with fatigue and his head feels like a rock – like a ball of snow – balanced on top of his neck.

There is no nausea, but food passes through him too quickly and he can feel the wood of this bench through his sit bones. Too soon to know if this is a side effect of his medication, or a symptom of advancing disease. It could be a cold, a virus, a succession of bad nights' sleep.

But his mind is clear, and this is an unexpected joy. To watch Heather and Mabel laugh and throw snowballs. Heather chasing

Mabel, arms outstretched like a monster. Mabel squeals in delight and the sound is crystalline.

Heather hefts the snowman's head onto his shoulders and twists it into place. She lifts Mabel up, so that she can add pebble eyes and a carrot nose. Her casual strength and energy. The stark and deepening contrast between what she has and what Adam has lost.

Heather points to a stand of trees in the distance, and while Mabel runs towards them, Heather joins Adam on the bench.

'What's Mabel up to?'

'Sent her to find arms. Can't have a snowman without arms. How you doing?'

'I was thinking.'

'About?'

'You two.'

They watch Mabel run into the trees.

'I think . . . it's probably not a good idea to send Mabel up . . . to my room in the mornings any more.'

'Why?'

'It's probably best,' Adam says.

'But you're . . . you're fine.'

'Now I am. But . . . '

'Okay.'

'I made my will,' Adam says. 'There's the house, then my sa—'

Heather puts a hand on his. 'Do I need to know?'

'No, I . . . I suppose not. It's all . . . there's a box in my room. All the papers.'

'Okay then.'

Mabel emerges from behind a snow-coated oak. She is dragging two very long branches.

'Except for inheritance tax.' Adam says.

'What?'

'It's a bastard. A real bastard.'

'Okay.'

'Unless . . .'

Heather turns to him. *What?*

'We should get married,' he says. 'I was thinking we should . . . get married?'

Mabel is still ten feet away, trailing parallel tracks in the snow where Mr Flakey's arms have dragged behind her. Young strength. Young ears.

'Who should get married?' she asks.

Heather stands and goes to Mabel. 'No one, baby. No one.'

Chapter 49

The park is quiet at this time of night, the sun a long time set, but it is aglow with reflected moonlight. Hitchens runs through the churned-up snow, woofing and barking at the moon and weaving in among the silent snowmen and snow-women. A community of frozen figures, stoic in the face of their limited time.

Hitchens bounds out of sight, and Pat stands still amid the snowfolk, feeling the cold silence on her skin.

She remembers making snow angels as a child, and as a teenager too. Pat looks around and sees not another living soul. She gets down on one knee and then the other, sits and eases herself onto her back, feels the wet kiss of melting snow on her neck.

'I know,' she says to an impassive snow-woman. 'I'll probably catch pneumonia.'

Pat fans her arms up and down at her sides, scissors her legs closed and open and closed again.

Getting up is more difficult, but she manages. Dusts herself down, shudders at the cold water running down her back.

And there it is: an angel in the snow. A perfect impression of Sister Patricia, her wings spread wide and white and beautiful.

Adam hears a dog barking and yipping at some far corner of the expansive park, but he sees no walker. Just a gathering of smiling snow figures. Some with scarves and hats. One or two with breasts. Mr Flakey appears happy among his own. Pebble smile still firmly in place. Simian arms descending at an angle all the way from his shoulders to the ground.

A silver thermos held in his gloved hands, Adam sits on the same bench he occupied earlier today. The park is eerie, but no less beautiful for it. He sets down the thermos, scoops up a handful of snow – no longer fluffy, but compacted, granular and sharp – and shapes it into a small ball.

Mabel is asleep in her bed; Heather soaking in the bath.

Adam tried to read a book in his room, but his mind was elsewhere. Out here, perhaps.

So one last walk in the snow, one last snowball.

Chapter 50

Tom reads in an attempt to fend off the mounting anxiety. Tries to lose himself in the dark poetry of *Richard III* as he waits for the doctor to call his name. But in thirty minutes of waiting, Tom has proceeded no further than page one.

'I have no delight to pass away the time,' says the deformed tyrant, and Tom thinks, *Yeah, man, I hear you.*

The hospital wrote to him after he missed his last appointment, urging Tom to rearrange at his earliest convenience. And when he didn't, they wrote again. Tom kept the letter but didn't respond. And then a buzzer and a voice on the intercom – a nurse come to visit him and, presumably, check that Tom wasn't decomposing into the carpet. Tom made tea; the nurse took blood, asked questions, then called the hospital and scheduled a scan and a follow-up appointment with Tom's oncologist. The scan was two days ago; the results will be in the doctor's office now.

'Thomas Johnson?'

Tom looks up to see his oncologist standing in the doorway of his office. Tom attempts to read the expression on his doctor's face, but has no more success here than he had with *Richard III.*

Tom closes the book.

'Take a seat, Tom.'

Where do you want me to take it, Doc? But Tom resists the quip.

'How have you been?'

'Okay, I'd say. All things, you know, considered.'

'The nurse said your pain levels have increased?'

'A bit.'

'A bit or a lot?'

'Yeah,' Tom says. 'The other one.'

'Have you been taking your painkillers?'

'I try to do without unless it gets *really* bad.'

'If your pain levels have increased, then . . .' That smile doctors do, with their lips curled inwards, the eyes telling a different story to the mouth. 'Then I'd say pain management should be our priority now.'

Now?

'The worse you let the pain get, the harder it is to get on top of it. I'm moving you onto a higher dose.'

'I'm not sure, what with me being . . . you know, *me*.'

'How long has it been since you took drugs recreationally?'

'Fourteen months, two weeks and three days. More or less.'

'Good.' The doctor types something on his computer while he talks. 'I'm going to give you a rolling seven-day prescription. Let's start there, yes?'

'You're the doctor.'

The doctor nods. *I am.* His hands go to a brown cardboard wallet on his desk. He looks up at Tom and does that smile. *They must teach it in medical school*, Tom thinks. 'So, let's talk about your scan.' He opens the folder.

'Can I . . .' Tom clears his throat. 'Do we have to? The scans, I mean. Do we . . . *need* to?'

'Well—'

'I mean, will it make any . . . difference?'

The doctor closes the cardboard folder.

'I'm in a play,' Tom says. 'Raising money for charity. A hospice, actually.'

'That's great. Anything I know?'

Tom holds up his copy of *Richard III*. 'Sort of a Shakespeare mash-up.'

'Sounds interesting.'

'It's in March,' Tom says. 'Pretty much four weeks from now.'

'Lovely.'

'Four weeks,' Tom says. 'You know what I'm saying?'

The doctor contemplates Tom for a moment before sitting back in his chair. 'Yes, Tom. I believe I do.' And he reaches again for his professional smile. 'And I . . . I'm sure you'll have a great night.'

Chapter 51

They have the hall to themselves.

'Is it too much?' Laura asks, the colour rising in her cheeks and neck. 'It's too much, isn't it?'

'It's amazing,' Tom says. 'It's perfect.'

The Ides of March are one day and one calendar month away, and the vicar was happy to give Laura use of the hall tonight. 'An extra rehearsal,' she told him. True neither exactly nor remotely, but anything that brings Tom and Laura closer can only benefit their performances as the star-crossed lovers. Besides, anything goes on Feb fourteen.

After last rehearsal she asked Tom if he fancied going out on Valentine's night. And she intoned the significant words with steep italics, to give Tom the impression she found the whole *Valentine's night* thing a bit naff. 'Otherwise I have to stay in with my folks. Sit between them while they watch *Harry and Sally* or whatever. So consider it a rescue mission,' she told him.

'Sure,' Tom said. 'I'll save you.'

'We'll do something low key.'

'It's my favourite key,' he told her.

Tom's bus passes the hall on the way into town, so it was a simple deception to get him to meet her here. He arrived twenty minutes ago. Laura has been here for almost two hours, making everything 'perfect'.

But despite Tom's polite reassurances that it's so, Laura is not convinced.

Their small folding table is set squarely in the centre of the room, although Laura now regrets not placing it closer to the stage. The drawn curtains would have helped create some sense of enclosure and intimacy. But here, they float, and their small voices echo. Whereas Prokofiev's *Romeo and Juliet* – frenetic, pompous, discordant – sounds incongruously large. Even at a low volume, the orchestral suite is too big for this hall. Too big for them. So much for 'low key'.

She feels silly, childish, exposed. But at least it's dark – the hall lit by a single standing lamp and one candle in the centre of the table.

Tom nods towards the lonely Bluetooth speaker sitting on a windowsill. 'Nice tunes.'

'Prokofiev.'

'Bless you.'

Laura smiles.

She chose *Romeo and Juliet* for obvious reasons, but can't bear to reveal the title of the piece to Tom precisely because it is so obvious. This whole thing had seemed like such a romantic idea when she first imagined it. But her imagination hadn't captured the revealing emptiness of the hall. The absence of other bodies feels like a spotlight and the lack of background chatter like scrutiny. As if every word and phrase she utters hangs above them where it can be weighed and replayed.

Tom takes a small slice of meatball. 'This is amazing.'

'My mum cooked it.'

The four words writ large in the air above their table.

'Well, my compliments to the chef.'

Laura had worried that in a restaurant, Tom would feel obliged to eat more than was comfortable, so she has prepared deliberately small portions to spare his throat. A three-prawn cocktail starter, miniature meatballs in spaghetti (the ping of the microwave ringing like a bell in the rafters of the church hall), a small chocolate mousse for desert. Child's portions, really, and this, too, adds to Laura's sense that this is more a game of 'let's pretend' than the romantic event she had envisioned.

Her parents were disappointingly supportive. Probably in response to Laura passing all her mock A-levels, and putting to bed any concerns that she has been focusing her attentions in the wrong direction. Whatever the reason, they offered no objections but only help. Her mother cooked the meatballs while her father pulled the folding table from the shed and cleaned it of cobwebs and deceased snails. And while Dad ironed a tablecloth, her mother did Laura's hair. A bit fancy, but it makes her look older and right now she is grateful for that.

'They want to meet you,' Laura says. Her tone adding: *How ridiculous they are! Right?*

Tom laughs awkwardly. 'They're coming to the show?'

'Plus every one of my aunts, uncles and grandparents. I mean, you'd think no one had ever stepped on stage before.'

'Well, you're their little girl.'

Laura blushes behind her make-up. 'Did you invite your mum?'

'Not yet.'

'But you spoke to her?'

'Yeah, couple of times.'

'And?'

'Early March,' he says. 'Unless she blows me out again.'

'She won't. She wouldn't.' But Laura's conviction is not reflected in Tom's eyes.

'We'll see. Anyway.' Tom raises his glass. 'Congratulations. Again.'

Laura tries not to look too pleased. 'They're only mocks. Still got to pass the real ones.'

'You will. You'll fly through them.'

And he's probably right. But it would appear cocky to say so. The exams don't worry her, they never have. She is more concerned about the impending tests and scans that will reveal whether her tumours have progressed or receded. Anything else is irrelevant. Almost anything else.

She sips her wine and watches Tom push a meatball around his plate. When her mother had suggested the dish, Laura's mind had flashed onto that scene from *Lady and the Tramp*. She imagined Tom and herself sucking on opposite ends of a spaghetti strand, their mouths drawn together until . . . they kiss. Not an easy scene to contrive when eating off separate plates, when using cutlery, when human.

'You don't have to eat it,' Laura says.

Tom cuts the meatball in half and then halves this again before taking a bite. He nods, smiles: *Delicious*.

'I'm sorry,' Laura says, 'I—'

'Hey.' Tom puts his knife and fork down. 'This is the nicest – *the* nicest thing *anyone* has ever done for me. Ever. So no more *sorry*, okay?'

'Okay.'

'And this really is delicious.' He picks up his fork and takes another bite of meatball.

Chapter 52

The last Valentine's card Adam is likely ever to receive is misspelled and clumsily made – *Happy Vanentines Day Daddy* – but it fills his heart in spite of, or perhaps *because of* the wonky letters and smears of glued-on glitter. He didn't expect a card from Heather, and is not idiot enough to think one from him might be appropriate. But he thought flowers might be acceptable. He handed them to her in a perfunctory manner after breakfast, declaring them to be from both him and Mabel. *Happy Valentine's Day*, he didn't say. 'Flowers,' he said. 'From us.'

Heather had kissed his cheek and left for work.

And now they're eating meatballs off their knees in front of the television. Adam and the mother of his child sitting side by side on Valentine's night and pretending that it's not. The TV isn't helping. Every channel a romantic comedy, a love story, a weepie. But it could be worse. The meatballs are good, Heather is relaxed, they have wine. Even the film is passable.

'How was work?' Adam asks.

'Usual. Teeth, bad breath, neck-ache.'

In a romantic movie, this would be where Adam flexes his fingers and says: *Neck-ache? Maybe I can help with that . . .*

'More wine?'

Heather lifts her glass. 'Sure.'

Adam needs to pee, but he's holding on. He's seen this movie before and pretty soon the couple will make love. It's awkward enough – sitting here, pretending this is any other February evening – without having to watch another couple make a meal out of each other. Without being reminded that the last woman Adam slept with was not the woman sitting beside him now.

231

So Adam is saving his lavatory visit for approximately one minute before the couple start undressing.

'How was rehearsal?' Heather asks.

'Usual,' he says. 'Snakes, poison, sword fights.'

Heather laughs, but whether at Adam's joke or the movie in progress is unclear. 'We have tickets now.'

'Yeah?'

'Are you . . . would you like . . . tickets?'

Heather turns to him. 'Of course!' She sounds mildly affronted. 'You must know that?'

Adam sips his wine.

'Adam?'

'I don't know,' he says. 'I . . . I wouldn't blame you if you didn't.'

She turns to the TV screen then back to Adam. 'Of course I'm coming.' She puts her hand on his wrist. 'Of course I am.'

On screen, the man gets down on one knee, produces a ring box from his coat pocket. And *fuck!* Adam had been so preoccupied with the impending sex scene that he had completely forgotten about the impending proposal scene. It's been less than a week since he suggested he and Heather marry to spite the taxman. And while her failure to answer doesn't constitute a romantic rebuff, as such, there is a lingering atmosphere of tension between them, roughly the size of a mature African elephant.

Adam clears his throat. Wonders why he felt it necessary to do so and then does so again.

'You okay?'

He nods. 'Did you think about . . . what I said?'

Heather doesn't answer.

'In the park,' Adam prompts.

'I just keep coming back to why you did it?'

'Why did I ask you to marry me? I thought I—'

'Not that. Last year. When you . . .'

'I d—'

'Don't say you don't know. And don't tell me' – marking the quote in the air – ' "We were in a bad place." '

232

'We weren't in a good place.'

'That happens, Adam. And you deal with it, or face it at least. You don't run to your ex-girlfriend.'

'I didn't run to her, and she's not my ex-girlfriend. Not really.'

'Just someone you used to fuck.'

'Heather.'

'What?'

Adam has asked himself why it happened a hundred times and more. Because he was bored, because there was bitterness and acrimony and an absence of passion at home. Because he was lonely, because he was weak. All true to a greater or lesser extent. But none of them adding up to a good reason.

He comes back, as he often does, to timing. It happened just days after the anniversary of his parents' death. His emotions were turbulent and raw, and Penny was anchored to that time. The memory of one thing evoking memories of the other – of grief and lust and guilt. And Adam comes back to this again. Was that a part of it, a part of the reason he cheated on Heather? Could it have happened with anyone else or at any other time? *It's almost plausible*, he thinks. And how very convenient to blame his infidelity on the death of his parents.

Adam shakes his head. 'It wasn't planned,' he says. 'We didn't . . . it just . . .'

Heather stands from the sofa. 'I'm going to bed.'

And on screen, the couple begin to undress.

Chapter 53

'Tell me something,' Laura says. 'Something you've never told anyone else.'

She is wearing a dress and heels. Slightly more make-up than usual; hair in a style he is yet to fathom – organised but only partially tamed. Mobilised, perhaps. The scar on her neck exposed, as are the hollows of her clavicles. Her pendant earrings catch and hold the flickering candlelight.

'You look stunning,' he says.

Laura colours, the red in her cheeks showing through her make-up. She almost looks away, but holds his eyes. 'I know. But that's not what I meant. Tell me something about yourself.'

Tom takes a spoonful of chocolate mousse. He smiles at Laura, acknowledging his transparent ploy to buy time. There's not much about Tom's life he hasn't told someone. Drug dealers, drug counsellors, doctors and fences and police. They've all heard some aspect of Tom's story.

Laura pours the last of the wine and leans back in her chair. *I can wait.*

Tom takes another spoonful of dessert.

His left hand goes to the tattoo on his right bicep. 'MUM' in some pseudo-gothic font – wide, and solid with blue ink. The heavy letters disguising the scar where, when Tom was twelve, she ground out a cigarette on his arm. He's never told anyone about that, but this isn't what Laura wants to hear.

The answer to her question, he supposes, should be embarrassing, clarifying or surprising. Certainly not horrifying.

Laura tilts her head, and again, her earrings reflect the light from their single candle. All this thought and effort on Tom's behalf. He smiles, because the answer to Laura's question – of course – is all around him.

'I've never been on a Valentine's date before tonight,' he says.

'Never?'

'Never had a Valentine's card. Never written one before tonight.'

He considers his virgin effort. The formal – 'Happy Valentine's Day' – in self-conscious opposition to the conventionally affectionate – 'Love Tom'. Measured against Laura's sincerity and candour – *I'm so happy we met. Laura x* – he is embarrassed by his reticence.

'I'm glad you were my first,' he says. 'Because I . . . I enjoy being with you. More than with anyone else I've ever known.'

Laura picks up her napkin and folds it into a neat triangle. 'Please don't bullshit me.'

'Never.'

'Because . . . I'm not even sure what this is. I mean, we're more than friends, right?'

He nods.

'So what are we, Tom?'

'We're . . .' He gestures across the table. 'We're us.'

'Crap answer.'

Tom laughs. 'It's complicated?'

'Thank you, Professor Obvious.'

Tom raises his hands. 'I don't know what to say.'

Laura unfolds her napkin, refolds it, puts it down. 'I know it's complicated. And I understand what we're dealing with. But there's nothing we can do about any of that. That's our lot, isn't it?'

'But you've got so—'

'Guess what, Tom,' and her voice rises just enough to make it clear that whatever comes next does not come lightly. 'I have cancer. And I'm sick of people telling me everything will be fine. Because they don't *know* that. And I'm sick of people telling me what's best for me. Like what *I* want doesn't count in any of this. Like what *I* want is silly or childish or unimportant.'

'I'm sorry.'

'You should be.' A pause. 'And . . .?'

'And . . . what do *you* want?'

'I want to be normal. I want you and me to forget about all the other stuff and just . . . be . . . normal.'

'Normal,' Tom says, as if trying the word on for size.

'It means being honest,' Laura says. 'I don't want a sympathy boyfriend. If you—'

'It's not sympathy.'

'I want a *real* boyfriend. I want *you* to be a real boyfriend.'

Tom inspects the backs of his hands, turns them over and pays similar scrutiny to his palms, as if assessing himself for authenticity. 'You deserve better.'

'Were you listening to a w—'

'But . . .' He holds Laura's eyes. 'But I won't tell if you won't.'

Laura smiles and feels herself blush to her collarbones, but it's good. It's perfect.

'So,' says Tom. 'Where were we?'

Laura picks up her wine. 'You were about to ask me to tell you something I've never told anyone before.'

Tom clinks his glass against hers. 'So tell me,' he says. 'Tell me something you've never told anyone else.'

Laura stands from the table, holds out her hand, gesturing for Tom to do the same. He takes her hand. Stands. Laura leads him to the steps at stage right, and from there she leads him through the wings and onto the stage itself.

The heavy curtains are drawn and the boards are deep in darkness. Tom understands this is not a time for glib asides, and so he remains silent as Laura leads him to the approximate centre of the stage and stops. She reaches for something, there is a click, and a single standing lamp casts a small circle of light. The lamp is covered with a pink silk scarf that colours the light.

The chaise longue is decked with cushions and draped with blankets.

'The thing I never told anyone,' Laura says, a hint of tremor in her voice, 'is I have a bucket list.'

She sits on the chaise, still holding Tom's hand, and he sits with her.

He kisses her gently.

'It's a very short list,' Laura says, and she returns Tom's kiss.

Chapter 54

Awkward by nature and given neither to idle chat nor deep discourse, Raymond was the quiet man of the group. His absence is a subtle thing. *But no less profound for it*, thinks Pat. The quiet ones bring balance, and she misses his steady presence today. At least his absence can be explained – if not understood. The same, however, cannot be said of Vernon.

Pat and Adam sit on the chaise. Ignorant of the gentle lovemaking that occurred on this seat two days ago, Pat is nevertheless aware of an increased intimacy between Tom and Laura. It's difficult to miss.

Laura leans against Tom as she holds her phone to her ear. She listens, shakes her head and hangs up. 'Still no answer.'

I'm sure he's fine is what Pat wants to say. But she isn't sure, and this thought is reflected in the faces of Adam, Tom and Laura. They can be no surer that Vernon is fine than they were sure Erin was fine just four weeks ago.

'Should I send another text?' Laura asks.

'I wouldn't,' Adam says. 'He'll . . . he'll reply when he can.'

Including today, they have three more rehearsals before curtain-up. Tickets have been sold and the proceeds promised. There are posters and flyers in coffee shops, bars and newsagents' windows. Raymond's lines have been reallocated, and all the parts are understudied. The honour of suffocating Pat now belongs to Vernon. But today, in Vernon's absence, Adam is the man with a pillow clutched in his hands.

He turns to Pat. 'One more time?'

Pat reclines on the chaise. ' "Will you come to b— bed, my lord?" '

' "Have you prayed tonight, Desdemon?" '

'I should think she prays every night,' says a hushed voice from the back of the hall. 'Her being a nun and whatnot. Sorry, I mean Sister, Sister.'

Vernon is standing at the back of the hall. Something like a large holdall on the floor beside his feet.

'You're okay!' Laura shouts. 'I called, but—'

Vernon holds a finger to his lips and nods at the item beside him. 'Sorry,' he says. 'Summink came up.'

He lifts the item by the handle, leaning away from its apparent weight for balance.

Adam goes to the edge of the stage and eases himself down. 'Is that . . .?'

Vernon nods.

Pat sees it now: not a holdall, but a child's car seat, a tiny pink-swaddled bundle inside.

'A baby?' says Laura.

'This,' says Vernon, 'is my very beautiful granddaughter. Decided to come early, din't ya?'

It's a struggle, but he manages to lift the baby seat onto the stage and the group gathers around.

Pat sits beside the sleeping baby, her legs dangling from the edge of the stage. In the reverential hush, she subconsciously matches the fast rhythm of the child's breathing. As if – *listen carefully* – her whispered breath tells an important secret. Vernon removes the baby's woollen hat, revealing a headful of soft blonde fuzz.

Pat touches her fingers to the girl's hair; a tear forms in the corner of her eye, swells and escapes. 'She's beautiful.'

Vernon nods: *I know*.

'She's perfect,' says Pat.

'When?' asks Tom.

Vernon checks his watch. ''Bout thirteen hours ago. Come straight from the hospital.'

Adam looks around. 'Just you?'

Vernon nods towards the door. 'Her mum's sleeping in the car.

How funny's that? Twenty-nine years ago, I drove her home from the same hospital, sleeping in the back. Now she's kippin' in the passenger seat. She had a long night. But it was worth it,' he says, touching a knuckle to the infant's cheek. 'Wasn't it, Veronica? Yes it was.'

'Veronica?' Laura says.

Vernon nods. 'Close enough, hey?'

The baby's hands are hidden inside knitted mittens, and Pat touches her finger to these. She looks at Vernon. 'Can I?'

Vernon nods, and Pat . . . so gently . . . slides one then the other mitten from Veronica's miniature hands. The child's eyes flutter open and then closed, as if indignant at this intrusion. The five friends laugh gently, and when baby Veronica flexes her delicate fingers – surely too small and too precise to be real – they laugh again. Her hands are thin and wrinkled, naked of the fat that will swell her fingers and dimple her knuckles. *The hands of an old lady*, Pat thinks. She touches her finger to Veronica's palm and the baby grips reflexively and with surprising strength. Her fingers are warm.

And Pat could sit like this forever.

But no sooner has she formed the thought than the baby relaxes her grip.

Vernon lifts his granddaughter from the car seat, one hand holding her tiny body, the other supporting her head. 'Doctor told me something in the hospital,' he says. 'She told me that babies born today – what with science and medicine and whatnot – they're more likely to live to a hundred than not. A *hundred*,' he says, bringing the child close to his face. 'The things you will see and do, little Veronica. *Yes*. The things you will see and do.'

He touches the tip of his nose to his granddaughter's, and the baby reaches her hands towards his face.

'Right,' says Vernon, turning to Laura. 'Want to hold her?'

'Oh, I . . . I don't re—'

'Just support her head.' Then, catching Pat's somewhat forlorn expression. 'You'll get your cuddle, Sister. But first things first; I need to show Adam here the proper way to smother a lady.' And with that, he goes to the steps leading onto the stage.

'You're not serious?' Pat says.

'Serious as cancer.'

'Vernon!'

'What?' he says, his face a parody of innocence. 'Anyway, Veronica's dad and my missus have gone to the supermarket. Champagne and whatnot. So reckon I'm good for at least fifteen minutes.'

Pat goes to the chaise and reclines. 'Do your worst, my lord.'

Vernon takes the pillow from Adam. 'I'll do my best, Sister. I'll do my best.'

Chapter 55

Sitting in his car across the road and a little way up the hill from the church hall, Raymond is relieved to see Vernon arrive for rehearsals. His old duelling partner is more than an hour late and the minutes — thoughts of Vernon's poor health over Christmas — have passed slowly for Raymond. He was moments away from crossing the road to find out if anyone had heard from the old bugger, but Vernon is here now and Raymond stays inside the car. He has a book and a thermos of tea — *like a cop on a stakeout*, he thinks, but the thought doesn't amuse him.

In the boot of the car Raymond has a toolbox, a sheet of MDF and a new tube of silicone. After the cast leave in an hour's time, Raymond will use the spare key to let himself in and then reseal the kitchen sink and see if he can do something about the gap under the front door which is letting out heat. If the vicar turns up, it won't look so unusual Raymond being there after a rehearsal.

All being well, he'll measure up the cracked windows, too. But he'll have to be a little more discreet about replacing them. If the vicar or his better half finds him fiddling with the kitchen sink they'll simply think him a daft old busybody, but if they catch him taking a chisel to the windows, they're liable to call the police.

Raymond watches the hall, imagining the five remaining actors rehearsing inside. Learning the lines that Raymond already knows.

Think on thy sins.

Inside the hall, these lines are directed at Desdemona, but in the car, there is only Raymond and he speaks the lines aloud and to himself.

As stakeouts go, this is an amateur affair. Any of the five might see him as they leave the hall. Perhaps they would ask Raymond

242

one more time to re-join their ranks. And would Raymond accept, or would he tell them why he cannot?

But thirty minutes later, the question proved itself redundant. He watched them leave, Vernon in his car and the others on foot. Laura and Tom were holding hands, and this, at least, made the old Scot smile. They walked straight past his car, but were too intent on each other to see him. Raymond watched until they disappeared from view, then he climbed out of his car and gathered his tools.

Chapter 56

The children sit on the floor, cross-legged and straight-backed. Effortless in their perfect posture. Adam on their teacher's chair at the front of the room, thirty small faces tilted upwards, waiting for wisdom or at the very least a funny story. Mabel front and centre, bouncing her knees in excitement.

'Hello,' he says. 'I'm Adam.'

Twenty-nine voices answer: 'Hello, Adam.'

Mabel giggles. 'Hello, Daddy.'

This is his first Parents' Day. The day when half a dozen mummies and daddies tell a class of fidgeting children why they have to leave the house in a bad mood at seven-thirty five mornings a week and occasional weekends. It must, Adam muses, be easier for the firemen, the dentists and the decorators of this world. *I save lives; I fix teeth; I paint walls.*

Adam was a management consultant. *I analyse my clients' business objectives, perform a market analysis and competitive audit. We crunch the numbers and sift the data.*

Not that Adam didn't enjoy his work. He found it both challenging and rewarding. But he has no funny stories, no heroic tales, and no idea how to make it sound interesting, or even comprehensible, to a group of six-year-olds with playtime on their minds.

If he were to tell them the story of his work life, it would go like this:

When I left university, I had a non-specific degree and no ambition beyond making money. One of my friends was applying for a job at The Mega Consulting Corporation, so I – lacking direction or a mind of my own – asked The Mega Consulting Corporation if they would give me a job too. They said yes. Me and all the other boys and girls at The Mega Consulting Corporation used to work very late, and then go to bars and drink too much wine and sometimes share each other's beds. And then my mummy and daddy died in a freak boat accident, so I stopped going to work but carried on going to bars for wine. Questioning everything, I decided I didn't like my job very much, so I told the boss I wouldn't go in any more. Instead, I went on lots of holidays to decide what else I might do. But I didn't do much thinking. Because I was too busy drinking wine, sniffing powder that made me feel funny, and sharing beds with people I didn't know very well. Then I met Mabel's mummy. And I fell in love with her, and she told me I should get a job or she wouldn't be my girlfriend any more. And you know the funny thing? I remembered that I actually liked working at The Mega Consulting Corporation. I was good at it, and it's nice to do something that you're good at. But, perhaps I worked a bit too hard because . . . well, what can I tell you, I'm a bit of an idiot.

He has rehearsed a version of this story. Lighter on the drinking and bed-hopping, but true to the central theme of 'find a job you like and you'll never work a day in your life'. But he has already sat through three variations (lawyer, brand manager, systems analyst) of this somewhat questionable (and progressively less convincing) riff, and as sincere as the advocates may have been, the children's faces remained blank and they certainly don't need to hear it again. So Adam takes the mental piece of paper on which his talk is written and runs it through his mental shredder.

'I'm not going to tell you about my job,' Adam tells the children. 'Because . . .' A deep breath. 'Well, I don't have one. Not any more.'

He looks over the heads of the children to the parents sitting on small wooden chairs at the back of the class. He smiles at Heather, and she returns this with a small twitch of the lips that may be nothing more than courtesy, or a suppressed cough. Sitting beside Heather, her friend Dianne sends him a wink of encouragement. And in the absence of anything else, this will have to do.

'I expect most of you know that I . . . I'm dying.'

He glances at Mrs Gibbons, just in time to see her wince. The other parents, too, are wearing the kinds of shocked expressions you would more normally see in response to a filthy joke at a christening.

Heather's head is dipped, her eyes aimed at her feet.

'Not right away,' Adam says, smiling. 'Not now. So nobody panic!'

The children laugh at this, and Adam is relieved to see Mabel is smiling along with her classmates.

'I have a sickness called cancer, you see. And it means that I will die a bit sooner than I'd planned.'

A young boy raises his hand. 'When did you plan to die?'

A murmur of laughter from the adults.

Adam pretends to think about this. 'Well, eighty-eight sounds like a nice big number, don't you think?'

A girl at the back raises her hand. 'My great-granddad is a hundred and two.'

'That's brilliant,' Adam says. 'Isn't that brilliant?'

Everyone agrees this is indeed brilliant.

'But here's the problem. Because I expected to live a long time – to eighty-eight, or even a hundred – I took what I had, my health, my family, my life, I suppose, I took all of those things for granted.'

Thirty confused faces.

'Taking something for granted is . . . it's when we have something good, and we forget to appreciate it. It's when we forget how lucky we are.'

The children fidget. One boy whispers to another who promptly laughs.

Heather meets his eyes. She might nod, she might smile, but any such gesture – if it exists at all – is a small one.

'Like our loved ones,' Adam says. 'Our mummies and daddies and friends – because they're always there for us, we sometimes forget to tell these people how special they are, how much we need and appreciate them. How much we love them.'

The children regard Adam with a mixture of defensiveness, incomprehension and mounting frustration. *This was meant to be fun.*

'Well I certainly did.'

He looks at Mabel, but his daughter is silent, thoughtful, her bottom lip held lightly between her teeth. Adam winks, and Mabel does her best – a lopsided wince – to respond in kind.

'I took what I had for granted. I forgot how lucky I was.'

He looks to the back of the room, and when Heather meets his eyes, she nods and she smiles and the message is unambiguous: *I understand.*

Dianne, too, catches his eye. She winks again, this time sending him a fleeting thumbs-up into the bargain.

'I forgot how lucky I was,' Adam says to the children. 'And now that my time . . .'

His voice has become unreliable, his eyes moist, a feeling of weight inside his mouth. And there is a real possibility he might cry in front of these children, ruining not just this Parents' Day, but possibly all Parents' Days to come. Children faking tummy ache, crying at the front door and begging their mummies and daddies: *Please don't make me go. That crying dying man frightened me!*

Adam focuses on Heather's face. Her cheeks are glossed with tears, but she forces a smile that says, *It's okay, Adam. I'm here, and it's okay.* Her smile tells Adam to continue.

'Now my time is . . . it's running out,' Adam says. 'And I realise that I should have been better to the people who are special to me. I should have been more patient, come home earlier from work, told more jokes, played more games and bought more flowers.' He looks directly at Heather. 'I should have said I love you more often than I did.'

A small voice: 'Why didn't you?'

Adam turns to the sincere little girl with her hand raised.

Because I was self-absorbed, impatient, unreliable and ungrateful. And because I always thought I could do better tomorrow.

'Because I was silly,' Adam says. 'I was incredibly silly.'

The child nods: *Right. Got you.*

Adam beckons to Mabel. 'Come here.' He says it quietly, because anything more might come with tears.

Mabel looks around to Mrs Gibbons for approval. Her teacher nods and Mabel goes to Adam. He grunts as he helps her up onto his thighs and feels the weight of her pressing into his bones. Her small body anchors him, both to his chair and this moment, and with his hands around his daughter's waist, Adam goes on:

'People say, some people say, you should live every day as if it's your last. And some people think that means you should do lots of crazy things, and have parties and dance and maybe eat too many sweets. Sounds fun, doesn't it?'

It sounds fun.

'But the next day,' Adam says, 'you have to do it again. And you might have sore feet from dancing, or tummy ache from all the sweets. Yes? Or a headache from too much wine if you're a mummy or a daddy.'

The children laugh.

'So I've been thinking about that. In fact, I think I'm a bit of an expert on it.'

'Because you're dying?'

Now Adam laughs. 'Yes. Because I'm dying.'

Someone at the back of the room sniffs, and when Adam follows the sound he sees Heather dabbing her eyes with her sleeve.

Adam kisses the top of Mabel's head. 'And here's what I think. I think you should live every day as if it might be your last with the people you love. Because one day . . . well, one day it will be.'

Heather wipes her eyes, but her smile seems true, rather than an act of will or gesture of solidarity. She puts the fingers of her left hand to her lips, as if loading them with a kiss, which she will now aim at Adam. But her hand doesn't move, and the kiss, if it was ever there, remains on her lips.

Adam looks at the fidgeting children and they regard him with muddled expressions that combine bafflement, unease and boredom. But mostly boredom.

Adam smiles at them, taking in their perfect skin and innocence. 'Thank you,' he says. 'Thank you very much for listening to
me.'

Soaking in the bath later, Adam is idly popping bubbles and thinking he should have stuck with the story about management consul-
tancy when Heather knocks on the door.

'Hello?'

Her head appears around the doorframe.

'You okay?'

Adam nods. 'You mean other than ruining Parents' Day?'

Heather says: 'I think you were very . . . brave.'

'I don't know.'

'It was important,' Heather says. 'It was . . .' She shrugs. 'It was
important.'

'I don't think they understood a word of it.'

'Mabel does. Or she will. I'll make sure of that.' She is still
standing in the doorway, the door only halfway open.

'We'll need a licence,' Heather says. 'If we're going to get
married.'

'Married?'

'You can get it fast-tracked. If you're . . . for special circumstances,' she says. 'A week. Ten days. So . . .'

Heather turns, goes to close the door. 'Anyway,' she says.
'Supper in ten if you want some.'

Heather closes the door and Adam sinks beneath the bubbles.

Chapter 57

Laura kisses his neck. She slides her hand from his chest to his belly, and Tom places his hand on top of hers, halting its descent. She wants to do it again, but Tom is exhausted and his flesh is weak.

They barely fit on his single bed, and if Tom were not so thin he doubts that they would. In a room above, someone shouts at some-otherone. A door slams.

'Sorry,' Tom says.

'Stop saying that,' she says. 'Just like a halls of residence, probably.'

Except you're unlikely to have some hairy howling bastard use the stairwell as a toilet. But from what Tom's heard of students, perhaps she's right.

Laura wriggles her hand free and slides it down between Tom's legs. His penis is flaccid and lifeless and this embarrasses him almost as much as his shoddy accommodation.

'Show me again,' he says.

'Again?'

'I want to see it,' Tom says. 'Indulge me.'

Laura rolls onto her side. 'Where is it?'

The floor is strewn with clothes: jeans, T-shirts, socks, underwear, two jumpers in a tangled embrace all of their own.

'There,' Tom says. 'Under your . . . pants.'

Laura stretches out an arm. 'Hold me,' she says, reaching back with her free hand. 'Don't let me fall into this abyss.'

Tom holds her hand, and Laura walks her fingers across the carpet until they arrive at the printed sheet of A4 paper.

Four black and white images arranged like some macabre Warhol. Each image a transverse section of Laura's brain, each dotted with three small white shapes. Numbers and letters printed in white on black: *Scan: 5634. Oblique. Pos: -14.3.* In the scans on the right side of the page, the white shapes are circled in yellow, and even at this reduced scale, it is clear that one of these malignant dots has been diminished in size and density compared to the corresponding image on the left-hand side of the page.

'Three point two millimetres,' Tom says. 'Amazing.'

'It's a start. Mum and Dad were carrying on like I'd been cured.'

You will be. 'Why didn't you say you were going?'

Laura shrugs. 'You know.'

And Tom supposes he does. He still hasn't told Laura about his own scan and he has yet to decide whether or not he will.

She takes the scan from him and places it on the bedroom floor. She kisses his neck, his shoulder, his chest.

'It's nearly seven,' Tom says.

'You should come.'

A pizza with Laura's parents to celebrate her scan results.

'No, this is their thing.'

'It's *my* thing, actually.'

'You know what I mean. I don't want to get in the way.' *What with me dying and whatnot.*

'Maybe I'll blow them out?' Laura says. 'Stay over?'

'Are you kidding?'

'No. Why?'

'Because . . . three point two millimetres, that's why.'

Laura pushes out her bottom lip. 'Killjoy. They'll think I've invented you.'

'They'll see me soon enough. Let's get the play done first.'

'You really should invite your mum.'

'One step at a time, hey.'

She slides her hand down Tom's side, and Tom suppresses a wince as her hand passes over the lump buried beneath his ribs.

'Nervous?' Laura asks.

Tom nods.

'I could come with you. If you like?'

Tom kisses her. 'Like I said; one step at a time.'

'Maybe *you're* inventing *her*.'

'If I was, I'd have invented her a little differently.'

A lot differently.

'But then you wouldn't be you,' Laura says.

'Which might not be a b—'

Laura puts a finger to his lips. 'And I love you,' she says. 'Exactly the way you are.'

Tom rests his head on Laura's chest. 'Remember when you asked me to tell you something I've never told anyone else?'

She strokes his thin hair.

'You're the best thing that ever happened to me,' Tom says. 'By a *long* way.'

Laura kisses him, whispers, 'I know,' and again, slides her hand down Tom's body, over his chest and hollow belly. And Tom is surprised to find his flesh is no longer weak, but strong, intent and very much alive.

Chapter 58

Pat has come to say goodbye. To her sleeping parents, lying close enough in their graves that it is easy to imagine they are holding hands beneath the layers of earth. For too long she has delayed this trip to the village where she grew up – the train ride is over three hours – but her days of procrastination, like all her days, are running thin. She is glad to be here now. It still feels like home.

And before the year is out, it will be home again. The arrangements have been made, and soon Pat will lie alongside her parents – within touching distance of her mother. This decision – beside which parent to spend eternity – was not an easy one. She loved them both equally and loves them still. She considered having her box placed between theirs, her mother to the left and on the other side the man she called Pops. But Pat doesn't want to come between these two who loved each other so much in life. In the end, she let practical considerations make the decision for her – it will require less, literal, upheaval, to place Pat beside her mother. And so that is where she will lie.

She reads the dates on their headstones, does the mathematics to which she already knows the answers: Eighty-six and eighty-eight. Good long lives both of them, her father dying just eight months after his 'Sunflower'. And both spared the sadness of seeing their daughter afflicted as she is.

Pat misses them, but she is not sad. Not for them.

'Good lives,' she says. And Hitchens, curled at her feet, grumps in agreement.

In three days, Pat will be a witness at Adam's wedding. Adam – lovely Adam – has been careful to point out that this is an arrangement rather than a romantic event, but Pat has detected a flicker of something in his eyes. *Happiness*, she thinks.

It's self-indulgent, Pat knows, but she feels sorry for herself. At a wedding many years ago, there was much hilarity when Sister Patricia caught the bride's bouquet. And although she hid it behind a pantomime of humour, it hurt and humiliated her, when she had to return the flowers so that the bride could throw them again. But no amount of bravado can soften the truth lodged in her heart, any more than it could diminish the tumour invading her brain. Pat wishes she had known love like her parents'. Wishes she had had someone to kiss her good night, to make her a cup of tea in the morning, and to call her Sunflower.

She stands, and Hitchens rises slowly to his paws. Pat steps onto the thin strip of grass between her parents' graves; she kisses the fingers of her right hand and lays them on her mother's headstone, then delivers a second kiss to her father.

'I'll see you soon,' she says.

Pat tugs on Hitchens's lead and they walk away between the quiet headstones for the long train ride home.

Chapter 59

Soon there will be a kiss. It was obvious, really, but somehow he had overlooked this key and excruciating detail. Until now.

The whole thing has taken just eight days to arrange. An irony when you consider that they have been together for ten years and close to seven of those engaged.

But eight days was enough. There was no dress to buy, no suit to hire. No bridesmaids to brief, beside Mabel. The witnesses – Pat and Dianne – were secured in the space of two emails. The venue – 'under the circumstances' – found a way to accommodate an additional fifteen-minute ceremony in their Tuesday morning itinerary. There are to be no speeches, and the prosaic vows have been lifted from a local government website. Heather's engagement ring will stand in as a wedding band. Eight days was more than enough.

And now they are here – Adam in his favourite jacket, Heather in a dress he has never seen before. Soon to kiss.

There has been neither hen do nor stag night. Last evening Adam went to bed early and read. He heard Heather turn in about an hour after that. This morning, they ate breakfast together as a family, fielding questions from Mabel:

Mabel: 'So you will be husbands and wifes now?'
Heather: 'Yes, Maybe.'
Mabel: 'Will there be cake?'
Adam: 'We can get cake.'
Mabel: 'Do you do dancing?'
Adam: 'Not today.'
Mabel: 'Will there be torn-up paper stuff?'
Adam: 'Paper?'
Mabel: 'For throwing.'

Heather: 'Confetti. No, sweetheart, no confetti.'

Mabel: 'Why not cafetti?'

Heather: 'We don't have any.'

Adam: 'They used to throw rice, in the *old days*.'

Mabel: 'Can we throw rice?'

Heather (a sigh): 'If you like, Maybe.'

Mabel: 'Yay!'

Mabel turns cartwheels now as the registrar invites Adam to read his vows.

'I do solemnly declare, that I know not of any lawful impediment why, I Adam Steven Campbell, may not be joined in matrimony to Heather Ellen Jenkins.'

The registrar turns to Heather, who gives her own declaration.

Pat brought flowers and Heather holds these loosely in two hands. Her nails have been painted a light blue. She went to the hairdresser this morning – 'it needs cutting anyway' – and she wears her hair down. And as Heather reads her plain legal declaration, Adam is reminded of everything he ever took for granted.

Feeling eyes on his neck, Adam turns and meets Dianne's gaze. She smiles without showing her teeth. Nods.

'Adam,' says the registrar.

Adam clears his throat. 'I call upon these persons, here present, to witness that I, Adam Steven Campbell, do take thee, Heather Ellen Jenkins, to be my lawful wedded wife.'

The government website stated that the bride and groom could then embellish these 'contracting words' with a promise. But any promise Adam might make, he broke a long time ago. And any vows going forward have a stark and looming expiry date. Besides, Heather would not thank him for trying to shoehorn sentiment into their wedding day.

Heather reads her own contracting words, her eyes straight ahead and unfocused.

Adam wants to tell Heather she is beautiful; feels the words – *You are beautiful* – form inside his mouth. But this is surely *verboten*.

The ceremony, such as it is, is almost complete. They have exchanged their dry vows in their sensible voices and nothing could be less romantic. But Pat is crying nevertheless.

'I'm sorry,' she whispers, and Mabel goes to Pat and holds her hand.

'I have rice,' Mabel says. 'You can share.'

Pat puts a hand to the little girl's face. 'Thank you,' she says. 'I'd love to share.' And Mabel dances excitedly on the spot.

The registrar smiles. 'Do you have a ring?'

Adam reaches into his jacket pocket and produces the engagement ring he first gave to Heather more than seven years previously. When everything about their lives was perfect. He slides it onto Heather's finger.

'I am happy to declare you husband and wife.'

And here it comes.

'Adam,' the registrar says, 'if you would like to kiss the bride, now might be a very good time.'

Adam, swamped with discordant emotions – sadness, regret, nostalgia and love, takes a half-step towards Heather. His eyes ask permission, and Heather, hesitating, gives a miniscule and cautious nod.

'You look beautiful,' Adam hears himself say.

Heather receives this with a tight smile.

He leans forward and kisses her, but Heather's lips do not respond. They merely receive the kiss as a courtesy.

'Thank you,' Adam says.

Heather nods. 'You're welcome.'

Mabel throws a handful of rice.

Chapter 60

His mother's hands shake as she tears open two packets of sugar to add to her coffee.

Nerves, he tells himself, but he knows this is not true. Tom has slept next to enough winos to know a bad case of the DTs when he sees it.

Her eyes are pinched and raw, her skin, even through a layer of make-up, mottled and traced with thread veins. Eighteen years older than Tom and closing in on her fiftieth birthday, his mother's excesses and disappointments are etched onto her face. If he didn't know better, Tom would put her age closer to Pat's or Vernon's. She bears only scant resemblance to the filtered images she posts on Facebook.

Tom arrived first, taking a table outside so he could see his mother approach. She was at the table, saying his name, before he recognised her. She is sober, though, and Tom imagines this required no small amount of willpower.

An act of maternal love.

They hugged and his mother kissed him on the lips. She held him at arm's length, inspecting him as if for damage. And then she hugged him again, this contact standing in for words while they each adjusted.

He brought flowers, and these sit on the table between them. Gerberas, the lady in the shop told him. His mother puts her hand to the paper wrapped around the bouquet.

'Nice,' she says. She lights a cigarette and takes a long, deep drag. Tom watches the coal glow orange then red. He wonders if she remembers putting a cigarette out on his arm because he dropped a glass. And if she does, can she smell his burnt skin every time she lights up? Maybe not, it was a long time ago.

'Smoke?' she says, offering the packet to Tom.

'Quit.'

'Right, course.'

'How have you been?'

His mother exhales smoke. 'Ups and downs, you know.'

Tom nods. He knows all about ups and downs. 'How's . . . Dave, was it?'

His mother waves her hand as if swatting a fly. '*Dave*,' she says, enunciating the name the way a cynic might mention *happiness*. She points her cigarette at Tom. 'How's the cancer?'

Tom nods. 'Not so bad.'

'What happened to your neck?'

'Surgery.'

His mother leans in to inspect the scars on Tom's throat. She puts two fingers to his neck and traces the line of the surgeon's incision from his ear to the collar of his shirt. 'Did they get it?'

'Yeah,' Tom says. 'They got it.'

His mother looks at her cigarette for a moment, then takes another long drag. 'Does it hurt?'

'I've got good painkillers.'

But Tom has yet to take one today. The pain is isolated in his throat for now, but he knows the pattern and in an hour or a few it will radiate to his jaw and teeth and the discs of his neck. The tablets will stop this, but they will dull his wits to approximately the same extent and so he is holding off for as long as he can.

His mother takes a sip of coffee. Her hands have steadied somewhat, but she still slops coffee onto the table when she puts her cup down. 'Fucking hands,' she says, mopping up the spillage with her sleeve.

Tom reaches across the table and soaks up what he can with a thin napkin.

His mother puts her lips to her fingers, and blows the kiss across the table to Tom. 'You're a good boy.'

'Debatable,' Tom says, and his mother coughs out a short dry laugh. 'I've been acting,' he tells her.

'On telly?'

He laughs. 'In a church hall.'

'You going to church now?'

'No. Just in an acting group. Shakespeare.'

'Lah-di-dah. Shakespeare, hey. Whatsit, "To be or not to be", right?'

'That's it. Here.' Tom passes two tickets across the table. 'You should come. Bring a friend, if you like.'

His mother looks at the tickets. 'Where's that?'

'Take you an hour on the train. Bit less.'

She puts the tickets down on the table, their corners sitting in a puddle of spilled coffee that wicks into the paper.

While his mother checks her watch, Tom steals a glance at his own and sees that it is not quite eleven-thirty.

'Maybe we should go to the pub,' she says. 'Introduce you.'

'Sure.'

His mother is already on her feet, lighting a fresh smoke. She grabs the flowers. 'Ready?'

'Ready.'

He picks up the damp tickets and holds them out to his mother. 'To be or not to be,' she says, shoving the tickets into her coat pocket. 'Chop-chop.'

Heather is dancing in front of the jukebox holding Mabel's hand and twirling her beneath one arm. Adam, Pat and Dianne sit at a nearby table, sipping their drinks and watching.

'So,' says Dianne, 'how are rehearsals going?'

'They're g— g— going,' Pat says.

'They're going well,' Adam adds.

'Are you c— coming?'

Dianne's eyes flick towards Adam. 'Haven't been invited.'

'Well let's r— r— rectify that, shall we? Dianne, would you like to come and see us m— m—murder Shakespeare?'

Dianne laughs. 'Well, when you put it like that.'

Pat reaches into her handbag and brings out a stack of tickets. 'Is there a M— Mr D— Dianne?'

'For his sins.'

'L— lovely.' Pat peels off two tickets. 'That'll be twenty quid.'

'You sure she's a nun?'

'She's a bloody good actress,' Adam says. 'So who knows?'

'Ha! I can hardly say my l— l— see what I m— m— hardly say tickets.' Pat's breathing becomes fast and shallow. 'Tickets t— tickets. Sh— sh— can't swim, Adam. Can't sw— s— s—'

Adam puts his hand to Pat's wrist. 'Pat, are you— slow down, Pat.'

'Adam,' Dianne says, 'what's going on?'

'Here.' Adam attempts to pass Pat's drink to her, but her hands are balled into fists. Her teeth are clenched, the tendons in her neck standing out like rope, spit and foam bubbling from the corner of her mouth.

Adam glances over his shoulder and sees that Mabel and Heather are oblivious to the unfolding scene.

Dianne gets to her feet. 'Adam! What's happening?'

'Call an ambulance, Dianne.'

'What's—'

'Do it now.'

Pat makes a hissing sound and collapses sideways, slipping from her chair and convulsing. Adam lurches forward, barely getting his hands beneath Pat's head before she crashes to the floor.

Mabel screams.

Chapter 62

Perhaps he'd imagined a scene like you get in those old black and white movies. A tearful farewell on the train platform. Tom leaning out of the window and waving as his mother trotted alongside, waving back and blowing one last kiss.

Never mind trotting, by the time Tom left the pub his mother couldn't stand without steadying herself against the bar. So Tom walked himself to the station, and waved at his own translucent reflection as the train pulled away from the platform.

His phone pings an incoming text from Laura:

How's it going? Hope having fun. Miss you x

The honest reply: *It went. Not really. Miss you too x*

But he doesn't want to get into it right now. He'll reply later when he's unravelled his thoughts. Right now the whole experience feels a little surreal. Troubling and disjointed.

Some drunks drink all day, and you'd barely guess. Others the drink hits them fast, taking them from zero to blotto in the time it takes them to empty a glass. As if all the accumulated booze simply needs reactivating. His mother falls – stumbles and staggers and falls – into the latter category of alcoholic.

By her second vodka tonic – and a big one at that – the flowers had been distributed among the regulars. His mother pushing gerberas behind red ears and into dry nests of over-dyed hair while she traded the sob story of her son for free drinks.

'Show 'em your neck, son.' Pulling his collar wide and parading him like a fairground freak.

'Say something in your voice, son. Say Shakespeare, so they can hear your voice.'

She wanted him to drink with her, but Tom knows a treacherous slope when he's standing over one. Besides, the pain in his throat was spreading, deepening, and he would need a heavy painkiller before much longer.

'Suit yourself,' she told him, when Tom declined yet another shot. 'You always did.'

'Painkillers,' he said, trying to salvage some credibility in his mother's eyes. But his mother simply rolled her eyes.

Tom suggested they go somewhere to eat, but his mother bought crisps.

After two hours she was flirting with a man called Dean who joined them at their table. Periodically Dean would whisper something into his mother's ear – his hand on her leg beneath the table – and his mother would respond in a drunken pantomime of scandal. Slapping his arm, recoiling in mock offence, but she never removed his hand from her thigh. Once, when Tom came back from the toilet, that hand was inside his mother's top.

Tom had a clean T-shirt and change of underwear in his bag, but it had become clear that he needn't have bothered.

Dean borrowed an ice-bucket from behind the bar, and marched around the pub encouraging the drinkers to drop a coin for Rachel's boy. No one refused. And when Dean brought three tequilas to the table, neither Dean nor Tom's mother noticed when Tom poured his into the carpet.

His mother was slurring her words and struggling to stand. Some of the other patrons were laughing at her. Tom offered to take her home in a taxi, but his mother refused. When Tom tried a second time, Dean gripped him by the shoulder and told him to leave her be. His grip was painful and his face threatening. 'She deserves to be happy,' Dean said, tightening his grip. 'After everything, yeah?'

'Yeah,' Tom said. 'Sure.'

He pulled on his coat and kissed his mother goodbye.

'Bye bye, Tommy,' his mother said, the words sliding over each other, her eyes unfocused.

'I'll see you at the play?' Tom said. But his mother only frowned.

'Don't forget your bag, *Tommy*,' Dean said, winking and waving sarcastically.

On the train, Tom takes a sip of water and his throat is painful from making himself heard in a noisy pub. His side hurts too – a dull throb as if he's been punched below the ribs – and taking anything more than a shallow breath is painful. If he takes a painkiller now it might just kick in before he arrives home.

Tom's fingers are trembling as he unzips the pocket on the side of his backpack.

Shit! He's so distracted by the creeping, gnawing pain that he's opened the wrong pocket, and his eyes are watering as he fumbles with the zip on the opposite side.

The box was new two days ago, containing exactly enough tablets to deliver Tom from agony twice a day for seven days. But as he pulls it from his bag, it's bashed and torn at one corner. As if his bag has been jumped on. Or the packet has been hastily removed and clumsily returned.

He opens the box and confirms what his heart knows; it's empty.

He remembers the glassy look in his mother's eyes. Remembers Dean sneering: 'Don't forget your bag, *Tommy*.'

He slams his fist on the table. 'Cunts!' and the word rips at his throat. 'Fucking fucking *cunts!*'

A middle-aged woman at the adjacent table flinches and looks at Tom as if he might do her harm. Tom looks away. He grabs his bag and stumbles up the swaying aisle towards the on-board bar. Because God knows, he needs something.

Chapter 63

Laura checks her phone, again. She can't sleep and the reasons are several.

Excitement, resentment, guilt, anxiety.

Excitement: a letter came from the university today, presenting Laura with an unconditional offer to study English Literature. She could set her exam papers on fire, collect a trio of Fs and they'd still take her. She should be happy. And her parents said as much. But this offer – no matter what it says in the letter – is not unconditional, is it? It's conditional on Laura having cancer and only a moderate chance of ever sitting her finals.

This offer has not been extended in recognition of her potential, but in acknowledgement of its lack. It's a sympathy vote. A little pat on the head for being almost dead. And that's your resentment, right there.

'We should celebrate,' her mother had said.

'What, being pitied?'

'I mean, this is what you want, isn't it, sweetheart?'

'Yeah, Mum, this is exactly what I want.'

'We could go for ice-cream.'

Laura sneered at the suggestion. In truth, she would have loved a scoop of salted caramel and another of pistachio. But pride wouldn't allow her this simple concession. Or maybe it was spite. Either way, she said no. And there's your great big scoop of guilt.

'Unconditional.'

She uses her index finger to trace the word along the inside of her forearm. Thirteen letters, and she wonders, is this too many for a tattoo? It's a big word in more ways than one. She imagines herself in some lecture hall, shirt rolled to her elbows, the tattoo visible as she scribbles notes into a lined notebook. Someone would ask what it means, and Laura could answer in any number of ways: it's about me, she could say; it's about life; it's about a boy I know. About a boy I knew.

University is still half a year away, but when Laura laid her head on Tom's chest, she didn't see six months in his stark ribs and sunken belly.

She checks her phone again, but he still hasn't replied. Maybe he's having too good a time. Maybe he's sick. Or maybe he regrets this whole business with Laura after all.

And there's your anxiety. So good luck getting any sleep.

Chapter 64

It's his wedding night, but Adam is in bed alone. Then again, what did he expect?

Nothing, he supposes. But he might have hoped.

By the time he got back from the hospital, it was past midnight and both Heather and Mabel were in bed. He found an envelope on the kitchen table, 'Mummy and Daddy' printed on the front. The envelope had been opened already, and Adam slid out the homemade card. *Happy wedding day mummy and daddy. I love you. Mabel.* This and a multitude of stars and love-hearts and crossed kisses.

Adam's wedding jacket lies crumpled on the floor, the lapel stained with Pat's blood. Despite his best efforts, Pat bit her tongue on the way to the floor. No stitches needed thankfully, but judging by the blood you'd have guessed otherwise.

A stroke, they told him. Minor, but a stroke nevertheless, and the right side of Pat's mouth is somewhat slack.

'I ruined your wedding,' she said.

And Adam told her, 'I ruined it long before today.'

They're keeping her in for tests, but whatever they find it won't be good.

Pat gave Adam her keys, and he stopped at her house on the way home to feed her dog. 'Everything's easy to find,' Pat had said, and this proved to be excruciatingly true. The cupboards and drawers were stuck with labels: *Glasses, Dishes, Dog food & dog treats, Knives, forks, spoons & so on.* He will go again tomorrow, feed and walk Hitchens and collect items from drawers labelled *Underwear, Pyjamas, Headscarves, Toiletries.*

Adam pushes a hand through his hair; it's thin now but he has lost no more since switching therapy. Maybe it's working, after all.

His fingers brush past something small and hard and Adam grasps it. A tiny grain of uncooked rice.

He climbs out of bed and fishes his wallet from his trouser pocket, then slides the grain of rice behind a credit card he no longer uses.

Standing in the centre of the room, Adam squats down and places a hand on the carpet, above the spot where he judges Heather to be sleeping.

'Good night,' he says quietly. 'Good night, wife.'

Chapter 65

Tom is drunk, but not drunk enough. Not drunk enough to sleep, and not drunk enough to blot out the swarming pain in his throat, tongue and teeth, in his skull, in his scalp, in his thousands of hollow follicles.

He has paracetamol, ibuprofen and other over-the-counter tablets, but – *call me a martyr, mother* – he has taken none of these. Perhaps he's afraid they won't touch the pain – because where would he be then? Where he would be then is well and truly fucked. So he sweats it out, he grits his teeth and punches his pillow. He howls out of the window, and somewhere in the building the werewolf howls back. This, at least, makes Tom laugh. But the laughter is painful, so Tom gives up on howling and makes do with sweating and punching and grinding and cursing the world beneath his breath.

They took every one of Tom's pills – *Every* fucking *one* – and his prescription doesn't renew for a further four days.

He could present himself to the pharmacist, wash his face and throw himself at the mercy of his GP, but Tom has a history of 'seeking', and they would ask questions. They would look at him with that expression they reserve for people like Tom. He could tell them he lost his tablets; that his bag was stolen, and they might even believe him. But more than likely they'll see a junkie trying it on. They might arrange an interview with addiction services. They might switch him to different pills. But these pills work. When he has them.

Tom already knows he will go without.

Call me a martyr, Mother, but I will go without the exact number of tablets you took from me. Even if it fucking kills me.

270

Chapter 66

Pat wakes from a deep narcotic slumber, and her first thought is that she is surrounded.

'Where?' she manages.

One of the men in blue pyjamas puts a hand to her brow. His touch is gentle but his skin rough. 'Hospital, darling. You're okay.'

When he takes his hand away, another man copies the gesture.

'Four,' Pat says.

'Four what, love?' two of the men say.

Pat's neck hurts when she turns her head. She is in a metal box, the four walls polished to a high shine. The sensation of movement.

'We're moving you,' the other two men say. 'Just in case.'

'I had a s— stroke,' she says, the fog beginning to clear.

'That's right, darling.'

Numbers on the wall. Arrows.

'A lift,' she says. 'We're in a lift.'

'Going down,' two of the men say, and Pat sees now that one is a reflection of the other. She herself is reflected in the wall. Stretched out on this hospital bed.

'Reflections,' she says.

The lift judders to a stop.

'Here we go, darling. Little bump.' And they wheel her into a quiet corridor.

'Where are we going?'

'Put you closer to the surgical ward,' the man with rough hands says.

'Surgical?'

'Just in case,' he says.
'In case?'
Her eyes begin to fall closed.
The man's voice fading. 'Just in case.'

Chapter 67

The performance is two weeks away. They have today's rehearsal and a full dress next week. Laura would rather they had two more weeks, or twenty, but right now she is more concerned with bodies than with time.

Pat is still in the hospital, and although she has assured Adam that she will be out in time for the dress rehearsal, there is no telling how coherent she will be. They have planned for this, of course, but they have no such contingency for Tom.

The rehearsal is fifteen minutes in when he finally appears.

'Afternoon,' he shouts from the back of the hall, and Laura can see immediately that something is off.

'Sorry I'm late,' he says. 'Late for my own funeral, hey?' And his laugh is hollow and forced.

Adam and Vernon are on stage as Tybalt and Mercutio, and Laura asks them to continue stabbing each other while she goes to greet Tom.

His clothes are a mess and he smells like he hasn't showered since she last saw him. Even so, she puts her arms around him, kisses him. But Tom is stiff and her kiss is not reciprocated.

'How was your mum?'

'Oh it was wonderful,' he says, clapping his hands together in an effete gesture. 'Peachy, perfect, just like in the movies.'

'Are you okay?'

Tom shrugs. 'Me? Why wouldn't I be *okay*? How could I possibly be anything other than *okay*?'

'You're acting strange.'

'Sorry, Laura. How d'you want me to act?'

She recoils, stung. 'Happy to see me, maybe?'

273

Tom forces a smile.

'Is it about Pat?' Laura asks.

Adam had emailed them all the day before, with news of Pat's stroke. There had been some back and forth, but Tom had remained conspicuously quiet.

'Is what about Pat? No. Nothing's about nothing.' His hands are shaking.

'You know she had a . . .'

'A stroke,' Tom says. 'Yes. I can read.'

'But you can't write a reply? Or pick up your phone?'

'Honestly, Laura, if I answered every message you sent me it'd be a full-time job.'

This is not Tom. Not the Tom Laura knows. So instead of indulging her urge to fire back, Laura bites her tongue and counts to five. 'I wanted to talk to you. Is that okay?'

Tom's eyes go to the floor, his jaw muscles hard and stark in his thin face. He stands that way for two or three breaths, as if pulled between belligerence and contrition and unsure which way to go.

Laura takes hold of his hand, waits until he meets her eyes. 'I had an offer.'

Tom processes this. 'Uni?'

Laura nods. 'Leeds. Unconditional.'

'What?'

'Unconditional. Doesn't matter if I pass or fail. I'm in!'

'Just like that, hey?'

'What do you mean?'

'Nothing. It just . . . it must be nice,' he says. 'Nice to be you.'

'Do you need to talk?'

Tom laughs. 'That might be the last fucking thing I need. No offence.'

'Have you been drinking?'

'*What?*'

'Drinking,' Laura repeats. 'Are you drunk?'

'I'm in pain, Laura. If you want to know. That's the thing with cancer. It fucking hurts.'

'Have you taken your tablets?'

'Oh, there's an idea. I completely forgot. But I'm a dropout, aren't I? Shit for brains. No one's going to give me an unconditional offer, are they?'

Adam calls from the back of the room. 'Everything okay?'

'Thanks, *Dad*. All good here.'

'Maybe you should go home,' Laura says. 'We can talk when you feel better.'

'Well don't hold your breath for that to happen. Hey, princess?'

'You know what?' Laura says. 'You're acting like a dick. Like a . . . a child.'

Tom barks a rude laugh. 'That's rich.'

'Fuck you, Tom.'

Tom steps back and bows deeply from the waist, as if receiving a shower of applause. 'Finally,' he says, 'you're beginning to sound like a grown-up.'

Chapter 68

They sit on a bench, looking across the beach towards the sea. Judith's eyes unfocused, as if she were staring all the way west to another continent. The sand is animated by a strong wind, shifting across itself in shallow hypnotic waves.

'Are you warm enough?' Raymond asks.

Judith doesn't answer. Raymond – memories of Desdemona – tugs her scarf a little more tightly around his wife's neck. He pats her fat hand and finds it warm. Her hands are always warm.

Raymond takes a chip from the cone and blows on it. 'Here,' he says, holding the chip to his wife's lips. Her mouth opens and the food vanishes.

The Mechanicals will have rehearsed today, and Raymond's sincere wish is that they didn't miss him. He dropped them in it when he left. But neither could he stay. And this is no one's fault but his own.

'I'm sorry we'll miss the show,' he says to Judith, and the wind moans her reply.

Raymond has told her about leaving the group. But not the reasons why.

'I'm ashamed,' he says, looking out to sea and avoiding his wife's vacant gaze.

Birds wheel in the air. They can smell the hot food, and Raymond throws a handful of chips in a long, high arc. The birds are on them before they hit the sand. And this man who is not given to displays of emotion has tears in his pale green eyes.

'But I need to tell someone,' he says. 'I need to tell you.'

Chapter 69

She grits her teeth against the pain, which is remarkable. The man had said it would hurt, but even so this has fairly taken her breath away.

'You okay, sweetheart?'

Laura tries not to look at the needle. 'Fine,' she says.

'Sure?'

She nods. 'Sure.'

But seriously, how do people manage this?

The tattooist tells her to relax, he wraps his gloved hand over her fist and shakes it gently. 'Relax,' he says, 'it will hurt less.' Her hand is clenched so tightly that she has to concentrate on opening her grip. 'There we go,' says the man. He clicks the trigger on the needle gun and applies it again to the inside of her forearm.

The word 'Unconditional' consists of thirteen letters, these stencilled along the inside of her left forearm in a modified Old English font. Mick, the tattooist, is still working on the first heavy letter; inking over it in slow strokes, adorning the verticals with painful serifs and brutal curlicues. She regrets not choosing a simpler letter set.

How to describe this pain? Hot, deep, alive. Mick said it would settle down, but it feels to Laura as if it's growing in intensity.

'Relax,' the man says, again shaking her clenched fist.

He dabs at her forearm with a piece of tissue, which comes away blotted with ink and blood.

'Do you have any water?' Laura asks.

The man doesn't tut, but she senses his frustration all the same.

'You're beginning to sound like a grown-up,' Tom had said. Which may or may not be true, but she still had to bring ID to this place. She had planned to bring Tom with her, and she imagines this would be a whole lot easier if he were beside her to hold her free hand and distract her with kind words or silly jokes.

After they fought, Laura contemplated not coming here. But then she reminded herself; she is doing this for her, not for Tom. She's a woman now, and she needs no one's help and no one's permission. Isn't that the whole point of the word, after all? *Unconditional*. All thirteen letters of it.

She's done her research, and nowhere does it say having a tattoo might compromise her therapy. Even so, her arm hurts so much it feels like damage. She imagines the ink infiltrating her delicate cells, spreading through her skin like black poison. She feels nauseous.

Mick returns with a plastic cup of water.

Laura thanks him and takes a sip.

'Okay?'

What else Laura found online was an article: *Tattoos and Don'ts – 7 things to consider before getting ink*. Items like: check the spelling, think about positioning, choose a reputable tattoo artist. And number 7, the old classic: *How will you feel about your tattoo in 10, 20, 30 years time?* Well that kind of presupposes you have another 10, 20, 30 years time, doesn't it? Laura had closed the article and immediately booked an appointment with Mick Ink.

'I . . .' Laura's lip trembles.

'Hey,' the man says, 'hey, it's okay.'

Laura tries not to cry, but the tears insist. As if her body can only take so much and hold so much. As if the day, the year, the ink in her skin have filled up every space inside her and are now forcing these childish tears from her eyes. From behind the mask of tough indifference she has worn for such a very long time.

'I have cancer,' Laura says, and Mick flinches. He sits back as if he thinks this might be contagious. 'I have cancer,' she says again, weeping freely now and not caring who sees or hears. 'And it's not okay.' Laura says. 'It's not okay.'

Chapter 70

Hitchens bounds towards them, tennis ball clamped between his teeth.

Take it, take it.

Mabel hesitates, extending her hand towards the ball then pulling it back when the dog huffs out a short excited note.

'Go on,' Adam says, 'it's fine.'

Heather, her arm looped through Adam's, whispers in his ear. 'You sure it's safe?'

'They love kids,' Adam says. 'But they c—'

'Don't tell me they can't eat a whole one, Adam. Because that thing looks like it could eat Mabel twice over.'

'Here . . .' Adam pulls the ball from the dog's teeth. It's not easy. 'He's a big softie. Aren't you, Hitch?'

Hitchens grumps and woofs. *Yeah, big softie.*

'Can I ride him?' asks Mabel.

'No,' Heather and Adam say in perfect unison.

Adam fits the ball into the launcher and throws it across the open field. Hitchens tears after the ball, and Mabel runs after Hitchens.

'How's Pat?' Heather asks.

'She *said* she was okay. But . . . it's not good, is it?'

Heather tightens her arm around Adam's. She is still wearing her engagement ring, but Adam is hesitant to attach any significance to this.

'What you're doing for her,' Heather says. 'It's very kind.'

'She's a friend,' Adam says. 'A good friend.'

'When does she get out?'

'Tomorrow.'

'You going?'

Adam shakes his head. 'Says a friend's picking her up. I've got a lunch.'

'Anyone I know?'

'Old friend,' Adam says.

And though this is true technically, it's an evasion nevertheless, and Adam wishes it weren't necessary. But it is, no matter how uncomfortable it makes him feel.

Hitchens returns at a gentle lope, his pace – deliberately, perhaps – slow enough that Mabel can run alongside. 'He's so *bouncy!*'

Hitchens lifts his paws onto the little girl's shoulders. His face is level with Mabel's and she can barely contain her joy at this.

'You're right,' Adam says from the corner of his mouth. 'He could easily eat a whole one.'

'I wish we had a doggy,' Mabel says, attempting to wrestle the ball from the dog's lethal teeth.

Adam looks at Heather, a question in his eyes. *Well?*

Pat understands that she can no longer look after this large energetic hound. She lacks the strength to walk him, and doubts her ability to feed him the right food at the right time. Yesterday, she told Adam she was ready to have Hitchens taken into kennels. And Adam told her there might be another option.

A dog like Hitchens, he thought, would keep his wife and his child safe after he's gone. And a dog like Hitchens would be a ton of fun besides. But the final call is Heather's. This walk a part of the decision-making process. They can either take the dog back to Pat's house. Or bring him home to their own.

'We'll have to walk him every day,' Heather says to Mabel.

'Walk who?'

'Hitchens,' says Heather. And Hitchens, as if suddenly grasping the situation, weaves between Heather's legs and rolls on the ground at her feet.

'Are we keeping him?' Mabel asks. 'Really? Hitchens? Are we, Mummy? Are we keeping him?'

'Yes,' says Heather. 'We're keeping him.' And Hitchens grumps and woofs and wags his tail like he's just remembered how.

Chapter 71

She picks up her phone and immediately puts it down.

She is not going to call Tom.

She is not going to message him. Her arm throbs from Mick Ink's needle, but his work is hidden under the sleeve of her shirt. She can't bear to look at it right now. And she sure as hell doesn't want to talk to her parents about it. *What have you done, Laura! How could you?*

The only person she wants to talk to is Tom. But she is *not* calling him. It's on him now. And how dare he talk to her like that?

Perhaps something bad happened with his mother. Or – and this, of the many things crowding her mind, is the one that worries her most – with his cancer. Something is wrong, that much is clear. She wants to tell Tom she is there for him. And she wants him to be there for her. And not just her – she wants him to be there for the whole group.

Pat is going home tomorrow and she will be at the dress rehearsal next week. 'Even if you have to p— prop me up, I'll b— be there.'

She sounded tired on the phone, and in addition to her stammer she has acquired something of a lisp. But she said she would be there and Laura believes her.

Tom, though, who knows if he's in or out? And even if he's in, how much use he'll be. He's no Romeo right now, and that's for certain.

Laura reaches for her phone. Turns it off, puts it in a drawer.

Her history homework book is open on the desk – *Discuss the changing role and status of women in the United Kingdom between 1918 and 1945.* So far her answer consists of a single word: *Women.*

And really, what's the point?

She unbuttons the cuff of her shirt and rolls the sleeve up to her elbow, revealing the small transparent dressing over her aborted tattoo.

A single, Old English letter **u**. But without the context of a dozen other letters it looks more like a pair of double-headed arrows. Representing what? Confusion, indecision, inertia.

Talk about embarrassing. She had cried so much, Mick couldn't get near her with the tattoo gun even if he'd wanted to. And it was pretty obvious all he wanted was to get this hysterical girl out of his establishment ASAP. Not great for business, after all. 'Come back when you've got your act together,' he told her, although not unkindly. He gave her a lollipop from a jar at reception. Probably intended to be ironic, which – all things considered – she supposes it was. Her tattoo being conditional after all; conditional on her not crying and bleating and losing her nerve like a silly schoolgirl. Stupid.

She says the word out loud: 'Stupid,' and she presses her thumb against the single letter in the crook of her elbow.

She accused Tom of being childish and he fired back that she was being a hypocrite: *'That's rich.'* A look of pure disdain on his face.

'Stupid,' she says again, louder this time, twisting her thumb hard against the fresh ink. Pain shoots up and down her arm like electricity. *'Fuck.* Fucking *hell.'*

Someone knocks on her bedroom door.

Laura rolls down her sleeve and wipes her eyes with the heels of her hands.

'Laura?' Her father knocks again.

He opens the door, peering around the frame cautiously before edging into the room. 'Everything okay, poppet?'

Laura nods.

He glances at the spread papers on her desk. 'Working hard?'

'Yep.'

'Need anything?'

'No.'

'Tea? Camomile?'

'I'm fine.'

'Sandwich?'

'Not hungry.'

'Hot chocolate? We've got marsh—'

'I said I'm fine! Will you stop treating me like a child! I'm fine . . .' And ever since she started crying in the tattoo parlour, it's like the tears are on permanent standby and in abundant supply. Laura shakes her head, sniffs back the tears and starts shuffling papers on her desk. 'I'm fine.'

Her father walks into the room and sits on Laura's bed. 'How's Tom?'

Laura fidgets with her shirt, attempting to re-button the cuff, but her fingers are trembling and the task is beyond her.

'It must be hard for him,' her father says.

'What?'

'Tom. He doesn't have . . . everything you have, poppet.'

She hates it when he calls her that. But . . . but the word, the name, it soothes her.

She turns to face her father. He pats the bed. And when Laura makes no move, he pats it again. Laura pulls the required face, then goes to sit beside him.

'You're a special girl,' he says. 'A special person.'

Laura rolls her eyes.

'You are. You're a fighter.'

'You used to tell me to toughen up.'

Her father's head drops, he makes a low noise at the back of his throat. 'I suppose I did.'

'Except . . . I don't feel very tough.'

He puts his arm around her shoulders; he places a kiss on her temple. 'You're tougher than anyone I know, poppet.'

Laura makes no derisive sound at this. She doesn't tut or shrug.

'And you owe it to *yourself* – nobody else – to yourself. To be the best, well, the best poppet you can be.'

'What if my best isn't good enough?'

'What are we talking about here? Exams, the play, something else?'

'All of it.'

'That's a lot,' her father says, reaching for her hand.

'I don't know if Tom's going to be in the play.'

'That bad?'

She nods. *That bad.*

He rubs the back of her hand. 'I'm sorry to hear that.'

'Yup. It sucks.'

'As Shakespeare once said.'

Laura laughs.

'You know, with everything you've been through . . .' There is a moment when it looks as though her father might cry, but – closed eyes, a deep breath – the moment passes. 'Most people would have just curled up into a ball. Not you, though. You changed course, studied, applied to university. Wrote a play.'

'Cobbled together, rather than wrote.'

'That all took courage, poppet. And those people, Adam and Pat and Vernon *and* Tom. They need you. They need you to be the brave one, see?'

Laura squeezes her father's hand in answer.

'Your best is good enough,' he tells her. 'Your best is amazing. Okay, poppet?'

'Okay, Dad.' She raises her hand to her eyes and her cheeks are sticky with dried tears.

'Laura.' Her father's voice is taut, urgent.

'What?'

He takes hold of her left wrist, carefully turning her hand palm up. 'What's . . . are you bleeding? It looks like you're bleeding.'

A spot of blood has seeped into the fabric of her shirt, flowering there like another spot of blood flowered almost two years ago. That one on her shoulder telling of the melanoma that was spreading through her body.

Her father goes to push her sleeve up, but Laura pulls her arm away from him.

'It's nothing.'

'Laura. It doesn't look like nothing.'

'Ink,' she says. 'It's just ink.'

'Poppet.' He's using his parent voice now. 'Show me.'

Laura begins rolling her sleeve back, pauses with the cuff half-way up her arm. 'Promise not to freak.'

'Laura, I—'

'It's nothing bad. Nothing *bad* bad.'

He takes her hand and pushes the sleeve all the way to her elbow.

She watches his expression as he frowns at the clear plaster dotted with blood and ink, the letter u still clearly visible beneath. He looks at her, confused.

'It's a tattoo.'

'A what? A tattoo?'

'Sorry.'

'A *tattoo*.'

The word sounds weird now, and Laura laughs.

Her father stares at the single letter as if waiting for it to do something or reveal its meaning. 'What is it?'

So she tells him. About the thirteen-letter word, Tom, the tears, the lollipop. About the absolute mortifying embarrassment of it all.

'Unconditional,' he says, under his breath.

'That was the plan.'

He lands another kiss on her temple. 'Well you can't leave it like that, can you, poppet?'

'I can't go back.' Blushing at the mere thought of it.

'I'll go with you.'

Her instinct is to refuse this offer, to say something smart or dismissive. But that's the mask she's been wearing and it's grown uncomfortable. Even so, the idea of walking into Mick Ink's with her *father*. She shakes her head but it's a gesture of resignation rather than refusal.

'I'll take that as a yes.'

'It's a yes. Thank you.'

'Maybe I'll get some *ink* of my own?'

Laura shakes her head. 'And that would be a no.'

'Right,' he says, standing, 'I expect you've got a lot to get on with.'

When he gets to the doorway, Laura says, 'Maybe I'll have that hot chocolate. If it's okay?'

'Marshmallows?'

'Always.'

Her father goes to leave.

'Dad?'

'Poppet?'

'Love you.'

Her father closes his eyes and takes a deep breath. 'I know, poppet. And I love you too.'

He closes the door, and Laura goes back to her desk and closes the textbook.

History can wait for one more day.

She opens her desk drawer, and removes the manuscript for *Shakespeare in Therapy*. She picks up a highlighter and begins marking all of Tom's lines: Romeo, Antigonus, Clarence, Polonius. The parts, if necessary, can all be reassigned. Laura will have to play the King in *Hamlet*, but if that's what it takes, that's what she'll do. She hopes it won't be necessary – hopes Tom comes to his senses and takes a long hot shower – but one way or another, this show must go on.

If she has to stand on that stage alone and play every part herself, then this show is going on.

Chapter 72

He was a massive dick today. And feels terrible about it. But maybe it's for the best. Best for Laura. It's hard for him to unravel. Thinking makes his head hurt. When his head hurts he can't sleep, and when he can't sleep he thinks . . . about his cancer, about Laura, about his mother, about his life, about his pain. Mostly about his pain. His prescription renews in three days. He thinks. But when he attempts the mathematics of this, his head feels like it might shatter. Three days, or two, or two hundred, it's a long way distant.

So in the absence of sleep and to stave off thought, he walks.

The pain ebbs and flows, and it's hard to know which is worse. The periods of relief are coloured by the dread of their end, and the waves of pain promise, at least, some relief to come. He is careful to not dwell on this. To not think.

Miles of left foot then right have brought him to the town centre. His legs and feet ache, and this is a welcome distraction.

It's close to kicking-out time and the streets are intermittently raucous. The isolated chants and shouts and outbursts of laughter only heightening the bracketing quiet.

Couples and groups and single people drift past. A mid-sized town this, just big enough to boast most of the attractions seen in the bigger cities: threatening teenagers, fighting drunks and cowering homeless.

Tom staggers as if intoxicated, but he has drunk little. This morning's hangover was a bitch with teeth and entirely counterproductive to the business of pain management. He has a small bottle of vodka, but he sips this carefully and sparingly.

At a cashpoint, Tom learns that all he has in the way of cash money adds up to £124.

He withdraws – without thought – £100, which is dispensed in four crisp tens and a trio of twenties.

Kicking-out time. The phrase doing double duty some nights. More than once, Tom has come awake to find himself or someone nearby on the wrong end of someone's shoe. Sometimes they piss on you. Alcohol and drugs won't heal your face or dry out your sleeping bag, but they certainly help a cold man care less.

He draws level with a man sleeping in a doorway. Tom folds a ten-pound note into quarters and carefully slides it into the cuff of the man's glove.

No thought, only instinct. Tom turns off the main drag, taking lefts and rights down dark and narrowing streets. A boy and girl huddled together in newspaper-stuffed sleeping bags watch him approach, their eyes like those of frightened animals in the low light. Tom hands a note to each, and the girl, nervous, goes to stand. Tom smiles and walks on.

The cold air feels good on his scalp, and maybe it has some anaesthetising effect.

He intends to walk until he can sleep. It is quiet and cold in these narrow alleys and Tom is tired now. Perhaps, if he found some good cardboard boxes, he might not die in his sleep out here tonight.

The alley opens into a wider street, some traffic, a bus stop, and across the road the train station. Tom heads towards the underpass, his footsteps echoing loudly in the concrete tunnel. It smells of dust and petrol and piss. A cluster of figures – maybe three, maybe four – halfway along one wall watch him approach. A man reaches into his backpack, removes something and conceals it behind his hands.

Tom addresses him. 'Know where I can score a bag?'

The man stands, his hands clasped in front of him. 'Forty.'

For his regulars, this man's dealer will hand out bags for a tenner. Anything above that, this man will keep, or, more likely, spend at the same shop. Tom doesn't begrudge the man his commission, but if Tom acts like a mug, this man might try and fob him off with baking powder instead of the stuff he needs.

Tom pulls a twenty from his pocket. 'More like it?'

The man takes the money. He sets off down the tunnel, cocking his head for Tom to follow.

' "Get me to an apothecary",' Tom says.

'Do what?'

'Nothing,' says Tom, following him into the shadows. 'Nothing.'

Chapter 73

Pat is right-handed, so of course it's her right side that has been weakened by the stroke. As she struggles to insert the key into her front door, the walking stick dangling from her elbow taps out her frustration against the wood.

Declan offered to do it for her, but Pat needs to know she can manage this simple task. Finally, using two hands, she turns the key and pushes the door open. The absence of Hitchens woofing and grumping, the silence that should be the sound of his toenails clicking on the floor – it hits her in the chest like a blast of cold air.

'Everything okay?' Father Declan asks.

Pat nods. 'Yes.' She lisps on her 's's now: *Yesh*. 'Okay.'

Pat plants her stick and shuffles into the hallway; Declan follows with her bag, closing the door behind him.

The old priest makes tea and brings it through to the sitting room.

'You found everything?' Pat says, a broad if lopsided smile on her face.

He laughs. 'I managed.' He takes a seat and pours the tea. 'So, have you thought about it?'

The tumour. Grown as tumours are wont to do, and interfering with the delicate vessels and circuitry of her brain. She's lucky, they said, that the stroke wasn't more catastrophic. But the next one – because there will almost certainly be a next one – may be worse. The next one could be fatal. They can open her up again and 'debulk' the tumour. This might help, it might buy Pat a little more time. But the tumour is lodged against a tangle of major vessels and the surgery is high risk. She could stroke out on the table. She could survive but lose her vision. Either way, her sand is running low. They can operate next week, but Pat would not be recovered in time for the play. And the play – well, the play is one of the few remaining things that lend value to her life.

Pat shakes her head.

'No, you haven't thought about it?' Declan asks. 'Or . . .'

'No more s— surgery.' *Shurgery*. 'No m— more.'

Declan's job involves knowing when to talk, when to listen, and when to ask an incisive question. He waits. Listens.

Pat sips her tea and manages not to drip any down her chin. A minor victory. 'I'll go m— my own way,' she says.

Declan leans forward. 'And . . . what way is that, Patricia?'

She smiles with the left side of her face: *You know what way that is.* 'Soon,' she says.

Declan sips his tea.

'Do you d— dis—'

He shakes his head. 'Who am I to disapprove?'

'Thank you. For coming.'

'I don't drive much these days. So it's nice to have an excuse.'

Declan sees this short exchange for the filler it is. Understands that it is a pause while Pat gathers her thoughts, or her courage. Candour comes at its own pace. Some run at it, the way they might run into cold waves. Others approach more carefully.

'Christmas,' Pat says. 'We t— talked about moving, about b— being h— human. I was—' The word, this crucial word evades her.

Declan sees the loss on her face: 'Disappointed?'

Pat laughs, and there it is, the word she wants: 'Jealous. I was jealous. But . . . I'm g— glad for you. That you exp— experienced what you did. If there is a G— a God . . . he made us the way we are. Made us want what we w— want.'

He glances about the room, at the variously labelled items: *Turns on TV, Turns on lights, Turns up heat.*

'I l— I loved you,' Pat says. 'I still l— love you.'

'Yes. I . . .' When he meets her eyes and smiles, she sees the young man that kissed her in the gardens of St Bernadette's. Declan nods. 'Yes.'

'I have a f— a favour. A favour to ask.'

He raises his eyebrows. *What?*

'Will you take me to b— to bed?'

Declan hesitates. 'Take you upstairs, you mean?'

Pat shakes her head. 'No. I want you to take me to b— b—'

'Pat. I . . . I'm an old man.' He laughs quietly. 'An old priest.'

She speaks slowly and deliberately, because now, more than ever, she wants to get to the end of a sentence without screwing it up. So she takes her time:

'I want you to . . . t— take off your . . . shoes and l— lie with m— me in my . . . bed. Tired. I want you to . . . h— hold me. And in the m— morning, Declan, when I w— wake up, I want you, I w— want you there . . . beside me.'

Declan places his cup on the low table, and then begins to unlace his shoes.

Chapter 74

He had warned her, but Penny's reaction has been no less extreme for it.

His first email was a short hello. *How are you and how have you been?* Some fluff about the weather. An apology for not writing sooner. *It's been a difficult year.* It felt rude or cruel to lay it all out there and then. So he signed off: *Hope this finds you well.* And waited for the reply – the same courtesies, fillers and apologies. The same presumptive hope: that her missive found him well.

So he wrote back and told her that, sadly, it did not.

He had deleted her name from his phone, but he recognised the number when she called.

Last year, they met on the anniversary of his parents' death. But this year they are meeting one day before that. Because the anniversary of his parents' death is now the anniversary of the day Adam cheated on Heather. He nearly declined the offer to meet, and later he came close to cancelling. But this felt cowardly, selfish, maybe both.

So they picked this day, this place.

Penny blots her eyes with a linen napkin. 'I can't . . . Adam. It's . . . it's just . . .' Her shoulders shake as she gives way to another bout of jagged sobbing.

Adam holds her hand. 'I'm sorry for not getting in touch sooner. It's . . . it's been rough.'

'Yeah, understatement of the year, Adam.'

She inspects the napkin in her hand, wet with tears and smeared with mascara. 'Well that's ruined.'

'Tell me something good,' Adam says.

Penny blows her nose into the napkin. 'I . . . honestly, Adam, I . . .'

'Tell me something good about you. Anything.'

'I went on a date.'

'That's good, right?'

Penny wavers her palm up and down. 'Older men,' she says with a sigh. 'Either they try too hard or they don't try at all. Like they've forgotten how to have fun.' She catches his expression. 'Present company excepted, of course.'

Adam has seen these couples – the divorcees and neverweds who know they are playing their final hands in this ridiculous and necessary game. He's seen them in restaurants and bars, dressed in their best and smiling like their future happiness depends on it. He sees them laugh at each other's jokes, watches the night draw on and the conversation turn – as it must – to their children and their failed marriages. To the reasons they are alone. *But, honestly, it's so good to be free.* He watches the women when the men excuse themselves to the bathroom, the way their shoulders drop, the way they fidget in their seats.

He sees Penny in all of this and he wants to tell her it will be okay. That she will find happiness because she deserves it. That any man would be lucky to have her in his life.

But he can't say this, because he can't deny the inevitable retort: *Just not you, Adam, hey?*

They were best friends and brief lovers, but they never worked the way Adam worked with Heather. All the answers, all the truths are painful now. So Adam keeps his platitudes to himself.

Perhaps she reads his mind. Or maybe she reads his face.

'I'm sorry,' Penny says. 'About . . . you know, fucking your life up and everything.'

Adam laughs. 'A nun said something similar,' Adam says. 'About my wedding.'

'*Wedding?*'

Adam nods. 'It's been . . . a crazy time.'

Penny holds his hand. 'How long have you got?'

'I don't know,' he sighs. 'Less than . . . if this treatment works, it could be . . . I don't know.'

Penny squeezes his hand. 'I do want to talk about that. If you want. But, what I meant was, how long until you need to get back to your *wife*.'

Adam laughs, the kind of true and good laughter that turns heads in a quiet wine bar.

'Can we get drunk?' Penny asks. 'Can we get drunk one last time?' And again the tears are coursing down her face.

'I'm not as good at it as I used to be.'

'Don't worry; I am.' Penny examines the wrecked napkin in her hands; creased, sodden and dirty with make-up. She smiles to herself, then looks up and meets Adam's eyes. 'I love you, Adam.'

Adam almost thanks her, but that would be a measly and insensitive reply. So Adam says nothing; he simply looks her in the eye and smiles.

'What do you say to ouzo?' Penny says. 'For old times' sake.'

'Old times,' says Adam. 'Sure.'

Chapter 75

The lights are off, and from outside the hall appears deserted.

On stage, behind the thick black curtains, Tom sits on the chaise, a blanket wrapped around his shoulders. A single lamp stands sentry in a circle of its own yellow light.

Getting in was easy. The front door is locked and alarmed, but – as they often are – the window in the men's toilet was unsecured. His ribs are scraped from wriggling head-first through the narrow aperture. His arms – weaker than the last time he attempted this manoeuvre – were braced on the sink, but they gave way when his hips cleared the window and he cracked his head a good one.

It seems, too, that the window frames have been recently painted, and he has white paint on his hands, a stripe running up the front of his coat and a matching pair along each leg.

But he's in and he's safe. Except from himself.

Tom thumbs the flint on his lighter; the flame jumps into life.

And how would sir like his heroin this evening?

'I believe I'll take it smoked,' Tom says. His voice is rough and it hurts to speak. His nose is running, and on top of everything it looks as if he has a cold.

Tom pulls the tinfoil from his pocket, already cut into two neat squares. (He bought the foil this morning, plus a packet of bacon he will never eat just for the sake of appearances.) One sheet, he folds into a trough that will contain the powder. The other, he rolls into a tight tube that will function as a pipe. He lays these make-shift implements at his side and again flicks the lighter into flame. But the heroin stays in his pocket.

He has carried this small polythene bag for twenty-four hours now. Has held it in his hand, opened it, inhaled its astringent aroma. Last night he slept with it in his hand and this morning he held it to the window and watched the light reflect off the fine white powder.

But he hasn't smoked it. Yet.

He hears a noise outside. A car, footsteps. And he freezes. He holds his breath, but there is no further sound.

He's skittish. He's paranoid. He's got the fear and he's got it heavy. The only thing worse than having nothing on the streets is having something. When you have something, it can be taken away from you. By stealth, or threat or a kick in the head. Today in his flat, listening to footsteps above and below, to the werewolf shouting at the sky, he waited for some boot to kick in his door. Because surely, they knew. Surely they could smell the contents of his little plastic bag.

The junkie fear intensifies after sunset. The voices surrounding him gaining in volume. The drinkers drunk and shouting and walking on heavy feet. So Tom filled his pockets with tinfoil and heroin, left the flat and walked until he arrived – as if on autopilot – at the church hall. At this safe place.

Twenty-four hours he's held this smack. A record. Previously he doubts he's held for more than twenty-four minutes before sending the powder coursing through his system. The sensation of a warm hand on the back of the neck. Of soft lips on his forehead and over his heart. Better than sex, they say. And here he is, on the chaise where he first made love to Laura, a bag of narcotic bliss in his lap.

The argument for taking it goes like this: I'm in pain, I'm dying, why the fuck not?

The argument against is more difficult to pin down. It pales before the incontrovertible logic of *why the fuck not?*

But still, the powder remains in the bag. He grinds his teeth.

'Am I being a massive fucking idiot?' His voice deadened by the thick curtain.

The arguments against include this stage, the play Laura has worked so hard to create and marshal. She emailed them all today, Tom included. She said dress rehearsal would go ahead on

Thursday. Adam said he would be there. And Vernon. And Pat. Lovely lovely Pat just one day out of hospital.

And Tom, cowering in the dark with a bag of junk. Striped with white paint like a convict, a skunk, a clown.

Tom stuffs his hand into the righthand pocket of his paint-smeared coat. Pulls out the Magic 8 Ball and shakes it with two hands.

'Am I pathetic?' His voice so low he barely hears it.

As I see it, yes.

'Smart ball,' Tom whispers.

His mother has called and emailed and messaged with declarations of over-sincere regret and soap-opera contrition. 'It weren't my idea, son. I told him to leave you one, son. I knew you'd get more. No harm done, son.' Tom rejects her calls. He leaves her messages unanswered, with the exception of a single short email:

I'm dying, Mum. It was good to see you one last time. Take care of yourself. Tommy x.

He deletes her replies unread.

'Was that harsh?' Tom asks the ball.

And against the odds, the affirming 8 Ball tells him, *My reply is no.*

Tom puts down the ball and picks up the baggie of smack. Opens it and tips half into the makeshift tray. He considers consulting the ball about what to do next, but he already knows what he's going to do.

After all, why the fuck not, right?

He puts the pipe between his lips, lights the lighter beneath the tray and inhales the rising coil of white smoke. The hit is instant and all-enveloping.

Waves of heat rolling across his skin, a cool whisper spreading through the crackling circuits of his mind, all sound fading to a gentle and pleasing hum . . .

The world softens, shrinks and fades to black.

Chapter 76

Lying in the bath, Adam listens to Heather's footsteps as she pads up and down the stairs. Changing the sheets on his bed and on hers. Sorting the laundry into darks and whites. She had asked about his 'date', her choice of words agitating Adam's sense of guilt.

'It was fine,' he told her. 'The usual.'

'You were a long time,' she said. Not an accusation, merely an observation. 'Mabel's in bed.'

'Yeah. It was . . . people want to talk, you know.'

'And drink?' A wry smile. 'Who was it again?'

'Henry,' Adam said. An impulse lie, the closest rhyme to Penny he could conjure on the spot. But what else could he say?

'Henry?' Heather frowning as she searched her memory for the name.

'How's Hitchens?'

'Like one of the family. Sleeping in front of the fire. Sad really.'

'How d'you mean, sad?'

'The way he's just moved on from Pat. It's a good thing, I suppose. But I'd expected more . . . I dunno, loyalty.'

His sense of guilt itching like an insect bite.

'I'll just . . .' Nodding up the stairs. 'I think I might jump in the bath.'

'Take your time,' Heather said. And then she had kissed his cheek. 'Take your time.'

Adam submerges himself beneath the water now, rinsing the shampoo from his short and patchy hair. Rinsing – he gets it – this thin layer of guilt from his conscience. Thin because what choice did he have? Thin because all they did was drink and talk and reminisce. But guilt all the same. For having enjoyed himself with Penny. For missing a precious bedtime with Mabel. For the lie – *Henry* – albeit a white one.

But it's done now. It's over.

He pulls the plug with his toe, lying motionless as the water drains away, revealing him in his wasted nakedness. He has the beginnings of a minor hangover: headache, dry mouth, a sense of background anxiety. And perhaps this is a suitable penance.

His clothes are in his bedroom, and Adam is embarrassed by his body. He has been waiting for Heather to go downstairs, but she is making her own bed now and Adam is cold in the drained bath.

He wraps a towel around his waist and another about his shoulders. He opens the bathroom door quietly and is two paces towards the loft stairs when Heather says his name.

'Your stuff,' Heather says. She is standing in the bedroom doorway, dressed in pyjamas. 'I . . . I brought your stuff down. Down here.'

Adam pulls the towel around his shoulders. 'In your room?'

'It's our room,' Heather says.

'I . . . thank you.' He feels some larger response is required. Larger in the sense that simple gratitude is not enough. Larger in that he does not understand the nature of this offering – is it reconciliation? And if so to what extent? Is this genial or conjugal? Or is it nothing more – or less – than simple kindness? Thank you does not seem enough, but his mind is swirling and these are the only words he can catch hold of: 'Thank you.'

'Anyway,' Heather says. 'It'll save on the laundry.'

'Right.'

She moves past him to the bathroom. 'Your pyjamas are on the bed.'

Chapter 77

When Tom comes to, he feels as if someone has removed his brain and replaced it with wet paper. A feeling of dullness, weight and torpor. The fuzzy, lacklustre depression of a heroin comedown. A feeling of having been hollowed out, squeezed, wrung. There is pain, but this has receded for the time being. A waning in its natural cycle; a direct effect of his fix; or maybe his faculties are too cloyed and apathetic to actually *do pain* right now if you don't mind. It would appear he's alive, at any rate.

He opens one eye experimentally, just enough to establish that it's still dark. Dark and soft and warm. As if beneath a heavy blanket. His mouth is dry and he licks his lips. Coughs. The acoustics sound off – a side effect, he supposes, of having one's head stuffed with papier-mâché. His skin itches too, and he wraps one arm around his shoulders to scratch. Strange. He was wearing a T-shirt, jumper, coat just a moment ago. But the garment under his fingers feels like a thin cotton shirt.

He goes to sit, but is somehow restrained. A weight across his chest, his belly, his whole fucking body. He is pinned down. Trapped. And the idea is panic-inducing.

Both eyes open now, but the darkness reveals little. He explores his surroundings with his hands. His eyes slowly adjusting to the darkness, he makes out swathes of white. A bed? He's in a bed. Beneath a white duvet as thick and heavy as an avalanche.

'Wha . . .'

He shoves the duvet down to his waist and levers himself onto one elbow. His eyes have adjusted enough now to establish that . . .

'Wha the f . . .?'

. . . this is not his bed.

. . . this is not his room.

. . . these are not his striped pyjamas.

He smells of soap and – a hand to his head – his hair is damp.

'The fuck!'

'You're awake,' says a low, Scottish voice.

'Raymond?'

'Aye.'

'*Raymond?*'

'I'll make tea.'

Raymond sits on a chair beside the bed, a mug held between two hands.

Tom, still in bed, is propped up on what feels like three hundred cloud-filled pillows. 'You washed my hair?'

'You were sick.'

'Sick?'

'Vomit. Quite the mess, I can tell you.'

'And you washed my hair.'

'I washed all of you. And you needed it.'

'I hope you didn't fiddle with me.'

Raymond shakes his head, a gesture that conveys both absolute denial and weary exasperation.

'I'm sorry,' Tom says. 'Bit weirded out is all. I . . .'

But where to start? He starts by taking a sip of his tea.

'What were you doing in the hall anyway?' Tom asks.

'Fixing the windows.'

'Oh.'

'They need replacing.'

'At midnight? By you?'

'Keeps me busy,' Raymond says.

'Most people do crosswords.'

'Never enjoyed them. What's your excuse?'

'Oh I just needed somewhere quiet to take my heroin.'

Raymond shifts in his chair. He contemplates his tea. 'I saw. And I threw it away, in case you're wondering.'

'Thank you.'

'You're welcome.'

'Is that a regular thing, son?'

Tom shakes his head. 'It was just . . . I was just . . . stupid.'

'We all make mistakes, son. But . . . that stuff'll . . .' *kill you.*

'Yes.'

'Want to tell me?'

'It's a long story.'

'And is this particular story over?'

Tom nods. *It's over.*

Raymond sits back in his chair. He sips his tea.

The conversation, such as it is, is soothing. Tom feels, in the presence of Raymond, a calm that he hasn't felt for a long time. The man's placid and neutral demeanour has a quality of – the only way Tom can articulate it to himself – clear water. Clear skies.

'Are you okay?' Raymond asks.

'Nothing a couple of good painkillers wouldn't sort out.'

'Where are your painkillers?'

'I . . . lost them?'

'Another chapter in this long story of yours?'

'Yep. I'm afraid so.'

Raymond makes a deep grumbling noise that sounds like sympathy or compassion.

'We miss you,' Tom says. 'You know? At the group.'

Raymond doesn't answer.

'If it's because of Erin, then we all knew wha—'

'It's not about Erin.'

'Seriously,' says Tom. 'Why are you fixing windows in the dead of night?'

'Long story.'

Tom nods: *Touché.* 'How did you get me here?'

'Put you over my shoulder. Chucked you in the back of the car.'

'Was that wise?'

'I don't think anyone saw.'

Tom laughs. 'No shit! I mean, you putting me over your shoulder. What with your . . . in your condition.'

Raymond has told his wife, and now he will tell Tom. He puts his mug down on the bedside table. 'The reason I left the group,' he says. 'It wasn't about Erin. It's about me.'

Tom looks alarmed. 'Did something happen?'

Raymond shakes his head. 'No. Nothing happened. I . . . don't have it.'

'Have what?'

'Cancer,' Raymond says. 'I don't have cancer.'

'You . . . you fucking *what*?'

'I don't have cancer. Never did.'

'You made it up?'

'I did.'

Tom puts his own mug down, spilling tea over the bedside table. 'You faked cancer?'

A nod.

'We believed you,' Tom says. 'We cared. What kind of person does that?'

'It was wrong.'

'No shit, Raymond. No shit it was wrong. Where are my clothes?'

'Washing machine.'

'Why?'

'Because they—'

'Not my *clothes*, Raymond. Why did you – I can't believe I'm even saying this – *fake* cancer?'

Raymond wipes his eyes with his sleeve. 'I went for a friend. I went to check Sam's thing for a friend.'

'Your friend had cancer?'

'Prostate. Spread to his spine, pelvis, lung.'

Tom picks up his tea. But his expression makes it clear that this is by no means a relaxing of hostilities.

'Kenneth,' Raymond says. 'Kenneth was referred by his doctor; he'd never actually met Sam. So when I walked in . . .' He shrugs.

'Sam assumed you were Kenneth.'

'Shakes my hand, invites me to take a seat.'

It's not difficult for Tom to imagine the scene. Raymond, awkward at the best of times, caught on the spot in a room full of terminally ill strangers. Sam, garrulous and insistent, still holding Raymond's hand and steering him towards a vacant chair.

'I told him I wasn't Kenneth, and Sam, he just shakes his head like it's some administrative error. Asks my name and invites me again to take a seat. So . . .'

'What about your friend?'

A small, nostalgic smile. 'Aye, he thought it was a hoot.'

'But he didn't go?'

'Not really his thing. Besides, he was . . . very tired . . . in a lot of pain.'

'Was?'

'Aye.'

Tom nods at this. *I'm sorry.* 'But you went back?'

'To explain. To tell Sam that Ken wouldn't be coming. Well, I suppose that's what I told myself I was doing.'

'But you didn't.'

'When you get to my age—' He winces at the faux pas. 'Sorry, I didn't . . .'

'It's fine.' Tom allows himself a short laugh. 'Cancer or no cancer, I was never getting to your age.'

If Raymond appreciates the humour in this observation, it doesn't register on his face. 'People,' Raymond says, 'they . . . you lose them. One way or another, you lose them.'

'You were lonely?' Tom hesitates over the last word, as if it were an affliction. As if it were something terminal, which – as the thought forms – he understands is not so far from the truth.

'It was just one hour a week,' Raymond says. 'I used to look forward to it.'

'Yes,' says Tom. 'So did I.'

'But when Erin . . . after Erin, I couldn't . . . it wasn't right.'

'You should have said something.'

'Aye.'

They sit quietly for a while.

Tom sets the mug down on the bedside table. Gently this time. 'I'm glad you don't have cancer.'

'Thank you.'

'Really glad.'

'Aye.'

Tom yawns. 'Time is it?'

'After two. You should try and get some sleep.'

Tom takes a fold of clean white cotton between finger and thumb. 'I won't have to try very hard.'

Raymond stands, hesitates. 'It's a big house.'

'Okay.'

'You'd have your own bed, your own bathroom. Hot water. Good towels.'

'What?'

'It'd be nice,' Raymond says. 'To have some company, I think.' He steps out of the room and pulls the door closed behind him. 'Sleep well.'

'Yes,' says Tom. 'I will.'

And he does.

Chapter 78

He is in bed with his wife, perhaps two hand spans of clean white sheet between them. Nothing less than an expanse.

They have made small talk. As if this were the most natural thing. As if they have not spent almost a year in separate beds. As if Adam weren't dying of cancer. As if they weren't less than one week married.

These fragile pretences lie between them. Lined up on the clean white sheet. So Adam reaches for one of them now.

'Why? Why now?'

Heather rolls onto her side, facing Adam, her hand dropping to the sheet in the hinterland between them.

'I was . . . I thought our wedding night would be . . . the right time, but . . .'

Adam is happy simply to be in the same bed as his wife, but he detects – or is he being foolish – the intimation of something more intimate in Heather's words.

'You're a good man,' she says. 'A good father.'

But not a good husband.

'I . . .'

She puts a finger to his lips, moves her hand onto his chest. 'You never made excuses. Never took the easy way out. And that's . . . it's honest.'

Her hand moves from his chest to his belly. 'So if you tell me that you love me, I'll believe you.'

Heather kisses him, shifts her body across the vanishing expanse so that they are close against one another.

'Do you love me, Adam?'

'I never stopped.'

Adam hardens. He didn't know if his body still could, but it responds to his wife's kiss.

'I've been lonely without you,' Heather says, her hand drifting down his body.

But this can't happen. The chemo polluted his fluids with toxic medicine and for all he knows the trial drug could be as bad if not worse. He can't do this without protection; and never has the word been more relevant.

Adam pulls his head back from Heather's. 'I don't think I can. Not tonight.'

Heather takes him in her hand. 'It's fine,' she says soothingly. 'You'll be fine.'

Adam shakes his head. 'Not me,' he says. 'The drugs. I might . . . I need to use a . . .'

'Oh.' His cock still in her hand. 'Oh.'

'But I can get some . . . maybe tomorrow I can get some.'

Heather appears conflicted. She goes to speak, then hesitates. 'What?'

'I might . . .' She bites her bottom lip in a gesture of pre-emptive apology. 'I might have one. Maybe?'

The only reason Heather would have condoms is if she used them with someone else. With Jamie. And as Adam pieces this together, he sees his inner thoughts reflected in Heather's expression.

'I'm . . . I'm sorry. That was stupid. I . . .'

Adam puts his hand to her face. 'It's fine. Honestly.' But even as he says the word, he feels himself soften in Heather's hand.

Chapter 79

He's slept fourteen hours of the last twenty, and had two hot baths in the scant time he's been conscious. He feels, if not like a new man, then a damn sight better than the man he was yesterday.

Last night, he slept for eleven hours under clean sheets in a double bed. When he woke, he found Raymond reading downstairs with the radio on low. They visited Tom's flat to collect clothes, his books, the Liberty scarf Laura gave to him and which Tom never gave to his mother. Raymond told Tom he can stay as long as he likes. *How about forever?* was the flippant answer on Tom's lips. Instead, he said, 'Thank you,' and packed every pair of socks and underpants he owned.

Next stop the doctor's surgery. Tom dozed on Raymond's shoulder until, after almost an hour, they were called into the doctor's office. Perhaps it was the steadying presence of the elderly and impeccable Scot, but Dr Gavin renewed Tom's prescription – which was by now only two days premature – with only minimal enquiry and a firm recommendation for increased vigilance regarding these 'rather potent tablets'. The recommendation was met with unequivocal reassurance from both Tom and Raymond, and five minutes after that Tom swallowed one of the rather potent painkillers with a mouthful of canned lemonade.

Final stop, a nursing home where Tom was introduced to Raymond's glassy-eyed wife. His 'old girl', Raymond called her. They sipped sweet tea, ate biscuits and held hands with the smiling vacant.

On the return trip to Raymond's house, Tom talked and Raymond listened attentively and without interruption. And when they pulled into the gravel drive in front of the three-storey house,

Raymond turned off the engine and said, simply, 'Do you have her address?'

'Yes.'

Tom went upstairs for bath number two. He shaved with one of Raymond's old-fashioned razors, wrapped himself in a large fluffy towel, sat on the edge of the double bed, shut his eyes, fell slowly backwards and slept for another three hours.

It's eight in the evening when Raymond parks his car two doors down from Laura's house.

'How do I look?'

'Better,' Raymond says. 'You look better.'

'Maybe I should have called. Probably I should have called.'

Raymond reaches across Tom and opens the passenger door. 'Shall I wait?'

'I'll get a bus.'

Raymond puts a twenty-pound note in Tom's hand. 'You'll get a taxi. And don't stay out too late.'

Tom laughs. 'I'll call when I'm leaving.'

'Aye.'

Tom steps out of the car. 'You don't think this is a mistake?'

Raymond smiles. *Possibly.* And then he nods towards the house. 'Lay on, Macduff.'

Chapter 80

Tom approaches the driveway slowly. There are lights on in the house, one in an upstairs window behind brightly patterned curtains.

None of which mean Laura is home. Tom turns to look for Raymond, but the old man has gone.

His eyes return to the upstairs window. Movement behind the curtains that could only belong to a teenage girl.

' "But, soft! What light through yonder window breaks?" '

Tom is still bruised from wriggling through the bathroom window at the church hall. It's safe to say his drainpipe-climbing days are behind him, but he can still fling a handful of gravel.

' "It is the east," ' Tom says, ' "and Juliet is the sun." '

Tom scoops up a handful of fine stones from the Hargreaves's driveway, takes careful aim and lets fly. The gravel is true and it patters pleasingly against Laura's window.

He waits.

Nothing happens.

Tom scoops up a second fistful of dirt. ' "I am too bold," ' he mutters as he draws his arm back.

'Romeo, I presume?'

'Shit!' A man standing at the half-open front door. 'I mean, sorry. I . . . ha!'

The man pushes the door fully open. 'Why don't you come inside?'

'Inside?' Tom says, as if the notion were a slightly eccentric one. 'Sure,' he says. 'Why not?'

Tom drops the gravel, wipes his palm on his trousers and shakes hands with Laura's father.

* * *

'Well,' says Laura's mother. 'This is nice.'

'Yes,' says her father. 'Very nice.'

The three of them sit at a round kitchen table, small enough that – should the mood take them – they could join hands and hold a séance. *To speak with the dead*, Tom thinks, supressing a smile.

'Shall I be mum?' asks Laura's father, nodding at the pot in the centre of the table.

Laura's mother, Ruth, snorts at his little joke.

The man of the house pours three cups of tea, adding the necessary milk and sugar according to requirements. Laura is upstairs, in the bath apparently.

'We've been dying to meet you,' her father says.

'I'd like to say Laura's told us all about you. But, well. She keeps close counsel. Doesn't she, Michael?'

Michael makes as if to zip his mouth closed.

'So,' says Michael. 'You're *Romeo*?' And he doesn't wink exactly, but it's the next best thing.

'Yes,' says Tom. 'And a few others.'

'We can't wait to see it.'

'Your daughter's . . . she's very . . . you must be very proud of her.'

Ruth nods. She dabs at the corner of her eye with an index finger.

'Extremely,' says her father.

'I . . . want you to know that . . . I respect her, Laura, very much.'

Michael nods. 'I should hope so.'

'And I know I'm . . .' Tom holds up his hands: *Look at me*. 'Probably not what you . . .'

Ruth takes hold of Tom's right hand. And then Michael takes his left. As if they are holding a séance, after all.

'You've made our girl happy,' Ruth says.

'Right,' says Michael.

'So you're just fine, Tom. You're just great.'

'Well I don't know about that. I mean . . . ha! I don't know
about *great*.'

'She's blossomed,' says Michael.

'She has,' says Ruth. 'Blossomed.'

'I don't think that's anything to do with me,' says Tom – still
suspended between Laura's parents. 'To tell you the truth, Ruth—'

Ruth snorts at the rhyme.

'To be perfectly honest, Laura's done far more for me. Far more
for any of us, really, than we've done for her. She's . . . you know . . .'

Michael nods.

'Special,' says Ruth.

'She's thirsty, is what she is,' says Laura from the kitchen
doorway.

She is dressed in tracksuit bottoms and a T-shirt. Wet hair, no
make-up, no effort on Tom's account. Nothing but her natural
confidence and remarkable hair. Her wise smile and playful eyes.

'How long you been there, poppet?'

'Just arrived,' she says. But there is a puddle of water at her feet.

Laura takes the fourth chair. 'You should put him down,' she
says to her parents. 'I mean, you don't know where he's been.'

Tom nods at Laura's hair. 'You're leaking,' he says, and he slides
an empty mug towards her.

Laura blushes.

'Am I missing something?' Ruth asks.

'Private joke. I'll tell you later.'

Ruth exchanges a look with Michael. *These kids!*

Laura smiles at Tom. 'You look better.'

'Yeah. I am.'

His eyes go to her left arm, to the word extending from the
crook of her elbow towards her wrist.

'Is that . . .?'

'A tattoo,' says Michael. 'Nice, isn't it?'

The skin is still inflamed around the heavy black letters.

'Unwritten,' says Tom, reading the word inked on Laura's arm.
'I . . .' He looks to Laura's mother, unsure what the party line is on

the Hargreaves's only daughter despoiling the landscape of her smooth and delicate flesh.

Laura's mother nods in encouragement.

'I like it,' says Tom. 'Very . . . poetic.'

'I thought so too,' says her father.

'And only nine letters,' says Laura. 'Which was a mercy.'

Michael stands from the table. 'I'll leave you two . . . you know, to it.'

Laura takes hold of her father's hand, pulls him back to his chair. She and Tom have much catching up to do, but it can wait a while. And besides, it's fun to watch Tom squirm. 'Stay,' she says to her father. Then, glancing at the teapot, 'Do we have any wine?'

Her father rubs his hands together. 'You know, poppet, I think we do.'

'Oh!' says Laura's mother. 'Lovely! I'll get the crisps.'

Chapter 81

They're eating cake again. Raymond, as ever, doing more eating than the others.

'I knew it,' says Vernon. 'I effing bloody well knew it.'

'L—l—l—'

'Liar,' says Tom on Pat's behalf. And he is careful to aim this where it was intended – at Vernon, rather than at Raymond.

Vernon plucks a raisin from his fruitcake and throws it at Raymond.

Hitchens – who up until now has been lying across Pat's feet, as if he is trying to hold her in place – jumps up and chases after the piece of fruit. He sweeps it up with a deft movement of his tongue, then lopes back to Pat, and lowers himself again onto her feet.

There has been much shock and teasing. A fair amount of laughter too, but none of the anger or recrimination Raymond had feared. Even so, he feels like a proper wally. 'I'm sorry,' he says again. 'I'm sorry I disappointed you.'

Vernon laughs a genuine and full-bellied laugh. Seated beside Raymond, he puts his arm around the Scot's shoulder. 'I'm the opposite of disappointed,' Vernon says. 'I'm . . . whatsit?'

'R— r— r—'

'Relieved,' says Laura.

'Exactly,' says Vernon. 'This is . . . it's . . . blimey . . . sorry I . . .' Vernon does his best not to cry, but the tears will have their way. 'Now look what you've gone and done. Silly old sod.' He wipes his eyes then replaces his arm around Raymond's shoulders. 'I'm the opposite of disappointed,' he says. 'The proper opposite of that.'

Laura nods towards the stage. 'Sure we can't convince you?'

Raymond shakes his head. 'I think I've done enough . . . acting.'

'Okay then,' Laura claps her hands together. 'We've got a shit lot to do, people, and just over seven days to do it in. So shall we crack on?'

Act V

Chapter 82

Raymond is at the church hall making final preparations – nailing down squeaky boards, checking the wardrobe and the props. Replacing light bulbs. Setting out one hundred and sixty chairs in uniform, perfectly spaced rows. All working together, they could have achieved this task in a quarter of the time, but Raymond – 'Laurence Olivier didn't lay out chairs' – was having none of that.

'I'll be back late,' he said to Tom and Laura. 'So don't . . . aye, wait up.'

They have the house to themselves. An old Ella Fitzgerald LP playing on a turntable in the dining room.

'I don't know who was more embarrassed,' Laura says. Her overnight bag is still in the hallway.

'No contest,' says Tom. 'Did you see him blush? Thought he might have a heart attack.'

'Don't,' Laura says. 'Just . . . don't.'

She sits at the large old oak table, a glass of wine in her hand. Two places are set with Raymond's best crockery and heavy-handled cutlery. Flowers doing their very best to escape from a plain glass vase. Every candle Tom could find is lit and flickering. And he found many. Candles on the table, on the sideboard, on the fireplace above a gently crackling log fire.

'I'm not much of a cook,' Tom says.

'I don't mind.'

'We'll see about that.'

Tom goes through to Raymond's kitchen. It's equipped with everything a chef could need and much more besides. Tom boils a kettle.

Among the arcana in Raymond's kitchen is a silvered serving dish complete with high-domed lid. It's wide and high enough to accommodate a good-sized bird. And the irony of this is not lost on Tom as he arranges two turkey-flavoured cup noodles in the centre of the tray.

He feels suddenly foolish. But . . . too late now.

Besides, he has a fire in the grate, Ella on the stereo, and a big tub of ice-cream in the freezer. And let's not forget, these noodles are excellent.

Vernon trims the hairs from his nose and ears. A task that – like shaving – takes considerably less effort thanks to the many cycles of chemotherapy. He checks his reflection in the bathroom mirror, and he could almost pass for living, he thinks. Some darkness under his eyes, but he'll turn in early tonight and the missus will sort out the bags with a touch of make-up in the morning.

He doesn't remember being this nervous since the night before his wedding. The difference between the two, he supposes, is that his wedding was the start of something. Of his life as a man, of his family. All of whom, including little Veronica, will be there tomorrow. Tomorrow, though, is the end of something. And he's more apprehensive about this than he is about forgetting his lines or missing a cue.

' "Being done, there is no pause," ' Vernon says to his reflection.

Othello talks of murder, but his words also speak to the unstoppable momentum of a terminal diagnosis. There is no *pause*, but rather an accumulation of hard stops.

Work stops, golf stops, curry with the lads stops. *Purpose*, Raymond thinks. You lose your purpose – beyond, of course, that great charade of courage and indifference. But these last months have been different; he's had a reason to get out of the house, made friends, been a part of something. He's been *living*.

Tomorrow night, though; tomorrow night, all that comes to an end.

*   *   *

322

Raymond sits in the front row of the empty church hall, a cup of tea and a slice of fruitcake on the chair to his right. A copy of *Romeo and Juliet* open in his hand. He checks his watch and it's close to midnight. Everything is set.

He approaches the crack at the foot of the stage into which a mouse once bolted. And where you find one mouse, you find more than one.

So Raymond brushes the crumbs from his plate onto the floor near the small opening.

Pat packs her bag.

Everything is clean; the floors scrubbed, the bathroom sparkling. No dirty dishes in the sink, no laundry in the basket. She has written a note, too, and this sits where these notes always do – in the centre of the kitchen table. It is addressed to Declan.

Pat has cleared the fridge of perishable vegetables, but has bought a fresh pint of milk so that he can make a cup of tea while he reads.

She walked Hitchens with Adam today. The big animal chasing and fetching the ball, while Pat and Adam went over their lines one last time. In the open air, with no eye on her and no expectation, she delivered most of them with only minimal hesitation. Perhaps, if there is a God – and soon she will know, or she will not – he will guide her tongue and clear her mind tonight. That would be nice. Hitchens seems content with his new family and this makes her more happy than sad, though both emotions are in play. Heather and Mabel – such a lovely pair – will bring Hitchens tonight. He's a good boy and too idle to make a fuss. Or so she hopes. It's curtain up in a couple of hours, so she will know soon enough.

Soon enough.

After the show she will decline the invitation to join her cast mates for a drink, claiming fatigue, or perhaps a headache. She will kiss them all farewell, and then Declan will drive her to the coast and walk with her to the sand. There – this has been promised – they will kiss each other and say one final goodbye. Declan will walk back to his car; Pat will walk into the sea.

She contemplates all of this with neither fear nor regret. She has lived a good life; a life rich with friendship, meaning and experience. And she has lived, yes, a good death, too – she has been a part of something special; made new and dear friends. She has woken up beside a handsome man; his lips the first thing to touch hers that bright March morning. The play will soon be played. Beyond tonight is decline and pain and a hospice full of nuns. No thank you very much. No, this is a good and fitting final act, and she is eager to embrace it.

Pat packs a small flask of whiskey into her bag. Later, alone on the beach, she will drink this as she undresses to her underwear. She will fold her clothes into a neat pile and then walk into the sea. It will be cold. But she will find her warmth as she kicks and swims into the waves, which will be rolling out towards the sea. Rolling out towards forever.

Declan will give her an hour before collecting her clothes and taking them back to Pat's house where he will find the letter, and a fresh pint of milk.

Chapter 83

There is love between them; he feels that. But they are yet to make love. Adam has been laid low with a cold – a minor thing – but in his weakened state it has hit him hard, sending him to bed early and feverish. *And perhaps this is no bad thing*, he thinks; with each passing day they are becoming more comfortable in the bed they share. And he feels better today; his head is clear and he is, if not strong, then strong enough.

'Nervous?' Heather asks him.

They are standing in the living room where the light is best, Heather's face inches from Adam's as she adjusts his tie.

'Terrified.'

'Just focus on us,' she says.

Mabel is upstairs in the bath, Hitchens napping in his basket in the kitchen.

'You look handsome,' Heather says.

'I'll take your word for it.'

She kisses him, then steps back to take him in. 'They got the blood out.'

He collected his jacket from the dry cleaner's on the way to meet Penny for lunch. It's been over a week, but the lie – of omission, of obfuscation – occasioned by that lunch sits on his chest, and he does not want to take this deceit to his grave. He will rectify the situation when the time is right. And when he figures out how.

'Almost,' Adam tells her. 'There's a little left on the lapel.'

Heather takes his lapels between her fingers, pulling the jacket straight. 'Wait' – she opens the jacket – 'the ticket's still in there.'

The dry cleaner's ticket is attached to the jacket's inside pocket with a safety pin, and Heather uses two hands to remove this. She smooths the material flat, feels something and reaches into the pocket, pulling out a crumpled receipt between two fingers.

'What's that?' Adam asks. But the words, as they leave his mouth, trigger the connections that tell him exactly what it is. The receipt from his afternoon with Penny. He feels a jolt of panic, but knows this is unfounded – it's simply a receipt, itemising drinks and nibbles.

He goes to take the slip of paper from Heather, but she has already unfolded it.

'Lunch,' Adam says.

Heather frowns as she reads the receipt. 'Ouzo?'

'Sure. I mean, when in . . . a Greek restaurant, right?'

'God. How many did you have?'

'Hah, yeah . . . me, not so many, but . . .' He shrugs. 'You know.'

'Whatshisname must have been legless.'

'Yep.'

'Harry, was it?'

So here it is, Adam. You can compound the lie or take the segue that fate has laid before you.

'Y— N—'

'What?'

'Nothing. I . . . I just . . .'

'Did something happen? With you and . . . Henry, that's it. Henry.'

Adam can feel his face moving through a series of involuntary expressions – he frowns, smiles, winces, sighs, opens and closes his mouth as if his circuits have been shorted. And perhaps they have.

Heather watches this display, her face going through its own routine of confusion, concern and slow-dawning comprehension. 'It wasn't Henry?'

Adam's head shakes itself: No.

'Who was it, Adam?'

'Don't get . . . it's not what it . . . not how it . . .'

'It was her?' Heather takes a full step back from Adam, as if recoiling from something painful, something repulsive.

'We . . .' Adam moves forward, but Heather holds up a hand. *Don't*.

'And then I let you back into my bed. The same night, Adam.'

'I didn't know y—'

'Do you know how guilty I felt that night? When I . . . I felt *awful*. And you let me. You just lay there and let me.'

'I'm sorry. Heather, I'm so s—'

'Did you kiss her?'

'What?'

'Penny, Adam. *Penny*. Did you kiss her when you were both pissed on ouzo?'

'No. I mean . . . on the cheek, I suppose.'

She sneers at him. 'You suppose?'

'If you'll just let me—'

'What? Explain?'

'She deserved to know. To hear it from me.'

Heather screws up the receipt and throws it at him. 'She deserves nothing. Neither of you do.'

'Heather.'

'Drop dead, Adam!'

Silence.

They stare across the space between them. Each contrite, each defiant.

Adam picks up the receipt from the floor. 'I'm working on it,' he says.

And he buttons up his jacket and leaves.

Chapter 84

So this is it. The Ides of March is upon them.

Four-plus months of planning, rehearsals, squabbles, setbacks and drama. All leading up to this point. Laura's parents are working front of house, collecting tickets and selling programmes. The cast peep around the curtains and watch their family members take their seats.

Vernon's family take up two full rows on stage left, and Laura's relatives, too, are here in force. The room is full of neighbours, friends, classmates and former colleagues. Staff from the hospice that will benefit from tonight's proceedings are present, as are the dozens of patients and patients' family to whom they have sold tickets. Word has spread.

Declan is seated in the front row beside Raymond's wife Judith and a carer from her nursing home. The priest holds Judith's hand, gently patting the back of it as he talks to the carer, saying something that makes her chuckle. Adam spots Mabel, sitting with Hitchens, Dianne and Dianne's husband — but there is an empty seat where Heather should be. He is still hurt, still remorseful. And if he returns 'home' tonight to find his remaining possessions in one more bin liner, then it will be no small surprise. Tom spots his oncologist plus one. He looks for his mother with some dread, but is relieved when he doesn't find her. Tonight is for him, for Laura, for Vernon and Pat and Adam and for Raymond too. They don't need his mother clattering through the aisles and making a scene. All Tom needs are the people standing beside him now, behind the curtain of this darkened stage. These are his family.

They had a final run-through this afternoon, and when they were done, they all wished they hadn't bothered.

Striving to better, oft we mar what's well, as Shakespeare had it.

But as Vernon pointed out, 'That's the beauty of Shakespeare. You can screw up the lines, and no one knows the difference. Innit?'

'Anyway,' said Tom. 'It's good luck. Bad rehearsal, good show. Don't they say?'

'Great,' said Laura. 'In that case we should be sensational.'

'At least no one said M— Mac— Mac' – a mischievous twinkle in Pat's eye – 'the Scottish Play.'

'Thank God for that,' said Adam. 'For a minute there I thought you were going to say *Macbeth.*'

Pat swatted him on the arm.

'We don't need luck,' Tom told them all. 'We've got cancer. And even Lady Fate isn't cruel enough to screw with a bunch like us.'

Laura kissed him. She whispered into his ear. 'I love you.'

'And I love you too,' Tom said, making no effort to lower his voice.

Standing in the wings now, Laura squeezes Tom's arm. 'Ready?'

'No.'

'Well, tough. Because that lot out there are and they're getting restless.'

'Perhaps one final p— prayer,' says Pat.

They come together and form a small circle in the centre of the stage, arms around each other's shoulders, heads bowed.

'Our F— F— Father, force of nature or otherwise . . .'

The others join her: 'Who may or may not be in heaven.'

They whisper the prayer slowly and with sincerity, landing together on the final 'Amen' and standing for a moment in silence.

'Okay,' says Laura. 'This is it.'

Raymond raises the curtain to reveal Adam lying on the chaise. Beside him, sitting in a chair, is Vernon. We recognise the set-up from countless cartoons and sketches as that of psychiatrist and patient. The scene is lit with a single standing lamp.

'So,' says Vernon, 'Mr . . .?'

'Shakespeare,' says Adam.

'So tell me, Mr Shakespeare, what appears to be the problem?'

'Death,' says Adam, and he pauses, allowing the word, the reason they are all here tonight, to float above the audience and settle.

'Ah, death,' says Vernon. And he turns to the audience with a wry smile. 'There's a lot of it about,' he says. And this earns the first laugh of the night.

The laughter has a soothing effect on all assembled, both on stage and off, and in that moment, Adam knows the show will be a good one. It's a shame Heather is not here to see it.

'I think I'm a bit obsessed,' says Adam as Shakespeare. 'I see it everywhere.'

'Well,' says Vernon. 'We are born to die.'

Shakespeare sits up a little on the couch. 'That's a good line.'

The shrink shrugs immodestly. 'Thank you. So, this obsession?'

'I see a man rolling a barrel,' says Shakespeare, 'and wonder, could a man drown in wine?'

The shrink makes a note. 'Interesting.'

'I see a man selling pillows, and imagine him smothering his wife.'

'Unusual,' says the Elizabethan psychiatrist.

'And at the baker's, I thought, *what if someone were to bake a* person *into a pie. Two people, perhaps.*'

'It would have to be a big pie,' says Vernon, and he gets the second good laugh of the evening.

'Why don't we begin with this business about the pillow?' says Vernon. 'Tell me more about that . . .'

Vernon reaches up to the lamp, and turns it off, plunging the stage into blackness.

Adam exits, and Pat takes his place on the chaise.

Vernon dons a hat and takes up a pillow.

While this business is underway, Laura narrates from the wings. Setting the scene for Othello's murder of Desdemona.

*   *   *

Vernon as Othello looks out across the audience, allowing his eyes to settle on each member of his family, baby Vee included. This takes a moment, but it's his moment and the crowd can wait. Call it tension, if it helps. He feels his family's love flowing towards him, and Vernon has seldom felt more happy, proud or fulfilled. His wedding day, the birth of his pretty chickens, and now this. This is right up there. A tear comes to his eye. It fits the part, and he embraces it. *Good theatre*, Vernon thinks.

Pat, from the chaise, clears her throat.

' "Will you come to bed, my lord?" '

Othello turns. ' "Ay, Desdemona." '

Pat will die on stage five times tonight, but her favourite demise is her third, that of Cleopatra. And not just for the gold headscarf. Although it is a very snazzy scarf. The Queen of Egypt, Pat believes, would approve. They are at the mid-point of the play, and any mistakes they have made have been minor, and likely missed by the audience. A stutter here, a dropped line there.

Laura lies dead at Pat's feet, killed by grief. When Pat says her next line – a comment on the ease with which her attendant has let go of life – she says it to Declan:

' "If thou and nature can so gently part
The stroke of death is as a l— lover's pinch
Which hurts and is desired." '

Death, Cleopatra says, is not so bad. Death, she says, is sometimes welcome.

Pat applies the snake to her breast, lowers herself gently to the stage floor and dies. Twice more she will die tonight on these boards. And then, one final time, in the cold and lapping waves. *Which hurts and is desired.*

These are Adam's favourite lines: Macbeth lamenting not merely the death of his wife, but the transience of life itself. He cried when he first read them (the first time, in fact, that he met his fellow cast members). But he mustn't cry tonight.

Granted, a well-timed tear might illuminate the truth and poetry of Shakespeare's words, but full-blown sobbing would only detract. And so, Adam turns away from Mabel's face, directing his gaze above the heads of the audience, to focus on the ticking clock at the back of the hall.

' "Tomorrow," ' he says, ' "and . . ." ' and then Adam freezes.

Standing beneath the clock, one arm hugging her chest, one thumbnail at her lips, is Heather.

Laura, as the recently deceased Lady Macbeth, lies motionless on the chaise. And as Adam prepares to deliver his lines, as he squares his shoulders and pauses . . . *a little too long?* . . . Laura steals a glance at the audience.

And her heart is pumping pure joy and pride. This, she now knows, is what she will do with the rest of her life, however long that life may be.

The fifty-pence coin is twisted into the waistband of her tights, but after the show, she will drop it into the collection tin that will be passed around to wring further funds from the hopefully weeping audience. Because the coin no longer holds any magic – statistically, Laura could be wherever, and worrying about where is simply taking up good, but relentlessly ticking time. She might live, like baby Veronica, to be one hundred. Or she might step out of the theatre tonight and – just like poor Doctor Sam – beneath the wheels of a number 57 bus.

Death will come when it will come.

So she will pursue this, not as if every day is her last, but knowing every day is a gift. Not acting; she knows with a self-awareness uncommon for a girl of her age, that her talents do not lie in performance. But the audience has responded to her words tonight. They have laughed and cried in all the right places. And not simply at Mr Shakespeare's work, but at Laura's comic interludes between young William and his shrink. She has an idea for a reworking of *Romeo and Juliet*, something with a spoiled heiress and a homeless man. But perhaps, instead of stepping on Shakespeare's toes again, she will attempt something original. The idea is both exhilarating and terrifying.

But, seriously, Adam has milked this pause for a little too long.

Sprawled on the chaise where she lost her virginity, Laura clears her throat, whispers Adam's next word:

'Tomorrow . . .'

' "Tomorrow, and tomorrow,
Creeps in this petty pace from day to day
To the last syllable of recorded time,
And all our yesterdays have lighted fools
The way to dusty death. Out, out, brief candle!" '

Adam has his rhythm now and feels confident enough, composed enough, to risk a glance at his daughter. Mabel waves and Adam accepts this with a subtle nod of his head.

Let her candle burn bright, he thinks. *Let it burn bright and long.*

He redirects his gaze to the clock at the back of the hall. To his wife, standing beneath it as the second hand marches on oblivious.

' "Life," ' he says. ' "Life's but a walking shadow, a poor player
That struts and frets his hour upon the stage
And then is heard no more. It is a tale
Told by an idiot," '

– he smiles at the audience, lets this line land –

' "full of sound and fury,
Signifying nothing." '

And Adam understands now, what that 'nothing' means.

It means death. That death, perhaps, is the ultimate meaning of life.

It is in any case unavoidable. And as such, that final *nothing* is nothing to fear.

Romeo cradles Juliet's head in his hands, and when Tom's tears fall, they land gently on his lover's sleeping eyes.

' "Here's to my love." '

His wrecked voice is small in the expanse of the hall, but the audience lean in when Tom speaks, and they hear truth in his fragile words.

He raises a small brown bottle to his lips. He drinks.

' "O true apothecary, thy drugs are quick." '

Tom considers all the back-alley apothecaries he has known, the quick drugs they plied. He could be sad, angry, bitter about this, but, on this stage, in this moment, he feels only peace in his heart.

He kisses Juliet's lips, and although this lady is meant to be dead, her lips – gently – return the favour.

' "Thus with a kiss I die." '

In the original text, there is a brief intervening sequence with Friar Lawrence – the true idiot of the play – and Romeo's man, Balthasar. But tonight, these lines have been excised, and Laura now comes gently awake to discover Romeo dead beside her.

' "What's here?" ' she says, plucking the bottle of poison from Romeo's hand, some warmth still in his lifeless fingers.

' "Oh churl," ' Juliet declares, ' "drink all and left no friendly drop to help me after?" '

Tom – his face shielded from the audience by Juliet's back – opens his eyes, winks once, and returns quietly to death.

Laura allows herself a smile before kissing Romeo one last time – ' "Thy lips are warm" ' – and sinking his dagger into her heart.

The stage is swallowed into darkness.

Vernon clicks on the standing lamp, illuminating himself and the patient on his couch.

'We are time's subjects,' he says ominously, ' "and time bids be gone." '

'Excuse me?' says Adam.

'Hour's up,' says Vernon.

'But there are so many more,' protests Shakespeare.

'Same time next week?'

Shakespeare gets to his feet. 'Well,' he says, 'if it were done when 'tis done, then 'twere well it were done quickly.'

'Come again?'

'Yes,' Adam says. 'Same time next week.'

'Oh, and one more thing,' Vernon says. 'Just a thought, but . . . you might think about writing some of this stuff down.'

Shakespeare puts a finger to his chin. 'Write it down?' he says. 'Now there's an idea.'

Vernon turns off the lamp for the final time.

Raymond pulls the curtain closed.

Chapter 85

When the curtain opens again, the audience are on their feet, clapping, crying, and, on Vernon's side of the hall, whistling and stamping their feet.

The Rude Mechanicals stand in a line of five, with Laura at their centre. She beckons to Raymond in the wings, and when he fails to join them she calls him again, making it clear that refusal is not an option. Raymond joins the line and the applause increases in volume.

Six in a row, they hold hands and feel the applause wash over them. They bow deeply, straighten and then bow again.

After some time, during which it seems the applause will never end, Laura takes one step forward, hands clasped together before her. The crowd settles and stills.

'Thank you,' says Laura.

She has seen actors make that action – two palms down – inviting the audience to sit. But standing here, a child really, the gesture feels conceited or contrived. So she waits. She says, 'Thank you,' again and waits.

She lets her neutral posture communicate that she has something to say. And one by one, the crowd sit.

'Thank you. This whole, mad idea started in Hillside Hospice. The hospice we are raising money for tonight. We' – she gestures to her fellow Rude Mechanicals – 'met in therapy with the wise, patient and charming Doctor Sam Brooks.'

Laura watches a murmur of recognition pass through the rows. She watches, in particular, an older lady with impeccably bobbed silver hair. She is flanked on either side by handsome men of between twenty and thirty – Laura doesn't know if it's possible to inherit a smile, but when these young men hear their father's name, his warmth shines through their faces.

'Dr Sam was helping us come to terms with our diagnoses,' Laura says. 'And to accept our mortality. To see death, not as something to be feared, but as an essential, inevitable, part of life.' Laura produces a folded sheet of paper from within the depths of Juliet's wedding dress. 'He gave me this. He gave one to all of us.' She reads from the page:

' "Of all the wonders that I yet have heard,

It seems to me most strange that men should fear;

Seeing that death, a necessary end,

Will come when it will come."

'A lesson Dr Sam shared in group and underlined in death.'

Laura glances at the sheet of paper in her hand. On the reverse is the speech – this speech – that she knows by heart. In the hand-written script, she goes on now to explain how none of this would be possible without Sam, how she wishes he could be here tonight. But if he were alive, then this play would not have happened. The truth, if she were to go this route, is that none of this would have been possible without his death.

Laura folds the sheet of paper and replaces it in the bodice of her dress. She turns her eyes towards the ceiling and says, simply, 'We miss you.'

Laura nods to her father – standing at the side of the hall and crying into a handkerchief. To gentle applause, he carries a bouquet of flowers to Dr Sam's wife, then returns to his spot.

'When we first met in this hall,' Laura continues, 'we were seven.'

And now – while the audience grasps this simple equation – Laura meets the eyes of Erin's husband and daughter.

'Erin,' she says, 'was one of the gentlest souls a person could hope to meet. She brought dignity, respect and' – Laura smiles – 'and muffins, to our small gang. She was the mother of this group, in more ways than one, and her passing came as a great sadness, if not an out and out surprise. Erin didn't get to say her lines tonight

as Gertrude, Iras, Emilia, Portia or Cordelia – but she was here . . .'
Laura places her right hand over her left breast.

Vernon steps forward, beside Laura, and performs the same gesture. 'And here.'

Then Pat, and Adam and Raymond and finally Tom: 'And here.'

Laura nods to her father, and now he presents a bouquet to Erin's daughter, Jenny.

Laura waits for the audience to settle one last time.

'A final thank you to the vicar, for giving us the use of this magnificent hall, and to his wife for the divine fruitcake. Thank you.'

As one, The Rude Mechanicals take a backward step, bow from the waist and vanish into the wings.

Chapter 86

While the hall empties, the cast loiters backstage, changing out of their costumes, drinking champagne from plastic glasses, celebrating their success and laughing about the dropped lines that no one noticed.

It is an excited and intimate huddle, but the actors are exhausted, not simply from tonight's performance, but from the weeks and months leading up to it. And now – with their work done – the cast is eager to join the folk waiting for them in the emptying hall.

Raymond goes first, to kiss his wife good night, and then to rattle a collection tin at the departing patrons. One by one, the remaining five empty their plastic cups, and follow him from the dim stage to the waiting light of their loved ones.

Chapter 87

Laura and Tom go first, and Laura is relieved to see that her extended family has been sent ahead to the Mermaid. She walks into her father's arms, while her mother takes Tom into hers. They hug and kiss and exchange dance partners to do it all again. As they leave, Tom collects Raymond who protests that he has chairs to stack and a floor to sweep, but all that – Tom tells him – can wait until tomorrow. Tom threads his arm through Raymond's, and the five step out into the clear night.

The hangers-on, Vernon's boys and girls among them, are stacking chairs when the former train driver emerges from backstage. His wife goes to him, eyes shining with pride, and while she wraps her arms around her man, his children clap and clap and clap. They clap until their hands sting and the layers of echoes reverberate around the hall like bells.

Pat and Adam are last to step from the shadows of backstage. Both have reasons for hanging back, but they have not shared these. Rather, they have lingered over the last of their champagne, taken their time as they gathered the plastic cups and empty bottle. They collected their bags; Pat's containing a small flask of whiskey – for warmth and for courage. And now they walk, hand in hand, into the main hall.

Declan and Heather are stacking the remaining chairs while Mabel throws a well-chewed tennis ball for Hitchens. For a moment, the two actors remain unobserved.

Pat hugs Adam, the way she has hugged them all tonight. A tight, prolonged embrace that will be their last, although the recipients of this warmth and love are ignorant of its finality. She kisses

340

Adam's cheek and gathers the word in her mind so it will emerge clean and intact: 'Goodbye.'

Mabel sees them first. 'Daddy!'

And as Mabel runs to her father, Hitchens follows, swerving his trajectory towards the woman who used to feed him the good stuff and tickle that special spot between his ears.

The dog wins the race, lifting his paws and letting Pat take them in her hands, as if they were dancing. Mabel wraps her arms around her father's thighs and Adam clutches her head to his belly.

'Mr Campbell? Adam?'

Adam looks up to see Mabel's teacher approaching them. He hadn't seen her in the audience tonight, and her sudden materialisation throws him.

'Mrs Gibbons?'

'Janet, please.' And she extends her hand first to Adam and then to Pat. 'I wondered, could I . . . a quick word?' And nodding towards Pat: 'With you both?'

Mabel runs off to join her mother, but Hitchens stays, eager to know what this is all about.

'It was beautiful,' Janet says. 'Wonderfully . . . moving.'

'Thank you.' Past Janet's shoulder, Adam sees Heather, waiting beneath the clock.

'I thought you made the whole thing very . . . accessible. Shakespeare . . .' – a pause – 'Death.'

'That was Laura,' Adam says.

'The young lady,' Pat adds.

'Years five and six are doing Elizabethan England,' Janet says. 'The plague, Walter Raleigh, Mary, Queen of Scots. Shakespeare.'

'That's . . . g— great.'

'They love the plague,' Janet says. 'Twenty thousand people . . . but . . . well, they love the plague.'

Pat and Adam exchange the briefest of glances.

'I think they would enjoy your play,' Janet says. 'I think they'd take a great deal from it.'

'The p— play?'

'If you . . . I don't want to impose, I know you're . . .' Janet takes hold of Adam's hand. 'It's special. It's very special.'

Adam looks at Pat. Pat look across the hall towards Declan.

'When?' asks Adam.

Janet's face opens up. 'Whenever,' she says. 'We'll work around you. Perhaps some time before the Easter break?'

'Which is when?'

'Two weeks tomorrow. This Wednesday could work?'

Adam laughs. 'I'd love to. But I'd have to ask the others.'

Janet looks at Pat. *And what about you?*

Pat feels the weight of the bag in her hand. She feels – or imagines she does – the weight of the moon, pulling at the tides. Pulling at her.

But one more week won't kill her. And now Pat laughs too.

Declan meets her in the centre of the hall.

'You were sensational,' he says, holding out his hand for Pat's bag. His face is weighed down with sadness, and Pat can see the effort it takes for him to smile.

'I was, wasn't I?' She passes the bag to Declan and takes his free hand in hers. 'B— buy me a drink?'

He frowns at her. 'We're not . . .?'

'Change of plans. T— tell you over a g— glass of champagne.'

Chapter 88

Mabel has gone ahead with Pat, Hitchens and the priest. Only Adam and Heather remain in the otherwise empty hall. Neither knows quite where or how to begin, so they tarry a while, stacking the last half-dozen chairs.

But this task, no matter how carefully they go about it, takes little time to complete.

Adam's feet echo on the floorboards as he walks towards his wife, stopping two full paces before her.

He smiles. He says, 'So.'

Heather casts her eyes around the empty stage. 'Sorry I missed the start.'

'You made it, that's all that matters.'

'And I'm sorry about earlier.'

'No need.'

'What I said. That was . . . I didn't mean it. I . . .'

'I understand. I . . . it must have been . . . a shock.'

Heather nods.

'It was . . .' *innocent.* 'Nothing . . .' *happened.*

All true, but these declarations of innocence simply recall the time when they were false.

'I called her.' Heather holds an invisible phone to her ear. 'The reason I was late . . . I called . . . Penny.'

The effect – of Penny's name on Heather's lips – is like an old ache flaring up. Then a thought – trivial, perhaps, in the bigger scheme, but the words speak themselves: 'How did you get her number?'

'You think I never went through your phone?'

Why? and *When?* Are the questions behind his teeth, but he has no right to ask, and the answers are either obvious or redundant.

'So you called her?'

'Been a long time coming,' Heather says. 'I'd had this whole . . . *hysterical wife* routine, I suppose. Chapter and verse and all the clichés.' Her voice trails off.

'But . . .'

'She congratulated me.'

'She what?'

'On our wedding.'

'Right.'

'And then she apologised. And then she thanked me.'

He forms the question with his eyes.

'For being there for you.' Heather's voice falters, tears catch and fall in the corners of her eyes. 'And then she cried. We both did. Just cried and cried and . . .' She shrugs.

'No chapter and verse?'

'Didn't get round to it. Next time maybe.' She steps towards Adam, takes his hands in hers. 'It was your parents' anniversary.'

It isn't clear whether Heather is talking about the events of a week or a year ago, but Adam gets the sense that the statement covers both.

'I'm sorry I didn't tell you. I . . . I didn't know how.'

'Maybe you could have tried' – she puppets her hand at him – '*talking*?'

'You always were the smart one.'

'Yes. But what you did, seeing her, saying goodbye . . . it was' – she shrugs – 'it was the right thing to do. It was noble. If that doesn't sound too . . . *Shakespearean.*'

Adam thinks of the men he has played tonight – villains and scoundrels and authors of their own misery. But no one noble.

Adam is not noble, but he will accept this new role that Heather has offered. It's a role he is ill-equipped to play, but he will do his best – he smiles to himself – he will die trying. 'Thank you.'

Heather nods: *You're welcome.*

'You okay?'

'I will be,' Heather says. 'A large glass of red wine and a packet of crisps would help.'

'In which case, I'm your man.'

He juts out his left elbow and Heather links her arm through his.

'And really,' she says, 'I'm sorry I missed the start.'

'What are you doing on Wednesday?'

'Wednesday? Why?'

'Come on,' he says. 'I'll tell you on the way.'

Adam has been dying for seven months, and whether he's getting any better at it remains a point of debate. But with his wife at his side, and spring just days away from bringing fresh blossom to the trees, Adam is looking forward to tomorrow. *And that*, he thinks, *is a pretty good start.*

'Cowards die many times before their deaths,
The valiant never taste of death but once.
Of all the wonders that I yet have heard,
It seems to me most strange that men should fear;
Seeing that death, a necessary end,
Will come when it will come.'

William Shakespeare, *Julius Caesar,*
Act II, Scene II

Epilogue

They performed for years five and six on a Wednesday. The audience reaction was less profound than in the church hall – some bafflement at the language, less laughter at the psychiatrist's couch – but the ten- and eleven-year-olds enjoyed the death very much indeed. Particularly the part where Tom was pursued by a bear.

Pat went under the surgeon's knife the following Tuesday. Declan was there when she was wheeled away to theatre, and he was there when she was returned to her ward four hours later, albeit too heavily sedated to appreciate this. The operation appeared to have gone well, but in the early hours of the following morning – around about the time the old priests and nuns preferred to slip away – Pat succumbed to a final and, as anticipated, catastrophic stroke. She suffered no pain.

She was buried in a plot to the left of her mother, the two caskets not more than an arm's length apart. After the other mourners left, Raymond, Vernon, Laura, Adam, Tom and Declan stayed back. And when they were sure no one was within earshot, they held hands and recited the prayer that Pat had written just for them.

In April, The Mechanicals performed for two additional primary schools within the borough. And in May they played for Raymond's wife, Judith. Like the schoolchildren, the residents of Rose Lodge Nursing Home were by and large bewildered by the performance, but the staff and relatives were generous with both their applause and their purses.

The following month, Laura received a letter from a lady with inoperable lung cancer. Vera had heard about The Rude Mechanicals from a man in her cancer bridge group, and, if Laura

349

was happy to share her script, Vera would like to set up her own chapter of the Mechanicals in Manchester. Within weeks, Laura had sent scripts to Southampton, Dorset and Abergavenny.

By now, the cast had grown to a robust – if not healthy – seven. And with the addition of a stage four breast and an advanced multiple myeloma, Laura was able to include several more deaths including the tearing apart of Coriolanus and the beheadings of Quintus and Martius.

'We've metastasised,' Tom whispered to Vernon at their regular Thursday rehearsals.

'God help them,' Vernon said.

Tom's health deteriorated following a bout of pneumonia from which he never recovered. By July, he had withdrawn from performing, but attended rehearsals when possible, sleeping in the corner and offering unsolicited advice from a pile of blankets.

He died three days after Laura passed all of her A levels with a brace of As and a single B. It was Raymond's belief that had it not been for Laura, Tom would never have lasted as long as he ultimately did. Of the seventeen titles on Tom's list – 'Shakespeare plays to read before I die' – he read all but *Cymbeline* and the final act of *Timon of Athens*, which he was anyway finding something of a slog.

He was buried with the Magic 8 Ball in one pocket of his overlarge suit. And, as per his request, the red Liberty scarf knotted about his neck.

His choice of funeral song – a popular one at cremations – confused the organist, as this was to be a burial. Laura knew that Tom would have enjoyed this final joke. And all confusion aside, the Bowie song sounded wonderful on the huge lead pipes.

His mother was sober at the funeral, but more than made up for that lapse at the well-appointed wake in Raymond's house.

They held Adam's wake in his home.

And while Vernon fed party sausages to Hitchens, Mabel was upstairs with her mother, opening the memory box left by her father.

He died in Hillside, thirteen months and two days after he first parked his car in the hospice grounds.

He stopped acting two months after Tom passed away, the same month Laura left for university. But Vernon and Raymond visited regularly, to talk about old times and bemoan their new recruits.

Penny visited on occasion, and Heather came every day with Mabel. When Adam was lucid, they played simple card games and listened to Mabel talk. Other times they sat quietly and watched the glitter fall in his jar of calm. Adam's final months were not without pain, but they were light on fear. And when death finally claimed him, Adam was ready.

Denied one more Christmas, Adam lived to see the supermarket shelves fill with festive swag. And one quiet night in mid-November – while Mabel stayed with her friend Holly – Heather and Adam listened to Christmas songs on the radio as Heather wrapped presents for their little girl and Adam signed his name on a thick stack of gift tags.

Vernon feeds one more sausage to Hitchens, and whispers into the mutt's ear: 'Outlasted 'em all, didn't I?'

A tear rolls down his cheek. But only one; Vernon is an old hand at funerals.

He lists their names: *Erin, Pat, Tom and Adam*. Raymond and Laura, too – him that never had it, and her that will kick its backside. Vernon's life – not to mention his inevitable demise – has been enriched by the influence of these Rude Mechanicals. And influence – he has learned – lives on. Influence can be immortal.

Raymond joins him on the sofa. In his left hand he holds two glasses. In his right, the bottle of thirty-year-old Scotch left to him by Adam.

'Old friends?' says Raymond.

'Aye,' says Vernon. 'Old friends.'

Behind the men, Lady McFluff swims in erratic loops, as healthy and vital as the day Adam brought her – if 'she' is indeed a she – home. He bought the goldfish to teach Mabel the lesson: all that lives must die. But while the fish did not, Mabel understands the concept all the same.

Upstairs, she empties the contents of her memory box. Some photographs, a collection of Adam's favourite books, films and CDs. A small jack-o-lantern lamp for Halloween, and a wind-up robot for Christmas future. Two letters: one to be opened now, and another for her eighteenth birthday. There is a beaded necklace that reads 'Daddy', which Heather fastens now around the young girl's neck.

'What's this, Mummy?'

Heather takes the silver thermos from the trunk and passes it to Mabel. The top has been sealed with grey waterproof tape. Mabel shakes the flask, and the liquid sloshes against the inside wall.

'Hear that?' asks Heather.

'Water?'

Heather shakes her head. 'Remember making a snowman with Daddy?'

Mabel nods.

'This is that snow,' her mother says. 'Isn't that cool?'

Mabel takes the flask from her mother and holds it to her cheek. 'Cool.'

She touches the bead necklace, as if reading the letters through her fingertips. 'I wish Daddy was still here.'

Heather pulls Mabel onto her lap. 'Yes,' she says. 'I do too.'

Vernon saw one more Christmas, although by this time he was unable to eat solid food and slept for upwards of sixteen hours a day. Not one for hospices, Vernon died in his own bed while his wife was downstairs watching TV. He had tried to hold on for his granddaughter's birthday, but as the great playwright had it: *We cannot hold on to mortality's strong hand*. And mortality slipped Vernon's grip just nine days before baby Vee gained her first number.

When Vernon had been diagnosed, the doctors had given him twelve months. And Vernon – sustained by family, purpose, and the immortal words of William Shakespeare – gave them twenty-three. *So how's that for statistics?*

Laura came back from university for the funeral, like she did for all of the others. This time, she brought a boy – a history undergrad called Malcolm. Raymond didn't care much for Malcolm, but he was happy to see Laura happy, and so kept his counsel.

Vernon's wake was too large to be held in the modest terraced house where he breathed his last, so his family hired the church hall that had been so central to the final fifteen months of his life.

Sitting on the low wall outside, while Malcolm talks football with Vernon's oldest son, Laura tells Raymond about the continued shrinkage of her mets, one all but invisible on her latest scans. *Unwritten*, she thinks, tracing a finger across the nine letters tattooed on her inner arm. The word has many meanings to this girl, this woman, who has experienced so much in such a short time. It stands for things undone, erased, lost and left behind. And for things not yet realised. The past and the future. It represents things unknown and unspoken. The people we take for granted. It represents hope.

Raymond loves this girl no less than a daughter, and her marvellous news moves him to discreet tears.

With Laura more than a hundred miles away, deep in study and heavily involved in the uni drama society, responsibility for running The Rude Mechanicals (now numbering eleven, though two are fading fast, and one couldn't 'act her way out of a game of charades') falls entirely on the Scot's square shoulders. Their next performance is scheduled for the Ides of March, just four weeks from now, and Laura promises she will be there. Raymond believes her. But he sincerely hopes she will leave the history student behind.

Epilogue #2

The noisy peoples have all left now and the mouse emerges from a small hole beneath the stage. The man has left crumbs again, and the mouse approaches these cautiously. She didn't get to be this old – almost two, and not so fast any more – by behaving recklessly. Half a lifetime ago, a people left food in a dangerous thing, and one incautious mouse was snapped almost in two. Snapped enough, at any rate.

But then, thinks the mouse, *All that lives must die*.

Isn't that what the peoples say?

Passing though nature to eternity.

Best not to dwell.

Because whilst life is both brief and fragile – no sense denying it – each new day brings the possibility of something good, and, who knows, maybe one more crumb of this very delicious cake.

'Good night, good night! Parting is such sweet sorrow,
That I shall say good night till it be morrow.'

William Shakespeare, *Romeo and Juliet*,
Act II, Scene I

[Exit]

Acknowledgements

Sincere thanks to the people who gave generously of their time and knowledge, sometimes under painful circumstances: Sonja Ashbury, Tracy Ellerton, Letizia Forrest, Iain Foulkes, Faye Gishen, Peter Glanville, Rollo Hawkins, Gavin Johnson, James Larkin, Paul Murray, Henry Makiwa, Gill Nuttall, Tina Powel, Victoria Reynolds and Sahil Suleman.

A special mention to Leesa Daniels – brave, bold and very funny.

And of course: Mark (Stan) Stanton for the tough love. Sarah Jones for tough love too, but also the more gentle variety – I needed it. My mother for faith and phone calls. My shrewd and patient editor Kate Howard. Amber Burlinson, Sorcha Rose, Sarah Christie and Joanna Seaton at Hodder for making it all happen – thank you.

And finally: Evie Jones for the Santa Claus joke and Ruby Jones for the Owinge Story. Thank you, girls x